MW00413498

Next Exit, Three Miles

CW Browning

Copyright © 2013 by Clare Wroblewski

All rights reserved.

Cover design by Dissect Designs / www.dissectdesigns.com
Book design by Clare Wroblewski

No part of this publication may be reproduced, stored in or introduced into a retrieval system, or transmitted, in any form or by any means (electronic, mechanical, photocopying, recording or otherwise), without the prior written permission of the copyright owner, except by a reviewer who may quote brief passages in a review.

This is a work of fiction. All of the characters, organizations, and events portrayed in this novel are either products of the author's imagination or are used fictitiously. Any resemblance to actual persons, living or dead, or events is entirely coincidental.

CW Browning
Visit my website at www.cwbrowning.com

Second Edition: 2018

ISBN-13: 978-1492135517
ISBN-10: 1492135518

Author's Note:

This book is dedicated to Jerry and Jenny.

Jenny, I am so grateful for your emotional support and practical, artistic advice. Your constant prayers have supported me and pushed me forward daily when I was tempted to give up. Having the encouragement of such a wonderful artist as yourself is priceless!

Jerry, you have always been willing to assist with the inevitable technical difficulties arising from technology. At all hours of the day or night, you have dropped what you were doing to repair my computers, educate me on Linux, and assist with formatting up to, and including, publication. Without you, I would still be writing long-hand!

It is only through your combined support that this dream was possible. Thank you.

Next Exit, Three Miles

"Greater love has no man than this, that he lay down his life for his friends."
~ John 15:13

Prologue

Alina Maschik looked up at the turquoise sky and breathed deeply. The cool mountain breeze felt good on her hot skin and, throwing her head back, she arched into a stretch, reaching her arms far behind her. Straightening again on an exhale, Alina lowered her eyes to the small community of huts nestled in the mountainside below. From this height, the bamboo roofs on the huts blended with the surrounding canopy of trees, causing the large open center of the compound to look very small and isolated. She sighed and stretched forward, bending from her hips and balancing her weight, keeping her back straight. Exhaling again, Alina wrapped her arms around her knees and, resting her forehead on her shins, felt the calming effect of oxygen flowing out of her.

This was her morning routine. Run four miles up the mountain, stretch, meditate, and then run back. She had been doing this for two years now. The cool air, coupled with the abundance of mountain creatures and raw beauty, never failed to take her breath away. The amount of peace that she derived from the simple experience of just *being* had healed old wounds that no doctor could ever see.

Wounds she hadn't even known were there.

Alina lifted her head and glanced down to the compound that had been her home for the past two years. Her eyes narrowed at the sight of Raven, her pet hawk, as he appeared suddenly and swooped once around the open courtyard. When she came to this place, he was a massive, wounded mess in the trees behind her hut. They were never sure what caused his extensive injuries, but no one was able to get close enough to heal him. After two days, he allowed her to take him in and nurse him. She gave him his freedom once he was well, but every night he returned to her. Slowly, Alina began to realize that he had accepted her and made her his. In turn, he was hers as well. He was her protector and her pet.

And he was *never* home at this time of day.

Alina scanned the miles of surrounding mountains, looking for some sign of disturbance, but there was none. Just Raven, perched on a tall post at the corner of the courtyard. Watching.

Alina sank to the grass and crossed her legs, closing her eyes and dismissing Raven from her mind. She centered her attention on the sounds around her and became very still. After a few moments, her breathing had slowed and she listened to the sounds of the forest resuming around her. A dark lock of hair brushed against her forehead as the breeze sighed around her. She was very still while she listened, first to her own shallow breathing, and then to her own consciousness. A branch popped behind her and she could see the mountain creature moving through the trees behind her. It paid no attention to her in its quest for food, but moved away from her quietly. Above her, a bird crowed in the trees while, slightly below her and to the right, a furry forager busily snuffled into the end of a dead tree trunk. Alina absorbed it all through closed eyes and open mind, her body relaxed and her muscles alert.

It was the sudden gust of wind that carried the faintest whisper of Raven's call. Alina opened her eyes and cut her gaze to the compound. Raven was still on the post, but even at this distance, she could see that his head was turned toward her. In her semi-aware state, Alina saw her pet clearly, looking straight at her with his piercing hawk eyes.

In one fluid motion, she was up and running back to the compound. Raven was calling her home for a reason.

Chapter One

Candlelight glinted off the cut glass, making the amber liquid inside sparkle mysteriously. Momentarily forgotten, the tumbler sat on a plain, mission-style coffee table, basking in the warmth of several candles while shadows engulfed the room beyond the table. The single occupant was absorbed in another world, his eyes closed, seated unmoving in lotus pose on the floor beside the table. His long legs were folded up neatly and his hands rested on his knees, palms up. His breathing was slow and steady, his body settled into the meditation comfortably. Images began to flicker through his mind behind his eyelids, almost like slides from an old projector. First they were fuzzy, as if there was interference with a faint signal. Then, slowly, they became sharper and more concise. His breathing slowed even more as the he studied the first images carefully.

The meditator saw the man walking towards him slowly, his dark hair cut short to his head and the gold chain hanging heavily around his neck. It was the man from the file. Angelo. In his mind's eye, his hand reached out and grabbed the chain, twisting it sharply to bring Angelo close to him. His hands grasped his head on either side and twisted sharply, the snap of the neck clear in his ears. However, just as quickly as the motion ended, that image was discarded.

The next image emerged. Angelo again. This time he was standing on a pier, waiting.

No.

The image changed again. Angelo was kneeling now, kneeling in front of him, facing forward. The Sig Sauer, with a silencer attached, appeared behind his head. The river flowed beneath them.

Yes.

That was acceptable. It was clean and had no possibility of any stray DNA inadvertently relocating somewhere that could be inconvenient.

That image was discarded and the next image emerged. This time it was another man, another face. He was getting into an older model Cadillac, some suitcases loaded into the trunk. The image paused there, the meditator considering it carefully for a moment before continuing. The Cadillac began to drive. The streets in the image changed rapidly until there was a train crossing. The image paused again and was studied. Residential houses were on one side of the tracks and businesses on the other. There was no other crossing for about a mile.

After another moment, the image was complete.

Cold, emotionless eyes opened slowly and the man on the floor exhaled softly. He stared at the candlelight thoughtfully, his mind still miles away at a train crossing.

Yes.

The word whispered through his mind and he reached out his long arm to the glass of amber liquid waiting on the table. He sipped the smooth bourbon in satisfaction.

Yes, that would do nicely.

New Jersey is the armpit of America. Not only is that its geographical claim to fame, but it is also a very good description of the quality of life in New Jersey. It is an over-crowded, smelly and notoriously famous pocket of land that alternates from smog-laden industrial areas to suburban niches to pine barren wasteland to rolling farmland. While it does produce the best blueberries and tomatoes in the country, it also produces the most toxic water known to man. And in exchange for very convenient proximities to cities, mountains, and shores, New Jersey also has the highest cost of living in the Union. Given this state of give and take, it's no wonder that most New Jersey residents live their life prosaically and with the same philosophy: Go ahead and throw it at 'em. They will take it standing up, and eat their pork roll sandwich too. This is because Jersey inhabitants are a special breed. They are survivors who have undergone carcinogen poisoning, high blood pressure, heart attacks, scrapple, and the mob. They can go just about anywhere and survive. But no matter where they end up, displaced Jersians never really get away from their roots. Jersey is like yellow mustard. Once it gets under your nails, it won't come out. Not until it's good and ready.

This realization was foremost in her mind as Alina drove over the Ben Franklin Bridge, crossing from Philadelphia into Camden, one of three major entry ports to South Jersey. She hadn't been back home for over ten years. The bridge was the same. Rutgers was still there, below her on the right, on the water front in Camden. In fact, even the toll booths were the same, right down to the dingy kinda-blue-but-not-really-seafoam-green worn paint. The distinct smell of the Delaware River blew through the open windows and Alina wrinkled her nose. After living in the mountains for two years, she didn't think the stench of pollution would ever go unnoticed again. It was, however, strangely familiar.

The cell phone chirped from the seat next to her, pulling Alina's attention away from her first sight of home ground.

"Yes?"

"I just left the house. The keys are under the flower pot on the left side of the garage," the male voice said. "Everything is ready for you, just the way you requested. As I said before, take your time and let me know. I'm willing to make you a fair offer."

"Thank you." Alina switched lanes to the left and headed onto the boulevard. "I'll let you know what I decide."

"I'll be in touch to let you know how to reach me once I'm settled."

"No need. I'll find you."

Alina disconnected the call and dropped the phone back onto the seat beside her. There was rustle from the back seat and she glanced back at Raven. He was re-adjusting himself on the perch inside a massive metal cage.

"Almost there, Raven. Just hang on another hour."

She turned her attention back to the road and merged onto Route 70, heading east. The landmarks were so familiar, and yet so foreign that she was somewhat discomposed. The drivers were the same though, and Alina switched lanes almost unconsciously, pressing the gas pedal down.

New Yorkers like to say that they can drive anywhere, but not just anyone can drive in New York. Alina wasn't so sure about New York, but she knew it was true for New Jersey. The speed limit is a suggestion only and the left lane is just another lane, not a passing lane. Having driven in many different countries since leaving Jersey, Alina had to admit now that most were not quite as aggressive as this small state. The reason was simple. People in New Jersey just didn't have time for manners or road etiquette. They had somewhere to be and that was that.

Alina tapped the brakes as a Honda Civic cut in front of her and she automatically switched lanes to avoid it. She shook her head almost imperceptibly. Not only had she been dragged back into civilization, but she had been dragged back to Jersey, of all places. The one place in the world that she truly had no desire to ever set foot in again, and yet here she was, speeding down Route 70 on her way to a house buried in the outer pine barrens of Medford.

It was truly ridiculous.

When she left ten years ago, it had been with the intentions of never returning. She joined the military and departed to start a new life. Her new life began in shadows, and continued in the dark and murky alleys of the military underworld. When she got out of the Navy and started working with the government, Alina had changed. She laughed a lot less and she watched a lot more. Her life before the military had become a distant memory, dreamlike in its quality, and she had all but forgotten Jersey and all the humor and carefree nonsense that life entailed. Now, driving on streets that had once been a part of her, Alina felt a strange and overwhelming sense of déjà vu. Trained to react to her instincts, she found the feeling unsettling. With a sigh, Alina silently reminded herself that it was only temporary and continued on toward Medford.

Angela Bolan stepped into her dark living room and flipped on the light. She closed the door behind her, dropping her purse and keys on the table inside the door. A bell jingled down the stairs, heralding the arrival of her roommate, and she smiled tiredly as she bent down to stroke the orange tabby cat rubbing around her legs.

"Hello girlfriend," she murmured. "How was your day?" The cat purred in response and then stretched. Angela chuckled. "That exciting, huh?"

She moved through the living room and into the kitchen, flipping on lights as she went. The red message light on her answering machine was blinking when she reached the kitchen, and she punched the button as she turned to the refrigerator. Angela nearly dropped the can of soda she was pulling from the fridge when she heard a voice she hadn't heard in ten years.

"Angela, it's Alina. I'm in town for a bit and thought we could catch up. I'll try again later."

The message switched off and Angela rushed to the phone to check the caller id. The number was blocked.

She stared at the phone in amazement. She had exchanged a handful of emails over the years with Alina, the last one being about a year ago. Alina never mentioned coming back to Jersey, nor had she ever given a clear idea of what she was doing with her life. For all intents and purposes, she had dropped off the face of the earth ten years ago.

Angela listened to the message again, then walked into the living room to drop down onto the couch, completely flabbergasted. Alina was back? In Jersey?

She got up and grabbed her cell phone out of her purse. If Alina was back, she must have contacted Stephanie as well.

Before she had a chance to dial, her phone started playing Jimmy Buffet. Stephanie was calling.

"You will never guess who I just talked to!" Stephanie yelled into her ear.

"Alina."

Angela plopped back onto the couch and sat back as her cat jumped up onto her lap. She absently stroked her hand down the tabby's back.

"She called you too?" Stephanie demanded.

"She left a message on my machine. I just got it," Angela said.

"She called me at the office. She caught me just as I was leaving. She's back in town for a while," Stephanie told her. "She wants to get together with us for dinner."

"What's she doing back?" Angela demanded.

"She didn't really say…and I was too shocked to ask!" Stephanie laughed. "Do you have plans tomorrow night?"

"Tomorrow is fine," Angela replied. "Even if I had plans, I would break them."

"Tell me about it," Stephanie agreed. "It's not every day your friend reappears from nowhere. I'll call her back and let her know you're in. I can't wait to see her!"

"Me too."

Angela hung up and shook her head. She was still stunned.

None of them ever thought they would see Alina again. Both Angela and Stephanie had received regular emails from her for the first year, then the emails became less and less frequent before tapering off to one every other year or so. Enough to let everyone know that everyone was still alive, but not much else.

Angela smiled slowly. She had always believed Alina would come back. Stephanie laughed at her and told her that their friend had moved on and was long gone. But Angela had known.

She stood up and turned to go upstairs and get changed.

She had known Jersey would call Alina back.

Next Exit, Three Miles

Alina turned off the road onto a long dirt driveway lined with trees. The house was set back three acres from the road, hidden from view by thick woods and underbrush. The drive curved to the right and wound its way through the trees before finally breaking through into the clearing where a modestly-sized, two-story modern structure sat in the wilderness. Alina scanned the area surrounding the house and was satisfied with what she saw. The dirt drive turned into gravel here, providing a little more curbside appeal. The immediate border around the house was clear of all obstructions, giving an unimpeded view from any of the windows and doors on the first floor. The lawn was flat and landscaped with flowers, but void of bushes or shrubs that would conceal a person. Lush, thick grass saved the yard from a stark appearance, however, and a bird bath perched waist high on a thin wrought iron pedestal in the center of the front lawn added a touch of whimsy.

The driveway curved in front of the house before continuing on and splitting in two. One half stretched along the side of the house to the back, while the other half turned back toward the road. Alina followed the left side and rolled along the side of the house to the back where a two car garage was set to the right and away from the house, facing the backyard. As in the front, the backyard was flat and void of any structures that could obstruct view until the trees and thickets began about half an acre from the back of the house.

Alina rolled to a stop and shut off the engine, glancing back at Raven. He lifted his head from his shoulder, where his beak had been buried, and pinned her with his black eyes. She smiled.

"We're here. You can go find your dinner now."

She got out of the SUV and walked around to the back door. Opening it, she angled the large cage sideways so that she could unlatch the metal door. Raven straightened his legs slowly and Alina opened the door, stepping back. With an abrupt whoosh, he launched out of the cage, spreading his black wings majestically and floating up to land on the roof of the garage. Alina tilted her head back in the waning daylight and looked up at him. He was surveying his new territory slowly, his hawk eyes darting over the area.

Alina turned back to the SUV, pressing the button on the key fob to pop open the back hatch. She pulled two large duffel bags from the back and walked across the drive to the backyard. A large deck stretched the length of the house, sitting three steps up from the ground. She stepped onto the smooth wood and walked across to the sliding door. Dropping the bags on the deck outside the door, she turned to look over the backyard.

As in the front, the visibility was fantastic until the line of trees began. Alina mentally picked out where she could set security cameras and watched as Raven lifted into the air and disappeared into the trees. He was off to find his dinner. She knew he would return when he was full. Alina didn't worry about him getting lost. He had followed her out of the compound and down the mountain easily enough. She tried to leave him in South America, in his home, but Raven had other ideas. He had even gone into the cage readily enough, accepting that it was the only way to travel with her.

Alina turned and walked around the house to the front door, her eyes moving constantly over the trees. The air smelled fresher out here, not as thick with fumes and dirt as it had coming over the bridge from Philadelphia. She really had forgotten how badly New Jersey smelled. It was like sticking your head in an exhaust pipe and turning the car on, taking a deep breath, and then plunging your head into a garbage can.

She unlocked the front door and stepped into the house, closing the door quietly behind her. Alina stood for a moment, taking in the silence and the feel of the house. She was standing in a very small entryway with a tiled floor that gave way to hardwood in the rest of the front of the house. To her left was a wide doorway leading into what looked like a den, and to her right was a sitting room. A staircase going upstairs was in front and to the right, and a hallway ran to the back of the house along the side of the staircase. Alina noted that she could see the back sliding doors from the front door and smiled. The open plan appealed to her sense of security. She liked this house more and more.

Alina went down the hallway and emerged into a large common room that was a living room on the right and a dining room on the left. The back of the house was carpeted from the end of the hallway and, clearly, this was where the family "living" was meant to take place. The sliding doors to the deck separated the dining room from the living room and Alina moved into the dining room. A picture window looked over the deck and there was a walnut table with four chairs around it and two more in the corners, suggesting a leaf could be added to the table. To her left a granite topped bar, capable of seating about four people, separated a large kitchen from the dining room.

Alina stepped into the kitchen, looking around. The floor was light gray and white stone and the counters were the same black granite as the bar. The Viking stove was stainless steel, as was the large refrigerator. In the center of the kitchen sat a granite topped island, with a stainless steel pot rack above it. Alina looked at it for a moment, then moved over to it and reached up to lift the stainless steel 6 quart sauté pan down from the pot rack. She placed it perfectly in the center of the island and stepped back to watch as the entire island moved silently and smoothly to the left, revealing a stone stairwell.

"Bravo, Marcus, bravo," she murmured. The stairwell opening was exactly 2 feet by 4 feet, just wide enough to step through, and Alina descended into the hidden basement. The first room at the bottom of the stairs was lined with counters topped with security monitors, servers and equipment, not yet connected. At the end of the room was another door, leading to a larger and more spacious room, lined with cages holding a variety of weapons. There were a few empty spots and all the cages were locked. Alina smiled slightly when she stood in the center of the room and looked directly up to find a set of keys taped to the ceiling, right next to a sprinkler head.

"Well that's original, at any rate," Alina chuckled.

Alina went back upstairs and grabbed her duffel bags from the deck, moving back to the front of the house to go upstairs, content that the most important section of her temporary command center was exactly as she had requested.

Stephanie Walker stepped into the restaurant and looked around. It was a busy Friday night and wait staff were rushing around between tables. A packed capacity crowd battled with the music piped in from hidden speakers overhead, vying to be heard over each other. The hostess smiled at Stephanie and Steph nodded back.

"I'm meeting two friends here," she said, still scanning the busy restaurant. The hostess came out from behind her podium and looked around.

"What do they look like?" she asked.

Stephanie glanced at the very thin, early twenties hostess. The thought crossed her mind that she would be shocked if the girl remembered anything, let alone two women that she probably seated close to half an hour ago, and Stephanie immediately felt a twinge of guilt.

"One is about my height, with light brown hair, and she is probably wearing a suit." Stephanie decided to give her the benefit of the doubt. "The other one has almost black hair, or she did the last time I saw her, and is a little taller than me."

"They came in about half an hour ago." The hostess swiveled on her high-heeled slides and headed toward the back of the restaurant. "I seated them in the back," she added over her shoulder. Stephanie followed with a raised eyebrow. This woman was a rare gem in the restaurant business. She followed her through the crowded and noisy bar until they reached the back. Two women were seated on opposite ends of a round table in a half booth on the back wall. One was, indeed, wearing a suit and had her blackberry in hand, typing away. The other still had dark brown hair that appeared black in most lights.

Her hair was longer than it had been ten years ago, brushing her shoulders in a thick, straight wave. She was dressed in a red shirt that draped over her shoulders and black pants. Stephanie paused for just a second, taking in the straight spine and squared shoulders. There was something about her old friend that made her pause: a radiating sense of power that made her look twice. Alina turned her head suddenly and Stephanie encountered dark brown eyes that were as familiar as they were strange. Stephanie pushed the sudden feeling of awkwardness aside and smiled at her.

"Alina!" she exclaimed, stepping up to the table. Alina stood up and accepted a big hug.

"Hi Steph," she smiled fondly at Stephanie. "It's been a long time."

"Too long." Stephanie slid into the booth next to Angela and set her purse on the seat next to her. "Hi Ang."

"How are you?" Angela scooted to the middle of the booth and Alina resumed her seat with her back to the wall.

"Exhausted." Stephanie tossed her hair out of her face and reached for the closest glass of water. "I'm sorry I'm late. I got held up at work. Did I miss anything?"

"We waited to order until you got here," Alina said, lifting her hand and motioning slightly. Stephanie stared, shocked, as a waiter materialized next to Alina. She glanced at Angela, who shrugged and grinned. "Are you drinking?" Alina asked Stephanie, pulling her attention away from the phenomenon of an attentive waiter.

"Absolutely. I'll have a Cosmopolitan." Steph looked at the other two glasses. "And bring another round for them," she added, noting that Angela's martini was almost empty and Alina's glass was half empty. The waiter nodded and disappeared. "What are you drinking?" Stephanie demanded Alina, leaning forward and looking at her glass. "Vodka?"

"Water," Alina answered. Stephanie stared at her.

21

"Water?!" she repeated. Angela laughed.

"I told you she's changed," she said. "Apparently, she doesn't drink anymore."

"I drink occasionally," Alina retorted, "but a clean body makes a clean mind."

"Oh Lord." Stephanie sat back and groaned. "You probably eat organic vegetables too, don't you? Where were you? California?"

"I've been a lot of places," Alina answered with a grin. "And yes, I do eat organic vegetables."

"I think the Philly cheesesteak idea is dead," Angela said in a stage whisper to Stephanie. Alina laughed.

"I will still have a cheesesteak," she said. "It wouldn't be right to come home and not have one. But only from Pat's. None of that Geno's nonsense!"

They fell silent as the waiter returned with the drinks and pulled out his pad to take their order. Cheeseburger and fries for Angela, Chicken Alfredo for Stephanie, and grilled chicken breast and steamed vegetables for Alina. Once the waiter had left, Stephanie looked at Alina and shook her head.

"Well, for what it's worth, you look fantastic," she commented. "Obviously the clean living agrees with you." Alina smiled.

"Thank you," she sat back and regarded Stephanie. "So, Angela filled me in on her stellar banking career. How about you? She said you got a promotion at work."

"Well, I don't know how much of a good thing that is." Stephanie sipped her drink. "The upside is I get more money. The downside is that I work all the time." She glanced at Angela. "Did you tell her yet?" Angela shook her head.

"Nope."

"Oh." Stephanie swallowed and cleared her throat. "Well, I have a partner now." She glanced up from her drink to Alina to find her watching her with those strangely detached dark eyes. "You know him." Alina tipped her head to one side and raised an eyebrow.

"Let me guess," she said. "John." Stephanie drank half her martini before nodding. Alina watched her for a beat and then sighed. "I heard he joined the FBI."

"He's a good detective," Stephanie said. "He's turned into a good guy. I almost never smack him now."

"Thing is, Alina, he knows you're back," Angela said, leaning forward. "There was really no way of hiding it from him." Alina smiled slightly.

"John is part of my past," she told them. "Don't worry." Stephanie laughed.

"I'm not. I just wanted you to be prepared in case you run into him," she sat back again. "So, tell me what the heck you've been doing with yourself for ten years."

"Well, I'm a consultant now," Alina said evasively. "When I got out of the military, I did some work with the government, then took a sabbatical. And now I'm back." Stephanie blinked and stared at her.

"Ok then. Ten years in three sentences. That works." She paused as the waiter reappeared with their food and set the plates out. When he was finished, a slight nod from Alina sent him on his way. "Ok. Two things." Stephanie picked up her fork and prepared to dig into the creamy pasta on her plate. "One, do you plan on sticking around this time? And two, what spell did you put on the waiter and can you teach it to me?"

"It's not just the waiter," Angela said, picking up her knife and cutting her huge cheeseburger in half. "It's also the hostess. Everyone seems to be afraid of Alina."

"I have to admit that if I didn't know her, I would be a little intimidated." Stephanie nodded. Alina raised an eyebrow and Stephanie pointed her fork at her. "You, my friend, look like you are dangerous. That is the only way to describe it." Alina laughed, but the laugh didn't quite reach her eyes.

"I'm just trying to eat my dinner and get used to Jersey again!" she protested. "You guys realize it smells here, right? I don't remember it smelling when I left."

"That's because you didn't notice it when you lived here," Angela explained. "We don't notice it either. Give it a few days and all that healthy pollution will clog up your nose and you won't smell a thing. Can you pass the ketchup?"

"So is that a no to number one?" Stephanie demanded. "You're not going to stay because of the smell?!"

"Let's just say that I'm trying Jersey out to see if we still like each other," Alina replied, handing Angela the ketchup. "No promises."

"Oh, come on." Stephanie laughed. "What's there not to love about Jersey? We have the shore, we have Philly...or New York, if you're a traitor...we have Herr's chips. Hell, we have Tastycakes!"

"And don't forget the nuclear waste and polluted water," Angela interjected before taking a huge bite of her burger.

"Well, yeah....but that just makes us a stronger species," Stephanie retorted with a laugh.

"You have Snooki," Alina pointed out dryly.

"That would be one of the results of the nuclear waste and polluted water," Angela mumbled, her mouth full. Alina grinned reluctantly.

"So, are you allowed to talk about work?" Alina asked Stephanie, changing the subject.

"Somewhat," Stephanie answered. "What do you want to know?"

"What made you late?" Alina asked, cutting into her chicken breast.

"Oh, that. A floater popped up in the Delaware, near the bridge in Riverton." Stephanie finished her martini and watched as Alina lifted her hand again. The waiter reappeared and took the two empty martini glasses, disappearing with the promise of two more. Stephanie and Angela looked at each other, and then at Alina. Alina was eating her dinner, oblivious to them. When Stephanie didn't continue right away, she looked up and raised her eyebrow. Stephanie hurriedly cleared her throat and went back to her pasta. A smile twitched at the corner of Alina's mouth.

"Anyway, the floater was identified as Angelo Cordeiro, a drug lord," Stephanie continued. "He also dabbled in guns and information, which is why he was on *our* agenda. When he floated up, I won the pool."

"Lucky you," Angela murmured.

"So the Bureau has taken over the investigation?" Alina asked, finishing off her vegetables and sitting back with her glass of water.

"Yes." Stephanie grimaced. "Well, with some assistance. Another agency has also been brought in." Alina was silent as the waiter came back with the two drinks. Once he had disappeared again, she looked at Stephanie.

"What other agency?" she asked. Stephanie shrugged.

"That's as much as I can tell you," she said. "And, actually, I don't know much more than that myself. Angelo must have strayed into much larger waters and pissed off some mighty scary people. But enough about work. Where are you staying?"

"A friend has a house in Medford that I'm renting," Alina answered, dropping the topic of Angelo. "He wants to sell it. I'll see how I like it."

"What's in Medford?" Stephanie demanded.

"Peace and quiet," Alina retorted. Stephanie looked horrified.

"What on earth do you want with that?!" she demanded. Alina smiled and sipped her water.

"Come on. How often are we going to get the chance to do this?" Stephanie demanded. Alina stood in the parking lot of the restaurant while they tried to convince her to go out for drinks. "Angela and I are lucky if we see each other once a month anymore, and I haven't seen *you* in ten friggin' years."

"She's right," Angela agreed. "Just come for a few drinks and then leave. It's still early." Alina glanced at her watch. It was seven-thirty.

"I'm not one for the bar scene anymore," she remarked. Stephanie scoffed.

"It's a fed bar," she retorted. "Not exactly the epicenter of single meet and greets." Alina was silent. That was the point. She had no desire to go into a bar filled with feds and lawyers.

"One hour. Give us one more hour," Angela coaxed, digging for her keys in her Gucci bag. Alina sighed inaudibly and nodded.

"One hour," she agreed. "I'll follow you." She turned on her heel and walked toward a sleek black car a few feet away.

"Whoa! What's that?" Stephanie followed her. Alina glanced at her.

"They call this a car," she replied dryly. Stephanie snorted inelegantly and walked up to it, peeking into the passenger's window.

"This is not just any car," she retorted. "It's a Camaro."

"It's a guy-car," Angela muttered behind them and Alina suppressed a grin. Angela was one hundred percent Jersey girl. She wouldn't dream of leaving the house without make-up, she lived in high-heels, and her nails and hair were always perfect. Her opinion of nature could be summed up in one word: outdoors. And that's where she didn't spend a lot of time. Unless it involved the beach, Angela had no time for nature. When they were younger, Alina often wondered why they were such great friends. As she got older, she realized that although Angela was very much a girly-girl, she had a temper and mind like a man. And that was where they were the same.

"It's gorgeous," Stephanie stated, stepping back and admiring the car. "Just what exactly do you do again?" she demanded. Alina laughed.

"I'm a consultant," she answered. "Don't worry. It's not stolen."

"I'm not grand theft," Stephanie retorted. "And if you think I'm not riding with you in this, you're crazy." She moved back to the passenger door and stood there expectantly. Alina glanced at Angela.

"I'll drive my own car, thanks," she said. "You can follow me."

Alina nodded and unlocked the car for Stephanie to get in. She went around to get in the driver side and watched as Angela walked to her car. When she reached her silver BMW, Alina started the car. The engine came to life with a roar and Stephanie sighed.

"It's not fair," she said. "I would love to drive something like this. Instead, I have a Maxima." Alina laughed and eased forward as Angela pulled out of her parking spot.

"So buy a new car," she retorted. Stephanie sighed again.

"Eventually, I will," she said. "Right now, I'm just too focused on work."

"So what's the story with this Angelo character?" Alina asked. Stephanie shrugged.

"We're not really sure yet," she answered. "He was hit professionally with a double tap to the back of the head and then chucked into the river with a cement block. There was storm a few days ago and the current must have pulled him loose. Forensics is working on it."

"And this other agency?" Alina asked.

"It's just that. Another agency." Stephanie frowned. "I don't mind working with other departments, but I'm not even being told what department it is! I was just told that the guy will be here Monday morning to help with the investigation. I'll tell you what, I'm starting to appreciate how local law enforcement feels about Feds now." Alina was silent and Stephanie glanced at her. "I just told you way too much, so I am trusting you to keep it to yourself."

"Of course," Alina replied.
"And, I still want to know what kind of consulting you do," Stephanie added. Alina smiled slightly and was silent.

Chapter Two

The bar was crowded when they arrived and Alina instinctively scanned every face in the crowd as they moved through it. Angela was forging a path to the bar and Alina followed. Stephanie brought up the rear, fighting to keep the grin off her face as they moved through the throng of over-worked attorneys and feds. Men had discarded their jackets, loosened their ties and ordered one too many Manhattans. The women still had their suit jackets and stilettos on, making a valiant effort to keep up with the men. All around them the conversation flowed in waves, and Stephanie watched as people unconsciously moved out of Alina's way without even noticing that she was passing. Stephanie watched the back of her old friend's head as they moved toward the bar and wondered again what she had been doing all these years. She moved with a confidence and precision that Stephanie had never seen before, almost as if she were untouchable, and people naturally responded to that forceful energy coming from her without the slightest realization that they were doing so.

"Stephanie, there's John," Angela called back over her shoulder, motioning to the back of the long room. Stephanie followed her gaze and picked out her partner in the back corner, his back against the wall, surrounded by a mix of co-workers and women.

"Typical," Stephanie retorted. Angela came to stop before the crowded bar.

"I'll get the first round," she announced, pulling two bills out of her purse. "What are you drinking? And Alina, I do mean alcohol."

"I…"

"No objections!" Stephanie interrupted her before she could speak. "This is a homecoming celebration. You can have at least one drink!"

"But I…." Alina opened her mouth again.

"No buts!" Angela retorted. "If you don't pick something, I will!" she added threateningly. Alina sighed.

"I was trying to say that I would have a vodka tonic with lemon," she finally got out. Angela and Stephanie started laughing.

"Ok then!" Angela motioned the bartender. "This lady will have a vodka tonic with lemon!"

Alina watched as the bartender leaned forward to hear the rest of the order before turning away to make the drinks. A heavy-set man next to her with sweat marks at his arm pits and a side-holster that had seen better days looked at her and nodded with a smile, moving out of the way so that she could take his spot at the bar. Alina smiled slightly in thanks and moved seamlessly into his spot. She watched as the bartender made their drinks, taking her attention from him only when she sensed, rather than heard, a presence behind her.

"And what brings you lovely ladies into this disreputable establishment?" a long forgotten voice spoke behind them, causing Alina's spine to stiffen slightly. She felt like she had been knocked in her sternum with the thicker end of a baseball bat, a feeling she hadn't felt in years.

"John, you aren't the only one who gets a night out once in a while," Stephanie retorted.

"I would never claim that I was!" John replied. "Hello Angela. How are you?"

"Same as always, John, awaiting your imminent demise," Angela retorted, accepting her drink from the bartender and reaching for Stephanie's.

"You're warming up to me. I can tell, you know," John answered with a laugh. Angela turned to hand Stephanie her drink.

"Whatever lets you sleep at night, darling," Angela shot back. Alina bit back a grin and reached out to accept her vodka tonic from the bartender. Then, with a deep sigh, she turned to face her past.

John Smithe stood before her, looking a little older and a little more solid than the last time she had seen him. There were new lines on his face and he had a certain grimness about the mouth that she recognized instantly as the habitual crease of a law enforcement agent. He still had the same sandy blond hair and the same pale blue eyes, but Alina noticed with detached interest that they no longer pulled a responsive twinkle from her. In fact, Alina was rather stunned to realize that she felt absolutely nothing for the tall man standing before her. The man that she had once been engaged to marry.

"Hello Alina." John smiled his best 'I'm-not-sure-how-I-should-act' smile and stepped forward to attempt a hug. Alina stopped him simply by looking at him.

"Hello John," she greeted him with a slight smile. "It's been a long time."

"Too long!" John agreed, motioning to the bartender for another beer. "Where did you disappear to? One day you were just "POOF" gone!"

"Now why does that sound so familiar?" Alina murmured, just low enough that John was the only one to hear. He looked down at her, his blue eyes inches from hers.

"Oh, now that wasn't very fair," he murmured back. "Don't tell me you're still holding a grudge over a boy's mistake ten years ago?"

Alina studied his face for a moment. He was standing close enough that she could feel his body heat and, at one point in time, that would have been enough to make her consider her response, and maybe even flirt a little. But not anymore. Alina saw before her a part of her past and nothing more. She smiled into his eyes.

"I've moved past that," she murmured. "And lucky for you that I have," she added thoughtfully, lifting her glass to her lips. A brief look of surprise flashed across John's face before an emotionless mask slid into place.

"Well, now that *THAT'S* over....whatever *THAT* was...." Stephanie pushed between them. "Can we play nice while she's in town, or will I have to keep you two separate?"

"You'll have no problems from me," John answered, handing the bartender some bills for his beer. "The past is the past." He glanced once more at Alina and smiled. "More's the pity," he added for her ears alone. Alina made no response and he took his beer and disappeared back into the crowd.

"Well, that went well, I think," Stephanie said cheerfully, holding her glass up. "To new beginnings."

"New beginnings." Angela laughed, raising her glass up and Alina smiled with grudging humor, touching her glass to theirs. As she lifted her glass to her lips, her eyes scanned the crowded bar again.

Suddenly her breath paused as she sipped the drink and her body stilled. There was that familiar feeling, one that had served her so well in the past. It caused a tingling at the base of her skull and the fine hairs on the back of her shoulders rose up as a chill coursed across them. Her military comrades had called it her sixth sense, but she always just thought of it as her instincts.

And they were all screaming now.

Alina lowered the glass and scanned the bar again, seeing nothing different since the last time she had looked. But something was very different.

Someone was watching them.

"Oh for God's Sake!" Stephanie exclaimed, setting her glass down on the bar and reaching into her shoulder bag. "You would think that they could leave me alone for at least one night!" she added, hauling out her cell phone. Alina glanced at Angela, who was shaking her head.

"You better drink up," she advised Alina before doing just that herself. "I'm actually surprised we went *this* long before a call. Our friend is a workaholic and everyone in her department knows it…and takes advantage of it."

"What about her partner?" Alina nodded toward the back corner where John was laughing at something the stocky man next to him was saying.

"John?" Angela snorted. "He ignores his phone until she calls him." It was clear that Angela's opinion of John had not improved over the years. She never had cared much for him, even when Alina had been about to walk down the aisle with him.

"I'm sorry, girls." Stephanie dropped her phone back into her bag and quickly drained her martini. "There was an accident at one of the train crossings and the senior agent in place thinks it may be related to my floater." She set her glass on the bar and reached into her bag to pull out her keys. Alina tossed back the rest of her drink, waiting for Stephanie to remember that she had driven her to the bar.

"Why don't we set something up for next weekend?" Stephanie suggested. "Is everybody free? Maybe dinner at my house? I feel bad, but I really have to run."

"I think I'm free next Saturday. I'll double check my schedule when I get home," Angela replied. She watched with a grin as Stephanie nodded distractedly and turned to leave, keys in hand. Alina raised an eyebrow and glanced at Angela. The two women stood there, watching as Stephanie started to make her way through the crowd.

"Ok. Alina, let me know about next week!" Stephanie called over her shoulder. "Bye!" And the crowd swallowed her up.

"How long do you give her before she remembers?" Alina asked, leaning back against the bar.

"Not until she gets outside and tries to find her car," Angela replied with a laugh. "You really could save her time by meeting her outside, instead of making her come back in." Alina sighed.

"Yes, but it's not nearly as fun!" she replied, and realized with a shock that she meant it. She was having more fun tonight than she had in years.

"Lina!" Angela nudged her. "Come on!"

"Oh fine." Alina straightened up and began moving toward the door. She still felt someone watching them and took one final look around. But the only person she saw was John, watching them leave from his back corner.

Alina got out of the car, taking in the scene of controlled chaos before her. They were at a railroad crossing in Palmyra along River Road, a few miles down from Riverside. Police cars were angled everywhere and large spotlights were trained on the intersection where a freight train hauling logs and metal containers was stopped. A crowd of emergency personnel was clustered in front of the train and Alina didn't have to look too closely to know what had happened.

"I hope they got the body out already," Stephanie said, walking to the front of the car and joining Alina. Although they couldn't see the car, there was no doubt that one was there. "I get light-headed when they have to pry them out."

"Understandable," Alina murmured, leaning backwards on the hood of her car and crossing her arms over her chest. "Does this happen often?"

"No." Stephanie sighed. "This is only my second." She straightened her shoulders and turned to head toward the crowd. "You don't have to stay. I can get a ride home from one of the others."

"It's ok," Alina answered. "I'm kind of curious." she added with a grin. Stephanie shook her head.

"Morbid," she retorted. "Let me see what the story is and I'll be back. I'll let them know not to bother you." Stephanie disappeared into the crowd of officials.

The track crossing was in a fairly busy section of town, with restored businesses lining Main Street on one side of the tracks and restored Victorian homes on the other. This intersection had a bank and an antique store on the corners of one side, and a pastry shop and dry cleaners on the corners of the other side. The streets were well lit on either side of the tracks and brick sidewalks told the story of restored elegance. Palmyra had worked hard to restore the town to its historical brilliance, and Alina was mildly surprised at the success. When she had left ten years ago, Palmyra had been a worn out and tired town. Now, it appeared to be making a valiant effort to clean itself up.

Alina straightened up and wandered toward the sidewalk. She noted the clusters of residents that were standing along the sidewalk, watching the drama being enacted on their doorstep. They were all chattering in low voices, trying to determine if anyone had actually seen the car get hit by the train. Alina moved into the crowds silently, observing everyone and getting another look at the accident from different angles. The right guard that came down to block the tracks when the train was passing had been ripped off its anchor, and one of the red flashing lights was shattered. Thick tire marks on the road led up to the tracks, and Alina paused to glance back and see where they started before continuing to move past the small pockets of residents.

"I was sitting drinking my tea with Harry when I heard what sounded like a backfire," a woman was telling her neighbor, "and then the most awful screeching."

"I thought it was Victors darn movie that he had cranked up so loud," the neighbor responded, shaking her head. "I yelled at him to turn it down, but he had already muted the TV."

"I hope there were no children in that car," another woman was saying. Alina moved away and back towards her car. Some teenage boys had walked up to it and were peering through the windows. She moved up behind them silently.

"It doesn't really transform," she said dryly. The three boys jumped and swung around.

"We know that," one said with a nervous laugh. "It's a sweet ride."

"It would be sweeter without your paw prints all over it," Alina answered. The boys shuffled out of her way and away from the car. Alina leaned against her car and looked around.

Someone was still watching her. She could feel it.

"Well, they have an initial confirmation on the body." Stephanie joined her a few moments later. "Looks like it's someone who has been on *my* watch list for quite some time." She leaned back against the hood and the two of them watched as the coroner's van came to life and slowly pulled away from the collection of emergency vehicles clustered around the tracks.

"And?" Alina asked.

"I have to wait for the official confirmation, but if it's him, this case just became a huge headache of red tape and supers breathing down my neck," Stephanie muttered. She glanced at Alina. "Are you sure you don't want to leave? I want to wait for some of these people to clear out of here so I can get a better look at the scene."

"I have nowhere to be right now," Alina assured her with a grin. "And if I did, I would leave. Did you see the shattered flasher light?"

"Yes." Stephanie followed Alina's gaze to the broken red light and guard rail.

"My guess is you'll find a bullet went through it, probably a .308 or NATO round," Alina said. "Probably fired from the roof of the antique store behind us. You'll find that two of the street lights are out too."

"What makes you say that?" Stephanie glanced behind them and followed the trajectory from the roof to the crossing with her eyes.

"Because it's what I would have done." Alina straightened. "This was a professional hit. It was clean and quick. The neighbors all heard the same version of the same thing in a very small space of time. There were no mistakes and no clumsiness."

"I leave you alone for ten minutes and you already have a theory for me." Stephanie shook her head. "What did you say you did in the military?" Alina grinned.

"I didn't," she replied. "You also might want to take a good look at the tire marks. I think you will find that they were made by *two* vehicles, not one."

"Where are you going?" Stephanie demanded as Alina began to walk away.

"The roof of that antique store." Alina winked at her. "I've made myself curious as to the probability of my theory."

"Not without me you're not!" Stephanie followed quickly. "This is *my* investigation! And you don't know anything about investigating."

"No," Alina agreed congenially. "But I love a good mystery."

Stephanie glanced at her suspiciously, but Alina's expression was concealed by the darkness as they moved quickly away from the bright flashing lights of the accident. She followed Alina as she moved across the street and down the sidewalk, along the side of the corner antique store. Alina was moving steadily, her eyes scanning the building and the roof in a single glance. They rounded the corner of the building and started up the road until Alina found what she was looking for: the fire escape ladder lowered from the roof.

"Are you afraid of heights?" she asked Stephanie, reaching out for the ladder.

"No."

"Good." Alina grabbed the ladder and went up quickly and silently. Stephanie followed and Alina winced at the sound of her clanking and huffing up the ladder. Stealth was apparently *not* Stephanie's strong point. Alina cleared the roof and moved to the side to allow Stephanie access. As soon as she joined her, Alina held up her hand to signal silence. Without really knowing why, Stephanie obeyed.

The roof was a massive expanse of inky darkness stretching before them. The lights from the road didn't penetrate this far above, and the sounds of the commotion below were a distant memory. Up here, it was silent and slightly ominous. They had some light from a half moon and a few straggling stars that had fought their way through the pollution-laden sky to shine faintly above. Alina scanned the darkness, still and listening.

"Here," Stephanie whispered. Alina felt something thin and heavy touch her hand. She looked down in some surprise at a mag light.

"Thanks." Alina switched on the light and angled it down at their feet.

The flat rooftop had been covered with a black tar coating fairly recently. It was smooth and not weathered yet. Alina raised the light a little and played it over the roof toward the front of the building. There was an air conditioning box midway between them and the front of the building. Over to the left was a ledge where this roof ended and the connecting roof of the building next door began. Alina noted briefly that the roof next door was much older and had gravel and debris covering it before she turned her attention to the right. A few yards to their right was another ledge where the roof ended. She stood for another moment, listening. The silence was almost oppressive.

Stephanie began to move forward toward the front of the building, examining the rooftop as she moved. Alina followed slowly, lighting her way with the flashlight and concentrating on their surroundings. She was confident that their shooter had long since disappeared, but Alina still felt something in the silence. It was that something that made her move into a protective position at Stephanie's back.

"There." Stephanie paused and pointed. Alina directed the light over her shoulder to the front corner of the antique store where Stephanie was pointing. "If you're right, that's the only clear shot from up here."

Alina nodded. That corner was the only spot that a shooter could take out both the crossing light and the street lights. The two women moved forward together, and then separated to skirt a wide area around where they imagined the shooter must have positioned himself. Alina played the light along the edge of the ledge, looking for the telltale scraping of a rifle barrel. She knew it had to be there. The roof was too new not to have allowed some sign of a high-powered rifle being fired repeatedly off the edge. On her second pass over the edge, the light paused and then went back. She held it steadily on the spot and heard Stephanie's intake of breath.

"Well, I'll be damned," she breathed. "You were right." Under the light was a half-inch wide gouge in the ledge, positioned in direct line of sight with the crossing intersection. Alina moved forward carefully and squatted down a few feet away to gauge the trajectory. There was a perfect shot to both the intersection and two dark street lights, one on each corner.

"You better get your boys up here," Alina finally spoke, standing up. From this height, the commotion at the crossing intersection looked very inconsequential and far away. "I

doubt they'll find anything, but it will help with a profile."
Stephanie nodded in agreement, staring out over the scene
below.

"Why take out the street lights and the flasher?" she
asked suddenly. "Why not just shoot the driver?"

"Too many unknown variables," Alina answered. "No
way to control where the car goes. If you take out the lights,
you can impair visibility, create confusion, and allow someone
else to direct traffic until you shoot the driver at the last
minute." Stephanie glanced over to Alina.

"The second car," she said.

Alina nodded and turned to go back across the roof
while   Stephanie followed thoughtfully. As Alina passed the
air conditioning unit, she caught a whiff of a familiar smell,
one that she had smelled recently, and that she suddenly also
remembered from her past. She paused with a frown and
turned toward the unit, playing the light over it thoughtfully.

"What is it?" Stephanie stopped beside her, following her
gaze curiously. Alina's lips curved into a slight smile in the
darkness.

"Nothing," she answered quietly. "Just a sense of déjà
vu. Nothing important."

Alina sat in the silent shadows on the deck, enveloped by
the darkness. The night sky was clear and the stars were
bright out here, the breeze carrying the scent of late spring.
An owl hooted off to the left and the song of tree frogs filled
the air. She watched the darkness, breathing deeply. Stephanie
had been confused tonight. Two bodies within the space of
twenty-four hours and no leads was a Federal agent's
nightmare. Alina shook her head slightly and lifted a cold
water bottle to her lips. She had made things worse by

pointing out the shooter and the second pair of tire prints. Stephanie would have found them eventually, but Alina discovered that she didn't have the patience to sit and watch the agency bumble around, even for a few hours. Stephanie was quiet on the drive home, and Alina knew that she had been processing her involvement at the crime scene. Stephanie would have questions now, but Alina didn't have time to humor her. Stephanie was Alina's main source of information at the moment, and Alina couldn't afford to have her miss a thing. She needed Stephanie to lead her to her quarry. She just wanted to get her mission over with and get out of Jersey. The old friendships and the old memories were reminders of her old life. She didn't want to remember that life.

Alina didn't know that girl anymore.

A movement in the darkness caught her attention. It was more a shifting of light and space, and she knew someone was there. Alina watched silently, her body still and her breathing slow. For several long moments, she sat silently waiting. When the man appeared out of the darkness, she slowly relaxed. Alina remained immobile as he moved silently across the yard toward her. She had no doubt that he knew she was there, even as she blended with the shadows around herself.

"*Viper.*" The quiet word drifted in the breeze. Alina felt the hair on her neck and arms raise at the name that she had not heard herself called in over two years.

"I knew it was you," she said as the man stepped onto the deck. He was tall, with broad shoulders, and dressed in black SWAT pants and a black t-shirt. His black combat boots made no sound on the wooden deck. He moved with the silent stealth and grace of a jungle cat, and Alina knew that he was just as dangerous. "This evening, on the roof, I knew you were there too."

"I hope I wasn't *that* obvious," the man replied, his low rich voice surrounding her like a warm towel. He moved across the deck to stand before her chair. Alina smiled slightly and stood.

"Not at all," she assured him, reaching up to wrap her arms around his shoulders in a hug. "Hello, Hawk." Alina brushed her lips across his cheek in greeting and stepped back to smile at him.

"It's been a long time," Hawk said with an answering smile.

"It always is." Alina picked up her water bottle and turned toward the sliding doors. "Come inside where we can talk."

Hawk nodded, and then froze as there was a *whoosh* of large wings and Raven swooped down out of nowhere. Alina grinned as Hawk instinctively ducked. Raven skimmed over his shoulder and came to rest on the back of the chair she had just vacated.

"Now, Hawk...you're not afraid of a real hawk, are you?" she asked dryly.

"Yours?" Hawk asked, straightening and glancing at the bird watching him with shiny black eyes. Alina tilted her head and considered Raven for a moment.

"Raven seems to think so." Alina opened the back door. "Come on. He won't hurt you unless you threaten me." She stepped into the dark living room and began walking toward the kitchen, not waiting to see if Hawk followed. He did, stepping into the house silently. He glanced back at the hawk sitting on the chair and closed the door.

"You certainly haven't lost your knack for surprising me, Alina," he said, following her.

"I'm glad I don't disappoint, Damon," she retorted with a laugh. "Would you like something to drink?"

"Water is fine." Damon glanced around the kitchen as she flipped on the light. His eyes took in the black granite counter tops and the matching island and bar in one glance. "Nice place."

"I would thank you if I didn't suspect that you had seen it already."

Alina opened the fridge and pulled out a bottle of water, tossing it to him. In the light of the kitchen, she examined him. His dark hair still fell over his forehead in a soft wave and his eyes were still just as blue. Damon Miles stood six feet two inches high and had shoulders as broad as a barn. His arms were muscular and his body was solid strength, a testimony to a healthy and very active lifestyle. He raised a dark eyebrow as he caught the bottle with one hand.

"I don't know what you're talking about." He opened the bottle and took a long sip, moving to a bar stool at the counter that separated the kitchen and living room.

"No?" Alina leaned against the island and watched him. "A few nights ago there was a breach in my security system when I wasn't here. A circuit that I carelessly left exposed."

"Really?" Damon looked surprised. "I hope you fixed the weak spot."

"I have." Alina moved over to sit next to him. "But next time, you may want to take care not to trip the sensors in the floors." Damon leaned his arms on the bar top and looked sideways at her.

"How do you know it was me?"

"Because you still smell the same," Alina stated. "What were you doing here?"

"Just taking a look around." Damon grinned. "I wanted to see if you had changed at all. Aside from one weak circuit, which took me an hour to find, you're just as thorough as you always were."

"I took a sabbatical. I didn't lose my mind," Alina retorted.

"There are some that would argue that, I'm sure." Damon winked. "Did you really go to South America?"

"I can't imagine you came all this way to discuss my whereabouts for the past two years," Alina replied. Damon grinned.

"No. I came to help you," he said simply. Alina raised an eyebrow.

"And why would you do that?" she asked politely.

"Because I was sent here." Damon drank some more water.

"I should have known this looked too easy," Alina sighed. "How much do you know?"

"I know that they tracked you down to South America and invited you to complete a mission that you unaccountably failed two years ago," Damon answered bluntly. "They think you had a breakdown. I know you better than that, so I'm open to suggestion on what *really* happened two years ago."

"Keep going." Alina drank her water and turned on her stool to face him. His rugged profile was cast in shadows from the light behind them and she took note of the short scar running from behind his ear to the beginning of his jaw-line. It hadn't been there the last time she saw him.

"London, two years ago," Damon said, without turning his head.

"Pardon?"

"The scar. It happened in London two years ago." He looked at her, his blue eyes dancing, and Alina's lips curved into a reluctant grin.

"Still a mind reader, I see," she murmured. Damon raised an eyebrow.

"It doesn't take much mind reading when you were staring at it," he retorted. Alina snorted.

"I wasn't staring."

"You were staring," Damon reiterated, sipping his water.

"So you know they pulled me back in from South America..." Alina prompted him back to the original conversation irritably. Damon laughed and turned to face her.

"Two years ago, you were supposed to take out a known terrorist named Johann Topamari, who has ties to the terrorist cell called Mossavid. For some reason, known only to yourself, you failed. It was the first time you ever failed and, quite frankly, I would love to know what happened. But I accept the fact that I probably never will, so moving on..." He recounted her own past to her matter-of-factly. "Following that, you dropped off the grid. Disappeared. Turns out you were on sabbatical, destination unknown, until one month ago when they found you. They pulled you back in because, after two long years, Johann has finally resurfaced, minus his security, and in the United States. You tracked him once. They are giving you a chance to redeem yourself. Did I miss anything?"

"Yes." Alina set down her water bottle. "Where do you fit into my continuing story?"

"Operating on US soil is more complicated than operating in Europe or the Middle East. The powers that be are concerned about containment."

"*You* are containment?" Alina's lips twitched. "How refreshing!" Damon grinned.

"I knew you would appreciate the irony," he replied.

"I work alone," Alina said.

"So do I," Damon retorted. "So it's a good thing that you have your assignment and I have mine."

"Since when did baby-sitting become part of your job description?" Alina demanded. Damon smiled. Alina stared at him, trying to intimidate him, and Damon simply stared back. "If there is something else going on here, I need to know," she finally said. Damon shook his head.

"Nothing that will interfere with you," he answered. Alina studied him, trying to determine if she believed him. Damon sighed. "We've known each other a long time. Are you going to tell me that, after all this time, you don't trust me?"

"It's not that I don't trust you." Alina picked her words carefully. "I just question why, if operating on US soil is so sensitive, they now have two of us doing it." Damon was silent for a moment and the sparkle that had been in his eyes ever since he stepped foot into the house faded.

"As I said before, you have your operation and I have mine," he finally said. "Our goals are temporarily joined." The sparkle leapt back into his dark eyes. "I have every confidence that we'll find a way to rub along together." A reluctant laugh escaped from Alina.

"Oh absolutely!" she agreed. "As long as you stay out of my way."

"My dear, I would never dream of getting in your way." Damon stood up and smiled down at her. "I have seen you work before and it truly is a thing of beauty." Alina nodded in acknowledgement and looked up at him.

"Where are you staying?" she asked.

"Not far." He grinned. "I'm sure you will find it." Alina smiled.

"Absolutely," she murmured, watching him move back toward the sliding door. A few seconds later he was gone. Alina picked up his empty water bottle and moved to put it in the sink. She switched out the lights and went up to bed thoughtfully.

Chapter Three

Alina slowly opened her eyes at the sound of her phone chirping. It was a little after seven on Monday morning and she was seated in lotus pose on the deck. The cell phone was a few feet away on the arm of one of the Adirondack chairs. Raven was perched on the back of the other one, hunched down and watchful. Alina stretched and reached out to grab the phone, smiling at Raven. He still only went away to hunt and then came straight home. He wasn't sure how he felt about this strange place yet, with all its hustle and bustle.

"Yes?" Alina answered the phone and slowly began to untangle her legs.

"Do you have a coffee maker?" Stephanie asked. Alina blinked.

"Yes."

"Good. I have bagels," Stephanie answered. "I'm out front."

"Come around back. You can park back here." Alina hung up and did one final stretch as Stephanie's gray maxima rolled around the side of the house. Raven lifted his head and watched as Stephanie shut off the engine and got out of the car, carrying a white bakery bag and her purse. Alina watched Stephanie as well, amused that even at seven in the morning, she still looked frazzled.

"Morning!" Stephanie called, slamming her door shut and starting across the lawn toward the deck. She stopped dead when she saw Raven watching her. "Oh My God! What is *THAT?!?!*"

"A hawk," Alina answered, laughing. Stephanie stared at him with wide eyes.

"He looks dangerous," she finally said. Alina nodded.

"He's a bird of prey," she said. "He can be very dangerous. But not unless you try to harm me. He's my pet."

Stephanie licked her lips and continued to stand there, frozen, staring at the black hawk. Raven stared back, unimpressed. Alina sighed and moved forward to meet

Stephanie. She reached out and took the bakery bag, then turned and led the way back up onto the deck. Stephanie followed reluctantly, keeping an eye on Raven the whole time.

"Do I even want to ask why you have a pet hawk?" Stephanie asked, relaxing slightly as they stepped onto the deck and Raven made no attempt to fly at her, claws barred.

"He adopted me," Alina answered simply, crossing the deck to the sliding door. "He was injured and I took care of him."

Alina glanced at Raven fondly. As if on cue, Raven straightened up and spread his wings in a stretch. Stephanie jumped and grabbed the back of Alina's shirt. Alina burst out laughing and opened the door as Raven settled back down on the chair contentedly.

"Is he *laughing* at me?!" Stephanie demanded, stepping into the house and closing the door behind her. "Did your bird do that on purpose?!"

"Probably." Alina chuckled and led the way into the kitchen. "So to what do I owe this pleasure?" Stephanie dropped her purse on the bar and looked around the kitchen and dining room curiously.

"Can't a friend bring bagels for breakfast?" she asked.

Alina set the bag on the counter in the kitchen and went over to the coffee machine on the counter. It was a super-automatic espresso machine that made full cups of rich coffee on demand. Alina had paid over two thousand dollars for it and didn't regret a penny.

"I drink espresso. Is that ok for you?" Alina turned to look at Stephanie. "If not, I have tea." Stephanie's eyes widened again as she moved across the kitchen to inspect the coffee machine.

"I've seen these in the gourmet kitchen stores," she remarked. "They're expensive! Is it worth it?"

"It is if you love your coffee," Alina answered. "Espresso or no?"

"I'll try it." Stephanie looked at Alina. "What did you say you did again?"

"Consulting." Alina placed a mug under the spout on the coffee maker and pressed a button. The machine began grinding beans, and a few seconds later hot espresso started streaming into the mug. "There's milk in the fridge and sugar substitute in the sugar canister," she added.

Stephanie grinned and turn to the refrigerator to pull out a quart of skim milk. She wrinkled her nose, but said nothing as Alina handed her the steaming mug of black coffee. Alina put another mug under the spout and pressed the button before turning to get plates from the cabinet.

"Shouldn't you be at the office?" she asked. Stephanie sipped the espresso and immediately grimaced. She began pouring milk into the mug.

"I wanted to come talk to you first," she answered. She tasted the coffee again and reached for the sugar canister. "This is really strong!"

"It's espresso," Alina retorted. She pulled two toasted bagels with cream cheese out of the bag and put them on plates. "I don't suppose this cream cheese is low fat?"

"No. You need some fat in your diet," Stephanie answered cheerfully. She added more skim milk to her coffee. "Everything in your fridge is fat free." Alina took her coffee from the coffee maker, grabbed one of the plates and headed back towards the deck. Stephanie finished doctoring her coffee, picked up the other plate and followed. "Aren't you putting milk in yours?" she demanded. Alina laughed.

"No. I drink it black," she answered.

Stephanie grimaced at her back and followed her outside. They went to the opposite end of the deck from Raven to a black iron bistro table and two chairs. Stephanie sat down and glanced at the hawk. He was paying no attention to them, staring instead at something deep in the woods to his left. She relaxed and looked at Alina.

"This is a nice house," she commented. "Are you going to stay?" Alina laughed.

"I've only been back a few days," she answered. "I don't know yet. Why did you want to talk to me?"

"Saturday night you were very interested in my investigation," Stephanie began slowly. Alina watched her as she took a bite of her bagel and waited patiently for Stephanie to continue. "If there is something I should know about you being back, I would appreciate it if you would tell me now." Stephanie finally blurted out. Alina swallowed some coffee and shrugged.

"I'm not with your mysterious assisting agency that is showing up today, if that is what you're asking," she replied calmly, her face not giving anything away. "When *does* your agent arrive, anyway?"

"He's there now," Stephanie answered, taking a bite of her bagel and watching Alina while she chewed.

She had been giving a lot of thought to Alina's reappearance after Saturday night and she knew that it wasn't just a coincidence. But Alina was giving nothing away, and Stephanie realized that she was going to have to wait for Alina to tell her why she had come back on her own. It didn't take a genius to figure out that it had something to do with her 'consulting.'

"Then shouldn't you be there too?" Alina asked mildly. Stephanie shrugged.

"John is briefing him," she answered. "I'm in no rush to meet the suit that is going to get in my way." Alina grinned.

"Maybe he's cute," she suggested, wiggling her eyebrows. Stephanie laughed despite herself.

"He's probably as cocky as they come," she retorted. Alina nodded and sat back, sipping her coffee.

"Probably," she agreed. "Why do you have another agency coming in on this again?"

"At first I thought it was because Angelo had ties to some international gun trafficking," Stephanie said after a moment. "But now I'm not so sure. It's Homeland Security that is sticking their nose in." Alina raised an eyebrow.

"National security?" she asked. "That's more than gun trafficking." Steph nodded.

"I know," she finished her bagel and eyed the half that was left on Alina's plate. "Are you going to finish that?" she asked. Alina shook her head, watching as Stephanie reached out and took it.

"The only reason I'm telling you any of this is because you helped me on Saturday night at the tracks," she said around a mouthful of bagel. "I don't know what you did in the military, or out of it, or for whom, but you know more about this mess than you're letting on." Stephanie held up a hand when Alina opened her mouth to talk. "All I'm saying is that I will share information with you, if you do the same."

"What makes you think I have any information to share?" Alina asked, setting down her coffee mug. "I was curious on Saturday. I told you that."

"Curious my foot." Stephanie snorted and washed the bagel down with the coffee. "You were deliberate. As long as you aren't working against me, and I don't think for a minute that you are, than we should be able to share information quite happily. Don't you agree?"

Alina was quiet while she considered Stephanie. She had connected the dots much faster than Alina had expected, but she found that it wasn't as much of an inconvenience as she thought it would be. Stephanie was clearly prepared to work loosely with Alina, and that was even without knowing why Alina was interested in her case. Things would move much faster if Stephanie freely gave Alina the information she needed. In return, she just had to keep Stephanie satisfied with any conclusions that she herself would draw eventually. It really was a win-win situation.

Alina tried to ignore the feeling of disquiet that she felt in using her old friend to help her complete her own mission. Years of working alone made her unused to this situation. Alina never had to consider how her actions would affect others. Now that had changed. She needed Stephanie. And Stephanie was completely unaware of it, but she needed Alina too. Stephanie had no idea what she was getting herself into.

"That seems reasonable," Alina finally spoke, dropping all pretense of non-involvement. "But how will you explain me to your superiors?"

"I don't need to," Stephanie replied. "You're a source." She stood up and stretched, then smiled. "To be honest, I am more concerned with how I'll explain you to John." Alina shrugged impatiently.

"I told you. The past is the past," she retorted. "You'll have no issues from me."

"It's not you I'm worried about," Stephanie retorted.

"Took you long enough to get here." John looked up from his computer screen as Stephanie dropped her bag onto her desk and set her coffee down.

"I had breakfast with Alina." Stephanie dropped into her chair and looked at him. "How's the visitor?"

"With the bossman." John got up from his desk and sauntered the two feet to hers. He leaned on it and looked down at her. "Alina, huh? How is she?"

"Just fine." Stephanie pulled open her bottom drawer and dropped her purse into it. "She does not send her love." John chuckled.

"I never imagined she would," he retorted. "She's changed," he added. Stephanie leaned back in her chair and looked up at her handsome partner.

"It's been ten years," she said. "She grew up." John shook his head.

"It's not just the time," he said. He played with a stapler on Stephanie's desk while he searched for the right words to say. "Her eyes are different. She's different. It's like...I don't know...like there is no emotion inside her anymore."

Stephanie was quiet for a moment. She knew what John was trying to say. She had seen it too. However, she wouldn't have said that there was no emotion. Just that it was very effectively hidden.

"Why do you say that?" she asked. "Because she didn't fall for your 'I've- changed-since-you-went-away-let's-be-friends' act?" John put the stapler down and stood up.

"Drink your coffee, Steph," he advised, heading back toward his desk. "Your claws are showing."

"Miss. Walker!" a voice called across the expanse of partial cubicle walls. Stephanie looked up to see her boss motioning from his office door.

"Better drink it fast," John advised, seating himself. "Don't want to make a bad impression on our colleague from Homeland Security." Stephanie picked up her coffee and headed toward the office.

"Ass," she muttered as she passed him. She heard him chuckle after she passed and grit her teeth. Sometimes she just wanted to punch him.

"Good morning, Rob." Stephanie walked through the open door into her boss's cluttered office. It wasn't a very large office. It boasted a desk that was covered with piles of folders and papers and two bookshelves that were also crammed with a mix of binders and folders. There were three filing cabinets, the tops of which held an assortment of tropical plants, and two chairs faced the desk. One was occupied by a man wearing a charcoal gray suit.

"Good morning." Rob Thornton moved behind his desk and motioned to the man in the suit. "This is Damon Peterson, from Homeland Security." The suit stood up and turned toward her. Stephanie found herself staring up into the brightest pair of blue eyes she had ever seen. "Damon, this is Stephanie Walker. She is the agent in charge of the case."

"Hello." Stephanie held out her hand and Damon shook it firmly.

"Good morning." Damon flashed a smile and Stephanie found herself smiling back. Lord, the man was good-looking! She seated herself and her coffee in the other chair and turned her attention to her boss. As soon as she sat, the other two men sat.

"We'll be working with DHS on this one, Steph," Rob informed her, sitting back in his chair and steepling his fingers over his stomach. "They seem to think your floater may have some connection with a terrorist they believe got into the States on a stolen visa." Stephanie blinked.

"A terrorist?" she repeated, swinging her head to look at Damon. He was sitting back in his chair, relaxed, watching her. He nodded when she looked at him.

"We believe he got into the States over a month ago. We have been working with local LEOs to try to determine where he is now," he told her. "I believe your floater was supplying guns either directly to him or to his go-between." Stephanie took a deep breath and let it out in a long sigh.

"Fabulous," she muttered. Damon chuckled.

"Of course, we could be wasting our time here," he added. "But we need to be sure. Robert has assured me of your co-operation."

"Of course." Stephanie nodded. "What I know, you'll know."

"Wonderful." Damon stood up. "Get me copies of everything you have and I will try to make this as painless as possible," he added with another flashing grin. Stephanie stood up and smiled.

"I never claimed it would be painful!" she protested. Damon winked.

"You don't have to," he replied. "I'm used to it. No one is ever happy to see us come into their office."

"What's this terrorists' name?" Stephanie asked as Damon turned to shake hands with Rob.

"Johann," Damon answered over his shoulder. "Johann Topamari. Thanks again, Rob."

"No problem." Rob shook his hand. "You're sure you won't set up here?"

"No, thanks." Damon grinned. "I've learned that it's more effective for me to work off-site. I have a temporary office set up with everything I need."

"Oh? You're not working here? With us?" Stephanie's spirits lifted somewhat. Damon looked down at her.

"I'll tag along, if needed," he said, "but I won't be hovering over your shoulder." He stood aside and motioned for her to precede him out of the office. "However, that being said, I'll know if you withhold anything from me, so I wouldn't advise it," he added as she passed. Stephanie looked up at him consideringly.

"You know, I think you would," she said slowly.

"Good! Then we understand each other," Damon said with a return of his smile. "That's a good base for a successful relationship." He held out his hand again, but this time there was a business card in it. "Numbers and emails are on the front and address on the back. I look forward to working with you."

"Well, I won't say the same because I try not to lie," Stephanie replied, taking the card. "But I have to say I feel much better about this than I did earlier." Damon laughed.

"I like honesty. It saves time," he said with a grin. "Did you get forensics back yet?"

"Not yet. I'm expecting it today." Stephanie turned toward her desk. "Have you met John?"

"Earlier. He gave me a run-down of our two bodies," Damon answered. "I'll leave you to get on with it. Forward me the forensics when you get them."

"Will do." Stephanie watched as he walked away, headed for the elevators. Women turned and watched him as he passed and she shook her head, turning to go back to her desk. She sank into her chair and picked up a pen absently, twirling it around her fingers and staring off into nowhere.

She had two bodies in the morgue, one of whom was suspected of supplying a known terrorist with arms and ammunition. As a result of that, she now had DHS looking over her shoulder. She had an old friend who mysteriously re-appeared suddenly from God-knows where, right on time for the first body to float up, and who was clearly no stranger to the finer points of sniper positioning. Stephanie sighed and threw her pen down on the desk. Add to that a bird of prey and an ex-boyfriend who was destined to cause complications, whether he meant to or not, and she was pretty sure that this was shaping up to be one of the more challenging cases of her short career.

And Stephanie had the uneasy feeling that things were just getting started.

Alina glanced at her watch and sipped her coffee. She was seated in a coffee shop on a side street in Haddonfield. It was a cute little coffee shop, with a cute little name and big comfortable arm chairs with low tables between them. It fancied itself a haven for artists and independent thinkers, and a section in the corner was set aside for either speakers or musicians. Abstract art mingled with framed replicas of long past political figures on the walls while Coldplay moaned out of hidden speakers. The owners had no interest in high priced cappuccino and chic tables. The coffee was reasonably priced and served in plain white mugs, and the chairs were mismatched and comfortable. This was meant to be a meeting area of minds and people who also happened to enjoy a good cup of coffee.

Alina glanced around in some amusement. She was sure that in the evenings the shop attracted just that sort of clientèle. However, at ten-thirty in the morning, she was fairly confident that she was the only childless woman there. Her fellow patrons fell into the sole category of busy, stay-at-home soccer moms, stopping for their mid-morning pick-me up. Alina turned her attention back to her folded over newspaper. When Hawk got here, she really must remember to ask him just how he had found this pretentious hole.

A few moments later, the bell chimed above the door and Alina lifted her eyes to watch Hawk stroll up to the counter and order himself a large, part this and part that, with a dash of something else monstrosity of a coffee drink to go. She stifled a grin. He was even dressed for the part, in low rise jeans and a faded green Gap tee-shirt. Her eyes briefly landed on his rear and Alina raised them again quickly as he turned around. One thing she had always acknowledged was that Damon had a mighty fine ass.

"Sorry I'm late. The contractors were late," he flashed a grin as he stopped before her and Alina felt her lips curving into an answering laugh.

"No worries," she said, tucking her paper back into her over-sized black leather tote bag and standing up. "I'll forgive you this time," she added with a wink. The girl behind the counter was watching them curiously, enjoying her own view of Damon's rear end.

"Do you need a refill?" Damon asked, taking in her short denim skirt and bright yellow halter top in one glance. His lips were twitching by the time they got to her matching yellow wedge flip-flops. Alina nodded, watching over his shoulder as the girl behind the counter immediately straightened up and snapped to attention.

"I would love one," she said. They walked back to the counter and Damon ordered her a large, 20 oz. straight espresso, black. He remembered her coffee preference. The man really never forgot a thing. The girl behind the counter gave Alina the same brief look of amazement that she had given her earlier when Alina had ordered the same thing.

"Are you sure you don't want to have some steamed water added?" she asked once again. Alina smiled.

"No, thank you," she answered. Damon chuckled.

"That would dilute the caffeine and we can't have that," he told the girl with a grin and a wink. She laughed and turned to get Alina's coffee. A few minutes later she handed her the to-go cup.

"God Bless you," she said to Alina. "If I drank that, I would be up for days straight." Alina smiled and took her coffee and she and Damon turned to leave the shop.

"That girl will forever remember you as the woman in yellow, who drinks straight espresso by the gallon," Damon said as they exited into the sunshine on the sidewalk. "Let's walk."

"And she will forever remember *you* as the guy with the great ass," Alina retorted, turning right and walking with him toward the main street that was filled with shops and bistros. Damon grinned.

"Will she now?" he demanded. Alina nodded.

"You know darn well she was staring," she answered. "How did you find that place, anyway?"

"Appalling, isn't it?" Damon asked cheerfully. "I fully expect it to go commercial and find one on every corner soon. Reminds me of a tiny hole in the wall in Amsterdam."

"I've never been to Amsterdam," Alina said thoughtfully. "Never had occasion to. Is it nice?"

"It's...interesting," Damon answered. "I can't imagine they would want you there. You would cause too much ruckus. It's turning into a modern day Casablanca. More spooks than tourists." Alina nodded complacently. She had never had any illusions about her job.

"So why the pressing need to meet?" she asked as they emerged onto Main Street and joined the mid-morning throng.

"I found out something that you might find interesting," Damon answered, sipping his coffee. He grimaced and tossed the full cup into the closest trash can. Alina grinned and handed him hers. He drank some thankfully. "Mmmm....much better."

"Why *did* you order that milky nonsense?" Alina demanded. Damon grinned.

"All part of the illusion, m'dear."

"Hmmpf," was Alina's only response. "I never mess with my coffee. The shoes were bad enough." Damon burst out laughing.

"When I told you to blend in, I really didn't think you would listen so well," he said, taking another look at the trendy skirt. "I didn't know you *had* legs!"

"You know exactly what I look like," Alina retorted, hiking her absurdly large bag higher on her shoulder. "What do you think I will find interesting?"

"Well, I got a call last night from your friend and mine, Harry...in DC." Damon got back to business and turned his attention from her legs to the pavement in front of them. "Turns out that he is a little concerned about some developments that cropped up over the bridge."

"Is he still playing cops and robbers for Homeland Security?" Alina asked, taking her coffee back and drinking. Damon nodded.

"Trying to. Apparently, something happened over at Three Mile Island."

"Three Mile Island?" Alina glanced at him, surprised despite herself. "As in...nuclear plant....one reactor shut down since the 70's....mother of all cold war horror stories...*that* Three Mile Island?"

"That's the one." Damon grasped her elbow lightly and turned her down an oak-lined side street. "I think the Church is down here, darling."

"I think you're paranoid, dear," Alina retorted, nevertheless slipping her arm around his waist. "No one is paying an ounce of attention to us," she hissed.

"I know," Damon answered cheerfully. "I just wanted to see what you would do."

Alina bit her lip to keep from laughing and pulled away.

"Will you be serious?!" she demanded. Damon laughed down at her, his blue eyes glinting.

"I'm always serious with you," he murmured with a wink. He turned his attention back to the street and guided her across to a Catholic church. They went inside and moved down the dimly-lit center aisle of the deserted sanctuary. Damon stepped into a pew three-quarters of the way to the front, and Alina briefly genuflected in the aisle before following him. They knelt on the kneeler together.

"I didn't know you were Catholic," Damon whispered.

"There's a lot you don't know," Alina whispered back. "Now tell me about the Island."

"A security guard lost his clearance badge last week," Damon replied, his head bowed as though in prayer. Alina kept her face forward toward the alter, her eyes alert.

"That doesn't constitute an incident," Alina answered.

"No," Damon agreed. "But the guard is now missing."

"Well, hell." Alina bowed her head and glanced at Damon. Brown eyes met blue.

"Your friend at the Bureau doesn't know it yet, but she's about to get dragged into one big mess," Damon said. Alina shrugged.

"She's already in it," she retorted. "Any ideas on the whereabouts of the guard?"

"Not yet." Damon lowered his head again and Alina did the same. "The badge was reported missing at night when he came back from a break and it was gone from his desk. He followed security protocol and then left for the night. He didn't show up for his next shift 2 nights later, and he hasn't been seen or heard from since he walked out the gates."

"Fabulous." Alina closed her eyes, her mind working rapidly. "When was his missed shift?"

"Friday," Damon answered. "Three days ago. They're looking for him, but they want you to be aware."

"And you're going to make sure, if the body surfaces, that Stephanie is brought in," Alina stated rather than asked.

"Of course." Damon chuckled. "She is one unhappy camper with me sticking my nose in, but I won't take it personally."

"Don't." Alina smiled slightly. "She has no idea who you are. If she knew you were with me, she would love you."

"Well, don't be too modest now." Damon crossed himself awkwardly and sat back on the pew. He felt, rather than heard, Alina chuckle. She remained kneeling for a moment, and Damon afforded himself of the unabashed pleasure of viewing her from the back. He always said that she had a fine body and he was thoroughly enjoying the opportunity to become re-acquainted with it now from his vantage point. After a moment, Alina crossed herself and joined him on the pew. They sat for a few moments in silence.

"I am not getting involved in a possible incident on the Island," she finally said. "I'm only taking care of my agenda, not theirs. Homeland Security is not, and never was, our job."

"I told them you would say that," Damon replied. They fell silent again, Alina brooding and Damon patiently waiting. He knew Viper well. He knew that she wouldn't sit by and allow a possible terrorist attack occur on US soil if she had the ability to prevent it.

"I was enjoying my sabbatical," Alina finally muttered, her tone coming as close to a whine as Damon had ever heard from her. "I hadn't necessarily retired, but the effect was the same."

"People like us never retire," Damon answered. "You know that."

They fell silent again. Alina knew he was right. They had been trained to become assassins. They worked on the "right side" of the law and in conjunction with the United States government. They were sanctioned at the highest level. But, essentially, they were trained to kill for a living. This was not something that allowed for a career change. She had always known that. Even if and when they retired, killers were still killers. Contracts were still made. Consulting was still done. The game was never really over. Not until your own time came.

"Tell me something." Alina looked over at him. "Did you volunteer for this? Or did I just luck out that it was you?" Damon grinned. Blue eyes met brown again.

"Both," he said with a chuckle. "No one else could have handled you."

"Oh, so *that's* what you think you're doing." Alina stood and picked up her purse, turning to move out of the pew. Damon laughed and stood up.

"I have my aspirations in life," he retorted, following her. Alina made a sound that sounded very suspiciously like a snort and began walking back up the aisle toward the door.

"Well, given the developments, I guess I'm stuck with you," she said as they reached the heavy wooden doors to the sanctuary. "But you might as well know, I am not thrilled with the situation. As much as I love you, I have never cared to be manipulated. You might want to pass that message on." Damon reached around her and pushed open one of the heavy doors, holding it open for her to pass out before him.

"Trust me," he said. "I already warned them." They stepped back outside into the warm spring sunlight. "But I'm a little hurt to actually hear you say it," he added. Alina looked up at him.

"It's nothing personal," she told him. "Think of yourself as Jafar's parrot. You're essentially harmless, but trouble is usually right behind you." Damon stared at her, torn between shock and laughter.

"I don't know which bothers me more," he told her. "You saying I'm harmless or the fact that you watch Disney movies!" Alina's lips curved into a slow grin.

"I told you, there are a lot of things about me that you don't know," she answered. She turned and started to head back to the main road. Damon followed.

"Apparently," he murmured, his eyes falling once again to her legs.

Chapter Four

Alina sat behind the wheel of her black SUV and surveyed the scene before her from behind her sunglasses. It was late in the afternoon and the sun was starting to cast shadows on the wide Susquehanna river. She had passed the bridge to the island about a mile back. Now she was parked on the bank of the river, staring straight ahead at the four reactor towers on Three Mile Island. Two were eerily dark, a testament to the reactor incident that had occurred over thirty years ago, resulting in the reactor being removed. The other two, however, were still in full use, with fluffy white smoke rising from the funnels.

Alina picked up her military binoculars from the seat beside her and surveyed the island, taking note of the security details and the fencing alignment. She studied the roads in and out, the buildings, and the parking lots. After about half an hour of studying the island, she set down the binoculars and picked up her iPad. A few swipes of her finger and she had pulled up all the local newspaper articles in the past two months. She was in the middle of scanning them when her phone chirped.

"Yes?" Alina said shortly as she picked it up.

"Whoa, cranky!" Angela's voice exclaimed. "Am I interrupting?"

"And if you are?" Alina asked, swiping to another page.

"Too bad," was the cheerful response. "Dinner? I had steak in mind. I know a fabulous steakhouse in Voorhees. Best steak in South Jersey." Alina paused in her reading. Angela knew how to get her attention.

"It will have to be later," Alina said, glancing at the display on her dashboard. "I'm about two hours away."

"Well, hurry up," Angela retorted. "I'm hungry. I'll call and see if I can drag Steph away from work long enough to eat." Angela hung up without waiting for an answer and Alina set the phone down slowly. She looked out the window again, gazing once more at the infamous island before her.

What was she doing? Alina tapped her finger on the side of her iPad. Her objective was to track down Johann Topamari and eliminate him, using all means possible. Nowhere in that objective had she made allowances for old friendships and steak dinners. The initial dinner? Well, that was necessary. She had to re-connect with Stephanie and get inside her investigation. That had a purpose. But this? Dinner with Angela had no purpose. Alina frowned. She had known coming back to Jersey was going to be complicated.

Viper stared unseeingly at the dead reactor in the distance. She had arrived in Jersey and everything had gone according to her plan, right up until Damon had shown up. Then everything had gone askew somehow. Now, she had the added pressure of having to accomplish her objective *before* some kind of attack on US soil took place. She knew Hawk was there to ensure that the public had no idea anything had occurred, but she knew him well enough to know that containment was not his specialty. He was a hunter. They both were. He was up to something, and she wouldn't know what it was until he was ready to tell her. Hunters didn't give themselves away.

The problem was that she liked Damon. She always had. They had clicked immediately in training camp, and in the years since when they had crossed paths, they had deepened that bond. They became as close to friends as people in their job could be. Now, they were working together. And Alina had never worked with anyone. Not since training camp.

A deep sigh escaped her. She had also, somehow, become part of a circle of friends again. Friends that she had walked away from ten years ago. She had changed so much since she had last seen them that Alina hadn't dreamed that they would be able to pick up their friendships right where they left off. Yet, somehow, that was exactly what was happening. How was this possible? Alina had been all over the world and seen things that she never wanted to see again. She was a completely different person now. She had made a notorious name for herself internationally and she had enemies around the world. Viper was *not* the sad little girl she had been ten years ago.

God help her, Alina suspected this whole situation was going to get even more complicated before it was over.

"Dinner?" Stephanie repeated vaguely, sitting back in her chair. John glanced up from his desk, his ears perking up. "Where?"

"That steakhouse I've been trying to get you to try," Angela answered. "I just spoke to Alina. She is two hours away, so you have plenty of time to finish whatever it is you're working on and get there."

"So what time are we thinking?" Stephanie looked at her watch and then back at the computer screen before her.

"About seven," Angela said. "I'll call you at six to remind you." She hung up and Stephanie looked at her phone, setting it down with a huff.

"I didn't say I would go," she muttered, doing a neck roll.

"Where are we going to dinner?" John asked, sitting back in his chair and stretching, Stephanie glanced over.

"I guess I am going to a steakhouse," she answered. "At least, if I can make any headway on this report."

"I love steak!" John said.

"You're not invited," Stephanie said without ceremony. "Where are you on Body Number 2?"

"Martin Sladecki." John pulled a legal pad out from underneath a pile of bank statements. "Age 57, owned a franchise of convenience stores named "Quick Stops" and worked out of Trenton. He has a sister who lives in Palmyra. It's a fair bet that that's where he was headed when he met with his accident." John got up from his chair and walked over with his notepad and his smartphone. "Sisters name is

Nancy. She's divorced with two kids." Stephanie sat back in her chair as John perched on the edge of her desk.

"Do we know his connection with Angelo yet?" she asked. John switched to his smartphone. He swiped the screen and hit a few buttons on the touchscreen before holding the phone out to Stephanie. She found herself staring at a picture of both Angelo and Martin.

"That's a picture of a picture in Angelo's house," John told her. "Both of the deceased and their respective wives. Looks like it was taken down the shore."

"Do we know which one?" Stephanie asked. John laughed and took the phone back.

"I may be good, but I'm not that good," he retorted. "The Atlantic looks the same from all the shore points. However, Matt, down in the lab, thinks he can at least pin-point *when* the picture was taken. He has the original."

"Well, regardless, all this proves is that they were friends," Steph muttered. "Anything else on Martin's businesses?"

"Yep." John picked up the notepad again. "All seven locations have been featured in investigations at one time or another for ties to the good, old-fashioned, Jersey mob. There was never enough evidence for charges, but on more than one occasion he was questioned in relation to money-laundering activities which, of course, you knew already. I am still waiting on all the reports from archives, but it looks like this has been ongoing since the early nineties. Each time we questioned him, he had a $500 an hour lawyer on speed-dial."

"That's expensive legal counsel for someone who drove a four-year old Cadillac," Stephanie commented. John nodded.

"Someone was paying the bills," he agreed. "General opinion was that it was Frankie Solitto, head of the Jersey Family. Of course, there is no confirmation of that."

"I've never known street gossip to be wrong." Stephanie picked up her pen and started twirling it absently. "So, we have a money-launderer for the Solitto family vacationing with a known arms dealer on the Jersey shore. Does Angelo have any ties to the Solitto family?"

"The opposite," John answered. "Frankie Solitto draws a very firm line between doing business with his Family and any other businessmen. It just isn't done. If you work for Frank, you don't work for anyone else, including yourself. Angelo wasn't working for, with, or in anyway around the Solitto Family. I can guarantee that."

"So Martin broke the cardinal rule and was working with Angelo?" Stephanie tossed the pen back onto the desk. "So Frankie Solitto had him whacked?"

"It's possible," John shrugged. "I'm going through Martins' bank statements now. Not an easy task." Stephanie nodded and pushed him off her desk.

"Then you better get back to it," she said. John headed back to his desk. "If the mob had them both whacked, our friend from DHS can go on his merry way."

"I thought of that." John sat down again. After a moment, he glanced up. "But it can't be that easy, can it?"

"Of course not," Stephanie replied. "It never is. But let's rule out one theory before starting over again."

Angela waved from the bar as Alina stepped into the crowded restaurant. It was a little after seven and the place was packed. The narrow wooden deck lining the front of the barn-shaped building was packed with waiting smokers, and the entryway was packed with the waiting non-smokers. More waiting patrons lined the walls around the hostess desk, making it virtually impossible to move in or out. It was a capacity-packed night.

Alina moved through the throng, heading toward the big square bar in the center of the restaurant where Angela was waiting with a red martini in hand. She had already scanned the crowds and knew where all the exits were and roughly how many people were seated and eating. She knew which ones were likely to be carrying concealed, and she knew which ones were members of law enforcement. What she *didn't* know was why she had agreed to come.

"Hi!" Angela kissed the air next to Alina's cheek and shifted over to make room for her at the bar. "I put our names in for the table in the back corner."

"How long is the wait?" Alina asked.

"Forty minutes as of twenty minutes ago. I just beat the rush." Angela smiled at her happily, her green eyes dancing. "I'm so happy you agreed to come! I can't get used to seeing you again!"

Alina smiled despite herself and suddenly knew why she had come. Regardless of who and what she was, Angela and Stephanie had helped make her into the woman that she was now. They were still a part of her.

"What are you drinking?" Angela asked.

"Just water right now," Alina said, motioning to the bartender. "I'll have wine with dinner," she added when she saw Angela was about to argue.

"Yes, well, there's something you need to know about dinner," Angela told her, looking suddenly uncomfortable. "You may want something stronger." Alina looked at her and the look on Angela's face told her all she needed to know.

"John's coming," Alina stated instead of asked. Angela put her drink down on the bar and put both her hands on Alina's arm.

"I had nothing to do with it," she hastened to explain. "Stephanie texted me about half an hour ago to say that she was on her way and was bringing John and that other agent that is working with them. I asked what I was supposed to tell you and this is what she sent back." Angela fished in her purse for her blackberry and held it out to Alina. Alina glanced down at the text on the screen.

Remind her that she said she would be fine with him.

Alina bit back a laugh. She could see why Angela wasn't about to give her the message verbally. Stephanie could have worded it a bit more tactfully.

"Really, it's ok." Alina looked over to the bartender. "A glass of water with lemon, please." She looked back at Angela. "Have you met the mysterious other agent yet?"

"Not yet." Angela tucked her blackberry away again and drained half her martini in relief. She had been dreading telling Alina about John. She didn't know what she had been expecting, but Alina was so different now, she hadn't known *how* she would react. "Stephanie seems to be more amenable to having him around, though. They must have come to some form of agreement on division of labor." Alina chuckled and accepted her glass of water from the bartender.

"He must be sitting back and giving Stephanie her space," she commented. Angela nodded with a grin.

"I'm expecting a little man who is about five foot three and as boring as they come," she confided. "My guess is that he's a paper-pusher who lets other people do the dirty work while he takes all the credit."

"That's a pretty harsh assessment." Alina watched as Angela finished her drink. Angela set the empty glass down on the bar and shrugged.

"I bet I'm right, though," she retorted. She picked up her slim clutch purse from the bar. "I have to run to the ladies room."

Alina nodded and watched as Angela disappeared into the crowd. As always, she was immaculate. Her hair and make-up were perfect, her nails flawless, and her high heels Jimmy Choo. Alina ruefully admitted to herself that she had always felt under-dressed when she was with Angela. She glanced down at herself and turned to lean her back on the bar so she could scan the crowds. She just had time to stop and change before heading to the restaurant. The black cargo capris and deep purple halter top that had seemed appropriate for a casual dinner with friends now seemed a trifle *too* casual. However, Alina could honestly say that she was perfectly comfortable being a little too casual. She could move freely in her loose pants, and the halter top hid the sheathed military survival knife that was nestled in the hollow of her back. The knife was usually strapped to her ankle, but the black patent leather and wood platform heels on her feet had necessitated a wardrobe adjustment.

Angela's name was called over the intercom and Alina straightened up. She started to move toward the hostess stand and caught sight of Stephanie and John stepping into the restaurant. Their suits were rumpled from a long day and John had discarded his tie, while Stephanie had unbuttoned the top four buttons on her tailored shirt. They both looked tired and hungry. Damon followed them in, looking crisp and fresh in black slacks and a deep blue button-down shirt. Alina's lips twitched. What was he up to now?

John caught sight of her first and said something to Stephanie. Alina motioned for them stay near the hostess as she moved through the crowd effortlessly. Her eyes met Damon's over Stephanie's head as she grew closer, and Alina saw the gleam of pure amusement in his bright blue eyes. Her own narrowed slightly, which brought a grin to his lips. Stephanie turned to him as Alina walked up and the grin disappeared before she could see it.

"Damon, this is Alina. She is a very old friend of mine," Stephanie introduced them. "Alina, this is Damon Peterson. He is working with John and I temporarily." Alina held out her hand to Damon.

"A pleasure," she murmured. Damon grasped her hand, his eyes gleaming again.

"The pleasure is all mine," he answered with an easy smile. Alina pulled her hand away and turned to face John.

"What a nice surprise!" Alina smiled smoothly.

"Almost like old times," John answered, looking down at her. Their eyes met briefly and Alina caught a whiff of an old familiar smell. The man still wore the same cologne.

"Not quite," Alina answered. She turned to give Angela's name to the hostess.

"John, behave!" Stephanie hissed behind her back. Alina heard John chuckle and she suddenly felt as if she was trapped in a farce.

"This way." The hostess told her, turning to lead the party to the back of the restaurant and the large corner table, partially obscured by a large potted cactus. The lighting was more subdued in this corner of the restaurant and two lit tapers cast a comforting glow over the dark scarred wood. It was quiet and partially set aside from the rest of the tables in the section. Alina wondered briefly if Angela had requested it with the thought that any scenes between herself and John would be less likely to be noticed back here.

Alina headed for the seat partially hidden behind the cactus out of habit. It had its back to the wall and afforded an excellent view of the rest of the restaurant. She reached it at the same time as Damon. She looked up into his blue eyes and he grinned ruefully. He pulled out the chair and motioned for her to sit.

"Thank you," she murmured, sinking into the chair.

"Great shoes," he murmured in her ear.

He took the seat next to her with a smile and Alina was suddenly glad of the poor lighting. A warming sensation was stealing up her neck and she strongly suspected that, for the first time in years, she was blushing.

"Where's Angela?" Stephanie asked, seating herself next to Damon. John sat on Alina's other side.

"She had to go to the ladie's room," Alina answered. "Here she comes now," she added, somewhat relieved to have John and Stephanie turn their heads toward Angela. John had looked at her curiously as he took his seat, causing Alina to wonder if he had noticed her warm cheeks.

"Hello, hello." Angela swirled up to the table and dropped into the last chair without ceremony. "Why, hello!" She caught sight of Damon and Alina watched her mouth drop open.

"Damon, this is Angela," Stephanie introduced them with a laugh. "Angela, this is Damon Peterson."

"Nice to meet you," Damon said with an easy smile.

"You can close your mouth now," John said blithely, reaching for one of the menus. Angela flushed.

"I have no idea what you're talking about," she retorted, snapping her jaw closed. "Did you find the restaurant ok?"

she asked Stephanie. Stephanie nodded without looking up from her perusal of the menu.

"GPS," she answered absently. "I am starving."

"I'm not surprised," John said. "You haven't eaten all day."

Alina picked up her menu and lowered her eyes to it, trying to ignore the patently curious man beside her. He was soaking in every comment and every look like a sponge.

"Typical." Angela looked at Damon. "You'll learn quickly that Stephanie is a workaholic," she informed him. "She just puts blinders on and forges ahead. I'm convinced that there are days she forgets to eat altogether."

"Sounds like someone else I know," Damon answered easily, setting his menu aside and smiling. "She's the same way. I have always maintained that she's trying to make up for the fact that she is a woman," he added with a grin.

Alina closed her menu with a snap. She set it down and glanced at him, her eyes flashing. Damon met her look blandly and her eyes narrowed.

"She may be," John said. "Stephanie, I mean." He hadn't missed the flash in Alina's eyes or the glance to the man next to her. He watched her lazily under his lashes.

"Don't be ridiculous." Stephanie finally looked up. "I work hard because I can't stand leaving anything undone."

"I, on the other hand, have NO qualms about leaving my work at work," Angela announced with a laugh.

"What do you do?" Damon asked.

"I work for a bank in the anti-money laundering department," Angela answered. "Fascinating, I know, but someone has to do it. I have no responsibility whatsoever. So I can, and do, leave work all the time," she added with a laugh.

"I wish I had that luxury," Stephanie said wistfully.

"Do you find it challenging trying to make a career in the FBI as a woman?" Alina couldn't help herself from asking. She was genuinely curious. Stephanie thought for a minute.

"It's not any more challenging than I would imagine it is making it in any other male-dominated field," she said slowly.

"I've been lucky in the sense that I have always had supportive bosses over me. I learned very early on that anything that I had to prove, I only had to prove to myself."

"That's an incredibly healthy outlook," Damon remarked. Stephanie shrugged.

"Yes, but I have been very lucky," she said. "There are other women who haven't been so lucky."

"Did you run into that problem in the military?" John asked Alina. Everyone looked at her. She shrugged.

"It was the military," she said, as if that was all that needed to be said.

The waitress came to take their orders and Alina was relieved to be out of the limelight for a moment. The sudden surge of remembered frustration that coursed through her at John's question had been unexpected. She had been able to overcome the feeling of inferiority that she experienced starting out in boot camp by becoming the best in her unit, but the memory of the anger and frustration from years ago caught her by surprise.

"Should I order a bottle of wine?" John's question pulled Alina back to the present. He was looking around the table questioningly. "It seems a little redundant for us all to order glasses."

"Sure!" Stephanie agreed. "I think I am done with work for the night."

"Oh my God, make it a bottle of champagne!" Angela chirped. Stephanie laughed.

"Oh, stop picking on me," she said. "Can't we pick on someone else? What about Alina? She looks like a workaholic too."

"No, she just looks dangerous," Angela retorted with a laugh.

Damon glanced at Alina in time to catch her slight, non-committal smile before she turned her attention to the waitress with her order. Damon flicked his eyes quickly around the table, fascinated. This was a part of Alina's life that he had never been able to discover, despite numerous attempts. She always kept quiet about where she came from and who she had been before the military. Stephanie and Angela's easy humor was clearly something that Alina had always been part of, and John was also clearly something more than what anyone had told him. Damon had seen him catch the flash in Alina's eyes earlier, and had been amusing himself by watching John watch her ever since. Alina actually had a past!

"I don't know if dangerous is the right word," John said when Alina had finished ordering. He looked at her consideringly, his blue eyes serious. "It's more of a look of....experience," he finally decided. "But I can see the danger hiding underneath." Damon finished ordering and turned back in time to see Alina's slight smile again.

"Interesting thought," she murmured. "I wonder what could have happened in my past to make me look dangerous?" she added, her dark eyes meeting his.

Damon raised an eyebrow slightly at the sudden silence that fell on the table. Stephanie sat back in her chair with a barely audible sigh, and Angela pretended to examine her nails while her eyes avidly watched Alina and John. Alina saw the sparkle of amusement that leapt into John's eyes.

"I don't know. I'm not the one who said you looked dangerous," he replied slowly before the amusement reached his lips in a slow grin. "Of course, there's nothing cast iron within reach."

Alina couldn't help herself. She leaned toward John and lowered her voice, forcing him to lean in closer.

"Oh, trust me," she murmured, her eyes meeting his. "I don't need cast iron to be dangerous anymore." Alina sat back slowly, satisfied to have caught the flash of surprise in Johns eyes before his mask of amusement slid back into place. Unfortunately, she could feel Damon's curiosity radiating from her other side. Alina accepted with an inward sigh that he was never going to let her get out of explaining this entire exchange.

"Speaking of dangerous," Angela stepped smoothly into the brief silence. "What did you do in the military, anyway?" she asked Alina.

Alina was silent as the waitress came back with their drinks. When the glass in front of her was filled with red wine, Alina reached for it almost thankfully. This dinner was getting more and more uncomfortable by the minute. Once the waitress left, she looked around the table. The only person not waiting for her answer was Damon, and he had such unholy laughter in his eyes that Alina couldn't trust herself to look at him again.

"I was in military intelligence," Alina finally answered. John's eyes widened in surprise, but Stephanie didn't look surprised at all. Angela's mouth fell open again.

"Seriously?" Angela was the first one to respond. Alina nodded, reaching for her wine again. She felt a little like she had just walked in front of a window naked and the whole street had looked in. There was a short silence before Angela threw her hands up in the air. "So what you're saying is...I'm the only one at this table who has never carried a gun to work!" she exclaimed.

Alina blinked and her lips twitched. Stephanie was rolling her eyes, John was looking at Angela like she had two heads, and Damon was clearly about to start laughing at any minute. Not one person at the table thought anything amiss with her having been military intelligence, and not one of them was a threat to her. Relief made Alina's lips twitch again, and then she burst out laughing. Stephanie and John started laughing, and then Damon. Angela looked around with wide eyes.

"What?" she demanded. "It's true! I feel left out."

"Angie, you really are something else," Stephanie finally got out. She looked over at Alina, whose shoulders were still shaking. "And you!" she pointed to her. Alina raised an eyebrow. "It's so nice to see you laugh again! Finally!"

Damon looked at Alina and watched as she shrugged. Her eyes were still alight with laughter and he suddenly realized that he had never actually seen her burst into uncontrolled laughter. There had always been something hooded in her eyes, somewhere that the laughter didn't quite reach. He sat back thoughtfully, reaching for his wine. This was certainly a different side of Viper.

And one that he strongly suspected she had long forgotten.

Chapter Five

"Frankie Solitto?" Alina stared at Damon over the top of her refrigerator door. "Are you kidding me?" Damon grinned and shrugged.

"It's right here in her report," he answered, dropping the folder onto the counter and walking over to join Alina at the refrigerator door. After dinner they had all gone their separate ways, and he had circled back and shown up at her back door. She had been waiting for him. "I don't suppose there is any beer in that fridge?"

"No." Alina handed him a bottle of water and pulled out another one for herself. "And you shouldn't be looking for one anyway. You'll get soft," she added with a grin, letting the fridge door swing closed and smacking him in his rock-hard abs. He raised an eyebrow as she passed him and glanced down at his flat stomach before following her.

Grabbing the folder off the counter, she continued into the living room. A large, over-stuffed, chocolate colored couch faced a fireplace and an over-sized leather recliner was angled off to the side. A flat screen TV had been mounted above the mantel, but Damon got the feeling it had never been turned on. This was not where Alina *lived*. The coffee table was dark wood, mission style, and void of a single speck of dust. There was one large jar candle in the center, and that was the only thing that showed any sign of use. It was a quarter of the way gone.

Alina dropped onto the couch and pulled her bare feet up next to her, curling into the corner gracefully. Damon settled in the recliner, his eyes dropping to the red nail polish on her toes. Somehow he could not begin to imagine Alina getting a pedicure...or even painting her nails herself. It was just completely at odds with what he knew to be her priorities.

He sat back and sipped his water, watching as she scanned over Stephanie's report. The house was saved from complete silence by the distant ticking of a clock in the front of the house. Damon looked around. He wondered if the house had already been furnished when she moved in, or if she had picked out the furniture. While tasteful, there was no personality in the rooms. Nothing gave any clue to the character of the person who lived here, with the possible exception of being extremely neat. Everything had its place. There was no clutter. No personal pictures. No magazines. No DVDs. Damon idly wondered where she had hidden the remote for the TV.

"This is the most ridiculous thing I have ever read," Alina finally muttered. She looked up, her dark eyes glittering. "I really didn't take Stephanie for a fool. This has to be John's input."

"Well, they don't have the advantage of your superior information," Damon replied with a shrug. "The way they lay it out, it could make sense." Alina raised her eyebrow.

"That Frankie had this guy Martin whacked because he was working for someone else?" she demanded. "Please. This reads like a bad, made-for-TV movie."

"Just to play devil's advocate, I could point out that the mob is still very influential in the northeast," Damon said.

Alina set the folder on the coffee table and opened her bottle of water. She looked at Damon. He was reclined in the recliner, his ankles crossed on the footrest, completely relaxed. His blue shirt made his eyes seem even more cobalt, and right now they were sparkling, just as they had been ever since he walked into the steakhouse.

"I won't dispute that," Alina agreed. "But I don't see Frankie whacking a long-term employee in such a public way. He was always more of a "make the fink disappear and then re-appear in a landfill" kind of guy. Stephanie knows that. *Everyone* in Jersey knows that."

"Maybe he suspected Martin was laundering for a terrorist," Damon suggested. "I hear the mob is very patriotic these days."

"You want to talk to Frankie Solitto!" Alina realized suddenly, after staring at him in disbelief for a moment. Damon grinned.

"Guilty," he confirmed. Alina sat back and stretched her arms over her head, arching her back with a yawn.

"Why?" she asked, lowering her arms. Damon shrugged.

"Are we laying our cards out on the table?" he asked. Alina smiled slightly and shook her head.

"Not entirely," she answered. "Consider it sharing information."

"I seem to be doing more sharing than you are," Damon pointed out. Alina grinned. "Ok. I want to find out if Frankie knew about Martin's extra-curricular activities, and I want to find out if he knew who they were for. And I want to find out before our Fearless Feds bumble in and mess it all up."

"How is this going to get me any closer to Johann?" Alina asked. For the first time all night, the sparkle faded from Damon's eyes.

"It may not," he answered truthfully.

Alina considered him silently, her eyes dark and shuttered. The mask was back in place. She was the professional again. Damon was back on familiar ground with this Viper, and he was conscious of a slight sense of relief. While it was amusing to see new sides to Alina, Viper was who he knew. And Viper was who he needed now.

"We had better get going then," Alina finally broke the silence. "The Fearless Feds will start their bumbling in the morning. Let me get changed into something more appropriate." She stood. "I assume you already know where he is?"

"At his house in Bucks County. He has a meeting this week with some of the Philly Family." Damon swung his legs down and got up out of the recliner. "Security is going to be a factor."

"I never thought otherwise." Alina turned to head upstairs. "Give me a few minutes." She glanced over her shoulder. "Do you have a change of clothes with you?" she asked. Damon grinned.

"Meet me outside," he replied. "I'll drive."

Alina sat in the passenger seat of the black Jeep Wrangler and watched the lights of Philadelphia sparkle in the distance. They were crossing the bridge to head north on I-95. When she had emerged from the house, Damon was waiting in the Jeep, dressed in black cargo pants and black tee-shirt stretched taught across his shoulders. They drove now in a comfortable silence, and Alina stared out the window at the inky blackness of the Delaware River below them. She felt more at ease now, dressed in loose-fitting black cargo pants and a fitted olive tank top. A lightweight black jacket concealed the .45 holstered at her back, and the knife was back in its proper place, strapped to her ankle. While she enjoyed wearing platform heels just as much as the next girl, it was nice to be back to work. Alina glanced at the strong profile next to her. And, she had to admit, it was nice not to be the one driving for once.

"What are you thinking?" Hawk asked, catching her glance in the flash of a street light high above them as he pulled onto 95. Alina smiled slightly.

"That it's nice to be along for the ride for once," she answered truthfully. "I think I'm enjoying the whole no-responsibility thing." Damon looked over and smiled.

"You think?" he said with a laugh. Alina grinned.

"Well, I don't see myself making a practice of this, but for just once, it's kind of nice," she retorted. Damon chuckled and turned his attention back to the road as they fell silent again. Alina returned her gaze to the billboards that were flashing by. She was surrounded by the fresh, woodsy scent that was all Hawk, and lethargy stole through her. She knew she could trust him, and with that knowledge came a sense of relief. Whatever Hawk was doing here, he wasn't working against her. She could relax and focus on what she had to do.

"So tell me about John," Damon said after a few more miles of silence. Alina sighed.

"I knew you wouldn't leave that alone," she muttered. Damon grinned.

"Cast iron?" he demanded, looking at her. "Really?"

"It was a teapot," Alina retorted. "One of those decorative Chinese things." Damon looked at her and his eyes were filled with laughter.

"Well, at least it wasn't a frying pan," he murmured. "What did you do with it?" Alina let out a long, loud sigh.

"I threw it at his head," she told him. "It split his forehead open and knocked him out cold." Damon nodded.

"I would imagine it would." He was quiet for a second. "What did you do after knocking him out?"

"Went down the shore," came the calm answer. Damon burst out laughing.

"Let me guess...." he said, looking at her. "Stephanie and Angela joined you." Alina nodded and shrugged.

"It seemed like a good idea at the time," she replied. "I called the paramedics and then left. John was smart enough not to press charges."

"So you know I have to ask why," Damon said after a moment, his lips still twitching. Alina nodded.

"I know." She looked over at him. "And since you weaseled your way into that fiasco of a dinner, I suppose you should know. John and I were engaged before I joined up. He had an affair and I caught them in our bed. It was a messy ending to a not-so fabulous relationship to begin with. That's all there is to it."

"Interesting." Damon turned his attention back to the road. "And now he works with Stephanie."

"I always said the Feds weren't too picky about who they hired," Alina said, leaning her head back against the seat. "Do you plan on driving like an old lady the whole way there?" she asked. "We could have been there ten minutes ago." Damon grinned.

"I thought you were enjoying the ride," he pointed out. Alina shrugged.

"That was before you slowed down to slower than my grandmother would drive, if I had one," she retorted. Damon laughed and lowered his foot on the gas.

"My apologies," he murmured.

Alina nodded complacently.

"Accepted," she answered as the Jeep sped up again.

Damon cut the lights and pulled off to the side of the road. They were in the mountains of Bucks County, where the houses were small compounds and the property taxes were small fortunes. Damon had stopped a good half-mile down the country road from Frankie Solitto's compound. Alina got out of the Jeep silently in the darkness and waited for her eyes to grow accustomed to the pitch blackness of the mountainside. Damon walked around the back of the Jeep and joined her silently. He placed his hand on Alina's elbow and guided her in the direction he wanted to go. Alina stepped into the trees with him before gently pulling her elbow away. Damon looked down at her and she motioned that she was going to circle around to the back of the property. Damon nodded and watched as she disappeared into the blackness.

She never made a sound. It was as if she simply vanished. Damon smiled to himself. Viper was one of very few people he could honestly say he trusted enough to work beside. And her stealth and skill were only part of the reason, he admitted to himself, as he began to make his way towards the front of Frank Solitto's massive compound. He moved silently through the woods, avoiding the sentries by the simple act of sniffing. Frankie's security apparently didn't buy into the new-fangled idea that smoking could cause death. They were easily avoided and, within minutes, Damon found himself outside the thick, ten foot stone wall that surrounded the house. He paused, wondering if Viper had found a way through the back yet.

Frankie had dogs. That was one of the reasons he had wanted her to come. Alina had a way with animals. None of them ever discussed it, but everyone who had trained with her had seen it. It was almost magical. Animals just understood her.

Damon waited for a moment. He caught the distant sound of an engine, and then the crunch of wheels on the dirt road leading up to the compound. Sliding into the shadows, he watched as headlights became visible in the darkness. A moment later, a dark SUV came into sight. The gates to his right creaked as they swung open ponderously, the motor that controlled them humming in the darkness. Damon watched the SUV approach the gates, but he couldn't see beyond the glare of the lights from the inner courtyard reflecting off the windows. He took mental note of the plates as the SUV rolled through the gates, and then the vehicle was lost from sight as the gates swung closed again. He heard voices on the other side of the wall, and a few moments later those were gone as well as the occupants moved indoors. Silence fell again to the night, and Hawk moved out of the shadows.

Viper materialized next to him. She motioned for him to follow her and led him a little farther down, where she proceeded to scale the wall effortlessly and disappear over the top. Damon followed, landing silently next to her. Directly in front of them were a collection of rose and lilac bushes. He smiled. Even if someone had been watching, their entry would have been concealed by the bushes and the shadows they provided. Alina grabbed his wrist and pulled him down behind one of the bushes.

"The dogs are on the other side of the house. They won't be a problem," she whispered in his ear, her breath tickling his neck. "The guard at the back is sleeping now. Frankie just received someone who looks like a courier. He was in the library at the back of the house, but now he's with the visitor in the front. He'll return to the library. He left his drink and cigar there. That will probably be your best bet."

"And the other guards?" Damon whispered back. Alina smiled.

"There are only two more and they're at the front," she answered. Damon nodded and they moved out of the shadows toward the back of the house. When they passed the body near the back of the house, he glanced down. The guard had been bound and gagged securely and his shoes removed. If he woke up, he wasn't going to be making a sound. Alina led him to the windows of the library at the back. He stood against the wall next to one while she did the same on the other side. Damon looked in.

The light on the desk was still on, and there was another lamp on near the door. The walls were lined floor to ceiling with books, most leather bound and some with paper dust covers. A big and heavy mahogany desk dominated the room from its position in front of the windows, and Damon noted the half-finished glass of scotch and the cigar burning in the ashtray. Papers were spread across the desk and a laptop was angled off to the side. Damon looked over to Alina and nodded slightly toward the garden. She nodded back, settling her shoulders against the wall and crossing her arms in front of her. There was a soft click of the window casing, and Damon disappeared silently into the library. Viper made herself comfortable, her eyes and ears attuned to the night surrounding her. Hawk wanted to talk to Frankie alone. Alina didn't know what exactly Damon thought he would learn, but she had every intention of finding out later. In the meantime, she would ensure their privacy from the outdoors.

Damon didn't have long to wait. After a quick inspection of the library, he made himself comfortable in the shadows of the corner to the left of the window, away from both lights. He had only been waiting for a few minutes before he heard voices in the hall.

"I don't care who sent him." Frank Solitto was saying as he opened the library door. "He's an ignorant worm. Get rid of him. And don't bother me again tonight." Frankie slammed the door and turned toward his desk.

He didn't immediately see Damon, which gave Hawk time to examine the head of the New Jersey Family. He was on the taller side, with wide shoulders and graying hair along his temples. Frankie looked good for his age, which Damon estimated to be in the late sixties. He hadn't allowed himself to get soft around the middle as most older generation Italians did, but appeared to be fit and solid. His jaw was still angular, but the soft skin of his neck was looking a little puffy. His olive skin was lined and his eyes were deep-set and alert. Damon could see why Frank Solitto still demanded such respect. He was an imposing force in and of itself, radiating power and confidence.

"What the..." Frankie caught sight of Damon as he got closer to his desk. "Who the hell are you?!"

"Just someone who wants to talk," Hawk answered softly. He shifted so that Frankie could see the gun at his hip. "I'm not here to start anything, but for your own sake, I wouldn't make any sudden moves."

"How the hell did you get in here?" Frankie demanded, his eyes flashing as he took in the gun on Damon's hip.

"Through the window," Damon answered readily. "I want to discuss Martin Sladecki."

"Oh, do you, now?" Frank shot back sarcastically. He started to move toward the desk and Damon clucked disapprovingly.

"I would rather you stayed away from your desk for the time being," he said, pulling the gun from his belt holster. "I don't feel that we've achieved a sense of trust yet," he added apologetically. Frankie stared at him for a second, then chuckled.

"Oh you don't, eh?" he asked. He crossed in front of his desk and seated himself in one of the leather chairs off to the side. "I don't suppose that has anything to do with the gun you're waving around?"

"Not at all." Damon smiled coldly. "It has to do with the semi-automatic pistol that you have in your desk drawer. And before you reach for it, I've taken the liberty of removing the gun from under the seat of that chair as well." Frank's eyes narrowed.

"Who the hell are you and what do you want?" he demanded.

"It doesn't matter who I am," Damon retorted, "and I told you what I want. I want to talk about your former employee, Martin." Frank snorted.

"Martin was a fink. A useless piece of nothing," he told him. "The only reason he was still on my payroll was because it was cheaper than NOT having him on my payroll, if you get what I mean."

"Did you kill him?" Hawk asked. Frank looked at him.

"No, I didn't kill him," he answered. "Why do you want to know?"

"Did one of your associates kill him?" Hawk asked. Frankie waved his hand dismissively.

"Of course not." A note of impatience entered his voice. "Martin was pushed into the path of a moving freight train in the middle of a residential area. Do you really think anything that indiscreet would be done by me or my associates?"

"No." Damon tucked his gun away again and crossed his arms. "But the Feds are going to be here tomorrow asking you the same thing, so someone thinks it's a possibility."

"The Feds?" Frankie looked up. "Again? What do they think, I got nothing better to do than worry about has-beens like Sladecki?" Damon shrugged.

"He was working for someone else," he pointed out. "Everyone knows that you don't allow that." Frankie studied Damon silently for a moment, and Hawk allowed him the time to think.

"You're not a Fed," Frankie finally said. "And you're not one of the New Yorkers. Why do you want to know about that piece of nothing?"

"Let's just say that my interest is...specialized," Damon answered. Frankie snorted and grinned.

84

"In that case, I'm glad I didn't try to take that .45 from you by force," he said, sitting back and crossing his long legs. Damon smiled slightly.

"I wouldn't advise it," he agreed.

Frankie pondered him in silence again. Damon stared back steadily.

"What's in it for me if I talk?" Frankie asked. Damon smiled.

"I won't kill you," he answered simply. Frankie took in Hawk's big shoulders and lean frame and studied him some more. He finally shrugged.

"I'll tell you more than I'll tell the damn Feds, anyway," he decided. "I like you, even if you did disrespect me by coming into my home this way." Damon bowed his head slightly in acknowledgement.

"There was no other way," he replied. Frankie nodded again.

"Well, then, what do you want to know?" he demanded.

"Who was Martin working for aside from your Family?" Damon asked. Frankie shook his head.

"Martin got caught up with bad people," he said slowly. "The one, Angelo, he floated up in the river about a week back. That's when Martin started acting funny. So I had him watched."

"Acting funny how?"

"Jumpy. Like he was waiting for something." Frankie shrugged. "I thought maybe he had started using, but it wasn't that kind of jumpy. Anyway, he cleared out and went down to South Jersey to hide out at his sisters."

"Hide from you?"

"Nah." Frankie shook his head. "He knew we were watching him. He knew we knew where he was going. He was hiding from someone else."

"The person who put Angelo in the river?" Damon asked. Frankie shrugged.

"That's what I figured," he said. "So I had my boys do a little snooping into this Angelo." Frankie stopped. Damon raised an eyebrow.

"And?" he prompted. Frankie sighed.

"I don't know why I'm telling you this," he muttered.

"Because I'm holding a gun to your head and you don't have much of a choice," Damon answered calmly. Frankie looked up.

"You know, you have a way about you," he told him. "You ever find yourself at a loose end, you come see me."

"I appreciate the offer," Damon said, his lips twitching. "Now tell me about Angelo."

"Angelo ran guns, among other things, for Bobby Reyes. Bobby runs all the guns on the east coast," Frankie said. "We came to an agreement a long time ago. We respect each other's exclusive entrepreneurial endeavors. In twenty years, I've never known Bobby to break that agreement. So I went to him. I asked him about Angelo."

"Let me guess." Damon shifted slightly. "Bobby had no idea what Angelo was doing. It had nothing to do with him."

"Not only that, but Bobby was looking for Angelo himself when he floated up because a specialized shipment had gone missing." Frankie waved his hand vaguely. "That's what Bobby called it. A "specialized" shipment. He was pretty sure Angelo had taken it and sold it outside Bobby's network, and that made Bobby nervous. And now, here *you* are, with a "specialized" interest."

"Who do you think Angelo sold those goods to?" Damon asked softly. Frankie was silent for a minute. Then he looked at Damon.

"You find the person who whacked Angelo and Martin and you'll find who bought that shipment," he told him. "And I'll tell you this much. It's not a member of any Family in this country."

Alina didn't speak until they were back in the Jeep and pulling away. Damon had exited the library and motioned for them to leave. Quickly. Alina had glanced back from the garden wall to see Frankie Solitto standing at the window, with his drink in his hand, watching them. She got the impression that he was giving them a head start, and that impression was confirmed about five minutes later when she and Damon heard men yelling instructions and a dozen lights lit up the woods behind them. They made it to the Jeep quickly and without incident, and Damon pulled into the road and turned around to head back down the mountainside. He switched on the headlights about a mile down the road, once they were out of sight of the compound.

"Find out anything useful?" Alina finally asked. Damon nodded.

"He didn't kill Sladecki," he said.

"We didn't think he had," Alina retorted. "Does he know who did?"

"He thinks he does," Damon said. "And I'm pretty sure that his meeting with the Philly Family is to discuss the situation." Alina looked at him sharply.

"How much have they guessed?" she asked.

"Oh, they've pretty much worked it all out," Damon answered. "The only thing they don't have is a name."

"Do you think they'll be a problem?" Alina asked after a moment. Damon glanced at her.

"Not if you move quickly," he replied. "Angelo passed on a specialized shipment to Johann. Frankie said Bobby Reyes, the dealer he stole it from, became aware of it a few days before Angelo surfaced in the river."

"So Johann's had it for at least a week now." Alina's mind was working quickly. "And he took out his money launderer. That means the money is in place."

"It's a little like following bread crumbs, isn't it?" Damon asked idly, heading back toward 95. Alina stared unseeingly out of the window.

"Except the breadcrumbs are running out," she murmured. "I don't understand something."

"What?"

"This is out of character for Johann," Alina answered after a short silence. "He's never systematically cleaned up after himself like this." Damon shot her a look in the darkness.

"He's never worked on American soil," he pointed out. Alina shrugged slightly and fell silent. Something just didn't feel right about all of this, but Hawk was right. She had to move quickly now. She had to find Johann before he used his specialized shipment, and now she had to find him before the Family found him first.

"Where are you on Johann?" Damon asked, pulling onto 95 and heading south. Alina looked at him.

"I'm making progress," she said guardedly. Damon glanced at her.

"How about you tell me about the progress and we see if I can add anything or help?" he suggested. "I know the concept of working as a team is foreign to both of us, but I'm pretty sure this is how it works." Alina was quiet for a moment, and then she nodded.

"You had better come in when we get back. It might be a long night," Alina finally said in resignation. Damon's eyebrows shot into his forehead and his lips curled into a grin.

"I think I'm beginning to see the advantages of partners," he drawled. Alina laughed.

"I meant so that you can see where I am with Johann," she exclaimed. Damon glanced at her.

"Of course you did," he murmured.

Chapter Six

Alina switched on the light in the kitchen and dropped her jacket on one of the bar stools. Damon followed her, his eyes going to the gun in her back.

"Coffee?" Alina asked, heading for the espresso maker.

"Please." Damon perched on one of the stools. He glanced at the clock. "We made good time," he remarked. Alina nodded.

"We did," she agreed. It was a little past one in the morning.

Damon watched as she pulled out two mugs and filled the hopper of the machine with espresso beans. A feeling of contentment washed over him, taking Damon by surprise. He suddenly realized that he was exactly where he wanted to be, for perhaps the first time in years. There was a feeling of closeness in the room, and it felt good. It felt as close to home as anything he had felt in a long, long time. Alina pushed a button and the grinder came alive, breaking the silence and jarring Damon out of his thoughts.

"What's the story with Angela?" he asked, shifting on his stool. Alina glanced over her shoulder.

"Angela?" she repeated. Damon grinned.

"Yes. Why is she the only one who never had to carry a gun at work?" he asked. Alina grinned.

"Angela has always just been Angela. She's a pure Jersey Girl, through and through," she told him. Alina pulled the mug out from under the spout and handed it to Damon. She picked up the other mug and turned back to the coffee maker. "She may speak flippantly about her job, but she is an assistant Vice President with the bank and worked hard to get there. Angela is our corporate vine. She won't stop until she reaches the top of the wall."

"She works in the anti-money laundering department?" Damon asked. "That's a little ironic." Alina nodded.

"Quite," she agreed. "I'm sure Stephanie's already pulled all the information she could out of her."

"I don't see how she fits in with the two of you." Damon sipped his coffee. "You and Stephanie are similar."

"There's more to her than you think." Alina removed her mug and sipped it. "Mmmm."

Damon grinned. He had felt the same way when he had taken his first sip of coffee. They were silent for a moment, each enjoying their espresso. Finally, Alina moved toward the island.

"Well, are you ready?" she asked. Damon nodded and watched as she reached up and pulled down a stainless steel pot and placed it on the island. He let out an appreciative whistle as the island moved silently to the side.

"Well done," he murmured, following her down the stairs with his mug in hand. When they reached the bottom of the steps, Alina pressed a button and the opening above them closed.

Damon slowly looked around, taking in the flat screen monitors and servers that lined the room. The steady hum from the machines was occasionally interrupted when a fan kicked on to cool one of the servers, and the room smelled like wiring and plastic. Monitors flicked through streaming images ranging from pictures, to satellite images, to real-time streaming video of the house and the grounds. In between the monitors were white boards of varying sizes, some holding newspaper clippings, others with photos, and others with notes jotted down.

"Welcome to my command center," Alina said, moving into the room.

It really was a command center, and he had completely failed to find it on the night he had come to investigate. He knew it had to be somewhere, and here it was.

"Impressive." Damon honed in on the monitor that was scanning through thousands of pictures. "Who are you looking for?" Alina followed his look and smiled.

"One of Johann's associates," she answered. She sat in front of a laptop and motioned for him to look at the bigger plasma at the end of the room. "You wanted to know where I was on Johann."

Alina opened a file on the laptop and a picture appeared on the plasma screen. A tall man with dark skin was walking through gates in an airport. He had a carry-on bag over his shoulder and his head was down. Dressed in gray linen pants and a navy loose-fitting shirt, he looked like just another tired traveler.

"Johann?" Damon moved closed to the plasma screen. He had never seen a picture of the infamous terrorist. Only a handful of people in the world knew what he even looked like. And Viper had managed to get him on camera.

"This was him entering the country at Philadelphia International," Alina said. "He came in about six weeks ago."

"How did you get this?" Damon looked at her.

"I hacked into the airport surveillance server," she answered. "It helped that I knew who I was looking for."

"He came in alone?" Damon asked, turning his attention back to the picture on the screen. He could only see part of his face.

"Yes." Alina clicked on another file and another picture joined the first one. This one was taken outside the airport as Johann was getting into a cab. He was looking toward the camera and Damon got his first good look at him. His face was lean and dark, and his eyes were very deep set. His hair was short and there was no trace of shadow on his face. He was clean-shaven and westernized.

"He arrived alone and didn't meet anyone at the airport. He left the country again a week later," Alina said, clicking again. Another picture popped up. This time he was dressed in jeans and a black windbreaker. He had a laptop bag over his shoulder. "Here he is heading into Canada. Toronto was the most likely destination." Another picture joined the other three. "Three days later, he came back into the country."

"All on the same visa?" Damon asked.

"No." Alina swung around and sipped her coffee, staring at the picture broodingly. "Philadelphia was on the visa that alerted DC, but he went in and out of Canada on a US passport. He wasn't particularly concerned with getting into the States undetected, but he sure didn't want to be caught going in and out of Canada. And he succeeded. No one knows that he ever left the country."

"Except you," Damon pointed out. Alina smiled.

"Well, that's my job," she retorted. "In any case, he went to Canada twice in a week and a half, and then he stopped traveling."

"How do you know?" Damon perched on the edge of the counter next to her chair.

"I'm watching all the most likely entry points," Alina told him. "I'm also scanning the government databases and surveillance satellites, as well as watching train stations, bus stations, local airports, etc. He hasn't left the country. In fact, I don't think he's left the tri-state area."

"He did everything he needed to do within two weeks of getting here." Damon sipped his coffee. "You think he brought an associate back from Canada?" He asked, his eyes going back to the database scanning faces.

"I think he brought *someone* back." Alina finished her coffee and set the mug down. "Here's what I learned two years ago." She sat back in her chair and looked up him. "Johann built his business on a very limited number of associates, and all those associates are loyal. His security personnel is made up of family. His couriers are extended family. This is not a man who works with other groups and he is extremely cautious."

"But he works with Mossavid, no?" Damon asked. Alina shook her head.

"He *is* Mossavid," she retorted. "Which is something no one in DC wants to accept. They think Mossavid is this big terrorist organization out of Syria with ties to Al Queda and agents all over Europe. In reality, it is a small cell of specialized terrorists, and it's led by *him*." Alina nodded to the plasma screen. "When I was hired to take him out two years ago, I was told that he was one of the leading terrorists in the organization. When I tracked him, I found out that he *was* the leading terrorist, but of a small cell made up entirely with family."

"He doesn't work for anyone," Damon stated. He was staring at the plasma. "So he has complete autonomy."

"Exactly." Alina turned to the laptop again and pulled up another file. She didn't put it on the plasma, but motioned for Damon to look at it on the laptop screen. "This is an excerpt of a memo sent from the White House, guaranteeing funding." Damon bent over her shoulder to read the document on the screen. "Washington guarantees funding for the war on terror and, specifically, on Mossavid."

"Well, that explains why they want to keep the impression that Mossavid is a larger organization than it is," Damon murmured. Alina nodded, trying to ignore the closeness of his cheek to hers. She could smell his aftershave and feel the heat from his body, and a rush of answering warmth went through her. Her pulse quickened. "It also makes more sense now why they want to make sure that there are no mistakes this time. That's a lot of funding...and no results yet," Damon added.

Alina nodded, not trusting herself to speak just yet. Damon turned his head to look at her, his eyes inches from hers. Alina felt another shock of awareness shoot through her as she met his dark blue eyes and her chest tightened. They stared at each other for a second, then his eyes dropped to her lips. Tension sprang up between them, sudden and powerful, and Alina caught her breath as it felt like her blood was hammering in her head. When Damon lifted his eyes again to hers, they had grown darker. They stared at each other for what seemed like an eternity, and then Alina managed to clear her throat.

Damon straightened up slowly with a slight smile and Alina let out a long breath. He grinned, his eyes still dark. He moved back to his perch on the counter and watched as Alina turned her attention back to the laptop hastily. The sudden, almost blinding, surge of desire hadn't taken him much by surprise. He had always felt something for Alina, starting way back when they had first met in boot camp, but he had a suspicion that *she* had just been caught completely off-guard. Damon took a few deep, silent breaths. He had to wait for her to work out this new wrinkle in her own time. He just hoped she worked it out fast.

"What doesn't make sense to me is why he would be killing off his network," Alina finally spoke, going back to Johann. Her voice sounded normal and her hands were almost steady when she swung around to look at Damon again. Her eyes met his again, but this time she was back to business. "It's not like him. It takes time to build a network. He had to have started this one months before he even got here, which is why I am pretty sure he had an associate over here already. He has traditionally left his networks in place."

"Maybe he doesn't anticipate needing them again," Damon suggested, looking back to the pictures of Johann. Alina followed his gaze.

"You think it could be a suicide mission?" she asked. Damon shrugged. Alina was thoughtful for a moment, but then she shook her head. "Mossavid has never shown a propensity for suicide bombings before," she finally decided. "But something must have him spooked. The only reason I can think for him getting rid of them so systematically is that he thinks they are a threat with information."

"And we don't know where he is now." Damon looked back at Alina. "Any ideas?"

"I know he's in the tri-state area," she answered. "The last location I have for him is in Center City, five days ago. I have nothing since."

"If he's getting ready to do whatever it is that he's planning..." Damon left the sentence hanging.

They both knew the end. If Johann was preparing for the attack on Three Mile Island and the preparations were in the final stage, he wouldn't surface again until he launched the attack. Alina looked back to the monitor that was scanning faces. She had to find the associate. That was her best path to Johann.

"I'll find him before then," Alina said softly.

Damon looked down at her. She didn't look determined. She just looked confident. He had no doubt that she would find Johann.

The question was whether or not he could protect her while she did.

Alina came awake slowly, the fluttering of wings pulling her from the depths of unconsciousness. Sunlight was pouring through the skylight in her bedroom when she opened her eyes, and shiny black eyes watched her from the perch high in the corner of the bedroom. Raven shifted his weight and bobbed his head in greeting as Alina smiled. She stretched slowly, yawning widely, and wiggled her toes under the warm and fluffy down comforter. The position of the sun told her that it was later in the day than she normally woke, and she hovered in that pleasant state between dreaming and full wakefulness. It had been after three when Damon had left and she came up to bed. It had been another hour before she finally fell asleep. She had tossed and turned, remembering the sudden and powerful desire that she had felt in the command center. Alina reflected ruefully now, in the bright light of day, that it was a good thing that Hawk had left when he had. If he had been within a mile of her last night when she had been tossing and turning, she would have ripped his clothes off quite happily.

And that was a problem.

Alina threw off the covers and got out of bed impatiently. Raven watched as she stalked into the adjoining master bathroom to have a shower. He seemed totally unimpressed with her display of irritation as he stretched his wings out before hunkering down for his morning nap.

Alina got into the shower and stood under a hot stream of water, letting the water ease the tension in her shoulders. She stared at the slate colored tiles of the wall and sighed. Who was she trying to fool? She had always had a soft spot for Damon. When they had been in training together, she had feelings for him. The few times that she had run into him over the years, she had always still felt a little electricity. Alina could always count on him to make her laugh when she needed to laugh, be serious when levity was out of place, and he always seemed to know exactly what she was thinking. He understood her. He always had. How many people could truly understand her?

Alina brushed the water out of her eyes and reached for her shampoo. She hunted down bad people and killed them. Plain and simple. This was not something an average man could know or relate to. Not only could Damon do both, but he understood the unique challenges that she faced with her own conscience and her own morality. He faced them too.

Alina had known coming back to Jersey was going to be complicated. Who would have thought it would be this ridiculous though? In addition to her ex and assorted friends from her past, she now had the added complication of an increasing attraction for the associate who had been sent by their respective bosses, essentially to babysit her. Alina's lips twitched. She could certainly appreciate the irony of the situation. If everything was happening on time and according to plan, Viper might even find it all amusing. But she had yet to locate Johann and the clock was ticking. There really wasn't time for these kinds of distractions.

Not that she had much of a choice, Alina reflected as she turned off the water and stepped out of the shower. She wrapped a towel around her head and looked at her reflection in the mirror. Life was certainly not predictable. She had learned a long time ago that even the best plans went hinky sometimes. Her eyes dropped to the jagged scar that ran at an angle from her right hip bone toward her belly button. It had been made by a knife three years ago when an unforeseen complication caused her to get a little closer than she would have liked to the security of one of her marks. Alina touched the scar absently. It was a constant reminder that not everything went according to plan.

She lifted her eyes back to her face and stared at herself thoughtfully. If everything *did* go according to plan all the time, life would certainly have the potential to be very boring.

Granted, when it came to her job and Johann, she wished everything would just fall into place. But Alina was honest with herself and admitted that the challenge of the hunt was what made her work interesting. She sighed and shook her head.

She was thinking too much and working too little. She had to focus on what needed to get done, and let everything else take care of itself. The sooner she got the job done, the better for everyone involved. Especially herself.

Angela got out of her car and looked around. She had stopped the car at the front door of Alina's house. She didn't want to just go waltzing up to the back door, even though at one point in time that would have been expected. She took in the large and flat front lawn and the surrounding trees. It had taken over forty-five minutes to get out here in traffic, and that was just too long. And the house was too far out in the woods. Didn't Alina get scared out here all on her own? Angela shook her head and turned to look at the house.

The house seemed nice enough. It was a sprawling two story structure with lots of potential...if it were closer to civilization. Angela wrinkled her nose and swatted away a bug that flitted near her face. She let out a gasp and jumped back when she saw that it was a huge bumblebee. The bee buzzed forward, sensing movement, and Angela ran around to the other side of her car, flailing her arms as she ran, trying to get away from the buzzing monster. The bee gave up and buzzed toward the daffodils that were growing a few feet away and Angela let out a long and relieved sigh. One of the many reasons she didn't do nature...bugs! She looked around a little self-consciously and then straightened her hair and went to the front door, ringing the bell defiantly.

Alina had already come up from the command center, where she had seen Angela on the security monitor. She had burst out laughing as Angela ran away from the bee, swinging her arms at her sides like a mad woman. Poor Angie. She was probably wearing some expensive perfume that smelled like flowers. The kitchen island was sliding back over the stairwell when the doorbell rang. Alina went to answer, wiping the laughter off her face as she opened the door.

"Angie!" she exclaimed, stepping back so Angela could step into the hall. "What a surprise!"

"I hope I'm not bothering you," Angela said, looking around curiously while Alina closed the door behind her. "I had a doctor's appointment, so I took the day from work. I thought I'd drive out here and see where you set up camp. You do realize you are *miles* away from civilization, right?"

"Hardly miles," Alina retorted with a laugh. "Come back to the kitchen. I was just about to make some tea."

"It took me over forty-five minutes to get out here!" Angela protested, following her down the hall and into the kitchen. Alina thought about her South American mountain retreat that was a full day away from civilization and smiled slightly. She wondered briefly what Angela would say to that.

"I like it out here," she said instead as they walked into the kitchen. Alina closed the lid to a laptop sitting on the counter as she passed it, hiding the security camera footage. Angela placed her designer bag on the counter and wandered into the sitting area curiously.

"This is a nice room," she said, looking around. "It will be nice to have fires in the fireplace in the winter."

Alina glanced over her shoulder. She paused, her eyes resting on the fireplace thoughtfully. She had a sudden mental image of snow falling silently outside and a fire raging in the hearth with Damon in the recliner next to it. Alina allowed her mind to explore the image briefly. She supposed she would be on the couch reading. The resulting feeling of longing that suddenly washed over her at the thought made Alina frown.

"Hey!" Angela snapped her out of her reverie, exclaiming from the sliding doors. "There is the biggest black bird I have ever seen hanging out on your deck!" Alina blinked and went back to making the tea.

"Raven actually isn't that big compared to other birds of prey," she remarked, clearing her throat slightly. "As hawks go, he's actually one of the smaller ones."

"You *named* it?" Angela couldn't drag her eyes away from the hawk. He was perched on the top of the banister that surrounded the deck. He had been staring into the trees, but almost as if he sensed Angela's gaze, he turned his head and stared back at her with his black hawk eyes. Angela had the absurd feeling that he was evaluating her.

"Of course. He's my pet." Alina switched on the electric kettle and joined Angela at the door. "He came with me." The trace of fondness in her voice wasn't hard to miss. Angela looked at her.

"Then why isn't he in a cage?" she asked logically. Alina shook her head.

"He would die in a cage. He's a wild bird," she answered. The thought flitted through Angela's mind that they were not just speaking about the bird anymore.

"You always did have a way with animals," she said, looking back at the hawk. "Is he dangerous?"

"Only if someone tries to attack me." Alina turned to go back into the kitchen.

"Do you feed him?" Angela seemed fascinated by the thought of a wild hawk as a pet. "Where does he sleep?"

"He hunts for himself and he usually naps on the deck or on the perch in my bedroom," Alina answered readily. "I altered the skylight so that he can get in and out. It didn't take him long at all to figure it out," she added with a laugh. Angela finally moved away from the door and seated herself at the bar counter.

"Doesn't the rain come in?" she asked. Alina shook her head.

"Not yet." She set a steaming china mug down in front of Angela. "But there hasn't been a real storm since I've been here, so we'll see what happens then." Alina got her own cup of tea and seated herself next to Angela.

"Mmmm." Angela sipped the tea appreciatively. "This is good."

"It is." Alina sipped the tea and welcomed the break from work. She had spent the whole morning tracing the known movements of Johann and reconstructing the most likely actions in between, based on what she knew of him and how he worked. It was a tedious and stressful exercise.

"So what kind of consulting does an ex-military intelligence person do in the civilian world?" Angela asked, her eyes resting on the closed laptop. Alina's lips twitched.

"Security," she answered vaguely. Angela raised an eyebrow.

"For private companies?" she prompted. Alina was silent. "Fine. Don't tell me. I don't need to know." Angela huffed. Alina laughed.

"No, you don't," she agreed.

"Does Stephanie know?" Angela asked after a moment. Alina glanced at Angela.

"Not really," she answered. "Although, I think she's made some guesses."

Alina sipped her tea again, waiting for Angela to get to what was bothering her. Clearly something was. The usually chatty woman was suddenly being very quiet.

"Are you working with the FBI?" Angela finally asked. Alina laughed.

"Hardly," she replied. "What makes you think that?"

"I don't know," Angela shrugged. "You just seem to be paying a lot of attention to whatever this case is that Stephanie's working on. And then this Damon guy appears, and you guys clearly know each other." Alina looked at Angela, surprised. Angela saw the look and laughed. "Oh please, Lina," she exclaimed. "Stephanie may be too preoccupied to notice, but I certainly wasn't. And, shockingly, I think John figured out that something was up as well. He was watching both of you very closely last night."

"I noticed," Alina agreed. She had noticed John's interest, but totally missed Angela's.

"Well, I'm not an idiot," Angela announced. "And it certainly doesn't take a rocket scientist to figure out that you and Damon are somehow connected to Stephanie's case. So is that why you came back when you did? Are you working with Homeland Security? And does Stephanie know?"

Alina was quiet for a moment, drinking her tea. She hadn't anticipated Angela as a complication, which was a miscalculation on her part. She knew that Angie was a quick study and she should have been prepared for this.

"No," Alina finally spoke. "I'm not working with DHS and no, Stephanie's case is not why I came back when I did."

"How do you know this Damon character?" Angela asked.

"We met in the service," Alina answered. "We were in boot camp together."

"Was he military intelligence too?" Angela asked. Alina sighed and set her cup down.

"No. He was a Navy SEAL," she answered. "However, I don't believe he thinks that his former occupation is relevant to his current one, so I don't see why anyone should know."

"Just like you don't see why anyone should know that you guys know each other?" Angela shot back. Alina looked at her sharply and Angela winked. "Hey, I don't judge. If I knew someone that gorgeous, I wouldn't want to share him either," she said with a grin. Alina forced a laugh.

"I had no idea he was Stephanie's mystery man until they walked through the door at the restaurant," she lied blithely. "That's all there is to it."

"Sure." Angela finished her tea and stood up. "Well, if you need any help with whatever you guys are working on, just let me know." She picked up her bag. "I feel kind of left out."

"For heaven's sake, don't." Alina stood up and pasted a carefree grin that she was far from feeling on her face. "It may all seem like a great big mystery, but there's really nothing to it at all. I'm doing security consulting now and Damon is working for Homeland Security. That's it."

"Well, you have to admit that the whole thing looks a little shady." Angela headed for the front door. "And I think you will find that John thinks so too."

"John is welcome to think whatever he would like to think." Alina allowed a note of impatience to creep into her voice. Angela laughed.

"Oh, he will!" she said, opening the front door. "But don't underestimate him, Lina. As much as I hate to admit it, he's turned into one hell of an investigator." Angela warned as she stepped outside. "Thanks for the tea!"

"Anytime. You know that." Alina stood in the doorway and watched Angela get into her car. She waved and watched the car disappear toward the road. Once the car was out of sight, the smile left her face and she closed the door thoughtfully.

Angela hadn't bought a word of what she had said. That much was obvious in her parting warning about John. Alina walked back to the kitchen slowly. Was Angela going to be a problem? She was smart, but Alina didn't think that she would do anything rash. Perhaps she did just feel left out as she had said. If that was the case, then maybe just thinking that she knew a secret would be enough to keep her happy.

Alina picked up the empty mugs and carried them over to the dishwasher. As much as she wanted to believe that, she knew that it was highly unlikely that Angela wasn't going to try to do some poking around herself. She had worked out that something "shady" was going on, and Alina knew Angela. She would poke around until she figured out exactly what that something shady was. This was going to cause another complication that Alina just could not afford.

"For the love of God, what next?" Alina muttered to herself, turning to go back downstairs into her command center.

Angela drove away from Alina's house irritated. While she hadn't exactly expected her to spill the whole story, she *really* hadn't expected Alina to flat out lie. But that was exactly what she had done. Angela may not know how to run an investigation or hunt criminals down, or know the first thing about handling a gun or about military intelligence (whatever *that* was), but one thing she *did* know was people. And she had known from watching Alina and Damon last night that, not only did they know each other well, there was no surprise on either side at seeing each other at the restaurant. She watched them through the whole dinner. Alina appeared very uncomfortable a number of times when some part of her past came up and, conversely, Damon had been unduly interested. Although they knew each other, Damon clearly knew absolutely nothing about her past. Angela thought that was interesting. She had also found it interesting that Damon seemed to be watching John just as much as John had been watching him. In fact, Angela had found the whole dinner fascinating. It was like watching an elaborate charade being played out over steak and wine.

However, this morning she woke up curious. She had driven all the way out to the sticks for answers, and was coming away empty. Angela winced as she bounced over a rough mound in the gravel driveway leading back to the road. Alina clearly didn't want her to know what was going on. Angela didn't think that it was necessarily that Alina didn't trust her. She thought it was more of a case of need to know, and Alina had decided that she didn't need to know. Angela slowed down as the main road came into sight ahead.

Well, Angela wanted to know. She had always hated the rare occasions when they were younger and Stephanie and Alina kept secrets from her. They usually involved some sort of birthday surprise, and Angela had always quietly gone about uncovering the surprise before the event. Angela loathed surprises, and she hated not knowing what was going on even more.

"I'll just have to find out myself." Angela decided out loud, stopping at the tarmac of the main road. She checked to make sure that no cars were coming before pulling out onto the road. She would just have to follow both Stephanie and Alina until she figured out what they were up to.

Angela turned on the radio, happier now that she resolved on a plan of action. And if she could figure out where he was staying, she just might follow up on the mysterious and gorgeous Damon character as well! If they didn't want to tell her what was going on, Angela would just find out for herself!

Angela pressed the gas down and sped down the road. She never noticed the tall shadow that had moved quickly into the trees at the edge of road as she pulled out. And she missed the flash of sunlight glinting off the lenses of a pair of binoculars, watching her speed down the road.

A few minutes after she had gone, a lone figure dressed in olive hunting fatigues moved across the road and disappeared into the trees opposite. A minute later, an engine came to life and a black Bronco pulled out onto the road, heading in the opposite direction.

Chapter Seven

Damon watched from the darkness as Alina moved past the sliding doors again on her way to the kitchen. She had been pacing for the better part of an hour, occasionally going over to her laptop and checking the screen before resuming her loop around the living room and dining room. The night was silent around him and Damon felt comfortable in the darkness, watching. Raven was on the roof of the house, watching as well. Every once in a while, he disappeared into the skylight, only to reappear a few minutes later. Damon concluded that Alina had rigged some kind of entry through the skylight into the house. He glanced up at the dark bird ruefully.

At least she lets one hawk into the bedroom, he thought. Damon hadn't heard from her in two days. He had been watching her for those two days, so he knew she was safe. But Hawk had to admit that he was bothered that she hadn't tried to make contact, not since that night in her command center.

Damon rolled his head a few times before shifting slightly. He was settled on a thick old branch of a tall old oak, about twenty-five feet off the ground. From this vantage point, he had an unrestricted view of the back of the house and down the right side to the front. He had to appreciate the lack of greenery and obstructions in the immediate area around the house. While it had been done with the intent of the occupant having a clear view of anyone approaching, it had the equal effect of allowing anyone outside to have a clear view as well. He had tried a few trees the other night, avoiding her surveillance easily now that he had seen the monitors and knew what angles were covered. He finally settled on this one. It had the most unimpeded view of those available.

Damon leaned his head back against the tree trunk and wondered why she was pacing. Alina had always had a lot of energy, but he couldn't recall ever watching her pace before.

He cast his mind back to when they trained for the Organization together. The tall guy...what was his name? Damon frowned slightly. Something dopey...they all made fun of it....Hubert? No. That was the drill sergeant from boot camp. Egbert! That was it! Egbert had done a lot of pacing in their training days, and Viper had caused most of it. She always played devil's advocate. She was always counter-planning. They would come up with a plan, and Alina would point out all the flaws and why it would never work. Damon remembered it used to drive Egbert insane. Old Egbert was dead now, killed in some god-forsaken Mexican foothill.

Hawk's ears pricked and he lifted his head. The distant sound of a motorcycle interrupted his reminiscence, coming from the woods in front of the house. Damon stood up and swung silently and skillfully up into the upper branches of the oak until he was above roof level. He raised the binoculars and scanned the woods. The engine was more distinct now and Damon finally located it. It was approaching the house from the road. He zoomed in on the rider, relaxing when he saw the jeans and loose teeshirt. He clicked a button and zoomed in on the standard issue 9mm at the riders hip. Damon dropped the binoculars back down to hang around his neck and dropped back down to his perch in the lower branch.

He watched as Alina closed the laptop and picked up a remote. She pointed it to the wall of the fireplace and Damon raised an eyebrow. So she watched the TV after all! Alina came out onto the deck as the motorcycle roared past the front of the house and around the side. The rider parked in front of the garage, and Damon watched as John took off his helmet and switched off the bike. Alina was standing on the deck, her arms crossed and her legs slightly apart in a defensive stance. Hawk suddenly wished he had thought to bring a listening device. He watched as John got off the bike and walked across the lawn.

"I tried calling, but you didn't answer." John's voice carried across the night.

Damon sighed silently. Alina *hadn't* been watching television like a normal person. She had the security monitors wired to it. She hadn't known he was coming. She had seen him on the TV. Damon shook his head slightly. Did the woman ever take a break?

"Usually that means someone is busy or not home," Alina answered, her voice clear and steady.

"Well, clearly you're home." John stopped walking at the steps to the deck. He rested one hand on the banister. "So does that mean you're too busy to talk?"

Alina looked at him in silence for a moment. He was dressed in jeans and a loose-fitting green tee-shirt. His FBI weapon was at his hip, and his badge was clipped onto his belt.

"Are you here in an official capacity?" she asked, motioning to the gun. John glanced down.

"No, but it doesn't leave my side," he answered. Alina sighed.

"I *am* busy, but you can talk," she told him.

In the tree, Damon grinned as John stepped onto the deck. *First line of defense crossed*, he thought. *Let's see if she lets you in the house.* Damon raised his eyes at movement on the roof. *Or if you pass Raven's test.*

Alina backed up, uncrossing her arms as John joined her on the deck. She motioned to one of the chairs.

"Have a seat."

"Thank you." John smiled at her. "I wasn't sure if you were going to try to punch me."

"You haven't done anything recently to warrant that," Alina retorted. There was a faint rustle and Raven swooped down suddenly out of the darkness.

"Holy Mother of God!"

John yelped and ducked, throwing his arm up defensively. Raven buzzed his head before landing silently on the deck banister. Damon bit back a laugh in the darkness. He knew from experience how startling it was to have the big hawk suddenly appear out of nowhere and swoop down on you, but that didn't stop him from thoroughly enjoying John's discomfort.

"What the hell is THAT?!" John exclaimed.

"THAT is a hawk," Alina retorted. "His name is Raven. Play nice or I'll have him pluck your eyes out."

"You *named* it???" John straightened up and stared at the huge black bird of prey who was staring right back at him.

"Of course I did." Alina moved past him to sit on one of the chairs. She sat back and crossed her legs. "He's a pet. And he makes a wonderful guard dog."

"I can see that." John slowly moved to the other chair and sat down, never taking his eyes off Raven. "Although, I wouldn't have thought that you needed one."

"I don't," Alina answered, smiling slightly. She watched in silence as John watched the bird. After a moment, she cleared her throat. "You may not want to stare too long," she advised gently. "He might take it as a sign of aggression."

"I can't help it." John finally tore his eyes away from the hawk.

"So, what can I do for you, John?" Alina asked. Her nerves had been on edge ever since she saw him on the surveillance camera. It infuriated her that he still had the ability to make her feel anything, but he did. She was filled with a nervous energy, not unlike anger mixed with passion. But Alina's feelings for John had long since died. She knew this was just the energy of memories.

"Well, I wanted to talk, just the two of us," John said slowly. "Without Stephanie or Angela weighing in on every word we say." Alina looked out over the dark backyard and nodded.

"Fair enough," she agreed. "There are probably some things that should be said...just between us."

Her eyes scanned the darkness out of habit, then paused briefly at a point in the darkness. Damon stopped breathing. She was looking right in his direction. He knew there was no way she could see him, but Damon held his breath anyway. He couldn't hear what was being said now, and more than ever he wished he had audio on the deck.

"Exactly," John said. He looked at her. "What are you looking at?" He turned his head to look out into the darkness. Alina shook her head.

"Nothing," she answered, standing. "Do you want a drink? I think I might have a beer or two."

"Sure." John stood up, but Alina pushed him back down into his seat.

"I'll bring them out," she said, moving toward the door. "Relax."

"Right. I'll just relax then," John agreed, turning his gaze back to the hawk that was still watching him. "Here. Alone. With a *big friggin BIRD OF PREY!*" He raised his voice to call after her as she disappeared into the house.

Damon chuckled to himself. Well, he had heard THAT clear enough. Damon watched as Alina went into the kitchen. She reappeared a minute later with two beers in her hand, which she set on the counter while she opened her laptop. He frowned. Oh, *now* she had beer. He shifted restlessly and the weight of his binoculars made him look down. Hawk smiled slowly and lifted them to his eyes, zooming in on the deck. He may not be able to hear what was said, but he could *see* what was said. Lip-reading was sometimes misleading, but he was too curious to pass up the opportunity.

Alina set the two beer bottles on the counter and opened the laptop. She hit the space key and then moved the mouse, turning one of the cameras in the back slightly. She focused it on the area in the woods where she had sensed something. There had been no movement there. None. That was enough to make her suspicious. She angled the camera around and zoomed in, but could see nothing. The trees were dark and silent. Alina moved the camera back and sighed, closing the laptop. If something was there, it was very well concealed. Maybe she was just being paranoid. She picked up the bottles with one hand and went back outside.

"Did you two come to an understanding yet?" she asked with a grin, handing John one of the beers. John snorted.

"Yes. We understand that we don't trust each other," he said, lifting the bottle to his lips.

Alina sat back down and glanced again to that still area of the woods. As if reading her mind, Raven stretched, and then turned his back on them to stare out into the night.

"Good." Alina sipped the beer. "Then you have a basis for a healthy relationship," she announced. John grinned.

"Is that what you call healthy?" he asked. "I seem to remember you saying that you couldn't live with someone you couldn't trust."

"See what ten years can do? I've grown," Alina retorted. John laughed, then sobered.

"While we're on the subject..."

"We're not," Alina said flatly.

"I *am* sorry for being such an ass," John continued, ignoring her. "I threw away the best thing that ever happened to me." Alina looked at him. For once, his expression was serious. "When you left, I realized that. But it was too late."

The words hung in the air between them, made all the more haunting by their suddenness. Alina sucked in some air and sipped her beer, absorbing the apology.

John turned his attention back to the yard. He had watched for some flicker of emotion in Alina's eyes, some acknowledgement of what they had shared. But there had been nothing. He had always been able to read her like a book. Now, however, he couldn't read anything. It was like there was no emotion left inside of her.

"You did," Alina finally spoke, bringing his gaze back to her. It sounded as if she was picking her words carefully. "But it turned out to be for the best. It forced me to make a life for myself."

"A life without me," John pointed out. Alina looked at him and, for a split second, John thought he saw the old Lina he had loved. In an instant, she was gone.

"Come on, John," she said, pulling her legs up beside her on the wide Adirondack chair. "We both know that was a bad relationship from the start. We're much better off now. You have a good career and I have a life that I am content with."

"Oh, no doubt," John agreed. "But I want you to know that I truly do regret what I did to you. I do hope that we can be friends."

"We'll see." Alina looked out over the backyard. "I may not stay."

"Yes. Stephanie said you are trying Jersey out again to see if it still fits." John leaned back. "Where did you come from?"

"Everywhere," Alina answered evasively. "I've traveled a lot." John glanced at her.

"With the Navy?" he asked. Alina hadn't missed the searching glance. She smiled slightly.

"Of course," she replied.

"Is that where you met Damon Peterson?" John asked smoothly. Alina looked at him.

"Wow," she said. "You sure don't mince words anymore, do you?"

"I didn't think there was a need." John angled himself sideways in his chair so that he could watch her.

Alina shifted to face him, resting the bottle on her thigh. Her eyes met his and she was a little taken aback at the calm look of perception in the blue depths. Alina remembered Angela's warning and had to admit that here, again, she had miscalculated.

"I do know, Damon, yes," she said. "And yes, we met in the forces. And no, Stephanie doesn't know. I don't see that it's relevant to anything." John nodded, his eyes hooded, watching her.

"I figured as much. It was pretty obvious at the restaurant the other night." He sipped his beer, his eyes never leaving her face. Alina stared back calmly. "Why don't you think it's relevant for Stephanie to know?"

"I just don't see that it's important." Alina shrugged. "I hadn't seen him for a few years. I had no idea he was even working for Homeland Security. When you guys walked into the restaurant, I figured he would say something if he wanted it known."

"And when he didn't?"

"Look. Your defense of your partner is touching, but completely unnecessary," Alina said bluntly. "It's very simple. Damon and I met in boot camp. He moved on to Special Ops and I moved on to military intelligence. When people are in special branches, it's not something that we generally want known. We're proud, but we don't want to invite scrutiny. It was certainly not my place to tell you all that I knew Damon from the Navy."

"Well, it's not like it's a bad thing," John said thoughtfully. "It's an honor to be in special branches."

"It's also like waving a red flag to a bull sometimes," Alina retorted truthfully. "People find out that you were in special forces, and then some people want to test you. It's a stupid thing, but there you have it. People are stupid. Damon had his share of stupidity thrown at him."

"Has anyone ever tested you, Ms. Military Intelligence?" John asked with a grin, dropping the subject of Damon for a moment.

"Yes." Alina wasn't fooled. She knew he would come back to what he wanted to say. And she had a pretty good idea what his "talk" was going to be about now.

"How?" John asked. Alina sighed.

"It doesn't matter," she replied, remembering an MMA fighter in a dark alley. She had left him with a broken leg and no pride. "The point is that it is not conducive to a peaceful existence."

"You had to have known when you told them..." John's voice trailed off at the look on her face. "Ah. I see. You didn't."

"No. Someone else had that pleasure." Alina lifted her bottle again.

"So even military intelligence has their showboats," John murmured. Alina shrugged.

"It's those stupid people again. They're everywhere," she replied. Her eyes wandered out over the darkness again. An owl hooted off behind her and Raven shifted his weight on the banister. Her eyes rested on him. Normally, he would be off hunting right now, but Raven didn't appear to be in a hurry to fly off.

"Well, that is something we can agree on." John looked at her again. "You know I have to ask this..."

"No. I am not working with Homeland Security." Alina turned her gaze back to his face in time to see his look of surprise. She laughed shortly. "John, just spit it out. What's on your mind?" John stared at her for a second, his "Fed" mask sliding into place. Alina had the sudden urge to smack it off his face. He looked like a cop.

"We went to talk to Frankie Solitto the other day. The body at the tracks was Martin Sladecki, one of his older goons," he said slowly. Alina just continued to look at him questioningly. "He knew we were coming. He had a nice little story already laid out for us...complete with corroborating witnesses."

"I probably shouldn't be hearing this," Alina murmured. "But please, do go on."

"Damon was the only other person outside our team that knew what we were going to do." John stated flatly. Alina let out an inaudible sigh. She hated when she was right. It took all the mystery out of life.

"Maybe you should look inside your team, then," Alina said gently. "I can assure you, Damon is most assuredly *not* on Frankie Solitto's payroll."

"I can assure you that no one on my team is either," John retorted. "But Frankie knew we were coming."

"So what do you think? That Damon and I are *both* on Frankie's payroll?" Alina laughed in genuine amusement. "Don't be absurd, John."

"Then how would you explain it?" John demanded. If he had still known Alina as well as he used to, John would have recognized the sudden glint in her eyes.

"There are any number of explanations," Alina announced, making herself comfortable. "The most glaringly obvious is that one of his employees was peeled off a train track in South Jersey. The first thing the FBI does in a situation like that is go to question the boss. Everyone knows that."

"Ok. There's one," John admitted.

"Two, it's no secret that Frankie has people in the police department. And, as much as you hate to admit it, he has them in the FBI too. It could have been a janitor or secretary that overheard something, for God's Sake," Alina continued calmly.

"Ok. There's two. But a shaky two," John replied.

"Three..." Alina went on as if he hadn't spoken. "Frankie has surveillance twenty-four seven. He would have seen your entourage coming long before you hit the front gates."

"Ok." John held up a hand. "Witnesses?"

"How long do you think it would take to tell someone on his payroll to lie?" Alina demanded. "Not long, my dear." John was silent. "Face it. You're looking for ghosts where there are none." Alina's eyes flicked to the silent corner of woods. "Sometimes, things just are what they are."

"I agree." John sighed. "I may have been looking for shadows behind doors. But do you blame me?" Alina looked at him for a moment.

"No," she said finally. "I don't. I can see that it must look odd, me showing up out of the blue and then someone I know suddenly gets sent from Washington to look over your shoulder."

"More than a little odd," John said. He stared at her thoughtfully for a long moment. Alina stared back. "How well do you and Damon know each other?" John asked suddenly. Alina blinked.

"Excuse me?"

"Well, you know...did you just pass in the hall?" John shrugged. "Did you fight next to him? Were you more than friends?" He watched as her eyes grew shuttered.

"We trained together," Alina answered slowly. Her mind was working furiously, trying to come up with something close enough to the truth without actually *being* the truth. "And, later, we did fight together."

"So you would have taken a bullet for him," John stated. Alina nodded.

"Of course. Were we more than friends? Of course." Alina shrugged. "You become family at some point. But if you're asking if we slept together, that is none of your business."

"I never asked that!" John protested with a grin.

"You implied it." Alina stood up, indicating that the conversation was over. "I would appreciate it if you would not tell Stephanie. I'm sure Damon will get around to telling her if he thinks it's important. However, I understand if you can't keep secrets from your partner." John stood up and drained what was left of his beer in one swallow.

"She'll figure it out eventually," he said, setting the bottle on the floor next to his chair. He stepped closer and looked down at her.

Alina felt nothing but caution as she stared into his eyes. This was not the John she had left behind ten years ago. Angela was right. He had turned into one hell of a perceptive son of a bitch. And he was clearly looking for answers. She could only hope that he had not found the right ones.

John stared down at Lina. She was more beautiful now than he remembered and he was more than a little annoyed that he had been such an ass all those years ago. But who would have thought that things would turn out like this? She was something special. She always had been. But now she was more. He couldn't put his finger on it, but she was more of everything now. More beautiful, more mysterious, more experienced, and smarter. Smart enough to tell just enough of the truth. He knew she hadn't been completely honest with him. He just didn't know which part was the lie. John lifted his hand and was somewhat surprised when she allowed him to touch her jaw softly. He slid the back of his fingers down her jawline slowly.

"Thanks for the beer," he said softly. "And for the talk."

"You're welcome." Her voice was just as soft.

"Maybe next time you'll invite me in," John murmured. Alina took a deep breath and stepped back, the spell broken.

"Into my parlor?" she asked with a slight smile that didn't quite reach her eyes. John grinned and let his hand fall to his side. He moved past her to the steps and stepped off the deck.

"I'm not a fly," he replied, starting toward the drive. He paused and turned back. "And you're not much of a spider," he added, his voice carrying across the darkness to the invisible figure watching from the darkness. "A snake, maybe. But not a spider."

Alina froze, her heart stopping for second before beginning to pound.

"A snake?" she shot back sharply. John grinned and started backing up toward the drive.

"Spiders spin a web. They're pretty upfront with their intentions," he informed her. "Snakes are sneaky little buggers. They don't like anyone to see them coming."

Damon sucked in his breath. Even at this distance, he could see the tension in Alina's whole body. Viper looked like she was ready to strike. He watched as her hand flexed at her side briefly, and then her body suddenly relaxed again.

"Well, either way, I don't think you want to go willingly into their parlor," Alina retorted. Damon heard John's chuckle.

"I think I can take you," John said confidently.

"We'll never know," Alina shot back. John just laughed and got on his bike. A second later the engine roared to life. He turned it around in the driveway and then, with a wave, he roared off.

Hawk was watching Viper. Long after John had gone, she was still standing on the deck. The tension was back in her body. She stood with her legs braced apart, staring out into the night. Damon lifted his binoculars once more. This time she wasn't looking in his direction. She was staring somewhere else. Somewhere not here, but in the past. Damon lowered the binoculars slowly and watched her thoughtfully for a moment. John had got to her. Somehow, something he had said, had gotten under her armor.

Damon had to force himself to stay in the tree and not go to her. She had to face whatever it was and deal with it. Herself. Damon felt a sinking feeling inside him as he realized that he wanted to help her and wanted to support her.

He wanted her.

The realization had been there all along, but Hawk nonetheless felt a sharp shock at admitting it to himself. He wanted Viper for himself. She was everything he wanted, and just enough of what would drive him crazy to make it interesting. Damon watched her, his mind reeling with all the difficulties in his situation and all the possible outcomes. It wasn't just a physical desire, which he had always known existed for her, but now it was emotional. He wanted to be part of her life. He wanted to make her laugh, and be there when she cried...if she cried. He wanted to protect her. And have her protect him. He groaned silently.

Oh Hawk, this is not a complication we need right now. Sex is one thing. What you're thinking is something completely different.

Damon sighed.

This was going to get complicated.

Alina stood on the deck long after the sound of John's motorcycle had faded away, her mind reeling. *A snake.*

The words kept coming back to mock her. When he had said them, her mind immediately grasped the fact that he couldn't possibly know that her codename was Viper. There was no way he could know. But her instinct had taken control for a split second. For that split second, tension had coursed through her body, tightening her muscles and causing her hands to flinch in reaction, ready to reach for her weapon in sheer instinctual reaction. But then, as quickly as the wave of shock had crashed over her, it ebbed away. Alina had flexed her hands, her vision clearing enough to see John's teasing laughter. She breathed now, long deep and calming breaths, staring into nowhere. His touch after all these years had shocked her into immobility. Then, following hard on that, *a snake*. Not very complimentary at any time to a lady, but then John was never known for his smoothness.

Alina stared blindly into the night. She had accepted who she had become a long time ago. She was good at what she did, and had come to terms with the fact that someone had to do it, so it might as well be her. However, there was no disputing that every once in a while, the grimness of what she actually did for a living would rise up and taunt her. It usually happened randomly; when she saw a wife and husband out for the day with their perfect children, living their perfect lives, blissfully unaware of what other people did to ensure their freedom to live their perfectness. ...*A snake.*

She had earned the nickname Viper during that tenuous period between training and activation, when they were sent out on their own with loose over-sight and given an objective. It was that final test, the one that determined if they would be accepted into the "elite" of the Organization. Her "oversight" had been so impressed with the way she conducted her tracking that he started using the nickname in his reports. It was only natural that it would then become her codename. They all had them. Hawk had received his in much the same way. There had never been any doubt that they would join the ranks of the elite. The only question had been how high up they would go. Viper had completed her objective a few hours before Hawk. By the time he learned she had beat him once again, she had been on a plane, alone, heading for the middle east. ...*A snake.*

At first she had been amused at the name Viper. She certainly didn't think of herself as a fast, poisonous snake. But as the months went by, and the jobs started piling up, she realized how accurate the assessment by that long-forgotten oversight agent had been. She *did* strike like a snake. She got in, got it done, and got out as quickly as possible. Alina didn't give herself time to form attachments or get to know the targets. She just got the job done and moved on. As time went by, she began to realize that the speed was her coping mechanism. It didn't give her time to think about the morality or immorality of what she did. The speed with which she worked helped her distance herself from the job, and not let it consume her.

It also ensured that she remained alone, with no friends, family, or connections.

Except Hawk.

After they completed their training, she hadn't seen him for over a year. Then, unexpectedly, they came face to face in a street in Paris, of all places. Alina smiled slightly as she stared out into the night. Damon took her to dinner, to a little restaurant near the Louvre. Neither had mentioned why they were in Paris. They ate dinner and laughed over people they had known and places they had seen. And when dinner was over, they parted ways again. Alina had left Paris later that night, feeling strangely like she had left behind a friend. She kept the linen napkin from the restaurant as a reminder that she was not completely alone, that there was someone else, a friend, who understood and was living the same life. It had helped with the loneliness that came with the existence that she lived.

Alina shook her head suddenly, her eyes coming back into focus. Her mind returned from the past and she sighed. She had no idea why she was suddenly so retrospective, or why she was reminded now, ironically, of how much she depended on Hawk for her sanity. The thoughts made her nervous. When this job was over, she would move on and so would Damon. This was just another interlude in their respective life paths. Alina tried not to dwell on why they kept running into each other. Sometimes things just were what they were, and that was all there was to it. However, as Alina turned to pick up the empty bottles and go back inside, she was honest enough to admit that it was getting harder and harder each time to say goodbye to Damon.

Alina paused at the sliding door and glanced back. Raven stretched, looking at her, and then suddenly lifted his wings, lifting up into the air and disappearing into the night. She watched him go silently, and then looked back out into the darkness. She wondered briefly if it would be possible to stay here, and travel freely, and not be questioned by Stephanie or Angela. She wondered, if Damon always knew where to find her, would she see him more frequently?

And she wondered how on earth she was going to say goodbye at the end of it all.

Chapter Eight

Stephanie stepped off the elevator at six in the morning, coffee in hand. After spending a restless night, she had headed to the office early to get a jump on the day. Sipping her coffee, she went down the hall towards her desk. The whole Solitto thing was bothering her. She knew it was bothering John as well, which was why she had been turning it over in her head last night. Unlike John, she wasn't so worried that someone had apparently tipped him off to their arrival. What bothered her was the fact that Frankie had seemed pretty unconcerned about who may have killed his employee. In her experience, the Family was pretty territorial over their own. If someone messed with one, they messed with them all. So why the unconcern? Did he know who did it? Did he already have plans in place to take care of it? Or *had* he already taken care of it? Were they going to have another body float up somewhere?

Stephanie came to a halt as she entered her nearly deserted department. One person was already there, slouched in his chair, fast asleep. Stephanie resumed her trek to her desk, staring at John as she went. He was never in much before eight. Yet, clearly he had been at his desk for quite some time. Paper coffee cups from the vending machine were littered across his desk, along with papers and file folders. His monitor was still up, the results of a search flashing silently. Stephanie's curiosity got the better of her. She set her purse and coffee down silently and tip-toed over to peek at the search results. Her eyebrows soared into her forehead when she saw the name at the top of the search file. She went back to her desk silently and stood for a second, staring at the sleeping man. What on *earth* was he up to? There was only one way to find out.

Stephanie dropped her keys onto her desk with a loud clatter and John awoke with a violent start, swinging around to peer over at her.

"Morning, Sunshine!" Stephanie said cheerfully. "What are you doing here, so bright and early?"

"I was following up on something." John locked his monitor quickly, obscuring the search results from her view. "I couldn't sleep."

"Uh-oh." Stephanie sat down and reached for her coffee. "What's her name? Wait....I don't want to know. It's probably Bambi, or something equally obnoxious." John yawned widely and grinned.

"Why so hostile?" he asked innocently. He yawned again and started fishing around on his desk, looking for something. "What time is it, anyway?"

"Just past six." Stephanie sipped her coffee and reached over to turn on her computer.

"Good God." John stood up and stretched. "I'm going to run out for coffee. Do you want some?"

"Got some." Stephanie held up her cup. John nodded and turned back to his desk for some more aimless shuffling. Stephanie watched as he searched through the mess. "What are you looking for?" she finally asked.

"My phone," John muttered, still searching.

"On the floor," Steph told him. John straightened up and looked at her. She motioned to the floor at the side of his desk, where his smartphone was laying on the floor, face down. He picked it up with a grin.

"Thanks." He headed for the elevators. "See you in a few minutes." Stephanie nodded, her eyes on her monitor. She went about her morning routine until the she heard the elevator doors ding. She waited until she heard them close and peeked around. He was gone.

Without hesitating, Stephanie got up and went over to John's desk. She looked at the chaos covering his desk and took mental note of where everything was before she started opening up file folders. Several were open case files on various Solitto members, past and present. There were a few cold case files. One that had been pushed toward the back of the desk, near the monitor, caught her eye. It was a thicker file on their terrorist. Stephanie picked it up, careful not to

122

disturb anything. John often appeared careless, but he rarely missed anything. She wouldn't put it past him to have some kind of order in all this chaos. The file was a new addition to the desk. It didn't have the same wear marks and coffee drops that the others had. If Stephanie had to hazard a guess, the file had probably been pushed back to protect it from damage. Stephanie glanced at her watch and flipped the thick file open, standing in front of John's desk. She had worked with him long enough to know exactly how long it took him to go to the corner coffee shop, flirt with the girls behind the counter, get his coffee, and come back. She had roughly ten minutes.

Stephanie had read the file on Johann already, but John was obviously looking for something. She glanced through the file quickly, her eyes scanning the pages. The laundry list of terrorist acts was substantial, but nothing they didn't already know, and she wondered why on earth John had pulled the file again last night. What was he thinking? She continued reading, scanning each page for some sort of keyword or phrase that would give her a clue as to what had led John to the file. Pictures of exploded store fronts and houses, dead women and children from school attacks, any number of office buildings and shopping areas with high body counts were packed into the file. She had felt sick the first time she had read through the file, but she flipped through all the pictures again, trying to see what John was looking for last night. Stephanie finally gave up and replaced the file where she had found it. She went back to her desk thoughtfully and had just sat down when the elevator doors dinged. John appeared next to her a minute later and set a white bag on her desk.

"Blueberry muffin," he said, heading back to his desk. Stephanie opened the bag and peeked inside.

"Thank you!" she said, pulling it out.

"No problem." John grabbed the back of his chair with one hand and swung it over next to her desk. He settled himself facing her and sipped his coffee. Stephanie tore off a piece of the muffin and popped it into her mouth.

"I have a question to ask you," John said after a moment. Stephanie nodded, her mouth full of warm muffin. She opened her email and scanned it quickly before turning her full attention to John. The office was still empty and she knew this was the best time to find out what was on his mind.

"Do you wonder what Alina has been doing the past ten years?" John asked her, his blue eyes meeting hers. Stephanie sat back in her chair and picked up her coffee cup.

"Not really," she answered slowly. "She was in military intelligence. I would prefer *not* to think about what she has been doing for the past ten years. It would probably turn my hair gray."

"Your hair is already turning gray," John said with a grin. Stephanie glared at him.

"From working with you," she shot back. "The way I look at it, if Alina wants to talk about where she's been and what she's been doing, then she will. Otherwise, I am just her old friend and I love her for who she is, no questions asked," Stephanie continued. "Why?"

"I went and saw her the other night," John said slowly. Stephanie's eyebrows went up and her lips twitched.

"*Really?*" she drawled. "And how did that go?" John grinned.

"I don't have any broken bones or new stitches," he retorted. "I thought we had to get some things out of the way and clear the air, so to speak."

Stephanie considered John thoughtfully. He was right, of course. The past had to be resolved between the two of them. There was never any question about that. Neither of them had ever truly closed the door on the mess that their relationship had become. However, Stephanie was somewhat surprised that John had recognized that fact.

"That was very mature of you, John," she commended him warmly. "You two needed closure. Did you work it all out?"

"I have no idea," John admitted ruefully. "She managed to control the entire conversation and I'm not sure how we left things." Stephanie burst out laughing at the confusion in his voice. Oh, she wished she could have heard the conversation!

"Well, I guess we'll find out." She sipped her coffee. "Did she tell you something about what she's been doing the past ten years? Is that what you want to talk about?"

Stephanie tried to get the conversation back on track. The seven o'clockers would start arriving soon and when that happened, John would go back to his desk and her chance of a glimpse into his head would be lost.

"She didn't *tell* me anything," John answered. "But I was able to surmise a little bit." He sounded irritated and Stephanie could relate whole-heartedly. Alina had picked up a habit of not saying anything and leaving it up to them to draw what conclusions they liked. It was extremely frustrating. It made her feel like their friendship never existed. Or, worse, that it didn't mean a thing to Alina anymore. "Don't you think it odd that she suddenly came back when she did?" John asked.

"I've been down this road." Stephanie waved her hand in the air and crossed her legs. "It could be coincidence, but I doubt it. Whatever she *is* doing, she's not working against us, so I've come to an understanding with her."

"Really?" John looked up. "When was this?"

"The day our mysterious Mr. Peterson arrived. I had breakfast with her." Steph finished her coffee and dropped the empty cup into the trash can, wishing now that she had asked him to get her another cup. "I know you think that I work too hard, and am therefore oblivious to everything going on around me, but I'm not. She was with me when I went to Sladecki's crime scene. She was the one who led me to the rooftop where our shooter blew out the lights. Alina put it all together while I was still examining the car."

"You never told me this," John said, leaning forward. "Why didn't you tell me this?" Stephanie shrugged.

"I didn't see that it made any difference," she replied. "The point is that the next day I went over there and had a nice little chat. She knows that I know that she's not just here

125

for Jersey's lovely weather, and we agreed that any information could be mutually shared."

"Mutually shared?!" John stared at her in disbelief. "Are you kidding me?! This is a federal investigation...or had you forgotten?" Stephanie rolled her eyes.

"This is why I didn't tell you," she retorted. "Yes, it is a federal investigation. And whatever Alina is doing here, she can help us with that investigation. I would rather be working with her than against her right now. At least that way I can see what she is doing."

John stared at her. His initial reaction subsided as quickly as it had surfaced and he saw the method behind Stephanie's madness. It was much easier to keep tabs on the enemy if you were working with them.

"So what does she know?" John's mind was working furiously.

"Not much, actually." Stephanie shrugged. "We haven't discussed anything since that morning, and we didn't know anything at that point."

"So she didn't know about the Solitto connection?" John asked. Stephanie shook her head.

"Nope." She raised an eyebrow. "She didn't. Does that mean that she does now?" John had the grace to look a little sheepish.

"I told her the other night," he admitted.

"Oh really?" Stephanie demanded, her eyes twinkling. "Discussing our *federal* investigation, were you?"

"Look, it was bothering me that Solitto knew we were coming," John said, lowering his voice as the elevator doors dinged, heralding the first of the seven o'clockers. He leaned forward in his chair so he could talk quietly. "The more I thought about it, the more it bothered me. So I went out to Alina's to see if she knew anything. It's just too much of a coincidence for me."

"And did she?" Stephanie leaned forward as well. John shook his head.

"I don't know," he answered honestly. "She fed me a bunch of half-lies and misdirections and I honestly have no idea if she knew about Solitto or not. She's hiding *something*, but whether or not it's that, I just don't know."

"Well, how did you approach it?" Stephanie asked.

"I hinted that she was working for him," John told her. Stephanie stared at him, her mouth dropping open. John glanced up and shrugged at the look on her face.

"Are you INSANE?!" she demanded, her voice rising. She lowered it again hastily. "No wonder she didn't tell you anything," Stephanie hissed. "Leave it to you to be such an ass."

"It's a possibility," John defended himself calmly. "You may not want to think about it, but she could very well be on Solitto's payroll. It would explain nicely why she came back when she did."

"John, I really didn't think you were stupid, but now I'm starting to wonder," Stephanie muttered, sitting back in her chair.

"Well, she laughed at me, if it makes you feel any better," John retorted.

"I don't blame her." Stephanie leaned forward and lowered her voice again. "I can tell you this much, Alina is either working for a government agency or for herself. Solitto couldn't pay her enough to work for the Family. That's just not who she is."

"Which brings us back to the original question. What has she been doing and what is she doing back here?" John retorted. Stephanie stared at him.

"What does it matter?" she finally asked.

"I think she's much more involved in this mess than either of us know," John answered. "And, following that line of reasoning, I want to know what she's doing and for whom."

"Well, good luck finding any of *that* out." Stephanie sat back again and returned to her email. "Alina will let you into her past when the cows come home, John, and not a minute before."

"That's why I am not asking her."

John pushed himself back to his desk as the elevator dinged again and released a full load of people. Stephanie glanced over at him. She didn't need to ask him what he meant. The search results on his monitor explained that comment perfectly. They had been for Alina Maschik.

And they had been classified at a level far, far above theirs.

Damon swallowed the last gulp of coffee from his mug and set it on the vanity before stepping into the shower. Sighing, he lifted his face to the hot stream of water. He had arrived home just before dawn and managed to sleep about three hours before his cell phone had woken him. He would be happy when Viper found Johann. When she did, she wouldn't stay home and then his camping sessions in the tree could come to an end. He was getting to know the tree frogs now by their respective calls, and Damon was pretty sure he might be starting to resemble one himself. Last night he had settled in the tree and hadn't moved for six hours. Raven had even flown by and looked right at him, as if he was mocking him. Alina came out onto the deck around ten and practiced yoga for an hour. That had been the highlight of his evening.

Damon reached for the shampoo. He didn't like waiting. He never had. And he *especially* didn't like waiting where Viper was concerned. If she was inactive, it usually meant a storm was brewing. John had been there two nights ago now and Alina hadn't had any other visitors. Damon was starting to wonder what he was even watching for, other than the occasional yoga practice. But until Alina got the information she needed to move forward, Hawk knew that every night his place was in that tree.

Damon finished rinsing and turned off the water. He pulled the shower curtain open to step out of the shower and found the object of his thoughts sitting on the back of the toilet with her feet on the closed lid. She smiled and handed him a towel.

"Morning Tiger!" Alina said cheerfully, her eyes dancing. "Late night? I thought you would have been up hours ago!"

Damon took the towel with a grin and wrapped it around his waist before stepping out of the shower, his eyes never leaving hers.

"You have no idea," he answered. Viper's eyes were glittering with laughter and she shook her head, clucking her tongue.

"You have to be careful at your age," she informed him. "You need to conserve your stamina." Damon bit back a laugh and leaned forward, placing his hands on the wall at either side of her head. He brought his face within inches of hers.

"Trust me. Stamina is not a problem," he murmured, his sparkling blue eyes locking with hers. Alina grinned.

"Good to hear," she retorted softly, not breaking the eye contact. After a charged moment, Damon chuckled and straightened up. He glanced at his empty coffee mug.

"At least you could have brought more coffee," he said, backing up.

"Oh I did!" Alina replied, breathing an unconscious sigh of relief. Damon clothed was dangerous at any time. Dripping wet and wrapped in a towel with a five o'clock shadow, Damon was devastating. "It's in the kitchen." She got off the back of the toilet and moved around him to head out of the bathroom. She glanced over shoulder, taking one last look at him.

"Get dressed. I found him."

Damon walked out onto the small balcony off the living room and joined Alina with his coffee. She was seated on one of the two plastic chairs that had been there when he moved in, her feet propped up on the iron railing, her head back and her eyes closed. Damon glanced at her and sat in the other chair, sipping his coffee. He had shaved and dressed in jeans and a black tee shirt. His feet joined hers on the railing.

"Where is he?" Damon asked after a minute, his eyes taking in the grassy courtyard below them. The apartments across the courtyard all had their blinds pulled tight against the sun and the only movement in the courtyard came from a pair of doves, moving around in the grass.

"Cherry Hill." Alina didn't open her eyes. "He's holed up in a house in a nice quiet neighborhood."

"Did you see him?" Damon sipped his coffee and looked at her. She looked tired with her eyes closed, but Damon could feel the energy coming from her.

Alina still didn't open her eyes, but she reached into the shoulder bag on the floor by her chair and handed him a small camera. Damon took it and turned it on. He opened up the only video file on the camera and watched silently as a black pickup pulled up to a modest two-story house. Lights shone through the windows downstairs, but the second floor was dark. A tall teenager got out of the truck and reached back into the cab, pulling out a red bag that looked to be about the size of a large pizza box. Damon watched as the delivery boy carried the large insulated bag and a 2 liter of soda up to the door. A moment later, the door opened and the camera zoomed expertly in on the face of Johann Topamari. Johann glanced around outside as the boy took two pizza boxes out of the bag. He then took the boxes and handed some bills to the boy. The whole process took less than thirty seconds. The door closed and the delivery boy walked back to his truck with the empty bag. The camera stayed on the truck until it had pulled away and then the screen went black.

"Pizza?" Damon asked, shutting off the camera and dropping it back into her bag.

"One large plain cheese and one large garden vegetable with cheese." Alina yawned and finally opened her eyes. "I confirmed with the pizza place last night. He ordered once before, same thing, and pays cash. He also tips generously."

"Well, that's nice of him," Damon murmured.

"And he requested the same driver," Alina added. Damon nodded.

"He would. It gives him an added sense of security," he said. "When did you shoot that?"

"Last night." Alina dropped her feet off the balcony and stretched. "And I have more." She stood up. Damon looked up at her and grinned.

"Of course you do," he agreed. Alina winked.

"I want to take you somewhere." She held out her hand and he allowed her to pull him up. "I'll drive." She picked up her bag and opened the sliding door behind them, stepping off the balcony. Damon followed her with a slight frown.

How the hell had she left the house last night and he had missed it?

Damon sat in the passenger seat of Alina's Camaro and surveyed the scene before him. They were parked on the top of a rise with the Susquehanna River below them. In the distance, across the water, was Three Mile Island. He lifted the binoculars Viper handed him and slowly studied the island. Alina was silent, her head back on the seat, her eyes closed behind her sunglasses. She hadn't told him what he was looking for. She hadn't even told him where they were going. They had left New Jersey and an hour and a half later, they stopped here.

The car was silent for upwards of half an hour while Hawk examined the island and Viper relaxed. Occasionally, Alina opened her eyes and glanced over at the strong profile in the seat next to her. Her heart would give a little flutter and she resolutely closed her eyes again. It was distracting enough to have him sitting in the small sports car next to her. She didn't need to add to it by watching him.

"It would be damn difficult," Hawk finally said, lowering the binoculars to his lap. "But not impossible." He looked at Alina, who still had her eyes closed behind her sunglasses. "What are you thinking?"

Instead of answering, she reached into the backseat and pulled out her iPad. He took it with a raised eyebrow and chuckled.

"Figure it out myself, is that it?" he murmured, switching it on. Alina grinned.

"You're a smart man," she retorted.

Damon glanced at her with a grin and watched as she settled herself back in her seat, closing her eyes again. He turned his attention to the iPad and stared at it for a minute. What on earth was he supposed to be looking for? He went to the browsing history and started going through the sites previously viewed. When he got to newspaper articles, he smiled. He skipped to the beginning and started following her path of reading. Comfortable silence ensued in the car, and Alina was just starting to doze off when Damon let out a low whistle. She opened her eyes and turned her head. He had angled himself partially sideways in the seat and was leaning against the door, the pad resting on his knee. She looked at the article on the pad and smiled. He had found it faster than she expected.

"Three Mile Island is a red herring," Alina said softly.

"This makes much more sense!" Damon replied, looking up. His blue eyes had a light in them that Alina recognized. It was similar to what she imagined a tracking dog felt when he got the first whiff of the scent. She had felt it when she realized what Johann was planning, and again when she had found him last night. It was the knowledge that the hunt was now on in earnest.

"This is more like what I know of Johann," Alina agreed. She pushed her sunglasses up on top of her head and reached out to take the iPad off his lap. "When you first told me about Three Mile Island, it didn't make sense to me. Johann has never shown any interest in actual landmarks or mass catastrophes. He was never dramatic. All his actions in the past have been geared toward undermining population security and breaking people's individual will. Don't get me wrong. He likes a high body count as much as the next terrorist, but he is more interested in destroying a person's sense of security."

"Well, that would certainly fall in line with the ideology behind the actions," Damon remarked. "If you break the will of the people, you can break the people. Warfare 101."

"Exactly." Alina shifted to face him. "There's never anything flashy about Mossavid or what they do. They are just very effective. So Three Mile Island just didn't sit right with me. I started thinking about what was *around* the Island. When I drove up here to take a look, I saw the same thing you just did. It's not impossible, but it's damn close. And Johann doesn't appear to have the resources to pull off something of that magnitude in place in the US. At this point, as far as we know, he has himself and one known associate. He would need more than that for an attack on the Island."

"He would need at least 4 on the ground." Damon nodded.

"So I started digging around." Alina motioned to the iPad. "Ever since the tsunami in Japan, critics have been attacking the evacuation procedures set in place in the US around all the active nuclear plants. The standard ten-mile evacuation process is under fire. The NRC maintains that any radiation plume would deteriorate beyond that, but critics are more concerned with the increase in populations within that standard ten-miles and the challenges of moving them instantly." Damon nodded.

"All Johann would have to do is present the *illusion* of an incident on the island and the highways would be clogged with more people fleeing the area than current evacuation plans are prepared to handle," he said, following her train of thought. "And the interstate is within that ten-mile area, which is the most likely venue of travel."

133

"And it crosses the river farther up, between Middletown and Harrisburg," Alina added. "Japan was a series of natural disasters that no one really expected would ever happen at the same time. I think Johann is working on the same theory. According to the papers, the First Lady is scheduled to visit Harrisburg on the weekend for a benefit. There's also a big music festival scheduled to go from Friday to Monday. The roads are already going to be crowded with traffic in and out of Harrisburg. If he creates the illusion of a disaster on the Island, causes widespread panic, then attacks the airport and train stations..."

"And attacks the bridges and highways themselves..." Damon continued.

"Then he could orchestrate possibly the largest attack on US soil since 9/11," Alina finished. Silence fell heavily between them and Damon turned his eyes to the island in the distance.

"He has to have more people working with him," he said finally. Alina nodded.

"Which makes it even more confusing why he would be killing off his team," she added. "I don't understand that. But he has to have at least three others working with him. They have to create the explosion at the island, and then in the space of a few hours, set off bombs in the airport and/or train station, *and* on the bridge and/or the highways leading into Harrisburg."

"This is all pure conjecture," Damon stated, glancing at her. She nodded.

"Yep," she agreed. "But I'm right. I can feel it. And I know Johann. This is right up his alley." Alina looked back at the Island.

"I can't alert Washington on a hunch," Damon told her. "You know that." Alina looked at him in surprise.

"You don't have to!" she exclaimed. "It's not going to happen. They won't be there to make it happen."

They were silent again as Alina stared out into the distance and Damon watched her. She had all intentions of completing her mission before the weekend, and Damon had no doubt that she would. Part of him still wanted to alert Washington to their suspicions, but the other part recognized that it was not an option. He turned his attention out to the Island. He had learned a long time ago that things were never easy, and he had grown used to it. So had Viper. Between the two of them, this was just business as usual. Damon wondered what Stephanie would do if she had an inkling of what they were thinking. His lips twitched. Good God. The Feds would be thrown into a frenzy the likes of which hadn't been seen since 9/11.

"Any word yet on that missing security guard?" Alina asked. Damon shook his head.

"Nothing."

"I want to talk to Bobby Reyes," Alina said suddenly, dropping her sunglasses back on her nose and straightening in her seat. Damon looked at her, surprised.

"Why?"

"I want to know what exactly was in that specialized shipment that went missing," Alina answered, turning the key in the ignition. The engine came alive with a growl.

"That's not our department," Damon pointed out as she pulled into the road and swung around to head away from the Island. "Don't go getting involved in multi-tasking, Viper. It's no good."

"I prefer to think of it as insurance," Alina retorted. "I want to know what Johann has up his sleeve."

"We know what he must have up his sleeve," Damon argued. "You know as well as I do what kind of firepower it would take to accomplish what we think he's going to do."

"True," Alina admitted after a minute. Damon glanced at her.

"It's gotten under your skin, hasn't it?" he said suddenly. "This is all too close to home for you." Alina looked at him irritably.

"Of course not," she snapped. Hawk raised an eyebrow.

"Bobby Reyes is *not* a good idea," he stated. "It's bad enough that Solitto saw me. If he ever wanted to find out who I am, it wouldn't take him long to discover part of the truth. And the same goes for you. Don't be a fool and throw away your invisibility."

"Why *did* you agree to play the DHS agent, anyway?" Alina demanded as they sped along, dropping the subject of Bobby Reyes for a moment. Damon glanced at her.

"It was the easiest way to keep tabs on the investigation," he replied easily. Alina glanced at him.

"I already had an in on the investigation," she pointed out. Damon was silent. "You lost your anonymity the second you walked into that FBI building. Why?"

"It seemed like a good idea at the time," Damon answered, flashing her a grin. Alina snorted. "It's serving my purpose right now to have a high profile," he informed her, "but it would *not* serve yours."

Alina was silent. He was right. Not only was it none of her business what shipment Bobby Reyes lost, but it was not in her interest to draw any more attention to herself. Hawk was also right about this hitting a little too close to home. It was one thing to track and eliminate targets on foreign soil. It was another thing to do it on home ground.

Her job was to find Johann and eliminate him. By the time the people whose job it was to worry about what was in that shipment came to investigate, she would be long gone.

Chapter Nine

Alina pulled off the road into the entrance of the long driveway leading through the trees to the house. Damon was quiet beside her. They hadn't spoken much on the rest of the ride back into Jersey, and Damon had even dozed off at one point. Alina glanced at him now. He was staring out the window and seemed pensive. She wondered, for probably the thousandth time, what he was really doing here. Every day she had more questions and no corresponding answers where he was concerned. Why was having a high profile in his interest? It was *never* in their interest to have large exposure to people, and most especially to people in governmental positions. The people in those offices didn't like to think about the existence of people like Viper and Hawk. They were bad for politics. So why had Washington agreed to put Hawk in place as an DHS agent, of all things? And why had he done it? He had thrust himself into the spotlight with the Feds and with anyone connected with the investigation they were conducting. Why? It was almost as if he *wanted* as many people as possible to see him and see what he was doing. But what *was* he doing? And why was he seemingly content to sit by and watch as Alina went about her business? He seemed much more interested in Alina's work than in whatever it was that he was supposed to be doing. Why?

Alina broke through the trees and the house came into view ahead of them. If it was anyone other than Damon, she admitted that she would probably think that they were there to take her out of the equation as soon as she had taken care of Johann. But Alina trusted Damon. She knew that whatever he was doing, he wouldn't harm her. She might not trust the boys in Washington as far as she could throw them, but she trusted Hawk.

"Stop when you pull around the side of the house." Hawk broke the silence, undoing his seatbelt and putting his hand on the door handle. Alina looked at him. "Someone followed us into the woods."

Alina obligingly stopped at the side of the house and watched as Damon jumped out and disappeared into the woods. She continued on to the garage and pulled her car inside, parking next to the black SUV. Viper calmly got out of the car and reached under the seat to extract her modified .45, slipping it into the holster at the back of her pants. She pulled her lightweight jacket on over top and headed out the side door of the garage, hitting the automatic door button on her way to close the garage door. Alina went straight into the trees behind the garage and then picked up the pace, doubling back in a wide arc to approach the house from the road again. She moved silently and quickly, her ears tuned to any sound out of the ordinary. She had known she was being followed all day, and she had a pretty good idea who it was. The fact that Damon had caught it was interesting.

Viper paused in the trees halfway between the road and the house. A chill snaked down her spine and she turned her head quickly, sinking to her knees silently. She scanned the trees toward the road, her breathing steady, her ears straining for any unusual sound. Something was wrong. She could feel it. All her instincts were screaming. Glancing toward the house, she detected faint movement and knew that Hawk was there. Viper turned her attention back toward the road. Hawk and their visitor were in front of her. But something, or someone, else was behind her.

Alina slowed her breathing down and crept to her left to take cover behind a tree. Closing her eyes, she drew her attention inward, until she could hear her own heartbeat. She took note of the sounds in the trees above her. The rustling of the wind through the upper branches mixed with the scratching of scurrying little furry feet, leaping from tree to tree. Wings suddenly came alive as a bird launched out of its nest. Underbrush creaked to her right as a small predator foraged under a tree. Vipers eyes slowly opened.

To her right, there was no sound.

She started moving stealthily to her right, reaching down to unstrap the guard on the knife at her ankle. Her eyes darted around the area, scanning the trees above and the ground below. Afternoon sun was filtering through the trees and she looked for tell-tale shadows as she moved silently forward, foot by foot, her senses alert for movement and sound.

Alina was moving on instinct now. Her heart was pounding, but her breathing was steady and her eyes were clear and alert. She paused to listen, taking note of where all animal movement ended and where the silence began. It was a few yards ahead and to the right. Viper began moving again silently.

Suddenly, from the left, came the sound of two motorized dirt bikes. They were coming through the woods quickly, the distinctive high-pitched whir getting louder by the second. Alina straightened up quickly, and then she saw it! A tall shadow flickered ahead and to her right, moving quickly toward the road. Alina darted forward, jumping over an old, uprooted tree trunk and running parallel with what she imagined was the route the shadow had taken. The dirt bikes came into view behind her and she glanced back. Two teen-aged boys were tearing through the woods joyfully at top speed, oblivious of her existence. Viper looked forward again, running swiftly. She had lost the shadow, but she knew it wouldn't have stopped.

Viper reached the end of the trees just in time to see a tall man dressed in hunting fatigues disappear into the trees on the other side of the road. She stopped behind a pine tree and leaned on it, breathing hard. A few seconds later, an engine caught and revved. A black Bronco pulled out of the woods a few yards away and sped away down the road. Alina stayed concealed behind the tree, watching it disappear. She was able to get a partial plate as it fish-tailed slightly coming out of the trees. SKD-4. It was enough to run a trace.

Alina bent down and secured the knife at her ankle before turning and jogging back through the woods. Whoever he was, he hadn't been following her.

He had been *waiting* for her.

Alina emerged into the front yard from the trees and grinned. Angela and Damon were seated on the front steps, side by side. Damon looked amused and Angela looked disgruntled. She was dressed in black jeans and a black stretch tee-shirt. Four inch stiletto black leather boots, which were now generously coated with dirt and grass, graced her feet. Alina bit back a laugh. A black baseball cap with a rhinestone P glittering on the front completed the outfit. Angela was trying to be incognito. Alina wasn't sure which was worse: the four inch stilettos or the rhinestone Phillies cap.

Her eyes met Damon's as she crossed the lawn towards them. He raised his eyebrows questioningly and Alina gave an almost imperceptible shake of her head. He frowned, his eyes darting past her to the woods, then back to her face. Alina flicked her eyes to Angela warningly and turned her attention to her friend.

"Angela, what on earth are you doing?" she demanded as she walked up to them. Angela pouted as much as a grown woman could pout.

"I don't know what you're talking about," she retorted. "I just came to see you." Alina glanced around.

"I don't see your car," she commented. Angela shrugged.

"I left it by the road. I thought the walk would be good for me," she said.

Alina stared at her, doing her best not to laugh outright. While Alina stared at Angela, Damon stared at her. His frown deepened. Her flushed skin told him that she had been moving rapidly, and there was an errant sprig of moss in her hair. She wasn't breathing heavily, but her tank top was damp. She had been running. His eyes went back to the trees. He hadn't missed her silent warning to keep quiet. Someone else had been out there.

"You loathe walking," Alina was saying to Angela. "Unless it's in a mall," she qualified. Angela stood up.

"Your monkey here snuck up behind me and scared the Bejeebus out of me!" she exclaimed in a hurt voice. "And now you think I was trying to spy on you."

"That's exactly what I think," Alina agreed with a laugh. "You've been following me all day. Come on inside. I'll make tea," she added, stepping past them and unlocking the front door.

Angela hesitated, as if trying to decide what to do. She finally picked up her black Coach bag from the step and turned to follow Alina into the house. Damon waited until they had cleared the door frame before standing up. He took one last look at the trees before turning to follow them, closing the front door and locking it behind him.

"I wasn't following you *all* day," Angela murmured, following Alina down the hall to the back of the house. She was absolutely mortified over getting caught. She had been creeping up to the front lawn when someone grabbed her from behind and clamped their hand over her mouth. She couldn't even move in their grip, let alone take a breath to scream. Angela didn't think she had ever been so scared in all her life. She had felt like she was being held in a solid vise. They had stayed like that for what seemed like forever until a familiar voice had asked her if she was lost. Damon had released her then, laughing when she swung around and tried to punch him. He had caught her wrist easily and the attempt had only made him laugh harder.

"You're right," Alina agreed soothingly, going into the kitchen. She started to take off her jacket, then thought better of it. She left it on as she went to the cabinets above the counters. Damon noticed the movement and his eyes dropped to her back as he settled himself on one of the stools at the bar. He could just make out the bulge of her .45. He felt a little better about the episode in the woods knowing now that she was armed.

"You didn't follow me to the coffee shop this morning." Alina turned from the cabinet with a box of tea in either hand. "Jasmine green or Orange Blossom White?" she asked them cheerfully. Damon couldn't stop himself from chuckling. Angela shot him a fuming glare before turning to Alina.

"Green, please," she said. "Can I use your bathroom?"

"In the hall, on the left." Alina motioned to the hallway and then looked at Damon questioningly.

"Coffee," he said. She nodded and turned to put the white tea back in the cupboard. As soon as she heard the bathroom door close in the hall and the fan switch on, Alina reached behind her and pulled the gun from her back. She flipped on the safety and opened a drawer, dropping it inside.

"Who was in the woods?" Damon demanded in a low voice. Alina took off her jacket and tossed it on the bar.

"I don't know," she answered just quietly. "Tall male in hunting fatigues. He knew enough to stay just outside my security perimeter," Alina added. Damon looked grim and she looked at him thoughtfully. "He drove a black bronco. I got a partial plate. I'll find him."

Alina turned back to the counter and Damon watched as she hit the button to brew his coffee. The grinder ground the beans loudly and he waited for it to finish before speaking.

"You have moss in your hair," he told her, smiling when she reached up and smoothed her fingers over her hair until she found the greenery and plucked it out.

"Thanks."

"No problem."

The bathroom door opened and Angela came down the hall. She looked much calmer now, and not so disheveled. Her hair was perfect again under the cap, and she looked back in control. Alina switched on the kettle and turned to get Damon's coffee.

"Ok. So I was following you." Angela seated herself at the bar next to Damon.

"I know," Alina retorted with a laugh, coming over to hand Damon his coffee. "Why?"

"Because no one will tell me what's going on!" Angela exclaimed. Damon glanced at her, his eyebrows raising. She looked at him. "Don't look at me like that, Mr. Hunk-O-

Mysterious. I have my own issues with you. Do Stephanie and John know you're working with Alina?"

"There's nothing to know," Damon answered calmly. "We're not working together. We're old friends."

"From the military," Angela stated. Alina looked at Angela.

"Angie!" she said warningly. Damon grinned.

"It's ok," he said, holding his hand up to stop Alina. "Yes. I was in the military with Alina. We trained together before I went into Special Forces and she went into Intelligence." His blue eyes were sparkling as they met Angie's. "I was happy to see her again. We lost touch for a few years."

Alina caught the sparkle in Damon's eyes and her own eyes narrowed suspiciously. What was he up to? He had something cooking in that head of his and she was pretty sure that this whole ridiculous charade was about to become even more absurd. The electric kettle switched off behind her and Alina turned to start making the tea.

"So you just happened to show up the same time as Alina," Angela said, watching him. He stared back.

"Coincidences *do* happen occasionally," he replied with an easy smile. "In this case, it was a happy one. One day hasn't passed when Alina hasn't been on my mind," he added with a grin. Alina dropped the kettle loudly back onto its base. Angela's mouth dropped open.

"You mean....you two..." her voice trailed off as she turned her attention to Alina's back. "Lina?"

Alina finished counting to ten before picking up the two mugs of green tea and swinging around to face them. Damon looked like the Cheshire cat sitting next to Angela.

"He's still trying to convince me," Alina said calmly, moving forward and handing Angie one of the mugs. Her eyes met Damon's dancing ones and she smiled sweetly. "We'll see how well he does," she added.

"Well, that explains *that*, at any rate." Angela looked from one to the other, sipping her tea.

"Explains what?" Damon asked, drinking his coffee before he started laughing at the murderous look in Vipers eyes.

"The tension between the two of you," Angie said, waving her hands. "I felt it at the restaurant, and I feel it now. You guys have some serious sexual tension between you."

"Angie, don't be an ass," Alina snapped as Damon choked on his coffee.

"No, you do!" Angie insisted. "I took a class in Chi last summer. I learned all kinds of interesting things, and I definitely feel some serious tension coming off both of you."

"Well, I won't argue with that," Damon murmured with a cough. Alina shot him a glare.

"Don't encourage her," she retorted. She drank some tea, then set the mug down. "Seriously, Angie, why were you following me?"

"I told you the other day," Angela replied calmly. "I feel left out. I think you and Steph and Damon are working together, and no one is asking me for any help."

"Stephanie gave me a whole report on money-laundering from you," Damon pointed out. Angela shrugged and waved her hand.

"So what?" she asked. "You guys are doing all this exciting stuff." Alina couldn't hold back her snort.

"What exciting stuff?" she demanded.

"That's what I was trying to find out," Angie retorted patiently. She sounded as if she was explaining something to a child. Alina blinked. She felt a little like she was on a tilt-a-whirl.

"Let me get this straight." Alina looked at Angela. "You're following me because you think you might miss something exciting?" Damon buried his face in his coffee mug again.

"Well, essentially, yes, I suppose so," Angela agreed. "Although, it was more of an attempt to find out what you're doing back and why you came back when you did." There was a short silence as Alina stared at her old friend.

"And did you discover anything?" she finally asked after she got her voice back.

"Only that you drive really far too fast for safety," Angela replied. She set her mug down and pointed to Alina. "Really, I have no idea what you're thinking. If anything happened, you could never control that man's car of yours."

Alina couldn't bring herself to look at Damon. She could tell by the way that he had his head buried in his coffee mug that he was enjoying this conversation way to much.

"I drive too fast?" Alina repeated, her eye twitching.

Damon got up suddenly and carried his cup over to the espresso machine. A minute later, beans started grinding loudly.

"Yes." Angela glanced past Alina at Damon. "And you don't get out much. You really need to get out more."

"I'll take that under advisement." Alina drained her tea cup and suddenly wished it was something stronger. "Anything else?"

"Nope, that's about all I discovered so far," Angela announced cheerfully. "But I'm optimistic."

"NO!"

The word shot out in unison from both Damon and Alina. Alina glanced at him and he turned back to watch the coffee stream into his mug. Angela raised her eyebrow, looking from one to the other again.

"Excuse me?" she repeated.

"No," Alina repeated. "You're going to stop following me." Angela looked at her.

"Why?" she asked. Alina stared at her silently. "Lina, you have to give me a reason. I want to know what's going on. If following you and Stephanie is the only way I'll find out, then I'm prepared to do it." Alina pursed her lips, then sighed.

"It's not safe," she said quietly.

Damon turned from the coffeemaker with his full mug of coffee and leaned back against the counter. He sipped the coffee and watched the two women facing off over the bar.

"Because of the investigation?" Angie asked.

"No. Because of...because of what I do," Alina said slowly.

"Your consulting," Angie stated, pushing her mug away.

"Yes." Alina raised her eyes to Angie's and, in that instant, Angela peaked past the mask and glimpsed the old Lina that she had always known. "Just...trust me."

"Ok," Angela agreed instantly. The mask slid back into place and Alina nodded.

"Ok," she repeated. Angela laughed.

"Ok." She glanced past Alina to Damon. He looked confused. "I'll leave you two to work out your tensions in peace, then. I strongly suggest sandalwood candles," Angie added, standing up and picking up her purse. Alina repressed the sudden urge to scream.

"Oh, we will," Damon assured Angela cheerfully. "Alina is just being stubborn."

"You know, over-confidence is never a good thing," Alina shot over her shoulder. Angela laughed.

"I have a good feeling about you two," she said, waving to Damon as she turned away to head down the hall. Alina followed her, gritting her teeth at the chuckle she heard coming from the vicinity of the coffeemaker.

"I'm glad one of us does," she muttered. Angela stopped at the front door and shook her head at Alina.

"I don't know what you're waiting for," she said bluntly. "Men like that don't grow on trees."

Alina just looked at her, then reached over to open the door. She stood to the side expectantly and Angela laughed.

"Ok, ok. I'll drop it." She stepped outside into the afternoon sun. Alina followed her out the door and closed it behind her. Angela looked at her in surprise. "Where are you going?"

"I'm walking you to your car," Alina answered. She grinned when Angela stared at her. "I'm curious to see where you hid it," she lied smoothly. Angela laughed and they stepped off the front step together.

"It *is* a good hiding place," she said, blissfully unaware of any reason for ulterior motives on her old friend's part.

When Alina returned to the house, Damon was standing on the deck, staring out over the back lawn. She stepped through the sliding doors and joined him at the banister. She had traded her tea mug for a water bottle and she handed a second one to Damon. They stood in silence for a moment, her shoulder brushing his arm. She lifted her water bottle to her lips, her eyes moving over the back yard while her mind raced.

There was another player. The question was whose team was he on? Was he one of Johann's men? Was he from Washington? Was he one of Solitto's goons? And why had Damon almost seemed like he was expecting it?

Alina rested the water bottle on the banister. The late afternoon sun had shifted to the front of the house, casting long shadows over the back. The light flickered over the lawn, and she lifted her gaze to stare farther into the trees. Pieces of the puzzle were starting to emerge in her mind but she wasn't sure where to put them. One thing was clear: everything kept coming back to Johann. Now that she had found him, she just had to finish the job and then everything else would fall into place.

"When are you going to Johann's?" Damon asked, uncannily addressing her thoughts.

"Tonight." Alina picked up her water bottle and moved away to sit on one of the Adirondack chairs. Damon turned and leaned on the banister, watching her with hooded eyes.

"And our visitor?" he asked.

"One thing at a time," Alina answered, smiling faintly.

Damon seemed to be on the verge of saying something when a beep came from his jeans pocket and he reached into it to pull out a blackberry. Alina looked back over the lawn as he turned away to answer the phone. She caught sight of movement in the trees and watched as a doe came into view.

The head turned and big brown eyes seemed to stare straight at Alina across the distance. Alina stared back, allowing the peace of the evening to fill her mind. After a moment, the doe turned and continued steadily on her way. Alina raised up her legs to sit crossed-legged on the chair, setting the water bottle on the wide arm. She rested her hands on her knees, cleared her mind of thought, and closed her eyes, breathing deeply. Tonight she would finish what she had started two years ago.

She had failed then.

She wouldn't fail tonight.

Cairo had been crowded two years ago when she arrived. It was always crowded in the smelly, over-populated city, but it had seemed to Alina to be even more so then. She followed Johann there, ignoring all the intel of his so-called Mossavid connection and ignoring her own conclusions regarding the cell. She had ignored the duplicity of her government and focused on her job. They never asked questions. They just did their job. That was what they were paid to do. And that was what Alina had done. Johann was no different.

At least, she hadn't thought he was any different at the time. As it turned out, he had ended up changing the course of her life that morning.

She found him in the city easily enough. He had been in a hotel and hadn't seemed overly concerned with keeping his movements secret. His security detail was extensive and they had been efficient. She was unable to attempt a sniper shot, which is what she would have preferred. Viper was forced to enter the hotel and improvise.

Now, in her minds eyes, she saw it as clearly as if it had just happened.

The lobby only had a few people scattered about, mainly tourists waiting for their bus and the occasional guest shuffling out of the dining room. It was mid-morning and the sun filtered through the windows in the lobby, casting bright long triangles of light over the worn tile floor. Alina was in the shadows, beneath a wide marble staircase leading to the upper levels, dressed in the long flowing burka of a local woman. The bottom half of her face was covered and the head-covering cast enough shadow over her upper-face as to make identification impossible. The elevator was nearby, and it dinged open just as Johann exited the meeting room where he had been closeted for almost half an hour. Three children rushed past Viper as she moved forward, out of the shadows.

It was the children who had saved Johann's life that day.

He had been coming out the meeting room, his head turned, speaking to someone right behind him. In her mind's eye, Viper clearly saw the Carotid artery, her target, in his neck as he turned his head. She moved with speed which threw his security detail off-guard. Her hand came up, the .45 ready to fire mid-stride. She knew exactly how many men she had to get through to make it to the side door that would be her exit. She had already averaged her likely success and injury rate. She knew how many clips she would use and how quickly she would have to empty them.

Viper was striking.

And then the children had swarmed around Johann's legs instead of continuing through the lobby.

Everything happened very quickly after that. Alina immediately lowered her firing arm, but it was too late. One of the guards and one of the children had already seen it. Chaos ensued instantly. An alarm was shouted, Johann was thrown to the floor and covered by the man closest to him, and Alina spun away as multiple members of his entourage drew weapons.

But not before recognizing the western face of the man Johann had been speaking to as he exited the room.

Within seconds, the children had been herded into the room with him and the door closed. The soft click of the latch as the door closed heralded the deafening eruption of gunfire. The lobby cleared out instantly and Viper was forced toward the back of the hotel. The following few minutes were nothing but a blur to her. She had taken one bullet through her outer thigh on her retreat, but managed to stop the damage there. By the time she had vaulted out the back of the hotel and into the alleyway, four out of seven of Johann's security detail were dead.

But the man she had come for was left very much alive.

Damon pressed the end button on his phone and turned back to Alina. She was sitting in her chair crossed-legged, eyes closed, hands facing upward on her knees. Her breathing was deep and Damon saw with one glance that she was far away. He leaned on the banister and watched her for a moment. Her dark hair rested on her straight shoulders and her long eyelashes were dark against her cheeks. Damon knew that Viper's whole body was a weapon. Yet, to look at her now, no one would ever guess it. She appeared relaxed and supple, at peace with the world. He thought back to when they first met in boot camp. She had been almost bewildered back then. But she had a belly full of anger and their drill sergeant had seen that right off. He had pushed Alina harder than the rest of the women in the unit, and she had excelled beyond even the men. By the end of the three month period, she had broken almost every record in the camp. The two that she had not been able to beat were the two that Damon broke himself.

Damon smiled to himself now. They had clicked as soon as they met in the mess hall and their friendship very quickly blossomed into a friendly rivalry. It hadn't taken that same drill sergeant two blinks of an eye to catch on to that, and he did everything he could to work them against each other. The result had been that Damon had never physically worked harder in his life. By the time they were getting ready to graduate, they had developed such a close relationship that, he remembered, everyone was fully expecting them to request the same orders so that they could continue their friendship. Their relationship had been built on respect and friendly rivalry from the very beginning. There had never been anything more, although many of their fellow sailors always thought differently. At graduation, they stood together simply as friends and sailors.

After graduation, they headed out to begin their military careers. After a year, he went into the SEALs and he heard that she had migrated into Military Intelligence. He lost track of her then, and it was a few years before he saw her again. They had both been in the classified training facility of the CIA for over two weeks before they finally saw each other in the hallway. Damon still remembered the look on her face. She stared at him, nonplussed, for a very brief minute before cursing loudly and hugging him at the same time. She informed him that she was done competing with him. The last time had nearly killed her. Damon had agreed whole-heartedly.

And so their friendship had continued, grown, and trust was added to the mix. Through the years, as they had run into each other unexpectedly in random parts of the world, it had always been as if no time had passed, and Damon learned not to question it. If he ever wondered why they kept running into each other, he had learned not to question that as well.

"What are you thinking?" Alina's voice cut into his thoughts. He grinned. Her eyes were still closed, but the tension of awareness was back in her body.

"Just thinking back over the years," Damon answered. Alina opened her eyes and looked at him. They were laughing.

"You make it sound as if we're eighty," she said, lifting her arms above her head and stretching. Damon laughed.

"We may as well be, with everything that has happened," he retorted, straightening away from the banister and moving toward her. She shrugged and lowered her arms, disentangling her legs and lowering them to the deck.

"That's true," Alina admitted, looking up at him. She reached out and took the hand he held out to her, allowing herself to be pulled up out of the chair. The touch of his hand was warm and comfortable, sending a shiver of

151

awareness up her arm. But when her eyes met his, she saw that the laugh had gone out of them. "What's wrong?" she asked.

"That was Stephanie on the phone," Damon told her after the briefest of hesitations. He released her hand. "They have another body."

Alina felt her stomach lurch in an unfamiliar, sinking feeling. She knew what he was going to say before he even said it.

"They think it's Johann," Damon told her.

Chapter Ten

Damon rolled to a stop near the curb and surveyed the scene before him. The quiet residential street in Cherry Hill was hard to miss, even though it looked just like all the other quiet residential streets in this development. Poplar Lane was closed off and local police had set up the perimeter, their cars with flashing lights blocking all traffic from entering. As Damon watched, two of the police cars slowly pulled out of the way to allow a coroner's van to roll through the makeshift barricade. He took the opportunity afforded by the temporary breach in the blockade to roll his Jeep up behind it and hold his ID out the window.

"Mr. Peterson. Miss. Walker is expecting me," he said shortly to one of the officers.

The young policeman took his ID and walked away from the Jeep to speak into the mouthpiece attached to his collar. Behind the perimeter, the coroners van rolled slowly down the street to come to a stop outside the house from Vipers' surveillance video. Spotlights were set up all around the house. A few neighbors were settled on their porches, watching the activity as people in suits and black windbreakers scurried around importantly. The entire scene was one of quietly controlled and efficient chaos.

Somewhere, behind it all, Viper was lurking. They had taken separate cars from her house and Damon was glad for that. Hot anger had been palpable after he told her the news, her legendary control slipping, and Hawk didn't want to be anywhere near her until she calmed down. She agreed that he should go meet Stephanie at the scene while she watched from a distance. Where, exactly, that distance was, he had no idea. But Viper had already pulled the Camaro out of the garage and disappeared down the drive before he thought to ask.

Damon caught sight of Stephanie as she stepped out of the front door, stripping off latex gloves as she spoke to someone over her shoulder. A uniform called something to

153

her and she looked up and right at Damon. She waved him forward impatiently. Damon took his foot off the break and rolled forward, holding his hand out for his ID as he rolled past the uniform who held it out to him, waving him forward importantly.

"You're just in time to take a look before they move the body," Stephanie called to him as he got out of the Jeep. Damon strode up to her, holding out his hand to shake hers. "I'm still waiting for a positive id. We may have to wait until God-knows when, unless your people have some information mine don't," she continued, shaking his hand briskly and turning to walk with him toward the house. "The problem is that no one has a picture of him, but based on height, weight, and physical description, I think it may be him."

"You don't sound sure." Damon detected the hesitation in her voice immediately. Stephanie glanced at him and smiled ruefully.

"There is a somewhat distinctive mark on this man's face," she admitted. "It doesn't come up in any of the physical descriptions of Johann Topamari that we have seen. John is trying to confirm that now." Stephanie motioned him to the side of the house. "The body is actually in the back yard," she explained. "We're processing the house now. It would be easier to walk around, if you don't mind."

"Not at all," Damon answered agreeably, following her down the side of the house toward the backyard. "What have you got from the house so far?"

"Not much," Stephanie answered. "The house is owned by a Joseph Greene, but he's been renting it out for years. The current lease is actually being held by a company in New York as temporary living for re-locating employees. We're checking with them. There were two people living here and no sign of female clothing. They never used the kitchen, lots of take-out containers. No desktop computers and no laptops. But there is a wireless router and an ISP box, so the laptop must be with the roommate. There were some atlases of Pennsylvania, Jersey, and Delaware. Other than that, nothing too spectacular. They were careful."

They came to the edge of the backyard and Damon found the entire backyard awash with white light from multiple spotlights. Several agents were milling around, going over the entire yard carefully. The body itself was impossible to miss. It was hanging from a tree in the center of the yard, each wrist tied up and secured to a thick branch, stretching the arms out tautly. The feet were hanging a good three feet from the ground. The throat had been cut and, judging by the enormous pool of blood on the grass, the body was left to bleed out.

"Not very pretty," Stephanie said after a moment.

"Not very, no." Damon started to move forward, then paused. "Is it safe to go this way?" he asked, motioning a path to the body. Stephanie nodded.

"Yes. We've finished with this side of the yard," she replied, walking behind him.

Damon nodded and moved toward the body. It was facing the neighbor's yard to the right, and a quick glance told him that the neighbors had a clear view from their deck. He moved forward carefully, his eyes scanning the yard briefly. A metal waist-high fence surrounded the yard and thick boxwoods ran the length of the fence to the left side. At the end of the garden, two more tall old oak trees, similar in size and age to the one supporting the body, loomed out of the growing darkness. The rest of the yard was neglected and what grass there was grew in patches. It was a tired looking yard, in need of care and attention. And now, it was in need of a priest.

Damon turned his attention to the body. He was aware of the medical examiner and his assistant, with their vinyl bag and heavy plastic sheet, waiting a few feet away. Stephanie motioned to them as he approached and they stood to the side, watching. Hawk stopped outside the pool of blood on the grass and looked up into the discolored face of the corpse.

A strange mixture of relief and uneasiness swept through him. The face hanging at an odd angle was *not* the face of Johann Topamari. Pulled out his phone, he snapped a picture of the face before stepping away. He nodded to the medical examiners and turned away. Stephanie watched as he typed into his phone quickly.

"I'll see what my people say," Damon said, looking up when he was done. Stephanie nodded and watched as the examiner positioned the plastic sheet and his assistant positioned a ladder.

"How on earth did they get him up there?" she wondered out loud. Hawk glanced up.

"It wouldn't be hard if he was partially drugged," he said. "Your tox screen will tell you. If he was drugged, but not unconscious, a strong man or two average men could have got him up there. The neighbors didn't see anything?"

"No." Stephanie turned and walked with him back toward the house. "They were away and just got back this evening. The husband walked outside and saw him. He called the police, who called me once they got here and saw the body. Thankfully, the senior investigator recognized it as similar to a description we sent out."

"I don't think its Johann," Damon told her as they reached the corner of the house and started toward the front. "But, of course, I'll wait and see what my people say." Stephanie looked at him sharply.

"How can you know?" she demanded quickly. Damon met her searching glance with a smile.

"I'm afraid I have a little more information as to his appearance than you apparently do," he answered blandly. "But I'm not going to trust my memory. I'll let someone else take the heat on this one," he added with a wink.

Stephanie pursed her lips and was silent.

Alina finished her initial scan of the light-flooded yard and directed her military binoculars to the figure strung up from the branch of the tree. She was balanced comfortably in the fat upper limbs of a maple tree a few houses down, in a backyard opposite from Johann's. The beacon of light a few houses away was impossible to miss. She took note of the scurrying agents and her lips twitched slightly when Damon and Stephanie come into the backyard. Damon was striding as if he owned the yard, and Stephanie was matching him stride for stride. Two egos unconsciously competing. Watching them would have been humorous if she didn't have a body, literally, swaying in the breeze.

Alina focused on the corpse, her heart thumping. As much as she tried to repress it, a mixed bag of emotions was flooding over her. Her hand shook ever so slightly as she adjusted the focus on the binoculars and started to zoom in on the face, apprehension making her fingers move more slowly than normal. A million thoughts flooded her mind, as they had been since Hawk told her on the deck that Stephanie thought she had Johann's body. Who had beat her to him? And why? And how? How could she possibly have failed a *second* time? Was Johann turning out to be her unicorn, impossible to catch? Washington had been quite clear about the ramifications if she should fail a second time. This was her atonement mission; her chance to correct a mistake on an otherwise flawless resume.

Viper zoomed in on the face of the body hanging lifelessly from the oak tree. Her brain registered the slit throat and approximate angle of the killers knife even as she recognized the face. Relief washed through her instantly, followed almost immediately by utter shock. Alina dropped the binoculars around her neck just as her phone vibrated against her thigh. She mindlessly reached into her cargo pocket and pulled out the smartphone, swiping the screen. Glancing down, she found herself staring at a close-up of the face she had just seen. Hawk had added one line to the photo.

Is this Johann's associate?

Viper lifted her eyes back to the brightly-lit yard. A cold numbness stole through her body, starting in the pit of her gut. The discolored, lifeless face was indeed that of the associate that Johann had brought back from Canada. It was also the face of his brother.

Alina knew, *without a doubt*, that Johann would *never* harm a member of his family.

Viper stared unseeingly at the beacon of light down the block. Her mind was a swimming jumble of half-thoughts and instinctual knowledge, almost paralyzing her as her heart pounded and her breath came quick and shallow. She allowed the thoughts and emotions to run riot for a full minute before she slowly and intentionally took a long, deep breath. Her heart skipped a few beats in protest, but she took another long, slow breath. Alina closed her eyes, blocking out the artificial white light, and took another deep breath. She concentrated on the fresh smell of the new spring leaves that surrounded her and the mustiness of the bark that she leaned against.

Slowly, she forced all thought out of her mind and her heartbeat gradually returned to normal. The numbing sensation that had consumed her started to fade away slowly. Viper allowed herself a few seconds to embrace the sensation of floating high above the ground before she allowed thought to come back into her mind. This time, the thoughts were ordered and rational. She opened her eyes, seeing clearly what her mind had grasped as soon as she saw the face on the corpse.

Someone was systematically taking out Johann's entire network with the intention of ending with Johann himself. It wasn't Johann tying up loose ends. It was *someone else*. And they clearly knew more than Alina did right now.

Alina lifted the binoculars again and watched as the medical examiner cut the body down. Adjusting the focus, she slowly began to examine every tree, every yard, every street, and every sidewalk within viewing distance, looking for any sign of surveillance. Within seconds she zoomed in on the front of a vehicle, partially hidden from view by a house, parked a block or so away from Johann's. It was the front end of a black Bronco.

She dropped the binoculars back around her neck and quickly answered Hawk's message before lowering herself to a bottom limb and dropping noiselessly out of the tree. Viper took off at a run, darting out of the yard and into the next one under the cover of the growing darkness, away from Johann's house. She had surveyed the neighborhood enough in the past twenty-four hours to know that she could loop around and come up to the Bronco from the rear in a matter of minutes. She knew that she would find it was the same Bronco from this afternoon. A calm focus took hold of her as Viper hopped a metal fence and ran swiftly along a row of rhododendrons, disappearing into the night.

Damon and Stephanie emerged into the front yard just as John was stepping out of the house. He handed a couple of evidence bags to a young woman and waved to them.

"I'm still waiting to hear on that ID from the lab," he said, meeting them. Stephanie nodded.

"Mr. Peterson sent it to his people too," she said. John looked at Damon.

"And?" he asked. Damon grinned.

"Still waiting," he replied. John grinned.

"Mr. Peterson doesn't think its Johann," Stephanie told John as the trio walked slowly toward the road. John glanced at Damon.

"Do you know what he looks like?" he asked sharply. Damon gave him the same answer he had given Stephanie.

"I have some additional information," he answered. "But I'm waiting for confirmation." John was silent for a second before he stopped walking.

"Well, if it's not your terrorist, then your job is done here," John said. Stephanie groaned.

"John, your tactfulness is outstanding," she muttered. "I hope you don't take that the wrong way, Damon. John isn't known for his social graces." Damon laughed easily.

"Not at all," he assured her. "He's right. If it's not my terrorist, I'll be out of your hair." John watched him through sleepy eyes.

"You'll probably be glad to get back to Washington in time for the weekend," he commented, encountering a laughing look from Damon's sharp blue eyes.

"Oh, I might stick around for a little while yet," Damon answered with an easy smile. "I'm getting re-acquainted with an old friend."

John's eyes narrowed slightly and Stephanie's ears perked up.

"Oh? You ran into an old friend here?" she asked. Damon nodded, reaching into his pocket as his phone chirped.

"Yes. Someone I knew a few years ago," he told her, looking down at his phone. "It's been nice to touch base with her again," he added, allowing his voice to fade away in the manner of someone who has been distracted by what he was reading. Damon saw John's jaw clench out of the corner of his eye and his lips twitched ever so slightly. John was easier to read than a book and Damon realized that he was thoroughly enjoying himself. Then his eyes focused on the brief message on his phone.

Yes. Meet you back at the house. Off to the races.

Damon frowned at the phrase he hadn't heard since those long-ago days at the training facility. Viper was going after something. Or someone.

Damon wasn't amused any longer. His first instinct was to go find her, but he immediately acknowledged the irrationality of that thought. He had no idea where she was or what she was after. His only course of action was to do as she said and go back to the house and wait. Hawk acknowledged the irony of being concerned for Viper's safety even as he tucked the phone back into his pocket. This sudden feeling of helplessness was completely foreign to him.

"Bad news?" John asked. Damon looked up. John and Stephanie were both looking at him with concern. "You look like you want to shoot someone," John added. Damon forced himself to smile slightly.

"Not good news, I'm afraid," he answered. "Your body isn't Johann Topamari, but it *is* one of his associates," Damon told them. He looked at John with a slight grin that he mustered up from somewhere. "Sorry, John. You're stuck with me for a little longer."

"Who is it?" Stephanie asked, stepping out of the way as some agents passed by with more evidence from the house.

"I should have a name by the morning. They don't want to commit without running through some more databases," Damon answered. "But you were right about the distinctive mark on his face. It *is* hard to mistake it."

"Johann did that to one of his associates?" John mused out loud. "That doesn't make any sense."

"It does if he's tying up loose ends," Stephanie said.

"I don't buy it," John shook his head. "I don't see him taking out his entire network."

Stephanie leaned up against the coroner's van at the curb. She looked like she was settling in for a long debate.

"Ok. Why?" she asked John simply. John shrugged and stood with his legs apart, balancing his weight as he stared at the sky thoughtfully.

"Why would he?" he said. "Building a network takes months, if not years, especially in the States. So why would he dismantle it now? Nothing in his file indicates any prior tendency toward suicide missions. And if he *was* about to commit a terrorist act, which we have absolutely no indication that he is, then why take out his entire network? It just doesn't make sense."

"So, let's say, for the sake of argument, that he *is* about to launch an attack of some sort," Stephanie said, crossing her arms and leaning her head back against the van. Both of them seemed oblivious now to Damon's presence as he watched them curiously.

Was this really how Feds worked? One leaning on a coroner's van and the other staring off into the sky? Despite himself, Hawk was fascinated. He was trained to think while moving. Never stop moving. If you couldn't think and move at the same time, you were dead. At this rate, he wouldn't be surprised if these two sat down for a cup of coffee and a danish.

"And, let's say, he built his network with the intention of dismantling it once he had launched his attack," Stephanie continued. "That would explain why he used a low-rung arms dealer and a has-been mobster."

"And that made sense when it was just them," John agreed. "But now we have an associate that doesn't fall into the category of 'disposable local asset.' That body is one of *them*."

"One of *them*?" Stephanie grinned. John shrugged.

"You know what I mean," he retorted. "It's of middle-eastern descent."

"I do feel obligated to point out that not all terrorists are of middle-eastern descent, nor is everyone of middle-eastern descent a terrorist," Stephanie said mildly. John stopped staring at the sky and rolled his eyes.

"Are we going to discuss semantics or the matter at hand?" John asked politely.

Damon chuckled despite himself.

"I think she's just trying to be socially diverse," he told John with a grin.

"So what you're trying to say is...." Stephanie went back to John's train of thought. "Johann built a network mixed with both local assets *and* trusted associates from his home country. And, while he may have planned to eliminate the local part of his network, you can't buy into him taking out his own countrymen? Is that about the gist of it?"

"Right." John nodded.

Stephanie straightened away from the side of the van as the medical examiner came into view, manning one end of the gurney carrying the topic of conversation.

"Ok." She stepped back onto the sidewalk and the three of them watched the progress of the gurney silently.

Damon was grudgingly impressed with how quickly John had rejected the idea that Johann would have done that to his own kin. As soon as he had seen that the corpse wasn't Johann, Hawk realized that someone else was methodically eliminating Johann's network. But John had instinctively grasped what Hawk knew only from Vipers research. Damon felt he could almost start to like the man. Almost. He wondered what Alina would say when he told her how quick on his feet her ex was turning out to be.

Damon again felt that almost overwhelming need to leave and find her. He frowned.

"What if..."

Stephanie's thought was lost in the sudden, deafening roar of an explosion.

Damon acted on sheer instinct, grabbing Stephanie and throwing them both unceremoniously to the trembling ground. He twisted his head to see flames shoot high above the rooftops one street over.

Chaos instantly erupted. Screams could be heard coming from all over the neighborhood and police started running in the direction of the flames. Damon jumped up, his heart pounding and blood rushing in his ears. He had only one thought: Viper.

"You stay with her!" he shouted to John over the noise, pointing to Stephanie.

John nodded and started shouting instructions to agents around them. Their priority was the crime scene, and as Damon ran down the street to come up on the scene of the explosion from the rear, he heard senior agents shouting instructions to secure the crime scene and evidence.

Hawk reached into his back holster as he ran, unsnapping the catch and pulling out his gun. His eyes scanned the area as he ran, looking for signs of Viper and anything, or anyone, that didn't belong. He ran through the side yard of a dark house and emerged onto the next street behind the roaring blaze.

The heat from the flames stopped him in his tracks and Damon threw up an arm to shield his face, his breath catching in his chest painfully as he stared at the massive ball of flames. At the base was a twisted mass of metal that once was an SUV. The flames, that only seconds before had been over three stories high, had lowered already to a manageable size, but the heat pouring from the wreckage told him that a military-grade accelerant had been used. He looked around almost frantically as police officers on the other side of the fire started shouting orders to each other.

Hawk backed up and started examining the blast radius, looking for anything that would indicate that Viper had been there. He tried not to think about the possibility of her being inside the inferno, and instead focused on the debris, searching for any sign that she had been injured...or worse. The fact that she had been here or in the vicinity was beyond doubt in his mind. The only question was whether she had *caused* the explosion, or been a target *of* it.

After searching fruitlessly for a few moments, he moved back into the shadows of a huge elm on the corner and lifted his eyes to scan the area. Sirens were already wailing in the distance as the fire department responded to the police summons, and the number of spectators was growing as people began to swarm to the second scene of chaos in their quiet neighborhood. The police started to form a human barricade in an arc around the fire, holding the curious at bay.

Hawk melted deeper into the shadows, watching. His heartbeat was returning to normal as his breathing slowed. There was no sign of Viper in the debris or in the surrounding crowds. He had to believe that she was fine. On making that determination, Hawk's mind automatically turned to the cause of the explosion. The use of the accelerant raised new questions and Damon scanned the area one more time, looking for something that he couldn't identify. When his phone vibrated, he felt a flood of relief. He didn't need to look to know that it was Viper.

A young policeman watched Damon from a few yards away. He recognized him as the man with the Feds that he had let in earlier. He called over to his buddy to tell him he would be right back, then turned to head over to Damon. He took two steps and stopped, looking around in confusion.

Damon had completely disappeared.

They called him "The Engineer." The people who hired him didn't know his real name. His reputation was extensive and solid, and that was good enough for them. He had never much cared for the name himself, but he was a practical man. He knew that the name inspired apprehension and fear, and so he allowed it. It was the only remnant from his military days that still existed. He had made sure of that. But when a reputation is built so firmly on a name, well, there was nothing to be done about that. He accepted it and never really thought much about it. To the men and women who hired him, however, the name meant everything. It guaranteed that they were getting someone who was invisible and didn't really exist. It ensured superior planning, flawless execution, and not a trace to be found. Most important of all, it meant that there would be no failure. The Engineer had an astonishing one hundred percent success rate and they paid very highly for his services.

The Engineer stood in the shadows and watched the scurry of activity following the explosion. He felt a certain satisfaction in seeing everything play out exactly as he had planned it. So much planning, so much patience, and now he was beginning to see it start to pay off. This was just the beginning.

He was drawing them all to him. He liked to think of them as his wayward children. They wouldn't come to him voluntarily, and so he had to orchestrate events and script their reactions, planning everything down to the last detail. Then, when they finally did what he wanted them to do, he would put them out of their misery. The Engineer wasn't a cruel man, after all. He was simply thorough. And, if his wayward children learned a valuable lesson to take with them to the next life, well, then he would be shown tolerance in *his* next life. It was for this reason that he was always very careful to draw them to him slowly. That way, they really did have time to think about their actions and realize where they were going. Perhaps they could learn from their journey and that of their friends.

He had known Viper would be here tonight. He planned it this way. He knew that she would come to make sure that the body hanging from the tree wasn't Johann. She wouldn't trust that agent from Homeland Security who was hanging around the Feds to make that determination for her. The Engineer frowned slightly. Mr. Peterson was an unforeseen complication. However, he was confident that he had adjusted accordingly. He was concerned with why Viper was spending so much time with a member of a government agency. She was too smart for that. She knew that none of them could be trusted, especially after that fiasco in Cairo two years ago. And yet, here she was associating with not only the mystery DHS agent, but also two Feds. This was certainly something The Engineer had not expected from the Viper that he had studied. However, he admitted to being somewhat delighted with this new facet to her. She was turning out to be much more complicated that he had first thought. There was much more to her than just a brilliant assassin. He wished he had more time to explore the intricacies of her character, but all his planning had to adhere to a strict time table. He was already a little off schedule because of Johann's erratic behavior.

He sighed and lifted his binoculars, scanning the neighborhood slowly. Johann had to be here somewhere. He would have heard of Ahmed's death by now. It was all over the police scanners and The Engineer knew that Johann monitored the scanners. He had planned for it. He was just waiting for him to show himself. He wanted him to see the severity of the situation and accept his consequences.

Oh, yes. He had planned it all out, down to the very last detail. And, when it was all said and done, everyone would move when and where he wanted them to...just like chess pieces.

He continued to scan the growing crowds and shadows. There was still no sign of Viper or Johann. And yet, they had to be there! He thought he had glimpsed Viper just before he detonated the truck, moving in the shadows near the corner where he had parked it. But when he had looked into the shadows where he saw the movement, no one was there. He was annoyed that he had missed her, but he was more concerned with Johann. The Engineer needed to know that Johann had seen Ahmed. It was crucial that he feel the pressure.

The Engineer turned his binoculars at movement behind the fire and watched as the DHS agent appeared on the sidewalk behind the inferno that used to be the truck. He focused in on him curiously as the agent threw up his arm to shield his face from the heat coming off the flames. Ah yes, the accelerant was burning away. Mr. Peterson backed up a few steps and then started walking around the blast radius, looking on the ground at the debris. The Engineer watched him for a moment, diverted. Was he really looking for something useful in the debris? He smiled slightly. Oh, the government agents were so very predictable. Always imagining that clues were everywhere. What on earth did Viper see in him?

He moved on, dismissing Mr. Peterson from his mind. The neighbors were starting to gather, being held back by a growing number of the local police force. The Engineer swore softly and lowered his binoculars. There was no use looking for him now. Johann wouldn't show his face with this many people around.

He had missed him.

A strange feeling of frustration took hold, choking out his previous satisfaction with the evening. This was a feeling he hadn't felt in years. The Engineer never failed. His plans always played out just as he had scripted them. He never miscalculated. And yet, there was no Johann and no Viper.

This was *not* the way he had planned it.

The Engineer tucked his binoculars away and melted into the shadows again, disappearing swiftly into the night, leaving chaos behind him.

Chapter Eleven

Damon got out of his Jeep and turned toward the deck. The house was completely dark. When he had come through the driveway and around the side, he thought that Alina wasn't back yet. Relief washed over him at the sight of her seated in one of the Adirondack chairs. She was sitting in the darkness, with only the faint light from the moon lighting the deck. Her legs were folded up to the side of her and she seemed to be staring off into the night. Damon moved across the grass toward the deck, watching her. He had the almost uncontrollable urge to run up to her and lift her into his arms, to feel that she was alive and warm and well. Instead, he moved steadily across the lawn. There would be time enough later to explore this unusual feeling that was panic mixed with relief.

Alina watched Damon get out of the jeep and come toward the deck. He was moving with his usual steady, jungle-cat grace and she drew solace from that familiar walk. She had been sitting there for quite a while, thinking, and now she was feeling numb. Her legs were numb from where they had been curled into the chair and her mind was numb from all the various scenarios that she had been running through in her head. Seeing Hawk come toward her now, calm and familiar, filled her with warm comfort. She tried to push the feeling aside, but she was just too weary. Alina let it encompass her as she watched him.

"You look like you've been sitting here for a while," Damon remarked, stepping silently onto the deck and looking down at her. She tilted her head back and looked into his face.

"I have. It's a good thing you came when you did. I'm not sure I can feel my legs," she replied bluntly.

Damon burst out laughing. Alina smiled and shifted her weight, gingerly untangling her legs and straightening them out of the chair. Damon set a hand on her shoulder when she would have tried to stand.

"You stay here," he said. "I'll be right back."

He moved past her to the doors and disappeared into the dark house. Alina didn't question him, but crossed her ankles and leaned back in the chair again. She returned her gaze to the woods at the end of the yard and listened as the night surrounded her. The breeze carried the fresh scent of earth and young leaves, the signature scent of a spring evening. The moonlight cast silver shadows over the grass and an owl hooted nearby. Rustling in the trees to the left was followed by the unmistakable chirp of a raccoon. Alina leaned her head back and took a deep breath, forcing herself to relax. She listened as the large raccoon scurried over to the trash cans at the side of house. A minute later, one of the lids fell to the ground and Alina smiled. She should probably get up and scare it away, but she couldn't be bothered. It was hungry and looking for food. It would leave when it realized that the cans were empty. She closed her eyes.

The owl hooted again and the trash can fell to the ground with a clatter as the raccoon scurried away back into the trees. A bat swooped down from the garage and fluttered quickly around the yard before going back to the eaves of the garage. Tree frogs sang to each other, becoming increasingly louder as the shadows deepened. Alina absorbed it all, trying to calm her mind so that she could think clearly. Tonight had been a revelation, and the anger that had been simmering below the surface had finally ebbed away, leaving restlessness in its wake.

"Here." Damon appeared next her with a mug in each hand. Alina opened her eyes and reached out to take the hot cup of coffee.

"Thank you," she said, lifting her head and sipping the espresso gratefully.

Damon sat next to her and they were quiet for a few moments, sipping their coffee. He hesitated to break the companionable silence, sensing that Alina needed it. The hot espresso burned a path of warmth to his belly and he leaned his head back, closing his eyes. The tree frogs were singing loudly to each other and Damon couldn't help thinking how much more comfortable it was here than in his tree.

"Stephanie is ok?" Alina finally broke the silence. Damon opened his eyes and glanced at her. She was looking at him with large, clear dark eyes.

"She was fine the last time I saw her," he answered. "I left her with John." Alina nodded and turned her attention back to the dark yard.

"You didn't..." Damon started after a long moment. Alina cut him off instantly.

"Nope," she said. "It was remote detonated before I even got to it."

Damon absorbed that for a moment while Alina sipped her coffee. The numbness in her head was starting to recede, almost as if she was coming back to earth after floating just above it for an extended period time.

"Was it the Bronco?" he asked. Alina nodded.

"The bastard knew I would see it," she answered shortly. Damon glanced at her. Her hands were steady, but there was no mistaking the cold anger in her voice. "He wanted to make *sure* that I saw it."

"Did you see it detonate?" he asked, his mind working furiously. Alina nodded.

"I was heading towards it," she answered. "As soon as it went up, I took cover. I canvassed the area, but couldn't find anything. He was either at a remote location or he was invisible."

"Or just very well hidden," Damon replied.

Alina paused. She wished she could have insisted that she would have seen him, but she was honest and knew she could not. The explosion had done just what it was intended to do, cause chaos, and in the contrasting darkness and brightness of the flames, Alina knew she could have missed a shadow.

"He isn't an amateur," she said after a short silence. "He used an accelerant. That explosion was designed as a distraction to draw Johann out. That's exactly what it did."

"Johann?" Hawk glanced at her. She had her head back against the chair and was staring out into the night.

"He was there," Alina said. "I saw him on the other side of the fire. By the time I circled around, he was gone. Whoever this spook is, he had this all planned down to the last detail."

"Why?" Damon asked, setting down his empty coffee mug and getting comfortable. "Why do you think he tried to draw him out? And where do you fit in?"

"He's mocking me," Alina replied shortly. "He's after Johann, but he must have been watching me all along. I don't know why. There's something..." her voice trailed off as she stared into the trees. Something was nagging at the outer edges of her mind, just out of reach of her consciousness. "There's something that I'm overlooking...something that I remember...."

Alina shook her head in frustration. Now that the picture was becoming clearer in her mind, there was a grayness that she couldn't fit in with the rest...something that was on the edge of her memory.

"Don't force it," Hawk advised. "It will come to you." He turned his attention to the night around them. "Let's start from the beginning. This afternoon in the woods. Let's start there."

Alina glanced at him with a slight smile. He had made himself comfortable on his chair and propped his feet up on the banister.

"Ok." Alina went back earlier in the day with him. "You and Angela were in front of me."

"Did you see us?" Hawk asked. Alina shook her head.

"No. I could hear you and sense your movement," she answered. Hawk turned his head to look at her and she held up her hand. "Don't give me that look. You've known me long enough to know that in nature, my senses are better than my eyes." Hawk grinned.

"I won't deny that," he murmured. They had called her a witch behind her back in training. Her sixth sense had been legendary. And then, of course, there was that strange knack she had with animals.

"You were in front of me. I was about to come up behind you when I realized that someone else was behind me," Alina continued. "I dropped to my knees and turned. I couldn't see him, but I knew he was there."

"Do you think he saw you?" Damon asked. Alina thought for a moment.

"I think so," she said slowly. "I never caught sight of him until he was out of the woods and crossing the road, but I think he was watching me."

"It was definitely a man?" Hawk asked. Alina nodded.

"Tall, dark hair, maybe a buck eighty. It was hard to tell. He was wearing hunting fatigues, but he wasn't any more than a buck ninety, I wouldn't have thought," she said thoughtfully. "He took off when some kids came through on their dirt bikes. I ran him down to the road and was just in time to see him disappear into the woods across the way. The bronco started up and came out a minute later."

"So he knew you saw the truck," Hawk said slowly. "And you think this was all carefully planned out?"

"I think so." Alina stretched and propped her feet up next to his on the banister, crossing her ankles. "It feels like it. I feel like he planned for me to know that he was there tonight." Alina searched for the right way to put into words what she was thinking. "I think he's been systematically tracking Johann and taking out his network. Then I arrived. I think he is letting me know that he's here, and that he is going to win."

"You think this is a *game* to him?" Hawk demanded, glancing at her. Alina shook her head, meeting his gaze.

"I think this is business to him," she replied calmly. Hawk stared at her in silence.

"You think it's another hit on Johann," he stated after a moment. Alina nodded.

"And I think I know who it is," she added.

"Are you crazy?" Stephanie demanded. She was staring at John from the passenger seat as he sped through the night. "We can't just show up on her doorstep at close to two in the morning."

"Why not?" John asked blandly. "We both have done it in the past."

"That was *ten years ago*, you ass," Stephanie retorted. There was silence for a moment. "She might not even be home."

"True," John agreed, switching lanes and zooming into the exit for Marlton.

"You're in Marlton," Stephanie muttered. "Alina lives in Medford."

"I'm taking a back road." John glanced at her. "Can you please stop trying to navigate?"

"No!" Steph shot back irritably. "I think this is asinine. We shouldn't be just showing up in the middle of the night. What we need to know can wait until a decent hour. And besides, I'm more concerned with where Damon disappeared to."

"I can guarantee Damon Peterson will not be far from Alina," John retorted grimly. Stephanie glanced at him.

"Why?" she asked. John shrugged.

"Call it a hunch," he answered. Stephanie's eyes narrowed.

"So help me, John, if you're dragging me out into the pine barrens at two in the morning out of some misplaced sense of *jealousy*, I will make sure that you never have children," she promised fervently. "What Lina does with her time, and with *whom,* is none of your concern anymore. You made sure of that ten years ago."

"Well, ten years ago I didn't know that she and her *"whom"* were going to waltz into my investigation and turn it into a nightmare," John retorted. If Stephanie's eyes could have rolled any higher, her eyeballs would have popped out of her scalp.

"Oh, don't be ridiculous," she muttered, watching as Marlton fell away and the quiet darkness of Medford loomed before them in all its wooded glory. However, she fell silent after that. There was just enough doubt that John may be right to cause her to stay quiet and allow him to continue on. They did have questions that needed to be answered and Stephanie was pretty sure that Alina or Damon, or both, had the answers they needed. She also agreed that if Damon was not with Alina, he wouldn't be far away.

Stephanie looked out the window at the dark trees flashing by. She knew everyone thought she was so focused on her work that she didn't see the obvious right in front of her nose. She had worked hard to ensure that was the common perception. But she didn't get to where she was now by not being observant. She knew as soon as they walked into the restaurant that night that Damon and Alina knew each other. She had felt the tension in the big body behind her at the hostess desk, and had seen the same look of wariness in Alina's eyes as she joined them. Her suspicion had been confirmed as soon as they got to the table and she saw Damon murmur something as he pulled out Alina's chair. The look that passed between them was not the look of strangers, but of two people who knew each other well. She hadn't jumped to the same conclusion that John had, however. She had watched them closely that night, and she had noted how every person who entered the room was examined by Damon. He exuded an aura of protective awareness, and Stephanie had left the restaurant with the distinct impression that Damon was more interested in Alina than in anything else. While John had clearly formed the opinion that Damon and Alina were working together, Stephanie suspected just the opposite. She suspected that Alina had no idea why Damon was there, and she believed that Damon was there for Alina.

"Have you heard from your friend in Washington yet?" John asked after a few miles in silence. Stephanie pulled her attention back from the darkness outside and her thoughts.

"Not yet," she answered. "She may not be able to find out anything. Homeland Security is tight as a clam, apparently. But if she can, she'll let me know the scoop on Damon."

"Did she give a time-frame?" John asked, turning onto the road that led to Alina's house.

"No, Mr. Impatient, she didn't," Stephanie retorted. John glanced at her with a grin.

"You really are cranky tonight," he remarked.

Her only response was to glare at him. He laughed and turned on his high beams, slowing down. The street was pitch black with few street lights and the woods were thick.

"Deer," Stephanie said, catching sight of the iridescent glow of eyes in front of them.

"I see." John stopped and they watched as not one deer, but four, ambled across the road. Once they had cleared the road, he increased his speed again. "So what's the plan when we get there?" he asked. Stephanie looked at him.

"You're asking *me?*" she demanded. "You're the one who dragged me out here! You come up with the plan!"

"Do you want to be good cop or bad cop?" John asked, glancing over to her as he slowed down and pulled into the long gravel driveway.

Stephanie stared at him, flabbergasted, for a long moment before returning her attention out the window. John grinned and waited. It wasn't until the house came into view that she spoke.

"I'll be the good cop."

Alina set the coffee mugs in the sink and turned to lean back against the counter. She watched as Damon slid the door to the deck shut and locked it. He had followed her inside without a word, glancing around the darkness outside before stepping into the house. Alina watched as he switched on the lamp in the living room, her lips twitching.

"Make yourself at home," she murmured. Damon heard her and looked over with a grin.

"Thanks," he retorted, settling into the recliner.

Alina was forced into a chuckle and she pushed away from the counter to walk over to her laptop. She opened it and typed in a few commands, setting the security system and redirecting it to the flat screen above the fireplace. Damon watched as a quadrant appeared on the screen, displaying real-time surveillance of the four most accessible entry points to the property.

"I've been wondering if you used the TV," he said. "Now I see what you use it for." Alina shrugged and walked over to settle onto the couch. She pulled off her boots and tucked her feet up beside her.

"I have a TV in my bedroom if I want to watch TV," she informed him. Damon raised his eyebrow and studied her.

"And what does Viper watch when she wants to watch TV..." he wondered, leaning his head back and watching her lazily.

"Oh, I'm a sucker for reality TV," she retorted with a wink.

Alina set her elbow on the arm of the couch and propped her chin in her hand, watching Damon. He was completely relaxed, his feet crossed at the ankles. His jeans were worn and faded, and his black tee shirt hugged his broad chest and biceps. Dark hair fell carelessly across his forehead and he stared back at her with a faint smile on his face. They stayed like that, in comfortable silence, for a few minutes, lost in their thoughts. The night was silent outside and the only sound in the house came from the ticking clock in the front of the house and the low hum of the refrigerator from the kitchen.

"What are you thinking?" Damon finally asked softly, watching as her dark eyes reflected the light. Alina shrugged, smiling slightly.

"I'm wondering why you keep popping up in my life," she answered readily, her eyes meeting his frankly. If Damon was surprised, he didn't show it.

"Is it becoming a problem?" he asked, his eyes laughing at her. Alina's lips curved into an answering smile of their own accord.

"Not yet," she retorted enigmatically. "But you seem to be a recurring theme in my life, Hawk."

The storm of emotions from the past few hours had left her, and in its place was that ponderous languor that follows such a frenzy of adrenaline and mental stress. Alina stretched comfortably and Damon watched her lazily with hooded eyes.

"I haven't seen anyone else that we were in boot camp with, or anyone from the training facility," Alina continued. "But you, you keep popping up."

She thought she caught the faintest glimpse of a flash in his bright blue eyes, but in a second it was gone and his eyes went back to their hooded twinkle.

"Do we have to assign reason to it?" he asked in a low voice. "I always thought it was kind of nice how I keep running into you."

Damon watched as something flickered in the back of her dark eyes and her lips parted slightly. He held his breath for a moment. Damon thought he caught a glimmer of something resembling longing in her dark eyes, but then, just as quickly, Viper's mask slid back into place. Her lips closed, her lashes covered her eyes, and Alina sat up abruptly. The comfortable spell was broken.

"It *is* nice," she told him with a quick smile. She stood up and stretched restlessly. "It's always good to see a friendly face."

Alina turned to go into the kitchen, afraid she wouldn't be able to conceal the sudden confusion she was feeling. She hadn't been prepared for the sudden rush of warmth and longing that had rolled through her. Initially, she had some vague idea of trying to find out what he was really doing here, but somehow she lost control of the conversation. The onslaught of emotion had been completely unexpected and Alina wasn't sure how to proceed. She was so used to setting emotions aside that Alina did what she knew how to do best. She went over to the counter and flipped on the faucet to rinse out the mugs, pushing the moment aside.

She never heard him move swiftly and silently up behind her.

"You make me sound like a Labrador."

Hawks' voice was low and just behind her ear. Alina started, surprised despite herself at how quickly and silently he had moved. A bolt of awareness raised the fine hairs on her neck and she could sense his body a scant inch behind her. If she tipped her head back, she knew it would rest on his chest. Almost instantly, her heart started thumping and she felt another shiver of awareness slice through her. She inhaled slowly, resting her hands on either side of the sink.

"What's wrong with that?" Alina asked, not turning her head. "I like dogs."

There was a low chuckle behind her and his hands came up to cover both of hers. She caught her breath and watched his long fingers slide between hers, the warmth of his hands spreading like fire up her arms. Alina felt like she was completely engulfed by Damon, even though only his hands were touching her. His smell and his heat surrounded her, making her almost light-headed with a sudden onslaught of desire so fierce that she could only catch her breath.

"Cute." His breath tickled her ear as he bent his head toward it. "You don't make me think of dogs," Damon whispered in her ear, his lips brushing against it as they moved.

His full attention was focused on the woman in front of him, his hunting instinct taking over. He watched through hooded eyes as his whisper caused all the little hairs on her neck to rise up and the pulse at the base of her throat to start beating wildly. Hawk felt a small measure of satisfaction at the small, tell-tale signs that she was feeling the same overwhelming desire that he was...and had been ever since he had stepped into the living room from the deck. He rubbed his thumbs lightly across the backs of her hands, the skin soft against his, and watched as goosebumps appeared on her arms.

Alina felt like someone had just poured fire all over her. Her heart was pounding and desire was coursing through her with such intensity that she was almost blinded by it. Then Hawk started stroking her hands with his thumbs and she was lost. Viper forgot all about Johann. She forgot all about explosions and mysterious strangers in the woods. Every thought was pushed out of her mind by this intense longing and desire. All but one. All she had to do was lean back, turn her head, and Hawk would give her everything she wanted right this second.

Alina wasn't thinking anymore. She was feeling. For the first time in years, she was actually *feeling* something.

Damon felt the tension of indecision leave her body on one single, silent exhale. He reacted immediately and was already leaning into her and starting to lower his head as she turned hers. Deep blue eyes met dark brown and Hawk was satisfied with the desire that he saw burning in her eyes. He lowered his lips to hers.

A single, very loud beep echoed through the silent house just as his lips touched hers. His head snapped up and around. Alina's eyes popped open and went straight to the flat screen above the mantle. The driveway quadrant was flashing. A car was approaching the house.

There was a moment of absolute, deafening silence after the alarm had finished slicing through the house. Alina's heart was slamming against her chest as she brought her eyes back to Damon's face. His eyes were a deep, dark cobalt, still clouded with desire. But the glimmer of laughter was lurking once again in their depths. They stared at each other for a split second, and then Alina giggled.

Her eyes widened in shock as soon as the sound came out and Damon raised an eyebrow, staring down at her as if he had never heard a giggle. His look of utter amazement made Alina giggle again and she pulled her hand out from under his to clap it over her mouth. She hadn't giggled in *years*! But the emotions bubbling up inside her were uncontrollable and she leaned back against the sink and gave in to the laughter that was welling up inside her. Damon stepped back with a grin, watching the outburst.

"Saved by visitors," he murmured. Alina took a deep breath and tried to stop the laughter.

"And the ex, no less," she replied. Damon looked over to the flat screen again.

"What's he doing here?" he asked. Alina shrugged and choked down the rest of her nervous laughter.

"I have no idea," she answered, reaching out and shutting off the faucet.

Damon turned his attention back to her at the genuine sound of disgruntlement in her voice. The eruption of laughter was fading and Viper was sliding back into place. Damon didn't say a word as he reached out and touched her lips gently with one finger. He smiled slowly as her eyes met his, and he was content. Deep in the chocolate depths, the passionate woman still lurked. She wasn't gone completely.

"We will continue that," he promised softly. Alina tilted her head slightly to the side, considering him.

"We'll see," she answered just as softly.

Chapter Twelve

When John and Stephanie pulled around the driveway to stop before the garage, the backyard was flooded with light from a spotlight fixed to the back of the house. Alina and Damon were both seated in the chairs on the deck, Damon with his feet propped on the banister and Alina with her legs crossed. Both appeared totally relaxed, just enjoying the night. Stephanie got out of the car and waved.

"Oh good! We didn't wake you!" she called as as she came around the back of the car and waited for John.

"Is she serious?" Hawk murmured under his breath.

"Be nice," Alina hissed back, standing up as John got out of the car and the two started walking toward the deck. They were both wearing their FBI windbreakers and the breeze caught both of them, blowing the jackets open and exposing the badge and the standard issue on both their hips.

"Why do I suddenly feel like a felon?" Hawk asked, standing up beside her. Alina glanced at him in slight surprise.

"Because that's their intention," she retorted, keeping her voice low. She watched them consideringly. "I think...wine," she added decisively. "It will keep them off their official high horse." Hawk smiled.

"That could work," he agreed. They stopped talking as John and Stephanie reached the deck.

"We were afraid you would be asleep," John said, his eyes cutting over to Damon. "But apparently not."

"I'm still something of a night owl," Alina answered smoothly. She waved them up onto the deck. "Damon was just telling me about the explosion," she added as Stephanie stepped onto the deck first.

"I didn't realize the two of you knew each other," Stephanie said, looking from one to the other. Damon grinned.

"This is the old friend," he told her. Stephanie looked sharply at Alina.

"You never said anything!" she accused her. Alina shrugged.

"I didn't think it was important," she answered. "We were in basic training together. It's nice to catch up again after all this time." Alina glanced at John and turned toward the back door. "You both look tired. We were just about to go in. It's gotten chilly out here. Come on inside."

"We won't stay long," Stephanie said, stepping into the living room behind her. "We just left the crime scene. I wanted to run some things by you," she added. Alina glanced at her, raising her eyebrow slightly.

"Really?" she asked in faint surprise. Stephanie grinned.

"You seem to have some experience in crime scenes," she replied.

"Not quite in the same capacity as you," Alina murmured dryly. She led her into the dining area and Stephanie set her purse on the table, shrugging out of her jacket and dropping it over the back of a chair.

"I was thinking of a glass of wine," Alina said, moving to a dark wood cabinet against the wall. "Would you like one?"

"Yes, please!" Stephanie watched as Alina opened the cabinet, revealing a large, well-stocked wine rack. "I thought you didn't drink anymore!" she exclaimed. Alina glanced over her shoulder.

"I never said I didn't drink," she pointed out. "Angie just assumed it."

"Good point." Stephanie grinned. "Where are the glasses?"

"Cabinet in the kitchen, next to the refrigerator," Alina answered, selecting a bottle of Shiraz. She glanced around. Damon and John were still outside. "Do I even want to know what they're doing?" she murmured, looking out the picture window.

Stephanie poked her head around the cabinet door and followed her gaze. Damon was near the back door, but John was still near the steps.

"You might not," Stephanie answered dryly, nudging the cabinet closed with her elbow. She set four wine glasses on the bar. "I think there is a touch of...something....there where John is concerned." Alina looked at Stephanie and set the bottle down on the bar next to the glasses.

"Oh for God's sake..." she muttered, heading to the back door.

She stopped when she reached the door. Damon was struggling not to laugh as John was staring at something. Alina followed John's gaze and almost burst out laughing herself. Raven had settled himself on the back of the chair between John and the door. Stephanie came around the bar and joined her.

"What's he looking...OH!" Stephanie caught sight of Raven. "Was he out there when we got here?"

"He was on the roof," Alina answered. "I really don't think he cares for John," she added, watching her pet. Raven was staring at John unblinkingly, giving every indication that if John tried moving toward the door, he wouldn't get very far. Damon reached over and slid the door open.

"We might have a little problem here," he said, struggling to keep the laughter out of his voice. Alina shot him a look that clearly said, *'Do you have to enjoy this so much?'* Hawk just grinned back at her.

"I see that." Alina stepped outside.

As soon as she stepped onto the deck, Raven turned his head to look at her. Alina stared at him for a moment, and then held out her arm. They all watched as he immediately lifted into the air and settled gently on her outstretched arm. She murmured something in a low voice and he bobbed his head, keeping his black eyes on her.

"Go in, John. He won't bother you now," Alina said softly.

Damon waited for John to step into the living room, never taking his eyes off Viper. The black hawk seemed mesmerized by her. She was murmuring to it quietly and Damon was fascinated. When she finally lifted her eyes to him, Damon caught his breath. Standing in the shadows, with the light from the house spilling out behind her and the black bird on her arm, she was a magical sight. They stared at

184

each other for a moment in silence before Viper murmured something and Raven lifted effortlessly off her arm, breaking the spell and disappearing back onto the roof. Damon dropped his eyes to her bare arm. There wasn't one mark from the hawk's claws.

"You never cease to amaze me," he murmured. He missed the teasing flash in her eyes as she stepped past him.

"Oh, you haven't seen anything yet," Alina murmured under breath as she went through the door. Damon's lips twitched and he followed her inside.

"That bird is a menace," John announced as Damon closed the door. Alina raised an eyebrow.

"That bird is doing his job," she retorted. "He doesn't trust you."

"That's harsh," John said, moving over to the bar. Alina shrugged.

"It's the truth," she said shortly.

"That was pretty crazy, what you just did," Stephanie spoke before John could respond. "You clearly haven't lost your knack with animals." Alina shook her head, moving around the bar and pulling a wine opener from a drawer.

"No," she agreed easily. "It's come in handy more than once." She removed the cork and poured wine into the four glasses while John prowled around curiously.

"This is nice," John said from the living room. Stephanie looked over her shoulder.

"Didn't you see it when you were here the other night?" she asked. John shook his head, pausing to peer down the hallway to the front of the house.

"No. We stayed on the deck," he answered. Stephanie looked at Alina and she shrugged.

"I was more comfortable outside," she said in response to the question in her face, lifting one of the glasses. Stephanie grinned.

"I don't blame you," she replied.

Damon watched through hooded eyes. John was clearly curious about the rest of the house but reluctant to look without an invitation, which was not forthcoming from his hostess. Stephanie, on the other hand, seemed to be going out of her way to be agreeable at two in the morning. *Good cop, bad cop*, he thought to himself, glancing at Alina. She was watching John with narrowed eyes.

"Why don't we sit in the living room?" Alina suggested. Stephanie picked up a glass and turned toward the living room.

"I am sorry for just showing up like this," she said as she followed Alina into the living room. John moved to the bar to take one of the remaining glasses.

"Well, as I said, I'm a night owl," Alina replied easily, heading for the recliner. "Damon had no qualms showing up out of the blue either. Don't worry anymore about it." John glanced at Damon and blue eyes met blue.

"Coincidence, you knowing Lina," John commented. Damon shrugged slightly.

"They *do* happen," he answered calmly, picking up the remaining glass of wine. "I have to say that I am thoroughly enjoying getting to know her again." Damon sipped the wine and started to move into the living room.

"I would imagine so." John followed him. "How long has it been since you two saw each other?"

"Too long," Damon answered with a quick smile.

Stephanie looked from Damon to Alina sharply before sitting on the couch. Damon looked like a cat that had found a bowl of cream. She focused on Alina.

"It must have been a surprise when he walked into the restaurant," she commented. Alina waited to answer until John sat down next to Stephanie.

"It was a nice surprise," she finally said with a smile, glancing up at Damon as he perched on the arm of her chair. "I never thought I would see any of the boys again," she added.

"Oh ye of little faith," he murmured.

Damon leaned back against the chair and stretched his arm along the back. His entire demeanor suggested a closer relationship with Alina than was being discussed, a fact that wasn't lost on one person in the room. Alina knew he had to have a reason, but she let him know that she didn't appreciate the implications by shooting him a glare and shifting away from him. He just smiled back at her blandly.

"Well, it's certainly one hell of a coincidence," Stephanie murmured.

"They *do* happen," Alina unconsciously echoed Damon's words and John raised an eyebrow.

"So he told you about the explosion tonight?" Stephanie asked, sipping her wine and settling back against the couch.

Alina nodded, her dark eyes moving between John and Stephanie. Stephanie looked open and relaxed, while John seemed to be brooding and watchful. *Good cop, bad cop*, she thought with a sigh. *How predictable.*

"Yes. An SUV, I think you said?" Alina looked up at Damon questioningly. Damon nodded.

"We were able to contain the crime scene," Stephanie told them. "But the SUV was toasted for a reason. I think someone was making a statement."

"One hell of a statement to make," Alina replied, sitting back in the recliner and curling her legs up beside her.

"It's the only thought that I can come up with," Stephanie answered. "The explosion was too far away to have been meant to destroy any part of the crime scene. Once everything settled down, nothing was missing from evidence or from the house. No one was seen trying to gain access to the house or the yard, so it wasn't meant as a distraction. That really only leaves someone making a statement, and I don't think that someone was Johann."

"Stephanie!" John muttered warningly. Stephanie rolled her eyes.

"What?" she demanded. "I can tell you right now, she knows all about Johann."

Stephanie's words fell heavily into the room, causing a moment of silence. Alina was amused. So *this* was how they were going to play it! John looked at Stephanie, and then at Alina. Damon's eyes were dancing as he looked down at her, showing that he was fully enjoying the whole production.

Stephanie was looking at her as well, a challenge clear in her eyes.

"*Do* you?" John demanded, drawing her gaze.

Alina paused for a moment, letting the silence lengthen. She considered both her old friends calmly. Between the two of them, they had clearly worked out what they thought was most of the truth. How much of the real truth was she willing to reveal? She glanced up at Damon and read a clear warning in his deep blue eyes. Her own narrowed slightly. They were all looking at her, trying to manipulate her for their respective reasons, and Alina was suddenly annoyed with the lot of them. Perhaps she was tired. Perhaps she was getting weary of all the cloak and dagger nonsense. Maybe she was simply tired of being manipulated. Whatever the reason, Viper made a quick decision.

"Yes," she said calmly. "I know all about Johann. I've been tracking him for over a month."

Her calm announcement made Damon let out an almost imperceptible sigh. John stared at her, his face inscrutable, and Stephanie blinked. Alina didn't think she expected to get that response so easily.

"Why?" Stephanie finally broke the heavy silence that followed that announcement.

"I can't tell you that," Alina answered bluntly, sipping her wine.

"Can't? Or won't?" John asked. Alina flicked her eyes to him impatiently and didn't answer.

"Ok." Stephanie set her empty wine glass on the floor. "That's what I thought. So this makes things easier. What do you know?"

"That you're in over your head," Alina answered promptly.

John made a noise that sounded close to a snort. Stephanie glared at him before turning back to Alina. She didn't look any happier with that blunt statement, but she appeared to be willing to listen.

"Why?"

"You have no idea what you're up against," Alina answered calmly. "Johann isn't just a terrorist. He's a figurehead. You can't treat him the same way you would one of your usual suspects. There are different rules now." Damon glanced down at her. "And frankly, you have no idea what they are."

"That's why I'm here," Damon injected smoothly. He stood up and motioned to John's full wine glass. "I think I saw beer in the fridge earlier. You look like you might prefer that." John looked a little sheepish.

"I would," he agreed. Damon grinned and walked over to take the full wine glass.

"So would I," he said, heading into the kitchen with the wine glasses. Alina watched him, wondering what he was up to now.

"Did you know he was the agent that was going to be sent to work with us?" Stephanie demanded. Alina looked back at her friend and shook her head.

"Not until he walked into the restaurant." Alina resisted the urge to cross her fingers behind her back. Stephanie seemed a little appeased by that.

"Well, that's something, at least," she muttered. "What do you know about the explosion?"

"Only what Damon told me before you got here," Alina answered. She raised her voice slightly. "Damon, bring another bottle of wine. Stephanie's glass is empty."

"She can have mine," John said quickly. "I didn't touch it."

"What do you think it was, if not a statement?" Stephanie asked, leaning forward. Alina looked at her for a moment.

"I think someone is trying to get Johann's attention," she said finally.

"Someone like who?" John demanded. Alina shrugged.

"If I knew that, I wouldn't be sitting here," she answered dryly. "There's another player, Steph. And, as much as I hate to say this, I think you both need to be very careful," she added.

Damon came back into the living room with two bottles of beer in one hand and John's full wine glass in the other. He handed Stephanie the glass and John one of the beers.

"Don't be ridiculous," John said, taking the beer. "Why would they be interested in us?"

"Because you're interested in Johann," Damon said, going back to his perch on the chair and stretching his arm along the back again. "I'm with Alina on this one. I think there's someone else after Johann, and I think they'll take out anyone in their way."

"His network," Stephanie said slowly. "You both think someone else is taking out his network."

"Now *that* makes sense!" John admitted, sitting back with his beer comfortably. "I've said all along that it doesn't make sense for him to be taking out his own network." Alina looked at him, surprised. He caught the look and shook his head. "You don't have to look so surprised," he muttered. "I've changed in ten years."

"Hmm." Alina clearly wasn't impressed and Damon bit back a laugh.

"But that means that whoever it is, is a professional. They must be..." Stephanie's voice trailed off as the full ramifications of what she was hearing sunk in. "Oh good Lord." She drank half her wine in one swallow and glanced at John. "Maybe we *are* in over our heads." John scoffed.

"Please," he retorted. "So we may need to add an assassin to our repertoire. It's something different, I'll give you that, but not impossible."

"We should tell Rob," Stephanie said, finishing the wine.

Alina watched her, half amused and half appalled at how quickly her old friend had just drained the wine glass.

"Maybe I *should* have opened another bottle," Damon murmured in her ear. Alina glanced at him, her eyes laughing.

"I think she's rattled," she murmured back.

"And tell him what?" John demanded. "That we think there might be an assassin running around, blowing things up and trying to get to Johann before we do? He would laugh himself silly."

"We don't have the resources to handle this *and* Johann," Stephanie retorted, her mind working quickly.

"I think we were just insulted," Damon remarked idly. Alina nodded.

"Yep," she agreed.

John and Stephanie looked at them in surprise. Obviously, neither of them had considered the possibility of a joint working relationship.

"This *is* one of the reasons I'm here," Damon pointed out. "Your boss would agree. I have the resources that you don't."

"What, exactly, are the *other* reasons you're here?" John asked. Damon smiled slightly.

"Those are not included among your resources," he answered softly. Stephanie sighed.

"John, you're going to have to suck it up and trust him," she informed him. "He's right. We're under orders to work with him. It's not our responsibility to ask why. And he does have more resources available to him in this instance."

"If it even *is* an assassin," John replied. "This is all conjecture. We could be way off base."

Damon felt Alina shift in the chair and prepared himself. Viper was getting ready to play devil's advocate.

"Ok," she said agreeably. "Let's explore other explanations," Alina offered. "You go first."

"Here we go," Damon murmured. Alina ignored him.

"Oh for heaven's sake," Stephanie exclaimed. "Don't encourage him, Lina. He hasn't changed *that* much and I don't want to be here all night listening to the two of you!"

Damon grinned.

"You have to deal with it too, huh?" he asked Stephanie. She rolled her eyes and shook her head.

"You have no idea," she told him. "He will argue just about any side of any argument until the sun comes up. He plays devil's advocate just for the sheer fun of it."

Damon motioned to Alina.

"She used to drive our instructor's crazy with the same thing," he agreed. Stephanie shook her head.

191

"They're impossible," she said, standing up.

Alina looked at John. His blue eyes were laughing and she smiled reluctantly. They had spent hours arguing for fun when they lived together. It was one of the very few things they had shared that Alina did not regret. Apparently, neither of them had changed very much in that regard.

Hawk stood up and caught the look that passed between Alina and John. His eyes narrowed at the familiarity and Damon frowned slightly. It was as if they were sharing something that happened long ago. That was part of Viper's life that he would never know, a part of her that was long gone.

Stephanie also caught the look that passed between John and Alina, and her eyes went straight to Damon's face. It was unreadable, but she would swear to it that he was annoyed. Picking up both her empty wine glasses, she turned to take them into the kitchen thoughtfully. There was clearly a significant relationship between Damon and her friend, and he seemed threatened by her past relationship with John. Stephanie could have told him that he had nothing to be threatened by, but she got the impression that he didn't even realize what he was feeling. In fact, Stephanie suspected that neither Damon nor Alina were prepared for the feelings that were obviously springing up between them. Stephanie hid a smile as she placed the glasses in the sink. If nothing else, this was turning out to be one enlightening evening.

"Alina, tomorrow morning I'm going to follow up on some leads at the office," Stephanie said, turning from the sink as the others moved into the dining room. "Why don't you meet me there for lunch? We'll compare notes."

Alina nodded.

"I can do that," she agreed.

"I should have a name for your third corpse in the morning," Damon said, setting his empty bottle on the bar.

Stephanie nodded.

"John's already had the remains of the fire moved to our forensics lab," she said.

Alina looked at John. He finished his beer and set the empty bottle next to Damon's.

"They're working through the night on it," he said, reaching for his jacket. "Matt promised me answers in the morning."

"Matt?" Alina repeated.

John nodded and pulled his keys from his pocket.

"Our forensics geek," he explained briefly. "Man's a wizard, but a little strange."

"He works in the basement," Stephanie retorted, putting on her jacket. "What do you expect?" she turned to Alina. "So tomorrow at 1. I take a late lunch," she told her.

Alina got the distinct impression that she was being given an order.

"Sounds good," Alina agreed calmly.

A few moments later, she and Damon were once again on the deck, watching as Stephanie and John got into the car to leave.

"You think she's a target," Damon stated as John started the car.

"I think she's in a dangerous position," Alina replied, watching as John turned the car around.

"I'm not sure telling them as much as you did is a good thing," Damon said thoughtfully as the car disappeared around the side of the house.

Alina turned to lean against the banister and look at him.

"It will put them on their guard," she pointed out. "And it will stop them from wasting time and effort on what we're doing," she added. Damon nodded slowly.

"Oh, that I agree with," he agreed. "It also explained my continued presence neatly. But how long before they question your involvement more closely?" he lowered his eyes to hers. "You're playing a very dangerous game, Viper."

"I can't have them become a casualty on my conscience," she said softly. "This is the only way I know to keep them safe."

"And who's going to keep *you* safe when they start to put two and two together and get four?" Damon demanded just

193

as softly. "Do you trust them that much? Do you trust them with your life?"

Alina stared at him. Did she? He was absolutely right. Once this was over and they had time to think, they would certainly realize that Alina was, herself, an assassin. They would be torn between their loyalty to old, past friendships and their commitment to the law. Of course, the plan was that she wouldn't be around when they finally realized that fact. But what if they worked it out sooner? Before this was over? *Did* she trust them with her life?

"Yes," Alina said suddenly with conviction.

Damon stared at her in silence, then nodded.

"Ok," he said. He lifted his hand to cup her cheek. "But God have mercy on them if you're wrong," he added harshly, his eyes becoming almost glacial, "because I won't."

Chapter Thirteen

Alina was in her command center by seven the next morning, hot coffee in hand. Damon had left directly after making that cryptic statement and she had gone in, reset the security system, and gone to bed with the strangest feeling of warmth in her soul. She couldn't remember the last time someone had been concerned for *her*. It had certainly been before she had even met Damon. But there had been no mistaking his sincerity. He had left her standing on the deck, bemused and speechless. And, when Alina laid her head on her pillow to sleep, a deep sense of comfort had lifted her into her dreams. She had been too tired to question it, and had allowed the feeling of being cherished to wash over her and carry her away.

When Viper woke a few hours later, her mind was sharpened by rest. She opened her eyes, and was hit suddenly with the clarity of thought that only comes upon first wakefulness. The memory that had been eluding her the previous night rose up before her clearly, as if she was back in time and experiencing it again.

Cairo!

Alina had sat up quickly with a gasp and Raven had peered down from his perch, disturbed by this sudden, uncharacteristic movement by his mistress. The man in the room behind Johann! She had spent two years focused on the identity of the well-known Westerner who had been meeting with Johann that day.

What she had forgotten was what she *heard*!

Viper knew the name of the man in the woods. She had known it all along. She heard it that day in Cairo, just before all hell broke loose.

Alina sipped her coffee and settled in front of her laptop. She was irritated with herself that she hadn't remembered it sooner, but there would be time enough to examine why she had disregarded her own memory later. She was now consumed with focus. Now was the time to work.

195

Now was the time to find out just who this Engineer was, and what she was up against.

Damon shut his laptop with a frown and got up restlessly. He went into his small kitchen to pour himself another cup of coffee and carried it back to the living room. His mind was racing, processing the information he just received from Harry. Harry had been digging around in the recesses of Washington and the minds of men who had been forgotten when the new regime took over. That untapped source of knowledge was endless, and Damon knew that Harry was just getting started. He stopped pacing in front of the balcony. The sun was coming up, bathing the outdoors in gray shifting light that, in less than an hour, would be dawn. Damon stared outside, sipping his coffee.

Hawk had been in Scotland when Harry first contacted him a few weeks ago. He and Harry had kept in touch fairly regularly over the years, so the contact hadn't been a surprise. Hawk always had the impression that Harry thought of both he and Viper as his protégées. They had both certainly learned more from him than from any of their other instructors. As any good mentor, Harry touched base occasionally with Hawk, and Damon had always just assumed that he did the same with Viper. However, when Harry suggested meeting in person this time, Damon had known something was wrong. Harry was going to be in Belgium for a few days at a summit. Damon had gone without any hesitation.

That meeting was why he was here now.

Damon watched the shadows on the balcony. Harry had been working for Homeland Security for over a year before he had stumbled across a situation. He became suspicious when he realized that some resources were being diverted. Upon investigation, he discovered that someone in the government was actually bringing a terrorist *into* the country. With no one else to trust, he turned to his best asset and Hawk agreed to help. Their information had been sketchy at best, but Damon took the reigns and told Harry to go back to Washington and let him take care of it. Harry had done so, promising to pass on any additional information as he found it. His new position in the government made things tricky, however, and Damon hadn't expected much. The information that he received since being in New Jersey had not been outstandingly helpful until now. Harry had certainly delivered this time. This latest intelligence confirmed Damon's suspicions and gave him the means to a name.

A name that Viper undoubtedly already knew.

Damon had all the pieces to the picture, except one. He turned away from the door impatiently and strode back to the laptop. Setting his coffee down, he flipped it open. There was only one place he could find out what he desperately needed to know now.

He had to go to Cairo.

John stared at Matt in disbelief. It was a little after eight in the morning and he had taken the elevator down to the basement, to the forensics lab. Computers and monitors lined one side of the large room, and mysterious-looking machines and big refrigerators were on the other side. Two long tables took up the center of the room, and on them was just about any device used for testing imaginable. Old-fashioned chemistry equipment jostled for space with state-of-the-art technology while music blared out from one of the computers. The master of all the chaos was dressed in wrinkled khakis and a lab coat. He had a widow's peak on his high forehead and his sandy colored hair always had a tuft sticking straight up at the back of his head. He was the genius of the building. All the agents deferred to his skill. If he said it was so, then science made it so, and there ended the conversation.

And right now, he had just finished telling John that the accelerant used in the explosion was made up of various chemical components that could only be found in one of two places. Both of those places were military bases inside the United States.

"That's impossible!" John exclaimed, staring at Matt. Matt pushed his glasses back up onto the bridge of his nose and shrugged.

"It's not impossible, John," he answered calmly. "It's fact. The traces of the compound left were actually quite good samples, considering the amount of burn-off everywhere else. They shouldn't have been left, really, but the pocket of air caused by the..."

"Yes, yes, I got all that the first time," John cut him off hastily. "But this bomb was set by a terrorist."

"Then it's a terrorist who has access to our military bases and their newest toy," Matt retorted. "What can I tell you? It's your job to find out the hows and whys. I just give you the whats. I'll put it all in a report and send it up to you today." Matt turned to go back to his computers. John frowned, turning to leave the lab. Matt's voice stopped him at the door.

"Oh! I almost forgot. I have something else for you." Matt turned around and went over to one of the tables, shuffling around in a mess of paper. John turned back and watched as Matt fished out a photo from under a pile of blown up images. "That picture you gave me a few days ago." John raised an eyebrow.

"The one of Angelo Cordeiro and Martin Sladecki?" he asked, walking over to Matt. Matt nodded.

"That's the one." He held it out to John and turned back to the other pictures. "It was taken in Avalon about 2 months ago, believe it or not." John's eyebrows soared into his hairline.

"It would have been freezing!" he exclaimed. Matt grinned.

"Yep!" he agreed.

They looked at the picture together. Both men and their wives were wearing short-sleeves with the ocean directly behind them. John looked at Matt.

"I don't get it," he said. Matt laughed.

"That's because you're not looking outside the box," he informed him. He picked up one of the blow-ups and handed it to John. "Look closer."

John frowned and looked at a blown-up version of the same picture. Both men were laughing, and their respective wives were smiling into the camera. The sun was shining on the beach and the waves were crashing onto the sand. John stared at the picture helplessly. Matt clucked his tongue and pointed to the waves.

"The beach is in the wrong spot," he explained. John wondered if Matt had inhaled too many fumes.

"I'm sorry?" he asked. Matt sighed.

"If they were standing *on* the beach, the waves would be directly behind them. If you look closely, they're slightly *below* them!" he told him. John's head snapped up. Matt nodded with a grin. "They aren't on the beach. They're standing in front of a glass wall in a *house* that is on the beach. Look." Matt pointed again. "You can just make out the reflection of the glass."

"Oh my God," John murmured.

"It gets better." Matt fished for another blown-up angle of the picture. "Obviously, there were other people there. Someone is taking the picture. But I thought this looked interesting." John had another photo shoved unceremoniously into his hand. Matt pointed to a shadow reflected in the corner of the picture. "So I tried to blow up just that portion. I didn't have much success on the shadow itself, but I did get *this*. It's a reflection from a mirror, I think, behind the shadow."

Matt handed him yet another picture. John stared at it, stunned. It was a grainy, blown up image of part of a face, reflected in a mirror. There was no doubt about the identity. The mark on the face was too distinctive. Matt nodded.

"It's that body you brought back with you last night," he said. "He was there too."

"That's damn good work, Matt," John said, looking up. His eyes had a light in them that Matt recognized. All the agents got that look when he gave them something they could use. Matt nodded complacently.

"I thought you'd like that," he agreed. John flashed him a grin and turned to leave, the pictures gathered in his hands.

"I owe you a drink!" he called over his shoulder. Matt snorted.

"You owe me a couple," he retorted.

But John didn't hear him. He was already gone.

Alina sat back and rubbed the back of her neck absently as she stared at the sketched image on the monitor of Dimitrius, also known as The Engineer. She had heard of him. They all had. He was notorious even before she had completed her first assignment. Alina never dreamed that her path would cross his. He was an Israeli ex-patriot, by all accounts. A mercenary for hire, if you had the money to pay him. No one knew much about him, only that he had deserted the Israeli special forces and gone into business for himself. Some people whispered that he was mad. Others said he was disillusioned. Yet others said he must be acting on religious zeal. Alina had read enough in the past three hours to draw the conclusion that it was probably a little of all three. She guessed that he was probably about five or ten years older than her and his experience was extensive. The rumors were that he never failed. Alina's eyes narrowed slightly.

He had never gone up against her.

She pushed her chair back and propped her feet on the counter, crossing her ankles and lowering her chin, deep in thought. She had been able to glean quite a bit of information from her various sources and Viper was confident that she had a pretty accurate picture of him. He charged exorbitant prices, even for their line of work, and it was paid without question. Alina realized now that her glimpse of him put her in a class of her own. She appeared to be the only one ever to have seen him. He was invisible, and the people who paid him seemed content to leave it that way.

Alina stared at a scuff on the tip of her boot. Not only had she seen him once, but she could have seen him a second time at the explosion. Now why was that? Was he getting careless? Or had he intended for her to see him? Alina was sure that he knew all about her and was baiting her. But to what end? She frowned. And why was he toying with Johann? He had clearly had numerous opportunities to get the job done. Why the games? She brooded on that thought for a moment. Damon's question popped into her mind.

"You think this is a game to him?"

Alina lifted her eyes from her feet as the truth slowly dawned on her.

"Of course," she breathed.

It *was* a game! He had turned the job into a game! Whether it was his coping mechanism or whether it was the result of a broken mind was immaterial. The fact was that he had never failed because none of his targets ever knew that they were in the middle of a carefully planned out *game*. Viper smiled slowly, lowering her feet to the floor.

She had always been rather good at games.

Damon let himself into Viper's house silently and paused to listen. The house was silent, but he knew she was here. He glanced around the living room and moved into the kitchen. He was just lifting his hand to the sauté pan when the island started sliding to the side. Damon dropped his arm and stepped back as Alina appeared in the opening, carrying an empty mug. Her dark hair was pulled back into a pony-tail and she was dressed in dark, khaki-colored SWAT pants and an olive green tank top. Her dark eyes met his as she stepped out of the stairwell.

"I'm not sure how I feel about you showing up in my kitchen unannounced," she murmured. Damon grinned.

"You knew I was coming before I ever got near the house," he retorted. "I was hardly unannounced."

Alina smiled and went to put the mug in the sink. She touched a button under the sink and the island slid noiselessly back into place.

"True," she agreed, turning from the sink to face him.

"Any luck yet?" he asked, leaning back against the island and crossing his arms.

Alina smiled slightly.

"Of course," she answered. Damon grinned.

"Are you going to share?" he asked.

Viper smiled back slowly. Her satisfaction was palatable and Damon couldn't stop the sudden rush of affection that he felt for her.

"It's The Engineer," she said softly. "Someone sent The Engineer after Johann."

The teasing smile was wiped off Damon's face and his eyes lost their twinkle.

"The man's a myth," Hawk said.

Nevertheless, his stomach lurched at her words and he felt a chill streak down his back. Alina shook her head.

"Oh, he's real enough," she answered. "He's Israeli...or used to be, and he gets paid an absolute fortune," she added, walking over to the refrigerator and pulling out a bottle of water. She held it up questioningly and Damon shook his head, his mind working furiously.

"If half of what I've heard is true, then I'm not surprised," he said, watching her as she twisted the lid off the bottle and took a sip.

Alina nudged the refrigerator door closed with her foot and went over to sit at the bar.

"Oh, I think it is," she said thoughtfully.

Damon stared at her for a moment, his heart pounding. The Engineer was a legend, and one that he had never really taken seriously. But if Viper said he was real and after Johann, then Damon had no doubt that she was right. He had never known her to be wrong.

He suddenly, desperately, wanted her to be wrong now.

"You don't seem very concerned," Damon remarked, realizing that she almost looked excited. She looked at him, faintly surprised.

"I'm sorry," she answered politely. "Should I be wringing my hands and saying, 'Oh what should I do?'" Damon moved to the bar and leaned forward until his face was level with hers and just inches away.

"This changes everything," he told her harshly. "If this guy is real, he isn't someone you can just dismiss."

"Oh, I'm not dismissing him," Alina replied softly. "I'm fully aware of what he is capable of and how dangerous he is. But I have an advantage. I know how to get to him."

Damon straightened up, raising his eyebrow. She had a plan. He stared at her for a minute before sighing, resigned.

"Do I want to know?" he asked. She grinned and shook her head.

"Probably not," Alina answered. "But suffice it to say that I am fairly confident that I have discovered the secret to The Engineer."

A look Damon remembered well from days long past crossed over her face and Hawk was slightly comforted. This was the Viper he knew, and he had complete faith in her. Blue eyes met brown in a brief look of understanding. There was nothing more to be said. He knew she would do her job. Viper didn't know how to fail.

"Well, if anyone could, it would be you," Damon said with a flash of a smile. He glanced at his watch and came around the bar to stand next to her. Alina looked up curiously from her perch on the stool. She took in the look on his face and her heart dropped. She had seen that look on his face before.

"You're leaving," she said flatly. Damon saw the flash of disappointment in her eyes before the emotion was effectively shielded and her gaze became unreadable.

"I'll be back in two days," he answered. He grinned. "By then you should have this all taken care of." Alina smiled.

"Perhaps," she replied.

She wanted to ask him where he was going, and why, but Alina had the feeling that Hawk would not be completely honest with her. Inexplicably, she suddenly didn't want to hear any lies from him.

"Well, don't go having all the fun yourself," Hawk murmured, looking down at her. He lifted his hand and touched her jaw gently. "I have to go confirm some information in person. I'll be as fast I can." Alina stared into his deep blue eyes. He was asking her to wait until he got back.

"I'll try," she agreed, surprising herself. Damon nodded slowly.

"That's all I can ask," he said softly.

Alina caught her breath as he lowered his head slowly toward hers. His eyes were mesmerizing, dark pools of blue, and the room seemed to melt away. All that existed was the faint scent of his body wash and the heat coming from his solid strength. Damon watched her lips part slightly and he turned his head to whisper in her ear.

"Be careful, Viper." He brushed his lips against her temple and straightened up, turning to leave.

Alina blinked, forcing the over-whelming feeling of disappointment away as she turned on the chair to watch him go. At the door, Hawk paused with his hand on the handle and turned to look at her. She was leaning back against the bar, watching him with dark, unreadable eyes.

He smiled slightly, lowered one eyelid in a slow, sexy wink, and was gone.

Alina moved along the crowded city street quickly. The city buildings rose imposingly above her to the left, blocking the sun and leaving the impression of a cement curtain. Traffic streamed by on her right, just inches from the curb, throwing up noise and exhaust and adding controlled chaos to the hectic lunchtime rush hour. She was on her way to meet Stephanie, and Alina frowned slightly as she moved past a group of men in suits that had stopped on the sidewalk, clustered around a smartphone. Ever since emerging from the parking garage a block away, the hair on the back of her neck had been crawling. Viper felt eyes watching her, but she couldn't see them. She knew she was being followed, could sense it, but couldn't detect anyone on the crowded city streets. Alina berated herself for the hundredth time for coming out into the open like this. She knew better than this, but she had allowed herself to agree to Stephanie's lunch demand. Now all her instincts were screaming at her. What had she been thinking?!

Alina glanced up at the street sign as she came to a stop at a crowded corner, waiting with a throng of people for the light to change. The crowd was a mix of office workers hurrying back from lunch and tourists trying to find their way through the city. Viper moved seamlessly into the center of the crowd, giving herself as much protection as possible. Stephanie's office building was on the next block, and she moved forward thankfully with the crowd as the light changed. She felt exposed out on the street and anxiety was beginning to gnaw at her control. Her heart rate increasing and her gut trembling deep inside her, Alina glanced around as she gained the pavement on the other side of the street. Half of her protective shield turned right and the other half continued straight, carrying Viper along with them. She still couldn't see anyone, but she knew he was out there.

Watching.

The FBI building took up half the block and, because this block was a no-parking zone, Alina didn't have the protection of parked cars along the street. She took a deep breath, flexing the fingers of her right hand. Her knife was nestled at her ankle, concealed by her heeled boots and black linen pants, and her .45 was under the matching loose jacket, but Viper was not comforted by their presence. Every instinct inside her was screaming to get out of the open and into a building. She watched Stephanie step out from glass doors ahead and forced herself to take another deep and steadying breath. She was almost there.

Stephanie looked both ways after stepping out of the building. Alina had called to tell her she was leaving the parking garage and to meet her out front because she didn't want to go into the building. Stephanie didn't blame her. It took forever just to get past the front desk, with all the security and metal detectors. Stephanie paused just short of the flow of human traffic and looked to her right. She saw Alina, a few feet away, dressed in a casual black linen suit. She smiled and turned towards her.

"Hi!" she exclaimed. "Thank God you're on time. I'm starving!" Stephanie informed her as Alina joined her. Alina smiled.

"Good," she replied, stepping out of the flow of people and into the concealing shadow of the alcove. "So am I! Where are we going?"

"A restaurant a few blocks from here," Steph answered. "They make a Cobb salad that's amazing." Alina nodded, glancing around. Her heart was still pounding and she just wanted to get moving.

"Which way?" she forced a big smile. Stephanie grinned and jerked her head in the direction that Alina had been heading.

"This way," she said, turning to the left.

A sudden commotion behind them made both women pause and Alina instinctively moved to protect Stephanie as she sensed someone running up behind them. In an instant, the premonition and unease were gone. Alina inhaled as she turned quickly and calmly to face the threat, placing one hand on the side of Stephanie's shoulder, ready to push her out of the path of whatever might be coming. The crowd on the sidewalk had shifted, making way for a figure in a beige trench coat and brown bowler hat, rushing through the crowd. Alina instantly registered the fact that the absurd figure was too short and slight to be The Engineer and her shoulders relaxed slightly. Then the figure stumbled suddenly, flying unceremoniously towards her. The ridiculous hat slipped to the side and Alina recognized Angela's face as her body came hurtling forward, her arms grasping at air. Surprise replaced the defensiveness as Alina quickly reached out to try to catch her friend.

Viper sensed, rather than heard, the shot.

It propelled Angela into her arms with more force than she had originally been traveling. She caught Angela with a gasp and her heart leapt into her throat as panic erupted on the sidewalk. The crowd of people around them instantly seemed to ebb away as someone screamed. Alina absorbed the noise of panic and commotion even as her mind reflexively tuned it out. Angela's face had a stunned look on it before her eyes slid shut and her body became a dead weight in Alina's arms.

Alina eased herself to the pavement quickly with Angela in her arms, face down across her lap. Her eyes shot up to the rooftops diagonal from them. Blood was starting to spread across Angela's back, and Viper followed the trajectory path with her eyes just in time to see the damning flash of sunlight against glass on a rooftop across the street, two blocks down.

Anger coursed through Viper, fury so strong that it almost blinded her. She sensed men running out of the building behind them and Stephanie yelling orders as she tried to keep the crowds back and away from Alina and her unconscious charge. Blood was flowing more rapidly now, soaking through the fabric of the coat, and Alina pulled her knife from her boot, using it to swiftly slice the back of the ridiculous trench coat open. The bowler hat was still hanging precariously on her head, concealing her face, and Alina tossed it aside impatiently.

"Oh my God! Angela!" Stephanie cried, dropping to her knees as Alina quickly ripped the coat apart, looking for the entry wound.

"Thank God," she breathed, locating the oozing crater in the center of Angela's right shoulder. She had a chance.

Alina looked up as Stephanie tore off her jacket. She grabbed it from her, folding it and pressing it into the wound. Motioning Stephanie closer, Alina gently eased Angela onto her lap. Then she took Stephanie's hands and pressed them down hard on the folded jacket.

"She's still breathing. Put all your weight on it," Viper instructed harshly, replacing her knife in her boot and jumping to her feet in one motion. Stephanie looked up at her, pressing her hands against Angela's shoulder blade, her face pale.

"Where are you going?" she demanded, taking in the blood on Alina's clothes and the grim look of fury on her face.

"Keep your phone on!" Alina replied evasively, turning and taking off into the crowd.

Stephanie watched her dart into the road and heard tires screeching and horns blaring as Alina ran through the traffic to the other side, where she disappeared into the crowd. Stephanie turned her attention back to Angela. Blood was already seeping through her jacket and onto her hands.

"Where are those medics?!" she yelled to one of the guards, fear making her voice sharper than she intended.

He lifted his hand-held radio and barked into it as the glass doors flew open behind him. John appeared, his tie blown over his shoulder from running.

"What the hell happened?!" he yelled, taking in the inanimate figure in Stephanie's lap and all the blood.

The distress on her face made him catch his breath, and his eyes went back to the body almost fearfully. Stephanie saw the sudden look of horror and apprehension and understood instantly what he was thinking.

"It's not her!" she said quickly. "It's not Lina."

"You were meeting her for lunch," John spoke as if he hadn't heard her, unable to tear his eyes away from the blood soaking through the jacket under Stephanie's hands. Sirens sounded in the distance, loud and insistent.

"Yes, and this *isn't Lina!*" Stephanie's voice broke through the haze in his ears. "This is Angela." John stared at Stephanie.

"Where's..." he began, but Stephanie cut him off as an ambulance came careening around the corner.

"That way." Stephanie motioned with her head. "GO!" She yelled when he hesitated.

John pushed through the crowds that were growing around the two women, breaking into the street as the ambulance lurched to a stop. Using the momentary pause in traffic to run across to the other side, he reached the sidewalk and glanced back to see medics running up to Stephanie and Angela. John paused and looked around helplessly. Where was he supposed to go? Where had she gone?

His heart pounding, John forced himself to stop and focus. He looked back at the front of his building and pictured Stephanie with a body in her lap, covered in blood. *A body face down.* His head snapped around and he started running along the sidewalk, looking up at the rooftops. He crossed a side road and slowed down, glancing back again to the crowd in front of his building, and then up again. He started running again to the next block, glancing back once more. Slowing down, he looked up again before darting into the building a few feet away.

John labored up the multiple flights of stairs in the stairwell, headed for the roof. By the time he reached halfway, he was gasping for air. Pushing to keep going, he fought through the screaming objections of his respiratory system. He had no idea what he would find on the roof, if anything, but John knew that he had to get up there as quickly as possible. An invisible force was pushing him upward and a few minutes later, he erupted onto the roof, his gun in his hands.

The sun was shining brightly above the city and a fierce wind whipped across the roof. John blinked in the sudden glare of light, shielding his eyes with one hand as he glanced around. A lone figure was standing at the front of the building, looking out over the edge, toward the FBI building down the street. John glanced around the rest of the roof before turning his attention back to the still figure.

"Lina?" he called breathlessly. Alina turned her head to glance back at him, her eyes dropping to the gun.

"You can put that away," she called back. "He's long gone." John holstered his weapon and walked forward to stand beside her, breathing heavily.

Alina had her hands clenched at her sides, tension making her shoulders tight. She had just missed the bastard. When she came onto the roof, she caught a glimpse of him as he disappeared over the edge of the back of the building. By the time she reached the edge, The Engineer had vanished.

"He?" John asked, joining her.

He followed her gaze and watched as the ambulance came to life. They were too high up and too far away to hear the siren, but he watched as the lights came alive and the emergency vehicle slowly eased into the traffic.

"The sniper that shot Angela."

Alina's voice was void of emotion and John glanced at her. The wind whipped her hair back from her head as she watched the ambulance, her face impassive. He knew she had to be feeling something, yet she looked as if she were simply discussing the weather. Her shirt was covered in blood, and there were smears on her jaw and her hands. John wondered if she was even aware of the blood.

"Why would a sniper shoot Angela?" John asked, looking back over the roof. "And why here?"

"He wasn't trying to hit Angela."

The statement hung heavily in the air. John looked at Alina and watched as she turned away from the edge of the building tiredly. The ambulance had turned the corner and disappeared. She brushed her hair out of her eyes.

"She tripped and got in the way," Alina added as she ran her eyes over the roof, knowing she wouldn't find anything left behind, but looking anyway out of habit.

"So who was he aiming for?" John demanded. Viper's cold brown eyes looked at him and he suddenly understood. "Stephanie," he said shortly. Alina glanced back the street and nodded.

"He was waiting for her," she said, almost to herself. "Angela got in the way." Alina paused, frowning, and turned back to the roof edge.

"What is it?" John asked, watching as she moved forward slowly and crouched down near the edge.

"Why did he miss?" Alina asked. John stood behind her.

"You said it yourself," he answered. "He was aiming for Stephanie and Angela tripped and got in the way."

Alina stared down the street at the FBI building. The flags in front of the building were barely moving, yet the wind up here was whipping her hair around her face. She continued to frown. He wouldn't have made such a stupid mistake and miscalculated the wind. No. The Engineer had missed Stephanie by a good three feet. Why?

"I wouldn't have missed," Viper murmured softly, still staring at the front of the building.

"What are you thinking?" John prompted, staring down at the back of her head. He hadn't heard her soft whisper and Alina didn't answer for a long time. She finally stood up slowly and when she turned to face John, he found himself staring at a stranger. This cold-eyed and methodical woman was someone he had never seen before.

"I want to know why he missed," Alina repeated. "That was a straight shot."

"Maybe the sun..." John looked over her shoulder down the street, his voice trailing off. Alina was already shaking her head.

"This man is an ex-military, Israeli-trained assassin," she told him. "They don't miss." John looked at her, his eyes slightly narrowed.

"How do you know he's Israeli-trained?" he asked sharply.

"I know who he is," Alina answered, moving around him and starting to head toward the stairwell door. John reached out and grabbed her arm.

"Wait," he said. Alina stopped and looked at him, "How do you know?"

"I..." Alina sighed. "He's known as The Engineer. I found out this morning," she added before John could ask. "I was going to warn Stephanie at lunch."

"You and Damon *have* been busy," John remarked. "He was at our office this morning. He had the name of our corpse, and he seemed to think that you would have the name of the bomber by nightfall." Alina's lips curved slightly.

"We don't waste time," she answered softly.

"Your resources seem to be extensive," John said, watching her. Alina met his gaze.

"They are," she answered shortly. "And don't look any further than that," she advised. John grinned.

"I doubt I would get very far, even if I did," he retorted. That made her smile, but the smile didn't quite reach her eyes.

"Not likely, no," Alina agreed.

"Damon asked me to keep an eye on you. He seemed to think you might need it," John told her, his voice low. "Why?" Alina stared at him for a minute before gently pulling her arm away from him.

"You take care of your partner," she said quietly. "She needs you more than I do."

"Damon didn't seem to think so," John replied. Alina raised an eyebrow and turned away toward the stairwell again.

"He didn't know she was going to become a target," she tossed over her shoulder.

John pressed his lips together and glanced back at the roof edge before following her thoughtfully.

Chapter Fourteen

Stephanie looked up from where she was ensconced in a chair in the corner of the hospital room, her eyes going straight to the monitors next to the bed. The figure in the bed had stirred. She set aside her laptop and stood, stretching her arms above her head. The sun was setting outside and the gathering gloom was starting to penetrate the room through the double glazed windows. She walked over to the side of the bed and looked down at Angela. She was still sleeping, her face void of any color and her long lashes resting on her cheeks. Stephanie turned away from the bed and switched on the lamp on the bedside table. She went to the window and pulled the heavy, serviceable rust-colored curtains closed and then returned to her chair.

Angela had been rushed straight into surgery when they arrived in the ER. Stephanie waited for three hours in the waiting room until the doctor finally came and told her that Angela had been moved to a private room in the critical care unit. The bullet had gone straight through her shoulder, surprisingly doing minimal damage. It shattered the scapula and grazed a rib before exiting cleanly through the front, above her right breast. None of the bone fragments had pierced her lungs, and the nerve damage appeared to be minimal. The doctor said frankly that it was a miracle the bullet hadn't taken a more destructive path. He warned that the risk of infection was the biggest concern right now and left her, still shaking his head in amazement.

Stephanie stared unseeingly at the bed. John stopped by earlier, bringing the news that their agents were canvassing the neighborhood. So far, they had found nothing to lead them to the shooter. That had been over two hours ago. She hadn't heard from Alina at all. Stephanie had kept her phone on, waiting for a phone call, but none had come. Where was she? Was she safe? Angela had clearly tripped and gotten in the way of the bullet. John said Alina believed the shooter had been shooting at her. But why?

"Miss. Walker?" the agent posted outside the room stuck his head around the corner of the door. Bill was one of the older, more seasoned agents. Recuperating from an injury that had forced him onto desk duty, he had jumped at the babysitting job just to get out of the office.

"Yes?" Stephanie came back from her thoughts with a jolt.

"I'm just going down to the cafeteria for some coffee," he told her. "Would you like some?" Stephanie shuddered.

"No thank you," she replied. "And if I were you, I would stay away from it. I had some earlier. I don't know what it is, but it is *not* coffee." Bill grinned.

"Right. Maybe I'll get a soda," he said before disappearing.

Stephanie knew that Bill was only here to get out and about again, but she was grateful for his presence. Until she had a better idea of what was going on, an agent was going to be outside that door at all times. Stephanie would rather it was a seasoned and mature one, rather than one of the young hotshots who thought they were above sentry duty. The figure under the covers moved again restlessly, pulling Stephanie's attention back to the bed. She got up and went over to it, adjusting the covers. Angela still slept, but it was a restless sleep. The drugs were wearing off.

"Looks like she'll be coming around soon."

Stephanie jumped and swung around, her heart pounding. Alina was standing directly behind her, looking over her shoulder at Angela. She was holding a brown paper bag with suspicious grease stains on the side in one hand and a carrier with two large soda cups in the other. Stephanie hadn't heard a sound.

"What....where did you come from?" Stephanie stuttered, embarrassed at her surprise. Alina's dark eyes moved from Angela to Stephanie's face and she smiled slightly.

"Pat's," she answered, holding up the bag. "It's not Cobb salad, but you did promise me a cheesesteak."

Stephanie let out a short laugh and reached out to take the bag. The smell of cheesesteak and fried onions wafted through the air and she was suddenly ravenous.

"I haven't even thought of food!" she exclaimed. Alina went over to the table and moved the laptop, setting the sodas on the table.

"I figured as much," she replied, pulling the second chair over from the other side of the room.

Stephanie pulled out the two sandwiches, wrapped in their white-gray hoagie paper, and dropped into her chair. Alina set her chair with the back against the wall, facing the bed, and sat down on the other side of the table. She unwrapped the steak sandwich that Stephanie handed her.

"Have you spoken to John?" Alina asked.

"Yes," Stephanie mumbled, her mouth already full. "And where have you been?"

"Busy."

Alina took a big bite of Amoroso roll filled with paper-thin steak slices, melted American cheese, and fried onions. Both women were silent for a moment, one enjoying her first taste of Philly in ten years and the other wondering how long it would be before she got a straight answer.

Alina chewed slowly, her eyes on the bed and the restless figure there. Her fury was gone and in its place was nagging guilt. She should have taken Angela more seriously. If she had...Alina stopped the thought even as it formed. If Angela hadn't been there to block the shot, Stephanie would be dead. Neither one was a situation that should have arisen at all. Viper had brought the Engineer into the lives of her old friends, albeit unknowingly. Now she had to be the one to protect them. Alina only knew one way of doing that.

"What's the verdict from the doctor?" she asked, poking a straw into one of the sodas. Stephanie wiped grease off her mouth with a napkin.

"He said she was extremely lucky," she told her. "The bullet went straight through her shoulder. Her scapula is shattered, but none of the bone fragments ended up in her lungs, which he seems to think is a miracle."

"Nerve damage?" Alina asked.

"He thinks it's minimal. He's more concerned with infection right now," Stephanie answered, sitting back in her chair and sipping the other soda. "Once she's out of risk of infection, they'll go in and see more. But right now, it looks like months of reconstruction and pain, but nothing more than that."

"Thank God," Alina breathed, picking up the sandwich again.

"The bullet grazed her ribs and then exited out the front," Stephanie continued. "Knowing Angie, I'm sure she'll have something to say about the scar that will be right above her breast," she added thoughtfully. Alina grinned despite herself.

"She can get a tattoo around it. It'll be hot," she said. Stephanie was surprised into a snort of laughter.

"Can you imagine?" she demanded, picking up her sandwich again. Alina was silent for a moment.

"Did you find the bullet?" she asked casually after a moment. Stephanie shook her head.

"No," she replied. "John has just about torn up the sidewalk," she added, glancing at Alina. She was staring at the bed thoughtfully. "Any ideas?" Stephanie prompted after a moment. Alina shook her head.

"It has to be somewhere," she replied. "When it turns up, let me know," she added. Stephanie nodded and they fell silent again. The figure in the bed stirred restlessly again.

"You haven't been home to change," Alina said suddenly. "I'll stay here if you want to go get a change of clothes."

Stephanie looked at her. Alina was still wearing the linen pants, but her blood-soaked white shirt had been exchanged for a black tank top, and the linen jacket for a light-weight, black windbreaker.

"John is bringing me the change of clothes from my desk drawer," Stephanie answered. "I always keep a bag there. But thanks."

Alina nodded, sitting back in the chair. The sandwich was gone and her stomach was full.

"Do I smell...cheesesteak?"

Angela's voice croaked suddenly from the bed. Alina was out of the chair and next to the bed instantly. Angie's green eyes were open and she was staring up at her groggily. Stephanie went to the other side of the bed.

"You're awake," she stated the obvious, checking the monitors. Angie turned her head to look at her.

"And you're eating cheesesteak," she retorted.

Alina felt relief wash through her at the disgruntled tone in Angie's voice. She was going to be just fine.

"How do you feel?" Alina asked, glancing at the monitors.

"Like I've been hit by a truck," Angela answered. "What happened?"

"You got hit by a bullet," Stephanie told her. "It went through your shoulder."

"Who shot me?" Angela asked, looking from one to another. "Why? What the hell?!"

"I'll go get the nurse," Stephanie said, glancing across the bed at Alina. Alina nodded and Stephanie left the room, leaving Alina to explain as much, or as little, as she saw fit. Angela stared at her, waiting. Alina shrugged.

"Someone was aiming at Stephanie and you tripped and got in the way," she told her flatly. "What were you *doing* there?"

"I don't know," Angela said slowly with a frown. "I remember seeing you turn around to catch me when I tripped, then that's all I remember."

"That's when you got shot." Alina twitched the blankets to straighten them out. "Were you following me again?"

"No." Angela yawned widely. "I told you I wouldn't. I was going to follow Stephanie, but then you showed up, so I thought I'd join you both."

Angela looked up at Alina, her green eyes the only color in her face. Alina stared down at her, fighting the sense of ridiculous laughter that was threatening her composure.

"You were dressed in a trench coat," she pointed out, her lips twitching. Angie started to shrug, then her eyes widened in pain and she groaned. Alina reached out and gently touched her left shoulder. "It's your right shoulder. It's shattered," she said quietly. "The pain meds are only going to do so much, so don't move it."

Angie nodded, unable to speak yet and closed her eyes. Alina watched her patiently, waiting for the pain to pass. After a moment, Angela opened her eyes again.

"The trench coat was my disguise," she said breathlessly. "Everyone always wears a trench coat in the movies."

"And a bowler hat?" Alina grinned. Angela looked disgruntled again.

"It was the only hat I could find that matched the coat," she replied.

"Of course it was," Alina agreed with a sigh. She fought back the laughter that was threatening again. "How long have you been following Stephanie?"

"Today was my first day," Angie answered. "I'm not very good at it, am I?" Alina grinned.

"No," she answered bluntly.

"Why was someone trying to shoot Stephanie?" Angie asked.

"Because of the case she's working on," Alina answered promptly. "Now, I want you to promise me something before she comes back with the nurse," she added urgently. Angela smiled slightly, her face drawn and tired.

"If I can remember it," she agreed.

"There is an agent on duty outside this room, and there will be for a while. It will be the same two agents, rotating shifts," Alina told her, leaning down so that Angela could hear her lowered voice. "I want you to tell me if anything changes, anything at all. If the agent on duty even looks funny one day, I want to know about it. If a new nurse walks by, I want to know about it. Understand?"

"Ok," Angela agreed, unusually serious. Alina nodded.

"My phone is always on. Just text me if anything changes," she said, straightening up as Stephanie came back into the room with a nurse bustling behind her.

"Awake now, are we?" the nurse said cheerfully. "Are you feeling any pain?"

"Yes," Angela answered miserably.

Alina moved away from the bed unobtrusively, watching as the nurse adjusted the IV and checked the monitors. Stephanie joined her at the table.

"Did you tell her?" she asked in a low voice.

"Not everything," Alina answered, gathering the hoagie papers and stuffing them into the brown paper bag again. "All she knows is that someone was aiming for you and got her."

"Shouldn't we tell her?" Stephanie asked. Alina glanced up.

"To what purpose?" she asked. "All she'll do is worry."

Alina picked up the bag of trash and her soda. Stephanie opened her mouth to say something, but Alina stopped her with her next comment.

"Besides, once I find him, it will be a moot point," she stated matter-of-factly.

Alina flipped on the light in her bedroom, walking over to sink onto the edge of the bed tiredly. She had thoroughly canvassed the area around her house and the security system was on. If anything over five feet tall breached the new perimeter, she would know about it.

Rubbing her neck, she kicked off her boots. She had left the hospital immediately after her cryptic comment to Stephanie, aware that she had said too much. Stephanie's eyes had narrowed and Alina had the uneasy feeling that her old friend was starting to put two and two together a lot faster than Alina had expected. She passed John in the hall, coming

219

from the elevators with a duffel bag in his hand. He looked like he wanted to talk, but Alina had stopped him by telling him that Angela was awake. He had nodded and continued on to the room while Alina left quickly. She pulled into the driveway a little before ten, exhausted and irritable. One word kept coming through the haze of confusion in her mind: Why.

Why Stephanie? Why not John? Why now? Why somewhere so public? Why had he missed? Why was he risking his game by adding new targets? *Why?*

Alina got up and padded into the bathroom, switching on the overhead fluorescent light. She stared at her reflection in the mirror and a pale face with dark rings under her eyes stared back. Discarding her jacket, she pulled her .45 out of her back holster and set it on the vanity. The holster joined it and Alina dropped her eyes to the soft square bulge at her side under her tank top. She looked at the water glass on the vanity next to the sink.

An elongated lump of metal with a flattened nose lay unobtrusively inside.

She supposed she would have to pass the bullet on to Stephanie, but she wanted to run ballistics on it first to find out what fired it. Alina looked back at her reflection and took a deep breath, lifting the bottom of the tank and gingerly pulling it over her head. The top came away from the gauze bandage on her side with reluctance and Alina saw what she already knew: she was seeping. She dropped the tank top onto the floor with her jacket and stared at the discolored gauze bandage in the mirror.

She hadn't realized the bullet had lodged in her side until after she left John on the roof and was heading back to the car. The anger and adrenaline had blocked the pain, and they had all assumed the blood on her shirt was Angela's. Once in the car, Alina pressed on the numbing stiffness on her side and the resulting pain made her gasp. By the time she reached the house, she was light-headed and woozy from loss of blood.

Alina sighed now and reached for the bottle of brandy that was still on the counter. She drank some earlier before sitting on the side of the bathtub and digging the bullet out of the flesh in her side. After getting the bullet out, she had poured hydrogen peroxide on the wound, covered it with a gauze bandage, and left the house again. Now, Alina poured some brandy into the glass she had left next to the bottle and sipped it, letting the heat burn a path down to her belly while she stared at the bullet thoughtfully. It was a 45mm round and she was lucky that it had decreased in velocity enough not to have gone straight through.

Setting the glass down, she slowly pulled the bandage away from the wound. The hole had partially closed up, but was still seeping. Alina dropped the bandage in the sink and opened up the cabinet to pull out a fresh one. After gently cleaning the wound with hydrogen peroxide again and wiping away the dried blood, she covered the hole again with a folded gauze bandage. She covered that with a larger bandage, expertly taping it down. She had just finished cleaning up when her cell phone rang.

"Yes?" she answered.

"What happened?" Damon's voice sounded in her ear, deep and masculine, with a lot of noise in the background. Alina raised her eyebrow, ignoring the sudden thump as her heart skipped a beat at the sound of his voice.

"What makes you think something happened?" she asked.

"Stephanie left a message on my phone," he replied. Alina rolled her eyes.

"The Engineer took a shot at Stephanie," she told him, sinking down on the side of of the tub. "He missed and hit Angela." There was a brief silence.

"And you?" Damon asked. Alina looked at her pale face in the mirror.

"I'm fine," she answered.

"Where is he now?" Hawk demanded. Alina was starting to make out the noises in the background. He was at an airport.

"I don't know," Alina admitted. "But I'll find him."
There was another short silence.

"I don't suppose you'll consider waiting until I get back
now?" Damon asked. Alina's eyes narrowed slightly and
irrational irritation washed over her.

"And why would I do that?" she asked softly. Even over
the phone, her voice sounded a little dangerous.

"Two guns are better than one," Damon retorted
shortly.

"I wasn't trained to work in pairs," Alina shot back.
"Neither were you," she added as an after-thought.

"Why so defensive?" Damon demanded.

"You're implying I can't handle the situation," Alina
answered, irritation propelling her off the side of the tub and
into the bedroom. She stalked downstairs restlessly, aware
that her pain was making her unreasonable but unable to
prevent it.

"I don't think you can't handle it," he replied. "I would
just be happier if I were there..."

"To keep an eye on things?" Alina finished for him,
reaching the first floor and heading to the kitchen. The
resulting silence was damning. A fresh wave of irritation
washed over her. "Wow. That may be the first time you've
insulted me."

"I'm not insulting you," Damon snapped. "You were
buried in the wilderness for two years..."

He stopped suddenly, as if realizing that he was making
things worse. Alina gasped and the irritation turned to anger.

"So I'm naturally a little rusty," she agreed, her voice
almost pleasant. There was a loud sigh in her ear.

"You're putting words in my mouth," Damon muttered.

"No, dear. You're doing that all by yourself," Alina
retorted, the anger making its way into her voice. She
slammed the sauté pan down onto the island and stepped
back as the island slid to the side.

"I haven't slept in thirty-eight hours. Give me a break,"
he said. Alina grabbed a bottle of water out of the fridge and
started down the steps to her lair.

"Don't tell me you're getting soft on me, Hawk," she answered silkily. "We used to go days without sleep."

"That was five years ago," Hawk muttered. Alina dropped into the chair in front of her laptop. "Sleep is the best weapon we have."

"Age must be catching up with you," Alina retorted. There was a short silence.

"Are you done with your temper tantrum?" Hawk finally asked. "Can we get back to business?" Alina inhaled sharply through her nose and clenched her back teeth.

"You can certainly get back to whatever it is that *you're* doing. I have to look up the instruction manual for my rifle. I'm not sure I remember how to clean it properly," she said waspishly.

"Now you're being ridiculous," Hawk informed her. "That's not what I meant and you know it."

"Well, you know, I haven't slept in a while and..." Alina broke off, a sudden thought breaking through her anger.

"Cute. Are you done yet?" Damon asked politely.

"That's it!" Alina ignored his sarcasm. "That's why he missed!"

"Excuse me?"

"The Engineer! He missed a clear shot." Alina balanced the phone between her shoulder and ear and started typing on her laptop.

"I thought Angela got in the way." Damon's voice was muffled for a moment and then the noise around him disappeared as a car door slammed.

"She did," Alina answered. "But it was still a clear shot. I wouldn't have missed....even after two years in the wilderness," she added.

"So you think he missed because he hasn't *slept?*" Damon asked. "That's weak, even for you." Alina grinned at his belated shot back, her anger forgotten as her mind tackled this new idea.

"That's exactly what I think," she replied. "I think something upset his game plan and he's being forced to improvise, but he's not very good at that. He's been forced out into the open and that makes my job that much easier."

"And this has to do with sleep how?" Damon punctuated his question with a yawn.

"You said it yourself," Alina replied. "Sleep is our best weapon. It keeps us sharp. He was anything but sharp today."

"That could be for a hundred different reasons," Damon pointed out. "But I do agree that something has pulled him out into the open and forced him to move up his game plan," he added thoughtfully.

"When I find out what that is, I'll find him," Alina agreed. There was another short silence on the phone.

"I don't like the way this is all heading. It's getting messy," Hawk finally said. Alina thought briefly of Angela, Stephanie and John and sighed.

"This was messy before I ever got here," she replied.

"Just be careful," Hawk said. Alina shifted slightly in her chair and allowed herself the luxury of grimacing at the pain in her side.

"I'm always careful," she retorted. "I've taken every precaution possible. I even increased my security perimeter."

"I meant cleaning your gun."

Damon disconnected after that outrageous remark, leaving Alina torn between laughter and outrage.

Chapter Fifteen

Stephanie came awake with a start and sat up, disoriented. The room was dark and the only sound came from the hum of a refrigerator in the kitchen behind her. The fog of sleep cleared from her head and she began to recognize the shape of the coffee table and the flat screen TV on the wall. She was in John's living room, on his couch, buried under one of his spare quilts.

Awareness came back in a flood. John refused to let her go home to her own apartment and, after a lengthy argument in the elevator of the hospital, she had finally agreed to go home with him. The clincher had been when he threatened to call their boss and have her placed in protective custody. She had absolutely no doubt that that would have happened.

Rubbing her eyes, Stephanie swung her legs off the couch with a wide yawn. She wasn't sure what had jogged her out of her sleep, but she was awake now. A flashing red light caught her attention through the darkness and Stephanie yawned again as she stood up and padded over to her smartphone. The message light was blinking silently and she unplugged the phone from its charger, taking it back to the couch. Settling down again, she scrolled through the emails until one caught her attention. It was from Shannon Gleason, her friend in Homeland Security.

Hi Stephanie,

I looked into that issue you asked me about. Funny thing about that. I hit a brick wall. My clearance is pretty substantial, but it only went so far. I did find out that a Damon Peterson does work with the agency, but I was unable to find any additional information. In fact, the whole thing is a little weird. No one has ever heard of him, but there is a trail of employment. It's almost like he's a ghost. It doesn't necessarily mean much. There are a lot of agents that are clandestine, to say the least. I'll try to find out more. I have to be careful though. I think someone has tagged my access and is monitoring my system usage. I'm sending this from my secure home laptop. Be careful. I don't know what's going on up there, but it doesn't smell right.

    SG

Stephanie frowned. She had known Shannon since they were in college together. She was the most laid back person that Stephanie had ever met. She used to say that her blood pressure had to be just one point above comatose. For Shannon to voice concern, something had to have happened to *cause* her concern.

Stephanie dropped her phone onto the coffee table and sat back on the couch, thinking. When she called Shannon earlier in the week to have her poke around and see what she could find out, she thought it would be a straight-forward yes or no answer. After all, Damon Peterson either worked for DHS or he didn't. Now it looked like it wasn't that easy. Stephanie didn't really know *why* she had asked Shannon to look into Damon's past, except that something just didn't feel right with him. He didn't have the "establishment" feel. Neither did Alina, but Alina wasn't claiming to be part of it. Stephanie trusted Alina, but she didn't know what to think about Damon.

She got up restlessly and went into the kitchen, flipping on the light. A brief inspection of the fridge revealed nothing much more than beer, ketchup, pickles, and some suspicious looking cold-cuts. Stephanie grimaced and pulled a bottle of beer out of the case lodged on the bottom shelf, letting the door swing closed. She hunted through the drawers in the kitchen until she found a bottle opener and popped the cap off. Her mind went back to Damon as she leaned against the counter and sipped the beer. He and Alina clearly knew each other well, but Stephanie had a gut feeling that they weren't used to working together. She had learned not to ignore her gut. It usually knew more than she did.

She drank some more beer, staring at the wall absently. If Damon and Alina weren't used to working together, then it was plausible that he *did* work for the agency and she did not. But each time Stephanie thought about Damon as an agency employee, something made her pause. She couldn't put her finger on it, but something made her sure that he was not. Alina clearly trusted him. Could her trust be misplaced? Stephanie drank some more.

What if Alina was wrong?

Stephanie sighed impatiently and carried her beer back into the living room, switching off the kitchen light. This was ridiculous. She had a terrorist running around planning God only knew what, bodies popping up left and right, an assassin slinking around and taking pot-shots at her, an old friend who was clearly not what she was supposed to be, and a suspicious hunk of gorgeousness that seemed to be looking over *everyone's* shoulder. Stephanie sank back onto the couch. *Assassins, terrorists, the Jersey mob...You really can't make this stuff up*, she thought tiredly. This was the stuff of movies. It didn't happen in real life.

Looking around John's living room, Stephanie wondered how she ended up here. A week ago, her biggest problem had been whether or not to take a vacation at the end of the month or wait until next month. Now, she had an assassin trying to put a hole in her head and a terrorist slinking around up to no good. Stephanie frowned again. She would call Shannon in the morning and find out what she knew and what was going on down there. Maybe she would be able to shed some light on this mess.

Alina watched as a black Lincoln town car slid out of the driveway and turned to roll down the road. That was the last one. She glanced at her watch with a yawn and started her engine. It was almost eight in the morning and she was parked in the trees outside the wooded driveway of Frankie Solitto's Bucks County house. Arriving to find that Frankie had company already, Alina had gone back to her SUV, waiting until the last of the visitors left. Once the last town car disappeared from view, she pulled out of the trees, rolling up to the driveway and turning in. She approached the gate, rolling her window down as one of Solitto's large guards walked up to the SUV. The man looked like a bull terrier in six foot human form.

"Tell Frankie that one of his visitors from the other night would like a word," she told him shortly.

He stared at her for a beat. She was wearing large sunglasses, which effectively concealed most of her upper face, and she made no move to remove them. He looked into the SUV, examined her for another minute, and then stepped back.

"Wait here," he said shortly.

Alina nodded once and rolled the window up again. She waited patiently as he disappeared into a little hut off to the side of the driveway and picked up the phone. Her eyes wandered to the wall and the gate in front of her. A camera was trained on her vehicle and she could see another guard inside the gate. A minute later, the bull terrier was back.

"He'll see you. I gotta check you before you go in," he told her, motioning her out of the car.

Alina sighed imperceptibly and got out of the SUV so he could run his wand over her. When he was finished and nothing beeped, he set it on top of the hood and reached out to pat her down. He never laid a finger on her. Before the bull terrier had any idea what was happening, he was face down on the ground with a boot on the back of his neck.

"Nice try," Alina said softly. "You can open the gate now." He gurgled as he tried to talk and Alina lifted the pressure on the back of his neck just slightly.

"You bitch!" he gasped out hoarsely.

Alina clucked her tongue and dropped the pressure back onto the back of his neck, effectively cutting off his oxygen and forcing his face into the grass again.

"That wasn't very nice," she told him.

Viper looked directly at the camera mounted on the gate and waited. After a minute, the gate swung open ponderously. Once it had opened, she removed her boot and lifted the wand off her hood, dropping it on the ground next to the gasping man. Without a backward glance, she got back into the SUV and put it in gear, rolling forward through the gate and into the stone courtyard.

Frankie Solitto's compound was much more impressive in daylight. The courtyard was paved in the same gray stone that comprised the six foot stone wall that circled the property, and it was lined with flower beds that, in the summer, would explode with color. A large fountain in the center propelled water high into the air, and two huge urns held matching fig trees on either side of the entryway. The old-world style house itself was clay and stone, and looked like it had been imported, whole, straight from Italy.

As she rolled to a stop, Frankie stepped out of the entryway and watched her get out of the vehicle. The guard she had noticed from outside the gate stood off to the side, his hand on a rifle, watching. Two large dogs came bounding around the side of the house toward her, and Frankie watched as his guard dogs rushed up to her, tails wagging and tongues out. Alina never took her eyes from the tall man as she walked toward him, beeping her car locked behind her. The dogs ran circles around her, barking cheerfully in greeting, and Frankie looked stunned at the behavior of his dogs.

"Those are supposed to be fearsome guard dogs," Frankie said as she walked up to him. "I've never seen them act like this."

"I have that effect on animals. It's not the dogs fault," Alina answered. She stopped in front of him and held out her hand. "Thank you for seeing me."

"You've got some guts," Frankie retorted, shaking her hand and turning to motion her into the house. Alina stepped into the cool hallway and removed her sunglasses.

"It wasn't my idea to visit the other night," she told him, turning to face him. Her dark brown eyes met his and she smiled. "I apologize for that intrusion."

"He's not with you?" Frankie asked after studying her in silence for a moment.

Sweeping out his arm, he directed her into a sunny room off to the left. It was a parlor of sorts, bright and warm with plants and chairs and little nick-knacks on side tables. Alina took it in at a glance before turning to face Frankie.

"No. He's out of the country on business," she answered. Frankie smiled slightly.

"Shame. I liked him," he said. He motioned for her to seat herself on one of the chairs and he took the one opposite. "You remind me of him. To what do I owe the honor of *your* visit?"

"I think you have some information that I need," Alina said calmly, crossing her legs. Frankie's smile grew.

"Is that so?"

"Yes." Alina regarded him steadily. "You know who took out Sladecki," she told him. Frankie raised his eyebrow.

"I do?" he asked.

"You do," Alina answered. "But you didn't want to tell my friend. That's OK. You take care of your own. I get that." Frankie sat back and looked at her.

"You're from Jersey," he stated. Alina smiled slightly.

"I know you've been working with the Philly family to find the person who took out Martin," she continued, ignoring the interruption. "Under normal circumstances, I would be perfectly happy to let you handle this in your own...unique way."

"Would you now?" Frankie came close to a grin.

"I would," Alina agreed, her eyes glinting for a brief moment. "But these aren't normal circumstances. I really need you to turn it over to me now."

"Just like that," Frankie said. Alina nodded calmly.

"Just like that," she agreed.

There was a stunned moment of silence as Frankie struggled between laughter and insulted anger. Alina waited patiently. He took in her serious face and dark, emotionless eyes.

"You're serious, aren't you?" Frankie finally exclaimed. Alina didn't bother to answer. "You're really walking into my house, telling me that you're going to take over MY business." Alina shook her head.

"No," she disagreed gently. "I am saying that it would be in your best interest to tell me what you know, and let me take care of it for you."

"And why would you be wanting to do that?" Frankie demanded, all traces of amusement gone from his face. Alina met his glare squarely.

"Believe me, Mr. Solitto, I'm not trying to insult you. But you have no idea who this person is, and this is *not* someone you are equipped to handle," she told him softly. Frankie stared at her for a beat.

"And you are?" he asked just softly.

The smile that curled Alina's lips sent a chill down Frankie's spine. It was the only answer he needed, but he got one anyway.

"Yes."

"Who is this guy?" Frankie asked, dropping all pretense of ignorance.

"Someone who does this for a living," Alina answered calmly. "He's more dangerous than you can possibly fathom. I know who he is, and I know what he's doing here. What I don't know is where he is now, and who arranged for him to join the party. I think those are the two things *you* know."

Frankie stared at her in silence for a few minutes before standing up. He walked over to the wall near the window and extracted a key from his pocket. Alina watched as he unlocked a metal box and flipped some switches. She knew he had just turned off all the surveillance monitoring the room. She felt a surge of satisfaction mixed with anticipation. Frankie was going to play ball. He closed and locked the box and came back to sit down again.

"I knew you guys weren't Feds," he told her. "You were both too smart and too sneaky. I don't know who you are or what you do, and I'm OK with that. But know this," he held up a finger and nodded to her. "I do this thing...it never leaves this room. No one ever knows we had this conversation."

The threat was clear and Alina nodded in agreement.

"The only reason I'm doing this is that, given the situation, I think you might be our best bet. I am concerned for my Family. The information we have...it's not good." Frankie sat back and watched her for a minute. "But you know that already." Alina nodded.

"Yes," she agreed.

"You know about the weapons. You know where they went to?" Frankie asked. Alina nodded and he smiled slightly. "Of course you do." Frankie fell silent for a moment, weighing just how much to tell her. "Well, at first, I thought that the person or persons who received those weapons was the person or persons who whacked Martin," Frankie explained slowly. "But then Joey came up here from Philly with a story he heard from *his* cousin, Marty. Marty is down in Washington, running some of the more lucrative business endeavors for the Philly family." Alina was silent, listening. "Marty was in the bar one night and he overheard something he probably shouldn't have overheard. He sat on it for a while, but when he heard about Martin, he came forward to tell Joey. Joey brought it to me in good faith."

"And what did Marty overhear?" Alina asked softly. Frankie looked up and shook his head.

"Something no decent American would have said," he muttered. Alina bit back a smile. "I'll save you the details. The terrorist you already know about anyways. Passports had been arranged for someone else, someone they called an Engineer. The general idea seems to be that even the people down in Washington are scared of this guy. They arranged for the passports and paid him a fortune to come in and take care of clean-up. Marty greased some palms and traded some information and came up with the two names on the passports." Alina caught her breath. Frankie looked up. "My associates found him in Philly, but now he's gone again."

"All I need are the names," Alina said softly, her heart racing. "I'll find him."

Frankie studied her for a moment before smiling slowly.

232

"You know, I believe you will," he murmured. "I hope that you come out of this OK. I like you as much as much as I liked your boyfriend." Alina grinned.

"I'm not sure that's a good thing," she replied. Frankie chuckled and waved his hand.

"I've been in this business a long time," he told her. "I've learned a lot. A lot about people. I've learned who you can trust, who you can't trust, and who you want on your side no matter what. You and your boyfriend fall into that category. I don't know if I trust you, but I sure as hell don't want you against me."

"That shows some wisdom," Alina answered, her eyes meeting his frankly. "I respect you, but I wouldn't lay odds against us." Her eyes sparkled briefly, arresting Frankie's attention. "It's been done before and they lost," she told him. Frankie chuckled.

"I'm not surprised," he retorted. "Well, I'll tell you the same thing as I told your friend. You ever want a job, you come see me."

Alina bowed her head in acknowledgment, and then raised her eyes to his.

"The names?" she prompted.

The glass hit the wall with a crash, shattering the morning silence. The tall man reclining on the sofa sat perfectly still after his momentary loss of control. His laptop was open on the cushion beside him and the last message was still blinking on the screen, taunting him. Dimitrius rested his arm on his upraised knee, staring broodingly at the screen.

He should have known better than to take this job, but the challenge had been too much to resist. His old nemesis, Johann, *and* the mysterious Viper, had proved too tempting. The amount of money that he was being paid was obscene, but Dimitrius had never really cared much for the money. It was like the cherry on a sundae. It was nice to have, and made it a finished product, but wasn't really necessary to the enjoyment of the dessert. The satisfaction, the challenge, and the ultimate prospect of success against these two people had made the deal worth it.

He should have taken into account who was paying him.

Dimitrius scowled, lifting his eyes from the blinking secure message on the screen and staring unseeingly at the wall where a large blotch of amber liquid dripped down the off-white wall. He was so tired! That momentary lapse of control should have never happened.

He got up from the couch and walked over to stare down at the broken fragments of glass. He hadn't slept now for three nights and his nerves were showing the strain. Not only had he missed a perfectly straight shot yesterday, but now his control on his temper was slipping, something he never allowed to happen.

Dimitrius turned impatiently and went back to the couch, putting the shattered glass out of his mind. The latest demand was even more ridiculous than the last. That was the problem with the Americans. They thought that they could buy everything...even their freedom. The original contract had been simple enough. It was a straight-forward contract for a kill. Nothing fancy, and how Dimitrius chose to proceed was up to him. But three days ago, they wanted to change that contract. Add another target. Add more money for the inconvenience.

The Engineer clamped one hand into a fist. They had no idea what amount of planning and preparation went into his games. They thought he was just another gun for hire, like their old Westerns, slinking around dressed in black and firing a six-shooter from dark alleyways. They had no appreciation at all for his genius, for his artistry. Did they think he became this successful just through *luck*?

He slammed the laptop closed impatiently. First they added the additional target. He hadn't been happy about their demand on timing, but he had agreed. He could meet their demands without disrupting his game too much. He always allowed for some unexpected events in his plans. It would have worked out without too much inconvenience, if he hadn't missed his shot. He was furious with himself. It was a straight-forward, clean shot. There was no excuse for missing. None.

But miss he had. And not only had he missed, but the bullet was still missing! A visit to the hospital ER had elicited the information that the bullet had gone straight through the womans shoulder. Dimitrius returned to the city block only to watch helplessly as the Feds had, literally, torn up the pavement outside their building. After about an hour of observation, he realized they hadn't found the bullet either. Normally, this wouldn't concern him overly much. It could have ricocheted off the pavement and into the gutter, never to be heard from again and no one ever the wiser to its origin. But this wasn't a normal game, and Viper wasn't a normal spectator.

If *she* had gotten hold of that bullet, then Dimitrius wasn't so sure of his anonymity any longer.

The Engineer clenched his fist and jumped off the couch again, striding around the room impatiently. The fact that the Feds were still looking for it implied that she didn't have it either and he was probably making too much of the whole incident. He got irrational when he was tired. He had to rest.

But now the pigs in Washington had gone and taken matters into their own hands with some woman down there who was asking questions. Dimitrius paused in his pacing as a fresh wave of anger washed over him. Instead of consulting him, they just jumped into the fray and pulled at a string. Now, his carefully laid plan was going to unravel faster than he could blink. Didn't they *realize* what they were dealing with? Didn't they realize how dangerous both Johann and Viper were?

He had to find some way to contain the damage within the next few hours or all the days of careful planning would be wasted.

Dimitrius clenched his fists again and turned abruptly to go back to the couch. First, he had to answer the message. He had to make it clear that they not do anything else to upset his plans. And then he was going to have to move up his timetable.

Time was no longer on his side.

Chapter Sixteen

Stephanie frowned as she pressed 'end' on her cell phone. She had been trying to reach Shannon all morning, with no success. Her cell phone was going straight to voice mail and Stephanie was starting to get impatient. She hesitated to try her at the office, since Shannon seemed to think that she was being watched, but Stephanie was starting to wonder if perhaps she should.

"Still no luck?" John asked, joining her at the door of the hospital. They were on their way to check on Angela, John sticking to her like glue. Rob had stopped them both this morning and made it clear that he wanted John with Stephanie at all times. Stephanie thought it was ridiculous and, while she acknowledged that it was for her own safety, the constant company was starting to annoy her.

"No." Stephanie turned to stride into the hospital. "I think I'll try her office when we're done here."

"Have you heard from Alina?" John asked. Stephanie shook her head and stopped in front of the elevators.

"No." She pushed the button and they both stared at the red up-arrow light above the doors. "Let's head to Avalon this afternoon. I want to look at that house." The elevator dinged and the doors slid open. They stepped inside and Stephanie pressed the button for Angela's floor. "It's amazing Matt was able to catch that reflection in the picture."

"I'm telling you, the man's a wizard," John agreed as the doors slid shut. "Do you think we'll find anything down there?"

"Possibly." Stephanie shrugged. "It depends on how many people are left," she added thoughtfully. "They have to be hiding somewhere. If you think about it, the shore is the perfect place. No one is down there this time of year and the rent is cheap. That makes it an attractive base of operations."

"Do you think Johann is really up to something?" John asked, turning to face her. Stephanie pursed her lips and tilted her head to the side.

"I think so," she said slowly. "Otherwise, why would he be here? The question is what? And where? And how can we find out?"

"I think Alina knows," John answered. "I think she knows more than she's telling you."

"I do too," Stephanie agreed. "But I can't make her tell me."

"Well, technically, we can," John murmured. Stephanie glanced at him.

"Right. You can be the one to pull the badge and try to bring her in," she said with a grin. "You let me know how that works out for you." John grinned back.

"Just saying it's an option," he retorted with a laugh.

"She's probably protected by some secrecy act that we've never heard of," Stephanie said as the elevator doors slid open. They stepped into the hallway to see the object of their frustration coming out of Angela's room.

"Speak of the devil," John murmured.

Alina moved toward them with that formidable mix of assurance and fearlessness that she had acquired in her years away from them. She was dressed in loose, dark linen pants and a casual shirt. Her sunglasses were on top of her head and, aside from that air of danger, she looked like any other woman found on the city streets on a spring day. Stephanie suddenly wondered what she looked like in fatigues. They had never received any pictures, not even when she graduated, and she realized suddenly that they had never actually seen her in uniform.

"Why the frown?" Alina asked, meeting them halfway. She was looking at Stephanie.

"I just realized that I never saw any pictures of you in uniform," Stephanie answered truthfully. John shot her a quick look before watching Alina's reaction. She looked amused.

"I'm sure I could dig some up if you would like," she told Stephanie with a very faint smile. "I didn't look all that different. Just the same, in fact," she added with a grin. Stephanie laughed.

"I don't know what made me think of it," she said apologetically.

"Sometimes we think of the damnedest things out of the blue," Alina replied smoothly, still with that faint smile.

John frowned. He didn't think he would ever get used to this new stranger that was Alina. The faint smile and the air of aloofness was the complete opposite of the open and friendly woman he had lived with years ago.

"I, for instance, was just thinking what a good couple the two of you make," Alina continued with a smile. Stephanie burst out laughing and John grinned.

"Oh please, don't even think it!" Stephanie exclaimed. "I would kill him in less than 24 hours."

"The idea has merit," Alina murmured, looking at John. "Definite merit."

"How is she?" Stephanie nodded toward Angela's room, changing the subject as John made a face at Alina.

"In a lot of pain," Alina answered. "They increased her morphine drip. There's no fever, though, so that's a good sign." Stephanie nodded.

"How are you? You look pale," she said, looking at Alina.

John suddenly noticed what Stephanie had already seen. While Alina's hair and clothes were perfect, her face was very pale and there were dark rings under her eyes. John's eyes narrowed and he frowned.

"I'm just a little tired," Alina answered with a smile. "I didn't get much sleep last night," she added.

"Where are you headed now?" John finally spoke. Alina shrugged slightly.

"Out and about," she answered evasively. "I'll touch base with you guys later today." Stephanie was already nodding.

"Dinner?" she suggested.

Alina nodded and then continued on her way. Stephanie and John continued on toward Angela's room.

"Dinner?" John demanded under his breath. Stephanie grinned.

"We all have to eat," she retorted, glancing back. She expected to see Alina at the elevators, but there was no sign of her in the hall. She had vanished. Stephanie looked around with a frown before following John into the hospital room.

Alina stood on the beach and took a deep breath. The salt air was fresh and the brisk spring wind whipped her ponytail around her head. She had changed her linen pants for long running pants, the casual shirt for a long-sleeved, designer sports shirt, and her city boots for soft-soled, all-terrain running shoes. Staring out over the expanse of blue-gray waves crashing onto the shore, she listened to the roar of the ocean and the screech of the seagulls overhead. The sun had disappeared behind a thick layer of clouds and rain was threatening. Still, Alina stood on the beach, breathing in the afternoon air with eyes closed, *feeling* her first sight of the Jersey Shore in over ten years.

She had missed it.

Alina didn't realize how much she missed it until she crossed the causeway from the mainland to the barrier islands, smelling her first scent of salt air as the trees fell away behind her. The same anticipation that she remembered from the past had welled up inside her as she drove over the last bridge and saw the lines of shore homes ahead. Beyond those lines, beyond the blocks of tightly knit neighborhoods, once you had traversed the streets, were the dunes. Once the sand dunes were sighted, the sound of the ocean drowned out everything. Then, and only then, were you *there*. You had arrived, and all the anticipation and excitement of going "down the shore" culminated in one deep breath of release. Everything was left behind. All that was in front of you was water, beach, sun and relaxation.

Alina took a deep breath now and stared out over the crashing waves. The ocean always demanded her attention and respect. No matter what country, no matter what shore, she was drawn to the water. It was untamed, unpredictable, and uncontrollable. And yet, it followed a natural sense of order, according to the seasons. Even in the chaos, there was order. Even in the violence, there was control. Even in the seeming endlessness, there was an end.

The stormy vastness of the Atlantic captured her imagination. There was a whole other world under there and the glimpse that they saw, crashing onto the beach, was just a drop. It was nothing at all. It always reminded her that she, in essence, was nothing compared to the massiveness and might of nature.

Alina took another deep breath, lifting one leg up behind her and grabbing her ankle. She glanced around as she stretched. The beach was deserted. She lowered her leg and lifted the other one, looking down the beach to her right. One of the addresses that she dug up from the names that Frankie had given her was about two blocks down, the back of the house directly on the beach. Alina dropped her leg and jumped up and down a few times. If anyone was watching, she looked like just another jogger, warming up before starting her beach run. She had left her gun in the car and had only her knife, strapped to her ankle under the running pants. She just wanted to take a look around. If she saw anything interesting, she would come back later, under the cover of darkness.

After a few more warm-ups, Alina started off down the beach at a steady jog. The sand was clean and free from debris. There was money here. The properties were privately owned and taken care of by contractors. The front of the houses were gated and set back from the road, while the backs opened directly onto the sand. Alina kept her face forward as she ran, but her eyes were scanning the beach and the back of the homes that she passed. A dog barked at the back sliding door of the first one, stopping as she passed by. The next one was dark and silent. Many of these properties were only occupied during the summer season. The rest of the year, the owners typically rented them out or left them empty. Alina ran by a third one, also dark and silent, and wondered what it would be like to have a beach house. Perhaps she would invest in one someday.

The next house was the address she wanted. There was a small deck on the right as she looked at the back, and sliding doors in the center. Her attention, however, was drawn to the left side of the sliding doors. The left-side, bottom back wall was made entirely of glass.

Alina glanced in as she ran by without slowing her pace. No curtains were hung inside and she had a clear view into the room. There was a couch, a coffee table, and what looked like matching arm chairs. As Alina ran by, there was movement toward the back of the room, a shadow crossing through a doorway.

Someone was there.

Alina felt a surge of excitement as she passed the house and continued on down the beach. Someone was there and she got the distinct impression that the shadow was a taller man. Was it him? Was it the Engineer? Or was it Johann? Had she run him to ground at last?

Alina's mind was spinning with possibilities by the time she exited the beach three houses farther down. She ran up the path through the dunes and paused when she reached the sidewalk. Her breath was coming fast and hard and her side felt like it had been swiped by fire. Bent over at the waist to catch her breath, Alina gingerly touched the bandage at her side. It was moist, but whether from sweat or because the wound had ripped open again, she couldn't tell. After her breathing slowed, Alina straightened up and put the pain out of her mind. She breathed deeply and started running again, this time along the pavement, back toward the glass house.

Alina slowed as she approached the waist-high, wrought-iron gate surrounding the front of the property. The house was set back a bit from the road and the postage-stamp front yard was cold and bleak. A black sedan was parked in the driveway that ran along the side of the house. There didn't appear to be any movement or life in the house and, apart from the sedan, it looked like any other house in the neighborhood, empty for the season. But Alina had seen a shadow.

One of her targets was in there.

She continued past the house and jogged back to where her SUV was parked a few blocks away. Alina opened the back and pulled out a bottle of water and a towel. Sipping the water, she mopped her face while she leaned against the open back. Her eyes scanned the street thoughtfully. She had to find out who was in the house.

Alina sipped the water again, her eyes drifting down the street to the empty house next to the glass house. They dwelled briefly on the realtor sign in the front yard. Capping the bottle decisively, Alina stretched her legs for a few moments before going around to get behind the wheel. She started the engine and pulled a U-turn, cruising down the street. She glanced at the sign, memorizing the phone number as she drove by, and continued on to the end of the street before turning away from the beach.

Two hours later, the sun was going down and deep shadows cloaked the quiet, deserted street. In the summer, the street would still be flooded with light and the sound of children playing and adults laughing. The smells of barbecue would fill the air. This time of year, it was eerily quiet as the night descended, reminiscent of a ghost town. If anyone chanced to look out a window and examine the shadows, they might have glimpsed a shifting of light that may, or then again may not, have been a figure disappearing into the shrubbery surrounding one of the empty homes. However, the odds of anyone doing so were so remote that Viper felt absolutely no qualms as she slipped around the side of the house to the back facing the beach. She paused and listened to the sound of the waves crashing against the sand. It was dark back here, away from the street lights, and the beach was silent and deserted.

Alina had changed into black cargo pants and a black windbreaker with multiple pockets, and a long, slender black bag was slung over her shoulder. She waited patiently, ensuring that the beach really was deserted before she moved over to the sliding door at the back of the house. Turning her attention from the crashing waves to the door, Alina pulled a long, paper-thin steel tool out of one of the side pockets on the bag. She didn't need light. She had done this so many times that it was second nature to her. Viper silently slid the door closed behind herself a few seconds later, slipping the tool back into the pocket. She paused in the still house, waiting for her eyes to become accustomed to the darkness inside. The electric was turned off and the resulting silence was almost eerie, but she welcomed it. Silence was only unnerving when it shouldn't be silent.

As soon as she could make out the shapes of the furniture, Viper started to move. She had checked out the glass house before coming here. The sedan was still in the same spot, and there was a light at the back of the house and more light on the second floor. She hadn't seen the shadow again, but she knew he was in there.

Viper moved through the bottom floor to the stairs and climbed them silently, feeling her way with one hand on the wall. Her rifle bounced lightly against her back and Alina smiled to herself slightly. Her old friend was comforting as it shifted gently while she moved. It had been with her for years and it never failed her. *Better than most men I know,* she thought to herself as she reached the top of the stairs. She immediately turned left and headed down the hallway, staying against the wall and moving silently.

Viper went into the last room at the back of the house. There were three windows, one of which faced the glass house next door. She went straight to that window and knelt on the floor, swinging the rifle bag off her back fluidly and setting it noiselessly on the floor beside her. She unzipped one of the side pockets in her jacket and pulled out a pair of binoculars, studying the house next door as she took off the caps. The second floor had a light on and she caught sight of movement through one of the large windows. Upstairs, as downstairs, there were no curtains in the windows. The occupant clearly knew the houses on either side of them were empty and they weren't concerned about privacy. Viper doubted whether either Johann or The Engineer had ever given a single thought to window treatments.

She lifted the binoculars to her eyes and adjusted them, bringing the hallway of the second floor into sharp focus. It was empty, but a light was burning at the top of the stairs. She scanned the roof and lower floor briefly before returning to the second floor. The master bedroom was facing her. It had two large windows on the side facing her and Viper took full advantage of them, examining the bedroom. Regardless of which target was in the house, both of them would have chosen that room to sleep in.

Viper patiently waited for any sign of movement. She could see most of the bedroom from her vantage point, but the bathroom was out of her range of vision. She moved her focus back into the hallway. Aside from the light at the top of the stairs, the hallway was dark as it stretched to the opposite side of the house. Moving her attention back to the bedroom, she waited.

While part of her was hoping for the chance to end the run of the clever assassin, Viper wanted to finish what she had come here to do. The whole situation had gotten out of control. Stephanie, John and Angela were far too involved, and now Damon had disappeared as well. While he could be doing anything, Alina knew that it was tied up with this debacle and that added him as a liability on her conscience as well. Four people that she cared about, all involved in one big mess. That was four people too many, especially when it was supposed to be such a straight-forward mission. Go to Jersey, finish what she started two years ago, and move on. Quick and easy.

Ha!

Alina frowned slightly as she waited patiently for movement in the house next door. If she had known that the lives of her old friends, and the life of Hawk, would be thrown so unceremoniously into the path of a killer like The Engineer, would she still have allowed herself to be pulled from her mountain retreat and back into the game? The lure of Johann had been strong enough to get her here, even knowing that she would have to face her past. But she could never have foreseen the mess that this had turned into overnight. If she could do it all again, Alina admitted to herself that she would not have contacted Stephanie. She would have found another way to get the information she needed. She had involved her old friends as an expedient way of obtaining information and now they were in as much danger as she was herself.

Do you trust them with your life?

Hawk's question taunted her and Alina pressed her lips together. She trusted Stephanie and Angela, but could *they* trust *her*?

Movement brought Viper's attention sharply back to the bedroom next door. She pushed her personal dilemma to the side as a tall man walked out of the master bathroom. Viper exhaled silently as she zoomed in on the lean face of Johann Topamari. A heady mix of relief and satisfaction washed over her as she watched him go to the closet and pull something out, tossing it onto the bed. It was a large duffel bag. Johann unzipped the bag and started putting clothing inside. He was leaving.

Viper set the binoculars down and rapidly unzipped the bag at her side. Her movements were quick and sure as she lifted out the rifle and assembled it quickly. She was glad that she had brought her smaller one. Johann was only about 100 meters from her. Viper attached the scope and the silencer last and cracked the window in front of her, inserting the barrel into the opening with one fluid motion. She lowered her eye to the scope and adjusted the sight, watching as Johann went to the closet again. He returned to the open duffel bag with a jacket, which he was rolling up to tuck inside the bag. Viper exhaled slowly and calmly adjusted the sight, switching target from his head to the center of his body. He was moving around too much to make a head shot viable. There could be no mistakes this time. She slipped her finger over the trigger.

Creeeak.

Vipers head shot up and her finger slid off the trigger immediately as a jolt of shock shot through her. Someone was on the stairs!

Alina pressed her lips together and pulled the rifle out of the window, her hands immediately disengaging the silencer and the scope.

Creeeak.

Another set of feet crossed the same step on the stairs. Two people were coming upstairs!

Viper disassembled the gun swiftly and zipped up the bag, working as fast and as silently as she could. She glanced through the window and into the bedroom next door. Johann was still at the bed, packing clothes into the bag. Viper grabbed her binoculars and held them up again in time to watch him zip the bag up and pick it up off the bed. She cursed silently.

That's twice now, she thought furiously. *There will NOT be a third time!* Viper watched as Johann strode out of the room, switching the light off as he went.

Her chance was gone.

"Can you *make* any more noise? Seriously?" a voice she knew well demanded from the top of the stairs.

Alina lowered the binoculars and put them in her pocket, frustration and anger making her hands shake slightly.

"There's no one here!" the second person retorted. "What does it matter?"

They were in the hallway now, moving toward the bedroom. Alina shook her head, clamping her teeth, and got noiselessly to her feet. She couldn't believe it. Two more minutes: One for her to take the shot, and one for her drop out of the window and get away. Two more minutes were all that had stood between her and the end of this whole thing.

247

Two people appeared in the doorway behind her and Alina didn't bother to turn her head. She continued to watch the house next door. The light in the hallway went out and then, a minute later, the one at the top of the stairs followed suit. Johann was moving downstairs with his bag.

"It looks like there *is* someone here after all," Stephanie said, her voice loud in the silent room.

Viper ignored her, staring out the window and trying to get a handle on the fury that was coursing through her.

Two more minutes!

"What a surprise." John sounded anything but surprised. "I told you she knew more than she was saying." They walked across the room to join her at the window.

"How long have you been here?" Stephanie demanded, looking across to the house next door. Alina didn't trust herself to answer calmly, and so she remained silent. Stephanie glanced at her, trying to see her face in the dark.

"There's movement on the bottom floor!" John exclaimed, turning around again and heading for the door quickly. "I'll see what I can see from downstairs!" he threw over his shoulder as he disappeared again, leaving the two women next to the window. Stephanie turned her attention outside again and they both watched silently as a light came on on the first floor. The light flicked out a moment later and the house went dark.

"Who is it?" Stephanie asked.

"You'll see for yourself in a minute," Alina finally spoke. She was surprised at the calmness of her voice, considering that she was still trembling with anger. She looked at her old friend. "He's getting ready to leave."

Alina turned away from the window and walked toward the doorway. She didn't need to watch Johann walk out of the house and drive away.

"Wait!" Stephanie's voice stopped her at the door. Alina looked back and watched as Stephanie stared out the window. "How do you know he's leaving?"

"He just finished packing everything up." Alina turned to leave the room. "He won't be going back there."

"It's Johann, isn't it?" Stephanie asked, still watching through the window. Alina continued out the door without answering.

Alina took a deep, calming breath and closed the back of the SUV. Her bag was locked back up in the special metal box next to the spare tire and the floor was replaced. She knew that both Stephanie and John had seen it, but neither had mentioned it. In fact, none of them had said much at all to each other. Johann had exited the glass house as Alina was going downstairs, and the black sedan pulled out of the driveway a few minutes later. John had taken a slew of pictures from the windows and Stephanie joined him in the front of the house to watch the car disappear down the road. By the time Stephanie realized Alina was leaving, she had been out the back door and headed down the beach.

Stephanie caught up with her on the dark beach a few houses down. Instead of demanding answers right then and there, she suggested Chinese for dinner. Alina agreed to meet at the house in Medford before heading off into the night, back to her car a few blocks away.

Getting behind the wheel, Alina closed the door and sat for a minute in thoughtful silence. She wasn't concerned with where Johann was headed. The tracking device she had attached to the sedan earlier would tell her everything she needed to know. Now that her anger had faded, she wasn't even so concerned with the fact that she had been unable to take a perfect shot. Alina leaned her head back and closed her eyes with a sigh. What she *was* concerned about now was what she was going to tell Stephanie and John.

Do you trust them with your life?

They had both seen the rifle bag. They both already knew that she had been military intelligence, and Stephanie would have definitely already surmised that she worked for a government agency. Alina's lips twitched. They probably both thought she was NSA or DHS. That would explain the bag and why she was following Johann. Alina opened her eyes with a slight frown. She wondered how close they were to the truth.

Damon seemed to think that it was only a matter of time, and he thought she had already told them too much. She knew that the odds were extremely high for them figuring it out, but Alina paused thoughtfully. Even if they had figured out that she was connected to CIA, and were over-looking the fact that she was working on US soil, what were the odds that they would really figure out the whole truth? Even if they suspected it, and Alina knew that they suspected a lot right now, they were Federal Agents. They needed proof before they could convict, even in their own minds. Had she given them any? Her presence there tonight could have been attributed any number of plausible reasons.

Alina grinned to herself. Knowing John as well as she did, he was surely going over all of those possibilities with Stephanie right this minute.

Alina straightened up and reached for the small backpack on the passenger side floor, her concern put to rest for the time being. While having them both show up this evening was more than inconvenient, she didn't think it would turn out to be catastrophic. There were still too many other possibilities for them to hone in on the right one.

Alina opened the outside flap of the backpack and reached in to pull out a square gauze bandage and a roll of tape. The tinted windows concealed her nicely in the darkness and, after a quick scan of the deserted street, she shrugged out of her jacket and eased her shirt up. She carefully removed the bandage from her side, setting it on the console between the seats, and ripped open the package of the new one. It was awkward working in the dark, but she managed to get the new bandage on and taped down fairly quickly. Alina shrugged back into her jacket, ignoring the discomfort in her side, and clicked on the overhead light to look at the bandage she had removed. She was still seeping.

Clicking the light off with a slight frown, Alina folded the old bandage, tucking it into the empty package from the new one. She put it into her bag, to be burned later with the trash, and started the engine. She wasn't healing as fast as she would like, and as Alina pulled away from the curb, she acknowledged that she should probably have stitched the wound. The run on the beach earlier had strained it and now she had to be careful about infection.

Just one more thing to worry about.

Chapter Seventeen

Alina pulled off her shirt and sank onto her bed tiredly. Her side was throbbing, making her irritable, and the last thing she wanted was for Stephanie and John to interrogate her. What she really wanted to do was take some ibuprofen with a shot of vodka and go to sleep. However, that was not an option. It wouldn't be until this was all over. Viper had to stay sharp. She didn't have time to pamper herself.

A scraping sound, followed by the rustling of wings, drew her attention up to the corner of the skylight. Raven settled onto his perch and looked at her with his shiny black eyes. He bobbed his head once and then walked to the edge of the perch, watching her. Alina smiled, comforted by her hawk's presence. She stood up and went to the closet to find a more comfortable shirt and, as she did so, Raven squawked. Alina glanced back at him.

"What's wrong, love?" she asked.

Raven bobbed his head again and squawked again. Alina frowned and grabbed the first shirt that her fingers touched. She pulled the loose red top over her head and headed back into the bedroom quickly. Raven bobbed his head again and then lifted up and disappeared through his access door to the side of the skylight.

Alina switched off the bedroom light and headed downstairs as a car pulled around the house and stopped in the driveway. Taking a deep breath, she walked to the back door to watch as Stephanie and John got out of the car. Raven had settled on the deck and Alina grinned. He was watching John with his sharp eyes. She opened the back door and stepped out onto the deck.

"Easy, Raven," she murmured, stopping at the banister where he was perched. "I'm not a fan either, but he's a necessary evil right now."

Stephanie and John came up to the deck, both carrying brown bags

"I'm starving," Stephanie said by way of greeting, one eye on the large hawk.

"Come on in." Alina motioned toward the door. John followed her, watching Raven.

"If you stare at him, it only makes it worse," Stephanie told him, opening the sliding door and stepping into the house.

"You know, my place is free of animals, birds, fish, and assorted bad guys," John told Alina as he stepped past her. "I'm just throwing it out there."

"I'm more comfortable here," Alina retorted.

She turned to follow him into the house, but at the door, she glanced back at Raven. He had turned his attention to the trees and she paused, her eyes scanning the darkness. Raven was unsettled, but she didn't know if it was just from the visitors or from something else. After a moment, Alina stepped into the house and slid the door closed.

"We got General Tso's, chicken and mixed vegetables, beef lo mein, and kung pow shrimp," Stephanie informed her from the bar where she was already opening the bags. "And we got spring rolls and egg rolls."

"Good." Alina moved into the kitchen. "I haven't eaten all day," she said, getting plates from the cabinet above the counter.

She handed the plates to John before turning to the other counter where her laptop was sitting. Alina flipped it open and pressed some keys, switching on part of her security system. Raven's unease had spread to her. If the Engineer was out there tonight, she wasn't going to make it easy for him.

"Do you want to eat at the table?" Stephanie asked. Alina closed the laptop and turned around.

"Sure. Let me pull the blinds," she said with a smile. John carried the plates to the table and Stephanie started handing him the white quart containers. "John, the knives and forks are in the drawer near the coffee maker," Alina told him, moving around the bar and toward the windows. John nodded and went into the kitchen.

"You don't have to pull the blinds," Stephanie muttered. "I doubt he's out there."

"Better safe than sorry," John said from the kitchen.

Alina pulled heavy beige drapes across the dining room windows and then moved on to the sliding doors. She looked out onto the deck. Raven was still perched on the banister, facing the yard.

"Raven is unsettled tonight," she said, pulling the matching drapes over the sliding doors as well. Once the windows were covered, she turned back to the dining room table. "It's probably just because you're here, but I would rather be safe."

"You're doing this on the whim of a bird?" Stephanie asked, dropping into a chair and reaching for a plate.

"He's a very smart bird," Alina retorted.

"Soda?" John asked from the kitchen. Alina looked at him like he had three heads.

"No," she answered bluntly. Stephanie laughed.

"I told you she wouldn't have soda," she called. John looked disgruntled.

"You used to live on mountain dew," he said to Alina. Alina shrugged.

"I also used to smoke a pack a day and live with you," she retorted. "There's water in the fridge."

"Grab me a bottle, will you?" Stephanie called, opening one of the quarts and piling rice onto her plate. "You don't mind my starting, do you?"

"Not at all." Alina sat across from her and reached for one of the containers. "I don't suppose you got brown rice?"

"It's over-rated." The response from Stephanie was muffled by a mouth full of egg roll as Alina reached for the rice. "You need good, old-fashioned, useless starch."

"You still look pale." John joined them at the table and reached for the lo mein. Alina raised an eyebrow.

"I still haven't slept," she retorted, reaching for a spring roll and opening the rest of the containers, looking for the chicken and vegetables.

"So how did you know about the shore house?" Stephanie asked, handing her the chicken. Alina took it with thanks.

"I got some information on some aliases your shooter may have been using," Alina answered truthfully. "One of them turned up that address."

"You didn't know Johann was going to be there?" John asked, piling his plate high with lo mein. Alina bit into her spring roll and shook her head.

"Not until I saw him packing a bag," she said. "How did you guys end up there?" she asked. Alina watched the quick glance that passed between John and Stephanie from under her lowered lashes.

"A picture that Angelo had in his house," Stephanie answered after a short pause. "Our forensics wizard was able to identify the location."

"The basement gnome?" Alina asked, looking up from her food. John grinned.

"One and the same," he said.

"Ironic that we both ended up there at the same time." Stephanie mused. "What are the odds of that?"

Alina was silent, thinking of her lost shot at her target. Ironic indeed.

"Did you see anyone else there?" John asked her. Alina shook her head.

"Just Johann," she answered.

"Were you expecting our shooter?" Stephanie asked, glancing up from her food.

Alina was amused. They had answered one question to their satisfaction. Now they were trying to explain the rifle bag. Really, they were both so transparent.

"I wasn't *expecting* anyone," Alina told them. "But I was prepared for anything."

"Do you really think he'll try again?" Stephanie asked, opening her bottle of water and taking a sip. "I mean, what does he have to gain by having me dead?"

"He's an assassin, Stephanie," John muttered. "He doesn't have to *gain* anything, except money."

"Ok then." Stephanie looked disgruntled. "Who would pay to kill me?" Alina and John both looked at her silently and she stared back at them. "What?"

"Well, Johann, for one," John told her. "He can't be thrilled that we obviously know he's here now."

"Stephanie, why don't you let me worry about who and why," Alina said, finishing the food on her plate and reaching for another spring roll. "You just worry about your case."

"I can't help it," Stephanie said ruefully. "I can't just sit around and let someone else do the work."

"You're not. You're doing your work and I'm doing mine," Alina pointed out logically. "I'm much better at working with people like that than you are."

"What kind of consulting did you say you did again?" John asked, reaching for an egg roll. Alina was amused.

"I didn't," she retorted. Stephanie grinned at John's disgruntled look.

"Where did the mysterious Mr. Peterson go?" she asked Alina, changing the subject. Alina raised an eyebrow.

"I thought you would know more about that than I do," she answered. John glanced at her.

"Doubtful," he said. "All he told us was that he had to go out of town and would be back in a few days."

"That's all he told me," Alina told them. She smiled slightly. "Contrary to popular belief, I don't have any claims on Damon, or he on me."

"Hm." Stephanie was clearly unconvinced.

Before Alina could respond, her phone started ringing. She frowned, pulling the phone out of one of her cargo pockets.

"Excuse me." Alina pushed her chair away from the table and stood up, walking into the kitchen. "Yes?" she answered.

"Just checking in." Damon's voice greeted her. "I'm about to get on a plane, so I'll be unreachable. Anything I should know about?"

"Nope." Alina leaned against the island. There was a short silence on the phone.

"Have you found him yet?" Damon finally asked.

"Which one?" Alina asked dryly.

"Johann," Damon clarified. "I'm holding out hope that the other one can wait another twelve hours." Alina's gaze lifted from the floor sharply.

"I'm close," she told him, aware that two sets of ears were straining to hear every word she said. "Twelve hours, huh? Baghdad?"

"You can do better than that." Damon sounded amused and Alina grinned despite herself. "How are the Fearless Feds today?"

"Eating Chinese," Alina told him shortly. "Did you get what you needed?"

"I got what *we* needed," Damon replied cryptically. "I'm boarding now. Be careful," he added.

"Always." Viper disconnected and stared at the opposite counter thoughtfully.

"If you want any shrimp, you better get in here," Stephanie called. "John's eating it all."

"He can have it," Alina answered absently. "I'm done."

"You barely ate anything." Stephanie appeared in the kitchen. She took in the thoughtful look on Alina's face. "Who was that?" she asked, nodding to the cell phone.

"Mr. Peterson," Alina answered, bringing her attention back to her old friend. "He's on his way back." Stephanie nodded, watching Alina.

"When will he be back?" she asked.

"He's boarding a flight now," Alina answered vaguely.

Stephanie nodded again, still watching Alina. The dark smudges under her eyes were even more pronounced than they had been earlier and her pallor was concerning Stephanie.

"Come and eat some more," she suggested. Alina glanced at her and turned to get some water out of the fridge.

"I told you. I'm done," she said over her shoulder.

"And I'm telling you that you're not," Stephanie retorted. "You look like hell."

"You might as well give up now," John said, sticking his head over the bar. "She has that tone in her voice."

"I'm tired, not hungry," Alina retorted, closing the fridge door and turning around with her bottle of water.

"Well, come and eat and then we'll leave so you can sleep," Stephanie said, motioning her back into the dining room. "And while you're eating, you can tell me what you know about Johann," she added.

Alina glanced at her as she passed her. Stephanie was smiling, but there was a look on her face that made Alina pause for a second.

"She's not going to leave until I eat, is she?" Alina asked John, sinking back into her seat. He shook his head and passed her what was left of the lo mein. Alina sighed imperceptibly.

"So let's talk about Johann," Stephanie said cheerfully after Alina had forked lo mein into her mouth. John grinned and sat back.

"Can she finish chewing first?" he asked. Alina swallowed.

"I told you the other night." Alina sipped her water. "I've been tracking him for over a month. I can't tell you much more than that."

"Do you know what he has planned?" John asked, turning serious. Alina shook her head.

"I have some theories, but nothing you can use," she answered truthfully. Stephanie considered her thoughtfully.

"What are your theories?" she finally asked. Alina raised an eyebrow and that faint smile crossed her face.

"Nothing you can use," she repeated. John sighed and reached for the last egg roll.

"Ok. So let's hear what I can't use," Stephanie suggested.

Alina was silent for a few moments, chewing thoughtfully. If what she suspected was true, Stephanie and John were going to find out soon enough. They were undoubtedly having Johann followed. It might not be such a bad thing to let them keep an eye on Johann while she focused on The Engineer. If they kept Johann in their cross-hairs, then she could focus on the bigger threat without worrying that Johann would disappear again. She had already missed one shot. She wasn't about to miss another opportunity through sheer pride.

"I think he's planned an attack on the transportation structure around Harrisburg and Three Mile Island," Alina finally told them. Stephanie and John stared at her.

"What?" John demanded.

Alina sighed and pushed away her empty plate. She looked from one to another and then sighed again.

"I can't believe I'm telling you this," she muttered. "I think that Johann is planning to stage a bogus attack on Three Mile Island, forcing evacuation protocol to be enforced. Once the roads are clogged, I think he plans to blow a bridge and hit the airport and maybe a train station or two," Alina explained. "The First Lady will be in Harrisburg this weekend, promoting one of her charities, and there's a music festival also happening in the city. It will be chaos."

John let out a low whistle while Stephanie simply stared at her. Alina could almost see the wheels in her head spinning.

"Angelo..." Stephanie murmured.

"Was an arms dealer," Alina continued. "And just before he floated up in your river, a very specialized shipment went missing from his boss, Bobby Reyes. Reyes believes that shipment was sold outside of his network by Angelo, and he was looking for him when he bobbed to the surface."

"Reyes didn't mention that when we talked to him," John murmured to Stephanie. She shook her head, almost absently.

"He wouldn't," she replied. She sat back and looked at Alina. "How did you find out?" Alina was silent. "Ok. So you're right. I can't use any of this. It's all speculation."

"I know," Alina agreed.

"Damn, but it sounds right on," John said after a short silence. Stephanie nodded.

"I think so too," she agreed. "Johann has to have others to help with the execution."

259

"My guess is that's where he's headed now," Alina said, drinking her water. "He's not going to take any chances, not with everyone he's worked with so far turning up dead. He would have stayed away from them until the last minute."

"Have we heard from that tail yet?" Stephanie asked John. John shook his head and pulled out his phone, pushing his chair back from the table as he stood up.

"I'll check in with them now," he said, walking away from the table. Stephanie leaned forward as soon as he was out of earshot.

"I'm not going to ask again how you got your information," she said quietly. "But is it reliable?"

"Very," Alina told her. "But you can't go in and handle this with the Agency and guns blazing. Trust me. He'll see you coming a mile away and he'll disappear. Johann is not stupid."

"You seem to know a lot about him," Stephanie said slowly. Alina almost smiled at the understatement. "What do you suggest?"

Alina looked at her for a moment, and then leaned forward herself.

"I can help you prevent this," she said quietly. "This is a unique situation. It's one of those times that the usual protocol won't work. If you want my help, you have it. But it has to be done my way."

Stephanie stared at her searchingly for a minute before shaking her head.

"I have to think about that," she answered slowly. "John would have to be on board with that. And my boss..."

"Trust me." Alina stood up and started to gather the empty food containers together. "When this is all over, your boss will have no idea that anything else was ever an option and you'll be a hero." Alina looked up and met Stephanie's gaze. "You would have saved the country from the biggest terrorist attack since 9\11. Do you really think they'll split hairs on how you did it?"

Next Exit, Three Miles

Alina stood at the bedroom window, staring out into the night. Stephanie and John had left an hour ago. As soon as they cleared the security perimeter, Alina armed her system and shut off all the lights. She went upstairs and changed her bandage, cleaning the wound again gently. The hole was starting to close now and the seeping was slowing down. She poured hydrogen peroxide into the wound and had watched as it bubbled up. By the time the clean bandage was on, Alina was feeling light-headed. She poured herself a glass of the brandy that was still sitting on her vanity and wandered over to the window with the glass. She had told Stephanie everything she could, and it was now up to her to decide how to handle it. If Stephanie and John decided to involve the agency, and all the bells and whistles that the agency brought with it, then Viper would lose her last shot at Johann.

However, if they played the game according to Alina's rules, she would get Johann and the Engineer, and Stephanie and John would get the credit for preventing a terrorist attack on American soil. Everyone got what they wanted. For Viper or Hawk, this would be a no-brainer, but for Federal Agents...well, they didn't think the same way. Viper was well aware that she had taken a huge risk tonight.

She sipped her brandy and watched in the darkness as a bat swooped through the backyard. If they *did* decide that they had to play the game by the book, she would have to take care of things herself. She couldn't fail again. If the worst happened, Alina knew she would have to take Johann over the assassin. Johann was her target. Johann was the reason that they were all here, dancing to the tune the piper was playing. It just infuriated Viper that the piper was a diabolical assassin who had no vested interest in anything, except maybe his own pride.

Alina wasn't proud of what she had accomplished in her career, but she was realistic. She knew that she presented a

261

challenge to a professional of Dimitrius's caliber, and she was honest enough with herself to admit a returning sense of competitive spirit inside her. But that was where it ended. He had targeted one of her own and put a bullet through another. Two people that she considered family. It wasn't a game to her. Now, it was business.

But first Johann.

Alina crossed the bedroom to her phone and swiped the screen. She touched an icon and opened the tracking dot that she had placed on Johann's car earlier. It was stopped in Pennsylvania, on the opposite side of the river from Three Mile Island.

Johann was in place.

She went back to the window and sipped her brandy again. He would have the others come to him once he knew it was safe. Johann would be even more careful now, after seeing his brother-in-law dead and hanging from a tree. He would have no qualms calling the whole thing off if he suspected that it might fail. Right now, he would be apprehensive and watchful, knowing that someone was systematically coming after him. Johann was far from dumb. He would have already figured out that it was an assassin that was picking off his team. He may have even narrowed it down to a few names, her own included. But he wouldn't see that as a reason to abort his mission.

Now, if the Feds bumbled in...

Alina sighed and turned away from the window. Again, it came down to Stephanie and John. Viper couldn't predict what Johann's next twenty-four hours would be until she knew how Stephanie was going to play it. Then she could plan.

She finished the brandy and set the empty glass on the bedside table with a yawn. She hated waiting. A rustle of wings and a clicking of claws heralded Raven's arrival as Alina sat on the bed, yawning again. Raven settled onto his perch, his watchful eyes trained on her. Alina glanced at him and smiled. Exhaustion was taking over and her side was throbbing. She sank into the pillows with a sigh.

Next Exit, Three Miles

Her last waking thought as she drifted into sleep was that her hawk was watching over her.

Chapter Eighteen

Alina glanced up at the flat screen above the mantle as a loud warning beep pierced through the silence of the living room. In the interest of self-preservation, she had moved her morning yoga practice inside this morning and was just beginning when the loud noise jarred her breathing. She looked up from her triangle pose to see Stephanie's car coming through the woods toward the house. Judging by the amount of dust it was kicking up, it was moving at a fast pace.

Alina sighed and straightened back into mountain pose, bringing her joined hands down into a prayer station at the center of her chest. She inhaled once more and then exhaled, releasing the tension in her shoulders and ignoring the nagging throb in her side. Turning, she went to the laptop on the coffee table and turned off the security perimeter, closing the laptop as Stephanie pulled into the clearing in the front of the house. She glanced at her watch with a slight frown. It was shortly after eight and Stephanie hadn't called to tell her she was coming.

Alina unlocked the sliding door as Stephanie got out of her car and headed toward the deck. She noted the lack of purse immediately. All Stephanie was carrying was her phone and her keys. Alina's frown deepened and she slid the door open.

"Where the hell is he?!" Stephanie demanded, stalking onto the deck and through the open door angrily. Alina raised an eyebrow.

"Where the hell is who?" she asked, sliding the door closed behind her and turning to face her old friend calmly. Stephanie dropped her keys and phone onto the bar and swung around.

"Your Mr. Peterson!" she said sharply.

Alina looked at Stephanie for a long moment in silence before walking over to pull one of the stools away from the bar slightly.

"Have a seat," she offered, slightly sarcastically. "Would you like some coffee?" she asked, moving around Stephanie and into the kitchen.

The mild reminder of manners wasn't lost on her old friend. Stephanie dropped onto the bar stool with a look of embarrassment, her flash of anger set aside.

"Yes, please," Stephanie murmured.

Alina turned on the espresso maker and studied Stephanie silently while the machine warmed up. Her friend was a mess. Her brown hair was pulled back in a half-hearted ponytail and she was wearing jeans and a teeshirt that looked like they had been thrown on at random. However, more telling of her state of mind than anything was the complete lack of makeup. That just wasn't done. Not in Jersey.

"Quit staring at me," Stephanie muttered, pushing her keys and phone out of the way and resting her arms on the bar. "I'm sorry I barged into your house." Alina turned to make the coffee.

"I'm sure you'll get around to telling me why you did in your own good time," she retorted over her shoulder. Stephanie glanced up with a flash in her eyes, but it was wasted on Alina's back.

"God, you sound like Sister Angelina from high school," she muttered. Alina was surprised into a bark of laughter.

"Good Lord." She took the full cup of coffee from under the spout and walked over to set it in front of Stephanie. "There's a name I haven't heard in years." She turned to the fridge and Stephanie watched her pull out the milk.

"Remember when she caught us sneaking out the window of the girls bathroom on the second floor?" she asked suddenly with a laugh. "She was outside waiting for us."

Alina was taken back in time with the memory. She remembered shimmying down the old rusted pipe as if it were yesterday. They had been so busy trying not to fall and die that neither one of them had bothered to look down.

Sister Angelina, the principal of the school, had been standing on the sidewalk below. Waiting.

"Jenny DiStefano told her," Alina said, setting the milk in front of Stephanie. "She was such a rat. Remember?"

"She ended up marrying Joey Forno," Stephanie told her, pouring milk into her coffee. Alina opened one of the drawers in the kitchen and pulled out a spoon, sliding it down the bar to Stephanie before turning to get the sugar. "He cheats on her something fierce."

"Serves her right," Alina said before she could stop herself. Stephanie laughed.

"She's still a rat," she said. "Angela ran into her at the hair salon a few months ago. She said that Jenny was acting like she's made of money, but everyone knows their house is mortgaged ten times over."

Alina set the sugar in front of Stephanie and turned to make her own coffee. Once she had a full mug in her hand, she turned around and went over to lean on the island, facing Stephanie.

"Talk," she said, sipping her coffee. Stephanie set her mug down.

"I have an old friend who works in DHS," she said slowly. "A few days ago, I asked her to poke around and see what she could find out about Damon Peterson." Alina raised her eyebrow slightly, but was silent. When it was clear that Alina wasn't going to say anything, Stephanie continued.

"She sent me an email two nights ago. She felt like something was wrong. She thought she was being watched. If you knew Shannon, you would know how unusual that was. She was never one to over-react or make a mountain out of a mole hill." Stephanie paused and looked at Alina again. Alina nodded slightly to show she understood. "I tried to call her all day yesterday with no answer. I finally called her direct line to her office this morning." Stephanie paused again and drank some coffee. Alina felt her gut tightening. She knew what was coming.

"Her assistant answered," Stephanie told her. "Shannon was killed in a car accident yesterday. Her car went off the road."

Alina exhaled slowly, her stomach dropping through her feet. She suddenly felt cold. Stephanie suspected Damon, but Alina knew that Damon was nowhere near Washington. She was pretty near positive that Damon had been halfway across the world in Egypt. But there *was* someone in Washington who would have every reason to stop Stephanie's friend from finding out anything about Damon or Alina, and that was the person who had brought a terrorist into the United States. Alina met Stephanie's look squarely and the two women were silent for a long minute.

"Well?" Stephanie finally broke the silence. "You have that look on your face."

"What look?" Alina asked.

"That completely unreadable, unemotional look that makes me want to scream at you," Stephanie replied shortly, picking up her coffee.

Alina was surprised at Stephanie's vehemence. She had no idea what she was talking about, but her irritation was evident.

"I'm not sure what you expect from me," Alina said calmly, sipping your coffee.

"Show some emotion!" Stephanie exclaimed, waving her hand in the air. "Surprise. Anger. Amusement. Anything!"

"Are you feeling ok?" Alina asked. Stephanie made a frustrated sound and finished her coffee in one gulp.

"No!" she cried. "My friend from college was killed yesterday under extremely suspicious circumstances, while trying to find out information about *your* friend from God-knows where, who is now missing in action. And all you can do is stand there looking bored!"

"I'm not sure that any of those are necessarily related," Alina pointed out dryly. She set her coffee down with a sigh and took Stephanie's empty mug over to the coffee maker to refill it.

"Shannon would not have over-reacted. If she thought she was being watched, then she was being watched," Stephanie stated defensively. "I don't buy the whole car accident that was an accident thing."

"Oh, neither do I," Alina agreed, looking at her while the coffee brewed. "But we differ on who, exactly, may be responsible for your friends accident." The machine stopped brewing and Alina brought Stephanie the fresh cup of coffee. "You're jumping to the conclusion that the person she was asking questions about is the person who is responsible."

"Wouldn't you?" Stephanie demanded, reaching for the sugar.

Alina watched as she started loading up her coffee with sugar. She blinked, momentarily diverted by the amount of sugar going into the coffee.

"Why aren't your teeth falling out?" Alina asked. Stephanie glared at her and Alina grinned, picking up her own cup of coffee.

"Ok. To answer your question, no. I wouldn't automatically assume that the one had to do with the other. However," she continued when Stephanie opened her mouth to argue, "I've been trained to look at things a little differently, so we can't really use me as a good standard. Let me put it to you this way. Damon wasn't in Washington yesterday."

"Where was he?" Stephanie asked, reaching for the milk.

"My best guess?" Alina sipped her coffee. "Egypt."

"You know that for a fact?" Stephanie demanded.

"Do you know for a fact that he wasn't?" Alina shot back softly. Stephanie paused. "You're convicting a man without knowing all the facts," Alina told her. "I'm very sorry for your loss, but your anger is directed at the wrong person."

"Why do you think he was in Egypt, of all places?" Stephanie asked after a moment.

Alina sighed and took her coffee over to the bar and sat next to Stephanie.

268

"I think he's gone to get the name of the person who hired the assassin to come after Johann..and now you," she said quietly.

"And that person is in Egypt?!" Stephanie demanded incredulously. Alina shook her head.

"It's complicated," she said with a sigh.

"Everything with you two is complicated! That's all I ever hear! No explanations, just that it's complicated or you can't tell me," Stephanie complained. "I was willing to give you both the benefit of the doubt, but now things are getting out of control. What the hell is going on?" Alina was silent. Stephanie stared at her and Alina stared back as the silence lengthened.

"So it's like that," Stephanie finally said. Alina shrugged.

"I've already told you too much as it is," she told her.

Stephanie drank her coffee, her frustration evident as the two women sat in silence. Alina glanced at her old friend. She wished she could tell Stephanie something, anything, to put her mind at rest. But, with the death of her friend in Washington, this had now gone beyond Stephanie's security clearance and into the realm of national security. Alina knew this, but she couldn't even tell Stephanie that much without telling her too much.

It all went back to Cairo and what she had seen and heard two years ago. The man in the room with Johann, and the assassin that they had been discussing as they walked out of the room. Everything was intertwined and, unfortunately, Stephanie had been drawn into the web as soon as that arms dealer had floated up in the river. Whether or not Viper had taken the job to come back to Jersey, Stephanie would have still ended up in this same position, with no knowledge of what, exactly, she was up against.

"Let me ask you this," Stephanie interrupted Alina's thoughts. "Do you work for *our* government?"

Stephanie's eyes met hers, and Alina smiled slightly. She was finally asking her the one question that Alina knew Stephanie had assumed since they had their conversation over bagels on the deck the day after Martin Sladecki caught his train to the afterlife.

"Yes," Alina confirmed. Stephanie nodded.

"Ok," she said. They lapsed into silence again and Alina knew that Stephanie was working through the pros and cons of working blindly with Alina. After another moment of silence, Stephanie sighed.

"I'm going home to get dressed and then go into the office," she said. "I'm going to find out where Johann is and get John to go with me for some recon. Then, I'll come back here with John." She stood up and collected her keys and her phone, turning to face Alina. "We'll go from there and decide what to do about Johann."

Alina stood up and it occurred to Stephanie that she looked neither grateful nor apologetic. She simply nodded and Stephanie left the house with the distinct impression that, regardless of what she or John did, Alina was going to do what she felt needed to be done. She had her own agenda and she was going to follow that, with or without the rest of them.

Stephanie wasn't sure how she felt about that.

Alina waited until Stephanie was gone before reactivating the security perimeter. She carried Stephanie's empty coffee mug to the sink and set in inside thoughtfully. A slight frown creased her brow as Alina absently refilled her own mug. Once it was filled, she reached up for the sauté pan and waited for the island to move aside. A minute later she was seated in front of her monitors, her laptop open, and the island back in place at the top of the steps.

Alina opened a folder on an embedded drive and typed in her security password. A second later, she clicked opened a picture, dragging it to one of the plasmas on the wall. Viper sat back with her coffee, propped her feet on the table, and stared up at the smiling picture of a man. Two years ago, he had been well-known in the western world. Now, he was a household name. Then, he had been busy clawing his way up the political ladder. Now, he was representative of an establishment; a force that could not be reckoned with.

He was a person beyond reach.

Alina's eyes narrowed and she sipped her coffee. The pieces of the picture were falling into place and at the top was Cairo. Damon had gone because he learned something that led him there. He learned something that made him suspect what Alina already knew. That meant that someone else was feeding Damon information. That, in itself, didn't alarm Viper. Just as she had spent years building up an information network across the world, so had Hawk; it was what they did. But she *was* concerned with how much his informant knew. Everyone who knew anything about Cairo was at risk now. The death of Stephanie's friend illustrated that fact perfectly. She hadn't known anything, but she had started asking questions about an unknown DHS agent who was in New Jersey. That had been enough to make her dangerous.

Alina sipped more coffee and frowned. Why was Damon here? And why was he posing as a DHS agent? The questions that had been haunting her for the past few days were back again, but with new urgency. Had Hawk been set up? And if so, why? Who would have brought him into this mess? Harry? Or was he protecting someone? Was he here to protect someone in Washington?

Alina stared at the picture on her screen. God, she hoped Hawk wasn't here to protect *that* son-of-a-bitch. That would be enough to turn her stomach.

So close! Alina dropped her feet to floor impatiently and went back to her laptop. She was so close to fitting all the pieces together! But Damon didn't fit anywhere, and neither did the agent in Washington. She could certainly see why Stephanie thought Damon was involved, but Alina knew better than that. She knew the man on the plasma screen was responsible, either directly or indirectly, just as he had been responsible for so many other useless and wasted deaths across the globe. The question was why? Was he protecting Damon? Was he framing Damon? Or had that agent simply become a liability because of her communication with Stephanie?

Alina paused and stared at her screen absently. Maybe Hawk had nothing to do with Stephanie's dead DHS agent. Maybe she had fallen into Stephanie's trap of not seeing outside the box. Alina sat back slowly. Maybe she was looking for a connection with Hawk because that was what made sense. But what if it *was* just something as simple as the fact that the agent had been in contact with Stephanie, and Stephanie had become Target Deux on The Engineer's list.

What if the man in Washington was just being paranoid and sloppy?

Alina stared at her laptop for a moment before reaching forward to hit a button, disconnecting the secure link she had just opened to one of her contacts in Washington. Her gaze went back to the picture on the plasma screen.

One day, she promised it silently. *All sins are punished one day*.

Dimitrius looked through the scope of his rifle and focused in on the little house in the woods. As far as houses went, he supposed it was as good as any. It was a one level rancher with a front porch that ran the width of the house. It sat on three acres of quiet property, buried in the wooded countryside of Pennsylvania next to the river. There was an old, dilapidated barn toward the back of the property and a lot of scraggly crabgrass mixed with bare patches of dirt. It looked as though someone tried to cultivate a garden of sorts in the front, but time and nature had triumphed over the effort. The land looked unkempt and wild, and the house didn't look much better. Dimitrius watched as a shadow moved around in the front room, wandering aimlessly back and forth in front of the window. A black sedan was parked in the front of the house, pulled off to the side, and Johann was inside.

Waiting.

Dimitrius lowered the rifle and picked up his binoculars, scanning the woods thoughtfully. The only restriction placed on his contract was that Johann had to complete his mission before he was eliminated, and The Engineer had planned everything accordingly. He would be here waiting when Johann returned. He had no doubt that Johann *would* return here when he was finished, there would be no other way out. The roads to the north, west and east would be clogged and impassable. The only way for Johann to make a clean exit would be to come back here, across the river. That was, if he even left. Dimitrius hadn't ruled out the possibility that Johann had planned his attack as a remotely activated strike. Not for the first time, he wished he had been able to determine the details of this attack that Johann had planned here in the States. But he hadn't been able to find out anything other than that it involved Three Mile Island.

Dimitrius raised his binoculars and looked in the direction of the river just beyond the trees. He couldn't see the Susquehanna from his vantage point over the house, but he knew it was less than a mile distant. Once you crossed the river, Three Mile Island was only a few miles up. He wondered absently how Johann planned to get past the security in the area. It was a daunting task, and one that he thought would have been impossible. But Johann had found a way in.

He turned the binoculars back to the woods surrounding the house, turning his attention back to the matter at hand. He had to decide what would be the best approach to his target and he scanned the woods before coming back to the clearing, pausing on the old barn thoughtfully. He was still weighing his options when movement caught his attention a few moments later on the access road that led to the house from the main road. Dimitrius turned the binoculars and watched as a white utilities truck bounced its way toward the house. It barreled up the road, throwing up dust in its wake, and came to a stop behind the black sedan. He watched as four men piled out of the truck and walked up to the porch. The front door opened and Johann was framed briefly in the door before he moved out of the way to allow the men to enter the house. The door closed behind them and Dimitrius lowered his binoculars again thoughtfully. Four men plus Johann. Before he strung Ahmed up from the tree, it would have been five.

The Engineer smiled slowly. So that was the plan. The other four men would take the fall while Johann got away across the river. He had probably planned for he and his brother to escape back across the river during all the chaos, and the others would be left to make their own way out of the area. Given the extremeness of the target, the likelihood of them doing so without being seen or caught was extremely remote. Johann and his brother would disappear, and the others would take the fall as the terrorists who attacked Americans on American soil.

Only now it was just Johann.

Dimitrius had to admit that it was perfect. Once on this side of the river, Johann would still have traffic to deal with, but it would be far less than on the other side, closer to the island. Not only would it be less chaotic, but he could be completely out of the area before any sort of organized response could be mounted.

Or he would be if he was alive.

Dimitrius lifted the binoculars again and studied the old barn to the back of the property. Once again, he was distracted by movement on the access road. He swung the binoculars over and watched as a black pickup entered the access road, slowed a few feet in, and then pulled into the trees. He frowned and watched as the pickup didn't move. After a moment, he caught sight of something moving near the parked truck. Adjusting his binoculars, Dimitrius inhaled sharply in surprise as he recognized the two Feds moving through the trees toward the house. Now how on earth had *they* found Johann? The woman stumbled on some undergrowth and her partner grabbed her arm to steady her before they continued on. Dimitrius glanced back at the house, and then back to the Feds. Damn! If they scared Johann off now, all his careful planning would be wasted!

Uncontrollable anger washed through the Engineer suddenly, like a red hot wave.

No! No! No!

First, the fiasco down in Washington with the DHS agent, and now this! His game couldn't take any more adjusting. If Johann even suspected that there were Feds in the woods outside, he would be gone in a flash. Dimitrius would not only lose his chance to finish what Viper couldn't do two years ago, but he would lose his target. For the first time in his career, he would fail.

Dimitrius dropped the binoculars and picked up the rifle. He adjusted the scope until the woman was solidly in his sights. She was moving slowly, trying to stay silent. Her black jacket was open in front, displaying a white button-down tailored shirt tucked into black pants. Dimitrius centered the cross hairs on her chest and slid his finger over the trigger. He took a long, slow deep breath and held the rifle steady on her.

She paused, motioning to her partner to stop, and lifted a pair of binoculars that she held in her hand. Dimitrius paused as well, lifting his head from the rifle sight and glancing at the house. His finger moved off the trigger. Johann was still there. If he shot the Fed, Johann would undoubtedly run. He pressed his lips together in indecision for a moment, returning his eye to the scope and watching her through the sight. She was watching the house, standing perfectly still. He couldn't have planned a better shot if he tried.

Dimitrius hovered his finger near the trigger, debating. After a long moment, he lifted his head and put the rifle down regretfully. He couldn't take the chance on losing Johann. She would have to wait until another time and another place.

"So let me get this straight," John said, glancing at Stephanie as he pulled into the dirt road off to the right when she indicated. "We're going to go after a terrorist who is planning an attack on US soil without the backup of the Agency, without even *our boss* knowing, on the assurance of an old friend that she can "handle" it?"

"Pull into the trees. I don't want them to hear the truck," Stephanie directed. John pulled off the road and into the trees, cutting the engine. They were in the middle of nowhere, following the GPS co-ordinates that the agents who tailed Johann last night had sent them. The agents were encamped a quarter of a mile away with their surveillance equipment. The night before they had managed to set up sound in the house and were listening in even now. "And yes. That's the gist of it."

"What about Fred and Paul in yonder surveillance bus?" John demanded. Stephanie shrugged.

"Obviously, they'll have to know. They're my responsibility. I'll take care of it," she answered calmly. She glanced at John as she pulled a small pair of binoculars out of her purse and put them in her jacket pocket. "You don't have to do it. I'm not trying to make you do something you aren't comfortable with."

"Oh yeah," John scoffed sarcastically. "Because I am so much *more* comfortable with hanging my partner out to dry on her own." He reached over and opened the glove box, removing his backup and an extra clip. "Where you go, I go. End of story."

"Good." Stephanie nodded. "Then that's settled."

She smiled and got out of the truck, closing the door softly. John got out of the truck, muttering to himself, and came around the front of the truck.

"What makes you so sure that Alina's got this?" he demanded as they started moving through the woods parallel to the access road. Stephanie pushed a branch out of her way.

"I don't know," she admitted. "She just seems like a totally different person when she's addressing this whole issue. Focused. Professional. I get the feeling that she's used to this sort of thing."

"What sort of thing?" John asked, stepping over depressed area in the ground that looked suspiciously boggy. "Law enforcement?"

"Not exactly." Stephanie grinned at the thought of Alina in law enforcement, federal or otherwise. "I can't explain it. I just think that she is more adept at this than we are."

"Have you at least found out who she works for?" John asked. Stephanie shook her head.

"She works for our government, but in what capacity, I have no idea," she answered. "And I'm not sure that I want to know. I think the less we know, the better off we are."

"Speak for yourself," John retorted. "I like to know what I'm working with." Stephanie glanced at him.

"You *do* know what you're working with," she said. "You're working with Lina, your ex. You know her as well, if not better, than I do." John shook his head in disagreement.

"I knew the old Alina," he retorted. "She's morphed into a completely different person. I have no idea who this new one is, or where she came from."

Stephanie opened her mouth to answer, but gasped instead as she stumbled over something in the underbrush. She would have pitched forward onto her face if John hadn't grabbed her arm and hauled her back.

"Thanks," Stephanie gasped, her heart thumping.

"No problem," John said, letting go of her arm.

They continued moving through the woods, more carefully now as they glimpsed the house through the trees. The subject of Alina was dropped as they both fell silent, listening for any sounds from the house. Stephanie stopped just short of the last section of trees before the clearing around the house and pulled out her binoculars. There were no curtains in the house and she had a clear view through the front windows from where she stood. She raised the binoculars to her eyes and adjusted them. Shadows were visible toward the back of the front room, but she couldn't make out much more than shapes.

"What do you see?" John asked. Stephanie shook her head slightly.

"Four, maybe five, people toward the back of the house," she answered, lowering the binoculars. "They seem to be standing around a table or something, but I can't really tell."

"Do you want to try to get closer?" John asked, moving to the side so that he could see more through the trees. Stephanie shook her head.

"No. I think I want to go back to Fred and Paul and listen to what is going on in there," she said slowly. She looked around with a shiver.

"What's wrong?" John asked, catching the shiver. Stephanie was frowning.

"I don't know," she answered. "I just felt like someone walked over my grave." John frowned and turned back toward the truck.

"Come on," he said. "Let's get out of here. Did you get the plates on that utility truck?"

"Yes."

Stephanie turned to follow him, glancing behind her as she did. She felt like she was being watched. Stephanie took one last look around and then followed John with a sigh. Alina had her spooked and now she was just jumpy. There was absolutely nothing there.

Chapter Nineteen

Alina turned on the shower and faced the vanity to take her hair out of its pony-tail. It was early afternoon and she had spent the morning studying maps of the terrain around the location where Johann was hunkered down. She had also pulled up satellite images of the entire road network in the twenty mile radius surrounding Three Mile Island. She had been planning on driving out there herself, but when Stephanie told her she was going with John, Alina decided to leave the physical recon to them. Instead, she focused determining the most likely entry and exit points for Johann and his team. It didn't take her very long to see, according to the maps and to the blinking location dot of the tracker on Johann's car, that his exit strategy could not include every member of his team. He had obviously planned for only he and his brother to get out. The rest of the team was expendable, and *that* told Viper all she needed to know about the whole operation.

Alina picked up a brush and ran it through her hair before turning toward the shower, her mind absorbed with the problem of Johann. Dimitrius would undoubtedly wait until after Johann had done his job, intercepting him on his way back across the river. That would be the best time, while chaos was erupting elsewhere and while Johann was feeling enough satisfaction to let his guard down just a bit. That's where Viper would choose as well, if she didn't care about the massive loss of human life that would ensue.

Steam was filling the bathroom from the shower and Alina stepped into the tub carefully, wincing as the hot water hit her face. She stepped back slightly, closing her eyes and relaxing as the hot water streamed over her. Stephanie and John would try to intercept Johann *before* he blew anything, leaving her in a position of having to work in conjunction with the Feds. Alina opened her eyes and stared at the shower tile through the water. If it came down to it, would Stephanie be able to pull the trigger?

Alina knew Johann would shoot first before running the risk of being captured. There would be no surrender for him. That's what made him so dangerous. There was no negotiating or bargaining with him. Mossavid was autonomous because Johann was uninterested in politics or in creating relationships that he could use in the future. His one foray into the realms of the civilized communications of the Western World had ended in disaster two years ago. His sole mission was to disrupt and destroy as many members of Christian Western culture as he could, and he was very good at it. The body count caused by Johann under the auspices of Mossavid was staggering. Viper had been brought back from her South American retreat to ensure that Johann was taken care of once and for all, and she had every intention of doing just that. However, if Stephanie accomplished it before she could, then she wouldn't complain. She would then be free to take care of Dimitrius.

But Johann had to come first.

Alina sighed and reached for her shampoo. She couldn't count on Stephanie pulling the trigger. She had no idea if Stephanie had ever even been in a position to fire her weapon in the line of duty, let alone kill a man. Alina learned very early on in her military life that different people reacted differently when it actually came down to pulling that trigger. Some were suddenly attacked with previously unmentioned morality, while others just simply froze and forgot everything they had ever learned on the firing range. She had no way of knowing how Stephanie would react. Viper had to plan on doing it herself.

Alina rinsed her hair and reached for her soap, her mind still trying to find a way to satisfy her own job, Stephanie's safety, and the safety of thousands of unsuspecting civilians. *It couldn't be easy, could it,* she thought. *"Go to Jersey! Finish the job with Johann. Redeem yourself. Then we can all move past this."* That's what they had said.

Yeah, ok. This is working out just like we planned.

Alina stepped back under the hot water and let it wash away the soap. She grit her teeth as the soap ran over the hole in her side, causing a momentary burn before the discomfort gave way to heat-induced numbness. Standing with her back to the flow, Alina allowed the water to wash away her tension. She had to re-focus and center herself, and then everything else would fall into place.

By the time she stepped out of the shower some five minutes later, Alina was in a much better frame of mind. Her thoughts were clear and she felt refreshed and ready to go to work. She towel dried her hair, wrapped the towel around herself, and turned to go into the bedroom. Alina stepped into the bedroom, and froze.

Her heart started thumping in a mix of surprise and pleasure at the sight of Damon stretched out on the bed, his arms crossed over his chest, propped up with pillows against the headboard. He was dressed in jeans and a tee-shirt and his bare feet were crossed at the ankles. He looked like he had been settled in for some time, dozing while he was waiting. His black hair was slightly tousled and a five o'clock shadow darkened his face, lending his rugged good-looks an edge of ruthlessness. His deep blue eyes took in her towel and damp hair in a swift glance before his lips curved into the sexiest smile Alina thought she had ever seen.

"You just made my day," he told her. Alina's lips curved into an answering smile on their own as her eyes locked with his.

"That was easy," she replied.

Damon chuckled and uncrossed his arms and feet, swinging his legs off the bed. He got up and came over to her, his eyes never leaving hers. Alina felt rooted to the spot, unable to move or think. She supposed she should move away and grab a robe or some clothes, but she couldn't seem to make her legs work. Damon stopped directly in front of her and looked down into her face. There was a soft smile in his eyes.

"I have been thinking about you for the past twenty-four hours," he said softly, lifting his hand to brush a length of wet hair away from her eyes. "It's so good to see you."

Alina caught her breath again and tried to keep her breathing steady as her heart thumped against her ribs almost painfully. She wanted to lean forward over the few inches that separated them and kiss him, but she didn't think she would be able to stop if she did. She suddenly realized that somewhere, deep inside, she had been afraid he wouldn't come back.

"I'm glad you're back," Alina admitted in a low voice.

Something flashed deep in Damon's eyes at her words. Satisfaction, perhaps? Happiness? Relief? Alina was left to wonder as he dropped his hands to her hips and gently pulled her to him as he lowered his lips to hers. It was a gentle and undemanding kiss, made that much more powerful by the simple expression of emotion behind it. Alina sighed into him as she lifted her arms to his shoulders, momentarily forgetting all about the towel. Her stomach dropped out inside her and she felt like the house could blow up around them and she wouldn't care. Just as long as Hawk was there, holding her up, everything else could fall apart.

But then, close on the heels of that warm and comfortable thought, came a stab of unreasonable panic.

Damon felt the change in her immediately. In a heartbeat, Alina's back stiffened slightly and something inside her withdrew. She was still holding him close, and her lips were still kissing him, but Damon knew she had emotionally stepped back. He ended the kiss and lifted his head, suppressing a small sigh. He understood her better than he suspected she knew herself. Viper was afraid.

Damon watched through half-closed eyes as Alina slowly opened her eyes. They were warm and dark...and unreadable. But for a few moments, he had *felt* her feelings. For now, Hawk was content.

His eyes dropped a few inches and he grinned. The forgotten towel had slipped down and it was only his own body that was keeping it up. Damon gently grabbed the edges and eased it back up.

"As much as I am enjoying this, you should get dressed," he said huskily with a grin.

Alina's eyes widened and she gasped as her hands took over the task of tightening the towel around herself again.

"Thank you," she said, glancing up at him. His grin grew as her cheeks flushed pink.

"You're welcome."

Damon stepped back and watched as she spun around and headed toward the large walk-in closet. His eyes dropped to her barely covered backside and her bare legs and he almost groaned. Turning away to sit on the bed, he glanced up into the corner where Raven was on his perch, silently watching him with his black eyes.

"You don't have these problems, do you?" Damon muttered. Ravens only response was to blink.

"Did you say something?" Alina poked her head out of the closet. Damon shook his head and she disappeared back into the depths of the closet. "How was Cairo?" she called.

Damon grinned. He knew she would figure out where he went.

"It smelled," he answered. Alina chuckled.

"It does smell," she agreed, her voice slightly muffled. "Too many people in too little space."

Damon looked around the bedroom while he waited for her to emerge from the closet. He had a lot to discuss with her, but he didn't want to do it yelling into the closet. The room was spotless and uncluttered, like downstairs. However, Alina had allowed something of herself to touch the bedroom. The down comforter was covered with a deep red cover and the curtains in the windows were sheers in a matching shade of red. A couple of books were stacked on the bedside table and Damon smiled when he investigated and found them to be spy novels. There were a few candles in the room, all clearly burned regularly, and a flat screen TV graced the wall opposite the bed. Unlike downstairs, the remote was on the bedside table next to the books. This was where Alina relaxed, and Damon felt comfortable here.

"Have you eaten?" Alina asked, emerging from the closet dressed in jeans and a loose top. Damon shook his head.

"Not since last night," he answered, his eyes dropping to her bare feet. Her toenails were still red. He didn't know why that pleased him so much.

Alina studied him for a moment, sitting there on the edge of her bed. He looked sexy. And exhausted.

"Why don't you come downstairs and I'll fix you something to eat? Then you can have a shower and sleep," she offered. Hawk looked up at her with a slight smile.

"No rest for the wicked," he retorted. "But I *will* take you up on the food and the shower," he added, standing up. Alina raised an eyebrow slightly.

"You'll take me up on the nap, too," she told him, walking in front of him out of the bedroom. "You're no good to me tired," she added over her shoulder.

Damon grinned at the back of her head.

"I wish you meant that the way I want right now," he murmured.

Alina chuckled as she headed down the stairs but offered no rejoinder. Damon sighed and followed her, settling onto one of the bar stools when they reached the kitchen.

"How are the Fearless Feds?" he asked, watching as Alina opened the refrigerator and pulled out a carton of eggs.

"Suspicious of you." Alina set the eggs on the island behind her and went back into the fridge. Damon watched as red onion, green pepper, baby spinach and cheese were unceremoniously added to the pile on the island. "You're on their Most Wanted list right now," Alina told him, kicking the fridge closed with her bare foot. Damon raised an eyebrow.

"Any particular reason?" he asked. Alina glanced at him.

"A DHS agent, an old friend of Stephanie's, was killed down in DC the day before yesterday," she said, pulling a wooden cutting board from a drawer in the island and reaching for a knife. "It was made to look like an accident. She was poking around, trying to get information about you at Stephanie's request."

Alina sliced the top off the pepper with one smooth motion and looked up to gauge Damon's reaction. He was staring at her, his face unreadable.

"Who was it?" he asked. Alina shrugged.

"A woman Stephanie was in college with, apparently," she answered, chopping the pepper quickly and moving on to the onion.

"What happened?" Damon demanded.

"The woman sent her an email saying that she thought she was being watched," Alina explained, making quick work of the onion and moving over to the sink to rinse the knife. "Stephanie swears that she wasn't the type to imagine things, so she became concerned when she couldn't reach her yesterday. She finally called her office directly this morning and found out that she was killed in a car accident. Stephanie immediately put two and two together and came up with five. She came in here this morning, ready to hang you from the nearest tree."

"Well, at least it's been an interesting two days for you," Hawk murmured. Alina glanced at him as she slid the knife back into her knife block.

"That I won't deny," she agreed with a slight laugh.

They were both silent as she took two eggs out of the carton and cracked them into a bowl. Damon watched as she whisked them up with a drop of cold water.

"Where's Johann?" he asked suddenly. Alina glanced at him under her eyelashes.

"In place," she answered shortly. Damon stared at her silently and she sighed. "He's hunkered down in a house across the river and a few miles down from the island," she clarified.

"Have you been there?" Damon asked. Alina shook her head.

"Steph and John went this morning. I let them do the physical recon," she said. Damon raised an eyebrow and stared at her. Alina glanced at him and saw the surprise in his eyes.

"It was a matter of letting them take over Johann so I can focus on Dimitrius," she explained. "They interrupted me last night. If they hadn't, Johann wouldn't be with us anymore," she added suddenly. Damon let out a low whistle.

"How did that happen?" he asked. Alina shrugged.

"They showed up at the same place at the same time," she told him. "Two more minutes and it would have been done and I would have been gone," she added, needing to tell someone who would understand. As soon as she said it, though, Alina regretted it.

Damon watched as she turned to put the egg carton back into the fridge. He didn't know what to say. Despite the light tone she was using, Damon knew Viper had to be furious. That was twice now that someone had prevented her from putting a bullet in Johann, and he understood her frustration all too well. Damon mulled over the idea of mentioning that failure builds character, but he was fairly confident that that was a conversation that would not end well.

Alina took a deep breath and closed the refrigerator door. She was going to have to turn and look at Hawk, now that she had just admitted to failing a second time with Johann. Alina was afraid of what she would see in his face. She was angry enough as it was, and the last thing she needed to see was pity. Turning away from the fridge, she looked across the kitchen to Damon challengingly, her chin raised just slightly. His face was unreadable, but his eyes were bright with understanding. They stared at each other for a moment and Alina was strangely comforted. Hawk wasn't judging her. He understood her frustration.

"And the Engineer?" Damon broke the silence, moving on. Alina went over to the island.

"I'll get him when he goes for Johann," she said, reaching up to the pot rack to pull down the nonstick frying pan.

In her distraction, she forgot her injury and reached up with her left hand. The stretch sent a sharp stab of pain through her side and Alina couldn't stop the grimace of pain that flashed across her face. She didn't need to look at Damon to know that he had seen it. He appeared at her side a second later and took the frying pan out of her hand.

"What happened?" he demanded softly, setting the pan onto the stove and turning back to Alina. "You've been favoring your left side the whole time I've been watching you."

Alina looked up into his face with a frown. She should have known he would notice something was wrong.

"It's nothing," she retorted. Damon raised an eyebrow in patent disbelief.

"You never were a good liar with me," he told her. "Let me see."

"No." Alina stepped back quickly, coming up against the counter. "It's just a scratch."

Damon ignored her, his eyes dropping to her left side. He reached out to lift up her shirt and she blocked his hand at his wrist swiftly. He looked at her with a laugh in his eyes.

"Really?" he demanded. They stared at each other, one laughing and the other defensive.

"It's getting better," Alina informed him. The laughter faded from his blue eyes.

"Let me see then," he said softly. "You're no good to me wounded," he added.

Alina's lips twitched, a laugh springing into her eyes. She sighed and nodded briefly and Damon lifted the side of her shirt. He inhaled sharply and lifted the shirt higher to get a better look.

"Oh, baby, this is more than a scratch," Damon breathed, shifting her to the side so the light was better.

Alina felt a rush of irrational warmth at the endearment. Damon suddenly grasped her hips and lifted her effortlessly up onto the counter so that he could get a better look. It was done before Alina could even take a breath. One minute he was bent over trying to look at the wound, and the next, she was seated on the counter while he gently probed the skin around it.

"You got the bullet out yourself?"

His voice was sharper than he intended, but Alina didn't appear to notice as she nodded. The entry hole was partially closed now, but the skin was red and irritated and when he pressed gently, moisture came out.

"It doesn't appear too infected, but this should have been stitched," he murmured.

"I thought it would close faster on its own," Alina said. "By the time I realized it wasn't, it was too late to stitch it."

"This happened when Angela was shot?" Damon straightened up and turned to get a piece of paper towel from the roll near the sink.

"Yes. The round went through her shoulder and lodged in me," Alina told him. "I was on my way home before I even realized I'd been shot." Damon nodded and gently pressed the paper towel to her side.

"Adrenaline," he said knowingly. "Where are the bandages? Upstairs?" Alina nodded and Damon lifted the paper towel away. "Sit still. I'll go get them," he said.

"I'm perfectly capable of doing it myself," Alina muttered, glaring at him. Damon just smiled at her.

"Yes, but why should you when I want to?" he retorted, turning and disappearing out of the kitchen and down the hall before Alina could think of an argument.

She sat there on the counter for a minute, stunned. *What just happened?* she wondered blankly. How had she ended up sitting on the counter, meekly waiting for Hawk to reappear with bandages? Viper frowned and dropped off the counter noiselessly. This was ridiculous. She was letting him into her head and that was unacceptable.

Alina looked at the bowl of eggs and accepted the fact that the omelet would have to wait until Hawk had finished playing doctor to his hearts content. She wandered over to the back door and looked outside. The early afternoon shadows were lengthening in the backyard and she watched as two squirrels chased each other across the deck.

"You just couldn't do it, could you?" Damon murmured in her ear.

Alina jumped and realized that the squirrels were long gone and she was staring outside at nothing, completely lost in her thoughts. Damon had walked up behind her without her even noticing.

"Do what?" Alina demanded, swinging around. She was startled at how close he was.

"Sit still," Hawk replied. "Come into the bathroom where there is enough light for me to see what I'm working with."

"I can tell you what you're working with," Alina muttered, following him nonetheless.

Damon switched on the bright fluorescent light in the powder room and motioned for her to sit on the sink. Alina complied with a sigh.

"You realize this is totally ridiculous," she said as he stepped into the small powder room. He seemed to suck up all available space with his broad shoulders.

"Humor me," he said shortly. "Can you take the shirt off?" he asked, motioning with his hand to her shirt. Alina raised her eyebrow.

"Wow. Does that work on all the women?" she asked. Damon's lips curved and his eyes sparkled.

"I can do it or you can, sweetheart," he murmured.

Alina made a face at him and lifted the shirt over her head, dropping it in the sink beside her. Damon thanked her, opening the bottle of hydrogen peroxide. He gently cleaned the wound and then folded a clean gauze bandage into a square and laid it on the hole. He covered that with another bandage and taped the whole down with tape.

"How did you get the bullet out?" he finally spoke when he was finished. When Alina didn't answer, he glanced up to see her looking sheepish. Damon straightened up and looked down at her, wiping his hands on the clean hand towel. His lips twitched.

"Spit it out," he said. "Tweezers?"

"I couldn't find them," Alina murmured, feeling her cheeks growing pink and hating herself for it. Damon saw the blush and started to grin.

"Pliers?" he asked.

Alina shook her head and reached into the sink for her shirt. Damon leaned against the door frame and considered her thoughtfully. The blush wasn't going away.

"Roach clip?" he guessed, drawing a laugh from her. She finished pulling her shirt over her head and got off the sink.

"Metal nail file," Alina murmured. Both his eyebrows soared into his forehead.

"I'm sorry, a what?" Hawk demanded incredulously. Alina shrugged and squeezed past him through the doorway.

"It was the only thing that was readily available," she muttered as she passed. Damon watched her walk away with a grin.

"Do you even know what a nail file is?" he called after her. His answer was the finger, held up without a glance back.

Hawk burst out laughing then, a rich, full laugh that echoed down the hall and struck right into Alina's heart. A grin tugged at her lips despite herself. She lit the burner under the frying pan and picked up the eggs, whisking them again briskly. When Damon entered the kitchen a moment later, carrying the empty bandage wrappers, she was at the stove, making his omelet.

"Where's the bullet?" he asked, throwing the wrappers into the trash under the sink and leaning against the counter next to the stove.

Alina glanced up into his face, a little disconcerted at the novelty of having someone in her kitchen while she cooked.

"Downstairs," she answered. "I ran ballistics on it this morning."

"Find out anything you didn't already know?" Damon asked. Alina shook her head.

"Nope."

She turned and retrieved the cutting board with the vegetables from the island and Damon grabbed a handful of peppers off the board as it passed him.

"Israeli?' he asked, popping the peppers into his mouth. Alina nodded and started adding the vegetables to the omelet.

"He's old school," she said. "5.56 Galil Sniper. He probably used it because the distance wasn't far. It was only about 500 meters, if that."

Alina set the cutting board aside and watched as the omelet bubbled up around the vegetables.

"You're lucky it didn't do a through and through and go right through you," Damon told her. Alina glanced at him.

"I'm lucky he missed," she retorted. Damon looked at her sharply.

"How so?" he asked.

"He was aiming for Stephanie," Alina said, reaching back for the cheese and pulling a microplane grater out of the drawer in the island. "If he hadn't missed, she would be dead." Damon watched her grate cheese into his omelet silently.

"I want to see the bullet," he said suddenly after a moment. Alina nodded and motioned to one of the cabinets.

"You will. You want to grab yourself a plate?" she said.

Damon turned and got the plate out of the cabinet. Alina slid the omelet out of the pan and onto the plate, and Damon smiled at her.

"You're too good to me," he told her.

"I know," she agreed. "Now eat it while it's hot."

Damon grabbed a fork out of the drawer and took his plate over to the bar. Alina rinsed out the frying pan while he started to eat and cleaned up before going over to sit next to him.

"Tell me what you found out in Cairo," she said. Damon glanced at her.

"You already know what I found out," he countered. Alina glanced at him.

"True," she agreed. "You could have just asked me. You didn't have to go all the way there." Damon forked some eggs into his mouth before getting up and going into the kitchen to get a bottle of water out of the fridge.

"You know it doesn't work that way," he said, coming back with another bottle for her. He handed it to her as he sat down. "The powers that be need proof."

"Were you shocked?" Alina asked after a moment. Damon looked at her.

"I'm more shocked that he made it onto Capital Hill," he said. "I wouldn't have thought you would let him get that far."

"It wasn't my business," Alina said in a low voice. "Sometimes the people need a hero. And when they do, they don't care about the past." She opened the water bottle and took a sip while Damon ate in silence for a minute.

"Did you ever tell anyone?" he asked. Alina shook her head.

"No," she said. "That's not something you tell anyone."

"But that's the reason you disappeared," Damon prompted. Alina nodded.

"When we start to question why we're being used, then it's time to take a step back," she said quietly. "I can accept that what we do is needed to preserve a very volatile sense of balance in this world. We do what governments can't, or won't, do publicly. But two years ago, I ended up in a place I shouldn't have been, acting on orders that were based on lies, and witnessing something that I was certainly never supposed to see."

"You know you were never meant to walk out of Cairo alive, right?" Damon asked, glancing at her.

Alina lifted her eyes to his and Damon recognized the look deep inside them. She knew. She had spent two years knowing that she had walked away from her own death sentence.

"Yes," Alina said simply. Damon stared at her for a minute thoughtfully before going back to his eggs.

"That's why they wanted you to come finish Johann here," he said after a minute. "They don't expect you to succeed here either."

"Oh, I'm aware of that too," Alina said with a slight smile that didn't quite reach her eyes. "Is Harry the reason you're here?" she asked suddenly. Damon glanced at her and she met his look squarely. "Harry would have sniffed out this whole debacle long ago. You're clearly being protected by DHS and the only one who can do that so effectively is Harry. He didn't send you for containment, did he?"

"Yes and no," Hawk answered after a long moment of silence. He finished his omelet and drank some water. "It's complicated."

292

Alina stared at Damon for a moment. She suddenly had a full understanding of Stephanie's frustration with the word complicated.

"So you're still not going to tell me," she stood up and picked up his empty plate, her eyes meeting his. "Just remember that blind trust only goes so far," Alina told him softly. Hawk nodded slightly and she turned to go into the kitchen with his plate.

"Go upstairs and have your shower and get some sleep," she said over her shoulder. "You look like hell."

Chapter Twenty

Alina pressed the disconnect button on her phone and closed her laptop with a snap. Hawk had gone up to take his shower two hours ago and hadn't come back downstairs. She descended into her lair and was in the process of consolidating all her files on her hard-drives when Stephanie called. The conversation had been brief. The bugs inside the house where Johann was staying had just confirmed: Johann was launching his attack tonight.

Alina stood up and quickly disconnected multiple cables from the back of the laptop and reached under the counter for the bag. She packed the laptop, network cables, and power cords into the laptop bag before tucking the external hard drive into a separate bag. She then reached up and started pulling cables from the LCD screens along the walls and, one by one, they went black. Rolling up the cables swiftly as she went, Alina tied them neatly and set them to the side before turning to the multiple hard-drives and the two servers.

Ten minutes after she had hung up with Stephanie, her command center was decommissioned and all the equipment was ready to move. Alina headed up the stairs and emerged into the kitchen. The afternoon sun had faded and the kitchen was dark after the bright fluorescent lights in her command center. She blinked a few times and then pressed the button under the sink to slide the island back into place.

Outwardly, she was calm, but the under-lying tension that had been present all day had morphed into that feeling of anticipation mixed with apprehension that Viper knew well. Once she was moving, the feeling would dissipate and calm focus would replace it. But for now, Alina took a deep breath in an attempt to settle the trembling that was attempting to creep into her belly and legs. She rolled her head a few times and took a few deep breaths, forcing herself to focus her attention inward, rather than on the next few hours. It was going to end tonight, one way or another.

And neither Johann nor the Engineer would go down easily.

The house was silent as Alina went upstairs. She went into her bedroom and came to a stop at the sight of Hawk, spread out on his stomach diagonally across her bed, fast asleep. He was wearing his jeans, and nothing else. Alina stared for a long moment at a long, jagged scar that ran right to left from the center of his right shoulder-blade to below the low waist of his jeans. It wasn't very old and she wondered how it happened. Viper knew she was covered in her own scars, but she had always thought of Hawk as almost invincible. Seeing the scar made her realize that he was human, just as she was.

Alina frowned and went into the closet silently, not wanting to consider their very real mortality. She changed into black cargo swat pants and a microfiber tank top, then picked up her black utility boots and went back into the bedroom. Damon was still sleeping. Alina glanced up at Raven and smiled slightly. Her pet hawk was also asleep, with his beak buried deep in his feathers. As she looked from one to the other, somewhere deep inside, Alina felt something as close to peace as she had she felt in a very long time. Frowning again, she pushed the feeling aside and set her boots down on the floor near the bed. She looked at Damon, considering the best way to wake him up.

"Is there a reason why you're standing there staring at me?"

Damon spoke, breaking the silence in the room and causing Alina to flinch in surprise. He opened his eyes and peered up at her.

"It's time to work," Viper told him simply.

She went over to the dresser to get a pair of socks. Damon noted her SWAT pants and tank top and rolled over, stretching with a wide yawn.

"What's the plan?" he asked, sitting up as she sat down on the side of the bed to put on her socks and boots.

"I'm meeting Steph and John at their outpost." Alina laced up one boot before removing her ankle strap and knife from the other one. She strapped it onto her leg before putting her right boot on. "I'll take care of Johann on the Island before heading back to his base on the other side of the river. Our Fearless Feds can handle the rest of his crew. I have a bigger fish to fry."

"The Engineer?" Damon asked. Alina nodded.

"He'll wait for him somewhere near the house," she said.

"That's what I would do," Damon agreed, standing up. Alina finished lacing up her other boot and stood up, her pant leg falling to cover the knife.

"Me too," she said. Damon headed toward the door as she went over to the dresser to grab her watch.

"I have clothes in the car. I'll get changed," he said over his shoulder before disappearing down the hall.

Alina moved into the bathroom and a few minutes later, her hair was braided and ready to be tucked away under a dark cap. She took a deep breath and considered her reflection in the mirror. The square bulge under the top at her side drew her attention, and Alina stared at it thoughtfully for a minute. She stretched in a full stretch to the right, arching her left arm over her head and leaning to the side. She frowned when the bandage at her side pulled taut and tape started to pucker away from her skin.

Well, that's not going to work, Alina thought, taking the tank top off impatiently. Opening the vanity cabinet, she surveyed her options and took out a long ace bandage. She ripped open the package and wrapped it around herself, effectively securing the bandage and giving her side more support. She pulled the tank top back on and looked at herself again. Her middle looked thick, but it would work. Without giving her injury or appearance another thought, Alina switched out the light and left the bathroom.

Viper was ready to go.

Alina dropped silently over the wall to land next to Stephanie. The Island was dark and silent in this area. The two reactor funnels, dead since 1979 when the Island had its infamous meltdown, rose imposingly into the night about 200 meters away, eerily silent in the darkness. In the distance, on the far side, the two functioning reactors spewed thick, white clouds into the night air, illuminated by the bright lights around that side of the compound. Stephanie jumped as Alina landed next to her, startled. She glanced behind her at the wall.

"Oh my God!" she hissed. "Where did you come from? You just scared the crap out of me!" Alina smiled slightly.

"Sorry," she retorted.

Stephanie took in Alina's black clothing and the black knit cap that covered her hair. She was wearing a light-weight black jacket with multiple pockets over what looked like a Kevlar vest, and a black strap ran diagonally across her body, holding a rifle bag on her back. A leg holster with what looked like a .45 was strapped to her thigh, and a pair of night vision goggles hung around her neck. Stephanie blinked, unsettled at the sight of her old friend in what appeared to be normal work gear for her.

"You look like you're going to invade a small town," she muttered, turning her attention back to the area in front of her. Alina glanced at her.

"Not tonight. Maybe next week," she replied.

Stephanie shook her head with a reluctant grin and the two women were silent for a moment as Viper surveyed the area. The edge of a cement peripheral road started a few feet away and she looked to the right in the darkness, toward the edge of the island.

"That's your best bet," Viper whispered, motioning to their right. "Go along the edge, past the funnels, and stay in the shadows. Do you have an exact location?" Stephanie shook her head.

"I know he'll be somewhere between the two pairs of funnels, but I don't know where," she answered. Alina nodded and glanced to her left.

"I'm going to cross over to the other side of that access road," she said, nodding toward the road that ran down to the main reactor compound. "I'll set up on a rooftop on the other side." Stephanie nodded.

"I'm still not happy about you not wearing a com unit," she said. "How are we going to communicate?"

"We won't need to. You'll be fine," Alina replied. She looked at Stephanie, dressed in jeans and a jacket, her 9mm Glock at her waist.

"Where's your backup?" Alina asked her, motioning to the gun. The blank look she encountered from Stephanie answered her question perfectly.

"What do you mean?" she asked. Alina blinked.

"You don't have a backup firearm?" she asked. Stephanie shook her head.

"I didn't think of it," she admitted. Alina shook her head and reached into her back holster, pulling out the modified Glock that she carried as a backup.

"That does *not* make me feel confident," she muttered, handing Stephanie the gun and reaching into one of her cargo pockets for the clips. "It's modified. It has a longer range and better accuracy than your standard issue. And it has a bigger kick-back to it, so be prepared for that."

"I can't take your gun!" Stephanie started to protest, but a cutting look from Alina's dark eyes silenced her.

"You can," Alina told her, handing her the clips. "And you will. I don't want your death on my conscience."

"That's a little dramatic," Stephanie retorted. "I'm wearing a vest. And this isn't exactly my first rodeo," she added.

"Good."

Alina nodded shortly and Stephanie was struck with how calm and focused her friend appeared. She was all business. Stephanie suddenly felt that there was no one else that she would rather have on that rooftop than this cold, efficient stranger.

Viper glanced at her watch. She had already done a sweep of the other side of the island and would have liked to have done one more, but they were out of time. According to Johann's time schedule, they had to get into position now.

"They never found the body of the security guard, so keep an eye out for two players," she told Stephanie. "The guard may be in on it."

"Got it." Stephanie nodded, tucking the gun away. Alina looked at her.

"Be accurate," she added. "Johann won't miss." Stephanie nodded again and Alina smiled slightly.

"See you later," she said, clapping Stephanie on the shoulder lightly before disappearing into the darkness.

Stephanie watched her go, disconcerted when Alina seemed to vanish into the darkness, as if the night was accepting her into itself. In an instant, Stephanie was alone and she headed to the right, staying deep in the shadows. John was a few miles up the river and getting into position at the train station, one of the main targets. It was a stroke of luck that Pete had been able to get the bugs into the house while Johann was sleeping last night. It was an even bigger stroke of luck that Johann had gone over the details of his plan in that meeting with his team earlier today.

Stephanie prayed that the luck would hold out tonight.

Damon's breath came quick and even as he ran through the trees along the river. He had watched Viper go into the water and made sure that she reached the island without incident, watching through binoculars as she navigated the security and climbed onto the island. Once she shed her wet suit, he turned away and started running to make his way the three miles or so downriver to Johann's house. He wanted to sweep a one mile radius around the house and find where the Engineer was hiding. If he got the opportunity, Hawk would take the bastard out himself and risk Vipers wrath later.

However, he knew the odds of finding him in the darkness would be slim.

The Engineer wouldn't be seen until he was ready to be seen.

Hawk hadn't accompanied Viper to meet with Stephanie and John. Viper didn't want them to know he was back yet and he was content to remain incognito for the time being. Things were complicated enough already without being drilled about his whereabouts for the past two days. Better to get this night over with, and then he and Viper could re-evaluate. Once they knew exactly what had happened down in Washington, they could better address the issue. But until then, Damon was staying well out of the way of the Fearless Feds.

When Viper told him that they managed to get a bug into Johann's temporary house, his first thought had been that the Feds were being played. However, as she explained the attack that had been laid out, Hawk grudgingly had to admit that this was exactly what someone of Johann's caliber would have invented.

The explosion on the island was, indeed, meant to be a catalyst to cause widespread alarm and panic. Once that had been established, the real attacks would begin. One bomb detonated in the train station a few miles away, towards Harrisburg, shutting down the trains. Another bomb detonated in the Harrisburg International Airport, shutting down the airport. And the final two detonated on the bridge spanning the river near Harrisburg, the bridge where the Pennsylvania interstate crossed the river. Those three locations, in that order, would cause a death toll the likes of which the US hadn't seen in over ten years.

Hawk leapt over a patch of swampiness without breaking his stride. Viper was trusting the Feds to prevent the real attacks while she took care of Johann, preventing the starter explosion. He wasn't quite as confident as she appeared to be in the skills of the agents, but he was letting her run the show her own way. Heaven itself knew how successful Alina was at planning. If anyone could make sure that this whole thing never saw the light of day, then it was Viper. That was her job.

And, in order for him to do *his* job, he had to allow her to do hers.

Viper settled onto her stomach on the pitch black rooftop and set her eye against the night scope of her rifle. It had taken her less than two minutes to set up, and now she scanned the area between the two sets of towers, looking for Stephanie. On her second pass, she spotted her friend moving out of the shadows and slipping across the deserted pavement to disappear behind another building that flanked a parking lot. Alina started scanning to the left slowly, searching for signs of movement. She knew Johann had to be in position. It was just a matter of finding him before he found Stephanie.

Viper scanned the area slowly, noting the cars in the lot and the movement of the security lights. She hadn't seen a guard yet, but she knew security was tight down there. Before four planes had changed the world for Americans forever, the public had been allowed onto Three Mile Island to tour the dead reactors and learn about nuclear energy and how the reactors worked. Now, the island was closed to visitors. After multiple security threats from Al Queda and other terrorist organizations, the security measures on this island had been upgraded and increased until it was just short of being a nuclear fortress. Even so, Viper thought dispassionately, it had been easily maneuvered.

Of course, they were aware that Stephanie was there. While Stephanie had agreed that alerting local authorities of the threat would cause more harm than good, she had insisted on putting the Island on alert. Alina had disagreed, but she conceded the point, knowing that she would be able to avoid the security long enough to complete her own mission. She understood Stephanie's concern. Should the unthinkable happen and they fail, the Island had to be prepared.

Viper passed over a white utility van in the parking lot closest to Stephanie, then went back to it immediately. She studied it for a moment. Pennsylvania plates, security tag on the side, and pass hanging from the rear-view mirror. It appeared perfectly legitimate. And yet....Viper frowned. She could have sworn she saw it move slightly as she passed over it a second ago.

Alina moved the scope to the right slightly, looking for Stephanie. A shadow moved near the corner of the building and Viper knew she had Stephanie. She moved back to the van. It was perfectly still now and Alina could detect no sign of life nearby. But she was left with the unaccountably strong impression that the van *had* moved slightly, as if someone inside the back of the van crossed from one side to the other. It was positioned perfectly, directly in between the two sets of funnels. If an explosion occurred in that position, there would be no way to tell from either riverbank whether the explosion occurred in the live reactors or the dead ones. The illusion of another "incident" would be complete.

"Come on," Viper whispered. "Show me where you are."

She moved the scope again, peering through the cross-hairs as she scanned the night, looking for movement. Her heart felt like it was pounding, but her breathing was calm and her palms were dry. A quick glance at her watch told her that it was time, and yet she could still detect no movement in that parking lot or in any of the surrounding buildings.

Viper lifted her head, casting her eyes thoughtfully toward the two towers that were happily spewing forth white clouds. Could they be wrong? Could Johann have actually found a way to target the live nuclear reactor?

As quickly as the thought came into her head, Alina dismissed it. It would be virtually impossible to get any form of explosive into the nuclear reactor, let alone detonate it. She was impressed that he had found a way to get an explosive onto the island at all, and if it had been anyone other than

Johann, Alina would have never believed it possible. She lowered her head back to the night scope. The explosive had to be out in the open and Viper was liking the odds on the van more and more.

Movement caught her eye and Alina watched through the scope as Stephanie moved out from behind the building, staying in the shadows, and started to move up the side. Alina had a clear shot to her friend. She watched as Stephanie stopped and pressed against the side of the side of the building. *She heard something,* she thought, as Stephanie remained completely still against the side of the building.

Viper moved the scope back to the van.

There! It shifted slightly!

Alina watched as the van continued to move ever so slightly and then became still. Seconds later, a shadow moved at the back of the van and Viper slid her finger gently over the trigger. Her breathing slow, Alina allowed all thought of bombs and nuclear reactors to fade from her mind. All that was real to her right now was the trigger under her finger and the target hundreds of meters away. She waited patiently for the shadow to come into view.

When it stepped into her line of fire a few seconds later, Viper focused in on the face and swore softly. The face was the wide, round face of a very large black man who had about forty pounds and half a foot on Johann. He was wearing a security uniform and carrying a lunch bag in one hand. He looked like just another guard coming on duty, walking from his car towards his job. Alina's lips curved slightly.

"Oh well done, Johann," she breathed softly, focusing in on the uniform. It was the missing guard, alive and well, and Johann made sure that he was the first one out in the open, testing the waters before he committed to blowing the explosive.

Viper slid her finger off the trigger. She would wait. She was there for Johann.

She moved the scope back to Stephanie. She was still there, against the building, hidden in the shadows. Alina knew she could see the guard now as he moved out from behind the van and into the open. He was walking toward the building that Stephanie was pressed against, headed for the door at the other end of the building, away from Stephanie. He didn't appear to have seen her and Viper waited, almost apprehensively. While she was there to put an end to Johann, Stephanie was there to stop an explosion and Alina had little doubt that Stephanie had come to the same conclusion she had about the van.

Stephanie waited until the guard reached the sidewalk before moving out of the shadows. Viper watched as she walked toward the guard, her arms at her side, her posture relaxed. Alina couldn't hear anything, but she knew when Stephanie called out to him. He turned toward her, stopping in his tracks. Stephanie was still moving toward him, her lips moving and one arm gesturing, as if she was asking the guard for directions or for assistance. The guard didn't move, but seemed as if he was waiting for her to get closer.

Viper slid her finger over the trigger of her rifle again, exhaling slowly.

It was all over within a few short minutes. As Stephanie approached the guard, Viper watched through the scope as he pulled out a gun and aimed at her old friend. Stephanie didn't hesitate, pulling her own gun and, in the process, revealing the badge on her hip. Viper imagined she must have identified herself because the guard fired.

The sound of the shot echoed around the compound, reaching Viper on her rooftop, and she watched as Stephanie's firing arm came up. Where the guard had shot wide, Stephanie's shot was true and the guard was thrown back a step when her bullet ripped through his shoulder. The gun flew out of his firing hand, skipping across the sidewalk in one direction, while the lunch bag flew out of his other hand and hit the pavement in the parking lot, sliding across the tarmac before coming to rest against the wheel of a motorcycle parked nearby. Stephanie was advancing on the injured guard, both hands holding her gun steady, when he suddenly regained his balance and lunged at her.

Stephanie was caught off guard but Viper raised an eyebrow, momentarily diverted by the awkward clumsiness of the tackle. It reminded her of a drunk man trying to throw a punch, off balance and lacking precision. However, the guard had momentum backed by sheer weight behind him, and Stephanie was thrown to the ground. Her weapon skidded out of reach and Alina winced as the guard raised his good arm and delivered a staggering blow to the side of Stephanie's face. Almost immediately, Stephanie's foot connected solidly with his chest and he was knocked away from her long enough for Stephanie to scrabble away on the ground. She reached into the back of her jeans, pulling out Alina's modified Glock just as the guard reached her gun on the pavement. He turned and fired.

The two shots rang out simultaneously, exploding in the night and sounding to Alina, up on her rooftop, like fireworks. They were immediately followed by two more rapid shots from Stephanie. The guard was thrown backward and fell to the ground, three rounds straight through his chest ending his fight.

Viper watched Stephanie get up off the ground unsteadily and walk toward the fallen man cautiously, her gun still aimed at him and ready to fire. Blood poured down her arm, evidence that the guards final shot had caught her arm. Viper was watching as she advanced on the guard, kicking the gun on the ground away from him, when, suddenly, there was movement behind Stephanie.

The scuffle with the guard had moved them into the parking lot and away from the building. Stephanie had her back to the building and Viper caught her breath briefly as a tall shadow separated from the building, moving forward silently. She didn't need to focus on the face to know that it was Johann. The stealth with which the figure moved was more distinctive than the face could be. He had moved with that same careful grace that long ago day in Cairo, when he walked out of the meeting room into the hotel lobby. Stephanie didn't hear him and was bending down to check futilely for a pulse on the guard, leaving herself completely exposed.

Johann stopped just outside the shadows and raised his arm, the silhouette of a gun steady in his hand, aimed straight at Stephanie's head.

Alina's breath stopped and her finger moved gently, almost lovingly, over the trigger as she centered the cross-hairs. Time seemed to stand still as Viper held her breath for a few beats, listening to her own heart beat. Then, she exhaled slowly as her finger pulled back on the trigger.

Johann never got to fire his shot. Stephanie swung around quickly as he hit the ground, a single bullet wound in the center of his forehead. She straightened up with a gasp. He had fallen straight backwards with the force of the shot and was laying on his back a few feet behind her. Stephanie saw the gun resting where it had fallen out of his hand and, all at once, her heart started to pound and she felt light-headed. She hadn't heard a sound as he came up behind her and she stared as blood started to pool under his head, almost fascinated by the speed with which it started to collect on the pavement. That quickly, instead of *her* being dead next to the traitorous security guard, one of the most wanted terrorists in Western civilization was lying dead, killed with a single round perfectly placed through his forehead.

Stephanie turned to look at the rooftops in the distance on the other side of the island. They were dark and silent, but Stephanie knew that from one of them, her best friend from days long past had just saved her life.

Alina lifted her head from her rifle as Johann hit the ground. It was over. Two years later, she had finished it. She took a deep breath and let it out again before mechanically and silently lifting her rifle off its mount. Viper disassembled it rapidly, her hands moving confidently and setting each piece carefully back into the rifle bag. Her heart beat was starting to slow down to a normal pace again and that old, familiar feeling of cold was settling into her gut. She had succeeded in her mission, but at a great cost. Another little part of her had died along with Johann.

Viper never tried to put into words or thoughts this yawning feeling of emptiness and cold that filled her in the minutes immediately following the death of a target. Regardless of how evil or contemptible the target, she found it impossible to feel satisfaction in the death of another human being. Later, after this feeling had passed, she would be satisfied with a job completed successfully, but never with the actual death. Each one left her cold. But Alina had learned to accept the feeling, embrace the regret, and then leave it behind with the target.

Within a minute, Viper had packed up and was disappearing back into the silent night, leaving behind the cold emptiness. The only physical trace that she had ever been there was the dead body of one of the most prolific terrorists that the West had ever known.

And the federal agent whose life she had just saved.

Chapter Twenty-One

A chorus of nightlife sang around her as Alina moved silently through the woods. Her night vision goggles allowed her to move quickly and confidently through the unfamiliar terrain in the darkness. She had just barely managed to get off the island before security had locked it down, leaving the way she had come – underwater. Alina discarded her breathing tank and propulsion device when she came ashore a mile down from the island. They sank quickly, pulled under by the swift currents of the Susquehanna. The wet suit had gone the same route, weighted down with rocks, and Alina ascended into the dark woods without a backward glance. She ignored the sounds of helicopters that started to churn above, headed for the island. Stephanie would take care of Johann, the security guard, and the authorities.

Viper had more business to finish.

She moved swiftly, constantly scanning the woods for any sign of Dimitrius. He was out there. It was just a matter of time before she saw him...or he saw her.

Alina knew that Damon had come ahead of her to try to secure the area. The quick recon that he had done, while she was meeting with Stephanie and John earlier, had unearthed a flat rock overlooking the house and barn. He was going to set up there to watch her back. At least, that was what he had planned. Alina had no idea if he succeeded or not. They had opted not to use com units for the same reason that she had refused to use one with Stephanie, it was too risky. The more electronic devices used, the easier it was for an opponent to locate you. Viper wasn't about to make it easy for the bastard. Like Stephanie, Damon had disagreed, but she had won in the end.

Alina glanced at her watch and stopped, leaning against the large trunk of a tree, while she caught her breath. Pulling a GPS unit from one of her jacket pockets, she checked her location. The house was just ahead, about another quarter mile down, and Alina tucked the unit back in her pocket.

As much as she hated to admit it, this was the first time Viper was going into any kind of confrontation without a clear plan of attack. She wasn't happy about the lack of planning. She would have liked more time to come up with something that was fail-safe, something that she was confident would work, but she had run out of time. Even an extra day would have given her more time to come up with something flawless, but this was how it had played out. This would be her only shot at Dimitrius. Once Johann's death was public, The Engineer would vanish and she would likely never get another chance. She had to make this work.

Alina started moving again, navigating the woods silently and coming up to the property from the direction of the river. She slowed down as she saw the break in the trees ahead and the house beyond it. Viper scanned the woods once more before stopping a few feet from the clearing. She took a deep breath and listened. The woods were dark and silent around her, and the moon was covered by clouds. A slight breeze ruffled the branches high above her before it fell silent again.

Too silent.

Viper reached down and unsnapped the holster on her thigh before moving forward silently. Her heart pounding, she took a deep breath as she stopped at the tree line, pausing in the shadows to scan the dark buildings. The house was dark and silent in the center with no sign of life, and the old barn loomed out of the night behind the house. Everything was silent and still. The night goggles didn't detect any human body heat in the vicinity and Alina frowned, scanning the area again. Nothing.

She moved forward silently.

A bolt of awareness shot down her spine seconds before the rifle bullet tore a chunk out of the tree she had just passed. Viper dropped low to the ground and spun back into the trees, moving on pure instinct. She came to rest behind an opposite tree, her .45 in her hands and her breath coming fast.

"Damn."

The word was exhaled on a single breath, her heart pounding. She peered around the tree trunk, her eyes going straight to the roof of the barn. It was the only structure capable of concealing a shooter so effectively. It was dark and silent, and the goggles still didn't detect any temperature comparable to a human there.

Alina ripped off the goggles impatiently and closed her eyes, breathing deeply. The night was silent again, making the memory of that lone bullet seem deafening. Alina willed her heart to stop thumping and concentrated on getting her thoughts under control. Something had fired a round straight at her from the roof of the barn.

Viper opened her eyes slowly. She gave herself a moment to adjust to vision without the goggles before standing, her back still to the tree. She held her gun with both hands, pointing down, and took a deep breath. Stepping out from behind the tree, Alina moved into the open again. She had only taken two or three steps before that shock of awareness shot through her again.

Viper turned swiftly, bringing the gun up and pointing it directly behind her.

A tall shadow had dropped noiselessly out of a tree in the woods and was advancing silently. He held a gun in one hand and a remote control in the other. Alina noted the height and the fatigues.

She was facing The Engineer.

Dimitrius stopped just short of the clearing. He held his gun trained on her and they stared at each other in silence for a moment, each examining the other with wary curiosity. Alina was somewhat surprised at his size. The Engineer was close to six foot three, but he was slim. She was vaguely reminded of a May pole, and this tweaked her interest. Given the legend, she expected someone smaller and more nondescript, someone who could disappear into a crowd.

"Ah, Viper." His voice was low pitched and his accent unmistakable to one who had spent time in the middle east. "You arrived sooner than I anticipated."

The silky texture of his tone filled Alina all at once with distaste and revulsion. Her momentary curiosity gave way to cold fury.

"I apologize." Viper's voice was calm, emotionless, and gave no indication of the tempest of emotion coursing through her. "I'm more than willing to go back and we can go again."

The tall shadow chuckled with true amusement.

"You're funny!" He sounded surprised. "Unfortunately, I'm on a tight schedule this evening. Therefore, I must decline."

"What a shame." Alina still held her gun trained on his chest. "I would have really enjoyed the replay."

"I'm sure you would," Dimitrius said agreeably. "Do lower that, will you? It's distracting me."

"After you," Alina replied cordially. She got the impression that he was grinning in the darkness.

"Which one?" he asked politely. "The one in my hand? Or the one on the roof?"

Alina's eyes dropped to the remote in his other hand and she felt the crushing wave of instant defeat. Of course! The rifle on top of the barn was being controlled by remote! And right now, she had no doubt that it was aimed directly at her. Icy fingers of hopelessness slid down her back and Viper knew it was over. Anger mixed with chagrin as she paused a moment before letting her left hand drop away from her right. She turned her firing hand palm-down and engaged the safety before letting the gun drop from her hand in surrender.

"Thank you," Dimitrius said politely. "Now, you kick that away into the underbrush and I will throw away the remote."

Viper never took her eyes from him as she kicked her weapon away from them both. It landed a few feet away in the trees. As soon as it had, Dimitrius tossed the remote into the woods behind him.

"There. Now we can have a civilized conversation."

"At gunpoint," Alina retorted, nodding to the gun still pointed at her. There was a slight shrug.

"Well, we can't have everything, can we?" Dimitrius motioned with the gun. "You know the drill. Toss away that rifle, please." Alina removed the rifle bag from her back and threw it in the direction that she had kicked her pistol. "Good. Now, hands behind your head. Fabulous. I think we'll go to the barn, if you don't mind. It's so much more comfortable than the great outdoors."

He motioned for her to turn around and Alina clamped her back teeth before turning her back to him. Her heart was pounding again and her exposed position made her breath come short and quick. She forced herself to take a deep breath and sensed, rather than heard, him move up behind her. A second later, she felt the cold steel of his gun pressed against the back of her neck. He was so close to her that his breath brushed the top of her head. If Hawk *had* managed to get up onto that rock without being detected, he wouldn't have a clean shot without going straight through her.

"Now, march soldier. Straight for the barn." Dimitrius pushed her gently.

Alina somehow managed to make her legs move and she began walking. With each step, her heart dragged a little more and her legs got a little heavier. Once they were in the barn, Hawk would have no shot at all. By the time he got to the barn from the rock, it would be over. She would have been executed and the Engineer would have done what he did best: disappear.

Alina felt more fear than she remembered ever having felt before. The professional in her knew that this death march was designed to instill just such a fear, lowering her reaction time and increasing the odds of undermining her will to fight. However, knowing the psychology behind the act wasn't any comfort to her as the cold steel of the assassin's gun propelled her forward to the end of her road.

Viper had failed.

Even as the thought entered her mind, Alina acknowledged that this whole thing had been a long shot. She had been confident that she could find and eliminate the Engineer, but she knew all along that it would be a do or die attempt. Hawk had known it as well, and that was why he had been adamant about her not even attempting it alone. And, as Alina put one foot in front of the other, she admitted to herself that if Dimitrius had not targeted Stephanie, she would not be here. The actions of a fellow international assassin were no concern of hers, unless she was ordered to put an end to them, and she had no such order. Alina admitted that she was here now, walking in the darkness toward her own death, as the result of her own emotions. She had allowed her emotions to take over and this was the inevitable result.

She had, indeed, failed.

And yet, Alina couldn't feel regret. She had acted on pure emotion, yes. But somewhere, deep inside her, she realized with a shock that she was *glad* she had done so. She was happy that she still had some emotion left inside her to act upon. The image of Angela's stunned face as the bullet ripped into her body floated into Alina's mind and she knew, without any doubt, that this had been the only course of action she could have taken.

Somewhere, inside the cold machine that she had become, something had melted when she returned to Jersey. The warmth and love of true friendships that had been long forgotten had thawed deep inside her, and Viper was reminded of the way of life that she was trained to protect. She may have failed according to the rules of the world she worked in, but Alina knew she had not failed herself. She had won. She had won part of her soul back. And she could not regret that, even as she was drawing closer to the barn.

They passed the darkly silent house to their left and Alina glanced at it curiously. That was where Johann had finalized his plans and, just hours before, he left with the intent of destroying thousands of lives. That intention was destined never to be realized. Alina recognized the irony in her own fate as they passed the house, her lips twisting slightly.

Perhaps her pride *had* brought her to this inevitable place, but she truly could not regret a single thing that she had done to get here. With that realization, Alina felt the fear that gripped her in its paralyzing vise fade away. She had always known that the odds of her dying comfortably in her sleep at an old age were slim to non-existent. If she had to pick a time in her life, this was as good as any.

At least she had been given the opportunity to feel again.

The barn rose up before them and, before Alina knew it, they were inside. Once they were through the doorway, Dimitrius stopped and allowed her to distance herself from him. He flipped a switch and a single, naked light bulb flickered on, hanging from a rafter above them. Stalls in various states of disrepair lined the back wall, some empty and some holding an assortment of old rusted buckets and tools. The loft above them was dark where the light didn't reach, and Viper saw that the ladder to the loft was broken, laying on the floor in one of the stalls. Nothing in the barn looked as if it had been touched in years. The musty smell of old wood and forgotten dreams surrounded her and Alina turned to face her captor resolutely. His dark face was cast into shadows from the light, but she had the impression that it would have been attractive if his eyes weren't so cold.

"Take off the hat and jacket," Dimitrius said, moving out of the doorway.

Alina pulled the knit cap off her head and felt her braid fall to rest on her shoulder. She tossed the hat away before shrugging out of the light jacket. Dimitrius nodded once she had discarded that as well.

"Good. Now your back-up."

"I don't have my back-up," Alina informed him. A dark eyebrow soared into his forehead in disbelief.

"Of course you do," he replied. Alina shook her head slowly.

"I don't," She said. Dimitrius frowned and moved toward her.

"You'll excuse me if I don't believe you," he said, reaching out and turning her around by her shoulder. His hand slid down her back, then around her hips and down each leg, looking for the back-up weapon they always carried.

He pulled her knife out of her ankle strap and threw it away before straightening up, turning her to face him again.

"You're wounded," he stated, stepping back and motioning to the bandage under her tank. Viper's lips curved into a cold smile.

"Courtesy of a wide shot," she replied. Dimitrius threw his head back and let out a bark of laughter.

"So that's where the bullet ended up!" he exclaimed.

"Not quite where you intended," Alina said coldly. Dimitrius looked at her in some surprise.

"Oh, but it was," he said softly.

The words hung heavily in the silence as if they had been shouted, and Alina felt hot and cold all at once. She stared at him in shock, reading the simple truth in his cold eyes. She heard herself suck in air in a soft gasp as her gut tightened and her vision seemed to blur for an instant.

She had been the target all along!

"You look stunned." Dimitrius' voice cut through the haze of swirling shock and Alina forced herself to focus on his smiling face. "Perhaps you should sit down."

"I'll stand."

Alina was surprised when her voice came out evenly, sounding almost calm. Dimitrius shrugged.

"Have it your way," he said agreeably. "You really had no idea? What a relief! I thought I might be losing my touch. You're the most challenging target I have ever faced. It took quite a lot of planning."

"Johann?" Alina asked, her mind racing. Dimitrius smiled.

"The contract was for both of you," he told her, lowering his gun to his side and relaxing slightly. "But I knew that you would succeed with Johann this time, saving me the trouble. And, believe it or not, I wanted you to succeed. You had such a distinguished career until you unaccountably failed in Cairo. I know how difficult it is to be flawless in this business. I wanted you to have the opportunity to redeem yourself."

"Well, that was very thoughtful of you," Alina remarked. Dimitrius ignored the sarcasm and shook his head slightly.

"You know, we can never choose when our time is up," he said slowly. "But I wanted to show you some respect in your last hours. I think you're fascinating. Such a brilliant killer, and yet you seem to have a sense of justice. I wish that we could get to know each other better, but of course, there isn't time for that."

"Why did you change your plans the other day in the city?" Alina asked, watching him from beneath her lashes. "You must have had this planned to end here, tonight. So why take the shot there?"

Irritation flashed across his face and Dimitrius spun impatiently to start stalking back and forth.

"He changed the contract on me," he exclaimed. "All of a sudden, you had them spooked. They didn't want to wait for me to take care of it the way I had planned. They wanted you done first and then Johann, after he set off the bombs." Dimitrius glanced at her. "I think they were afraid of you. Then some DHS agent started asking questions and they got careless."

"Who hired you?" Alina demanded, raising her head and looking at him squarely. Dimitrius stopped and looked at her.

"You know I can't tell you that," he replied. Alina raised an eyebrow.

"I think I've earned the right to know who my murderer is," she retorted. Dimitrius studied her for a moment, and then smiled slowly.

"I think you already know who he is," he said softly.

His dark eyes met hers and Alina felt as though she was being sucked into their very depths. He was right, of course, she did know. And he knew that she knew. And the understanding and empathy that was in his dark eyes was the first sign of emotion that she had glimpsed inside him. They stared at each other for a long moment, the silence enveloping them, and Alina had the strangest sense that he was reluctant to end the moment.

"Such a waste," he murmured softly.

Alina didn't blink or look away, but her lips curved slightly in acknowledgment of the compliment. She didn't hold out any hope of a reprieve. They were both professionals.

"Would you like to turn around?" Dimitrius asked, raising the gun again. Alina shook her head, facing him. She held her chin up and her shoulders squared.

"I would rather face it, thank you," she answered calmly and Dimitrius smiled slightly.

"Of course," he agreed, taking aim. "I *am* sorry," he apologized.

Alina nodded slightly before lowering her eyes to a random spot on the floor. While she wanted to face her executioner, she didn't want his cold face to be the last thing she saw. Alina focused on a large crack in the floorboard near his foot. She wondered what would happen to Raven. She supposed Hawk would take him. They seemed to have formed a bond of sorts and she thought he might enjoy the novelty of a namesake. Alina was suddenly very sorry that she hadn't kissed him first this afternoon in the bedroom. She should have let him see how much he had come to mean to her. There was so much she suddenly wished that she had said and done, and the sheer panic of never getting the chance now threatened to disrupt her composure. Damon's deep blue eyes took the place of the cracked floorboard and Alina inhaled slowly.

The shot was deafening, reverberating through the barn and shaking the old rafters. The noise rang in her ears and Alina flinched, her heart jumping into her throat. It took a second for her mind to register the fact that she was still standing. And still breathing.

Her eyes flew up and she watched as Dimitrius fell backwards. He was dead before he hit the old wooden floor of the barn, the high caliber round passing directly through his heart. Alina stared at the gaping wound in the center of his chest, her mind clamoring to grasp what had happened. When the blood started to flow across his chest, she realized that she wasn't breathing.

Sucking in a sudden gasp of air, she spun around and looked up. There, in the shadows at the edge of the loft, Hawk lowered his rifle slowly. His blue eyes met hers and Alina simply stared at him numbly, her mind empty of all thought. Damon sat up from his stomach and swung his legs over the edge of the loft, dropping down into the barn. Alina watched him land on his feet and move toward her with that jungle cat grace that was so uniquely his own. She heard something that sounded very suspiciously like a cross between a gasp and a sob, and then her legs buckled right out from under her.

"Easy." Damon caught her in his arms and pulled her close, holding her up against himself. "Easy now."

He wrapped his arms around her and the numbness in her legs gave way to an uncontrollable trembling. Alina realized with a shock that her whole body was shaking violently, and that the sob had come from deep inside her. She didn't know if she wanted to laugh or cry or scream, and she couldn't seem to catch her breath. After holding all her emotion so tightly in check for the past hour, it was as if some invisible gate had been raised and she couldn't control the shaking. She couldn't control anything anymore. She barely heard the words that Damon was murmuring, but the soothing pitch of his voice washed over her and Alina could only rest her head on his chest and wait for the violent tremors to pass.

Damon closed his eyes, resting his chin on the top of Alina's head. She was shaking uncontrollably and all he could do was hold her tightly and try to absorb as much of the trembling as he could into his own body. He inhaled deeply, moving one hand up to the back of her head. Relief was coursing through him, pure elation that she was alive and in his arms. He had come so close, so very close, to losing her. Damon had never seen anything so brave in his life as the way she had faced her own death, with her back straight and her head high. Not once had she allowed any tremor of emotion to break through and show the Engineer that he had won. Dimitrius had paused in appreciation when confronted with her silent fearlessness, giving Hawk the clear shot that ended his life.

Damon opened his eyes and looked at the body of the The Engineer, laying in a growing pool of blood on the barn floor, the gun that would have ended Vipers' life on the floor next to his lifeless hand.

The hunter had fallen prey to a Hawk.

Alina didn't even realize that Damon had moved them outside until the cool night air touched her face. He had picked up her discarded jacket, hat and knife as they passed them in the barn, and Alina watched them swing from his free hand. She didn't look back at the barn, but allowed herself to be led across the dark yard to the edge of the property. Damon led her to a hollowed out, uprooted tree trunk and she sank onto it gratefully. Crouching in front of her, he took both her cold hands in his warm ones, rubbing them briskly.

"Look at me," he said. When Alina obeyed, he smiled slightly. "It's over."

Alina nodded, breathing fresh air deeply. The flood of uncontrollable emotion had ended and the violent shaking had subsided to a slight trembling in her hands. She felt drained and exhausted.

"How did you get in the loft?"

Alina broke her silence, her fingers stirring in his large hands. Damon squeezed them gently and moved to sit beside her on the tree. Clouds still covered the moon and the wind had picked up. She shivered, rubbing her arms, and Damon draped her jacket around her shoulders. Alina smiled in thanks, slipping her arms into the sleeves. She reached out and took the knife from his hand and bent to slip it back into its holder on her ankle.

"When I came to secure the perimeter, Dimitrius was at the rock. He was testing the rifle with the remote," Damon told her. "Once I realized that the rifle was mounted on the barn, I had some idea of what he was planning. I got into the barn and I was going to disarm the rifle altogether. But then he came to make an adjustment to it." Damon shrugged. "All I could do was wait, stuck in the loft. There are holes in the walls up there and I had a clear view of what was happening, but I didn't have any kind of shot without going through you."

Alina nodded, silent as she stared into the night, all the pieces of the puzzle falling into place.

"Harry sent you to protect me, didn't he?" she said suddenly. "He knew the Engineer was being hired for me."

"Yes." Damon nodded, playing with the black knit hat in his hands. "He contacted me a month ago in Scotland. He didn't know how to protect you. He knew you would go after Johann again and there was no way to stop you. It was the perfect set up."

"So he gave you the DHS alibi and you shadowed me, waiting for Dimitrius to show up," Alina said slowly. "That's why you were in such a high profile position. You *wanted* them to see that you were here too."

"I wanted to make it clear that you weren't alone. I wanted to force them to act," Damon said. "And it worked. They panicked and forced Dimitrius to change his plans and move everything up. Unfortunately, an innocent agent in Washington DC started asking questions about me around the same time that they realized who I really was." Alina nodded, staring at the dark house in front of them.

"And they were afraid she would alert the FBI," she murmured. "Stephanie could have put it all together and they couldn't risk that much exposure."

Damon was silent and Alina buried her hands in her jacket pockets. She stared unseeingly at the house, listening to the sounds of the night around them, her mind spinning. All this time, she had been at the center of the whole thing. All the questions, all the manipulations, all the planning...it had all been to silence *her*.

Damon glanced at Viper. She had her hands buried in her pockets and was staring straight-ahead with that unreadable look on her face. He sighed inwardly and waited.

"Harry is in danger now," Alina said after a few moments of silence. Damon nodded and the cool night air brushed against his face. An owl hooted nearby, the sound echoing in the quiet yard.

"Yes."

"And you just saved my life," she added after a moment. Damon glanced at her, his lips twitching.

"Yes."

Alina was silent again, lapsing deep into her own thoughts. Damon stretched, looking up into the black sky. He knew what she was thinking, knew what she was turning over in that head of hers. If he had an ounce of sense, he would cut bait and walk away now. He could disappear forever on what he had accumulated over the years and they would never even know where to start looking. Hawk knew she could as well, but she wouldn't run. Ever. And, he thought with a deep sigh, neither would he. Not while she was still out there.

"You're going after him, aren't you?" Hawk asked softly.

The night sang around them, but neither of them were listening now. Viper looked at him, her eyes dark and her lips drawn together in a grim line.

"You know I have to," she answered just as softly. "This has gone too far. Targeting their own agents and their own citizens? This has to stop."

"You know it's impossible," Damon told her. They stared at each other in the darkness, and Alina's lips curved into a grin.

"The only reason you say that is because it's never been done before," she retorted. Damon chuckled quietly.

"Well, then we had better find your rifle and side arm," he said finally. Alina grinned. "By the way, where *is* your backup?" Damon demanded, standing up and turning to reach out his hand to her. Alina placed her hand in his and allowed him to pull her to her feet.

"I gave it to Stephanie. She didn't have one, if you can believe that," she answered. "It turned out to be a good thing, too. She needed it."

"That was a good gun. You've had it since the beginning," Hawk said as they started toward the line of trees where Dimitrius had caught her. It seemed like an eternity ago now.

"I'll miss it," Alina agreed with a sigh. "But maybe one day I can get it back."

Damon glanced down at the note of sadness in her voice. Viper was looking ahead, but he knew it was with a view of the past. And that past had irrevocably changed now, becoming entwined with the future. Damon was still pondering this new development when Alina slid her hand into his. He looked at her with a smile, his fingers closing around hers warmly.

"I'm glad you're with me," Alina told him softly.

Damon smiled slowly and stopped, pulling her into his arms.

"There's nowhere else I would rather be," he answered truthfully.

Alina smiled slowly as his lips touched hers. Maybe it hadn't been everything that she wanted to say, and maybe it wasn't everything that had gone through her mind in the seconds before she thought she was about to die, but it was more than she had ever told him. She had him in her arms, and it was a start.

And Viper had always been partial to Hawks.

Next Exit, Three Miles

Other Titles in the Exit Series by CW Browning:

Next Exit, Pay Toll

Next Exit, Dead Ahead

Next Exit, Quarter Mile

Next Exit, Use Caution

Available on Amazon

About the Author

CW Browning was writing before she could spell. Making up stories with her childhood best friend in the backyard in Olathe, Kansas, imagination ran wild from the very beginning. At the age of eight, she printed out her first full-length novel on a dot-matrix printer. All eighteen chapters of it. Through the years, the writing took a backseat to the mechanics of life as she pursued other avenues of interest. Those mechanics, however, have a great way of underlining what truly lifts a spirt and makes the soul sing. After attending Rutgers University and studying History, her love for writing was rekindled. It became apparent where her heart lay. Picking up an old manuscript, she dusted it off and went back to what made her whole. CW still makes up stories in her backyard, but now she crafts them for her readers to enjoy. She makes her home in Southern New Jersey, where she loves to grill steak and sip red wine on the patio.

Visit her at: www.cwbrowning.com
Also find her on Facebook, Instagram and Twitter!

58053594R00181

Made in the USA
Middletown, DE
04 August 2019